BOG-MYRTLE AND PEAT

TALES CHIEFLY OF GALLOWAY

GATHERED FROM THE YEARS 1889 TO 1895,

BY

S.R. CROCKETT

KENMURE

1715

"The heather's in a blaze, Willie,
　The White Rose decks the tree,
The Fiery-Cross is on the braes,
　And the King is on the sea.

"Remember great Montrose, Willie,
　Remember fair Dundee,
And strike one stroke at the foreign foes
　Of the King that's on the sea.

"There's Gordons in the North, Willie,
　Are rising frank and free,
Shall a Kenmure Gordon not go forth
　For the King that's on the sea?

"A trusty sword to draw, Willie,
　A comely weird to dree,
For the royal Rose that's like the snaw,
　And the King that's on the sea!"

He cast ae look upon his lands,
　Looked over loch and lea,
He took his fortune in his hands,
　For the King was on the sea.

Kenmures have fought in Galloway
   For Kirk and Presbyt'rie,
This Kenmure faced his dying day,
   For King James across the sea.

It little skills what faith men vaunt,
   If loyal men they be
To Christ's ain Kirk and Covenant,
   Or the King that's o'er the sea.

ANDREW LANG.

PREFACE

There is a certain book of mine which no publisher has paid royalty upon, which has never yet been confined in spidery lines upon any paper, a book that is nevertheless the Book of my Youth, of my Love, and of my Heart.

There never was such a book, and in the chill of type certainly there never will be. It has, so far as I know, no title, this unpublished book of mine. For it would need the blood of rubies and the life of diamonds crusted on ivory to set the title of this book.

Mostly I see it in the late night watches, when the twilight verges to the cock-crowing and the universe is silent, stirless, windless, for about the space of one hour. Then the pages of the book are opened a little; and, as one that reads hungrily, hastily, at the bookstall of an impatient vendor a book he cannot buy, so I scan the idylls, the epics, the dramas of the life of man written in words which thrill me as I read. Some are fiercely tender, some yearning and unsatisfying, some bitter in the mouth but afterward sweet in the belly. All are expressed in words so fit and chaste and noble, that each is an immortal poem which would give me deathless fame—could I, alas! but remember.

Then the morning comes, and with the first red I awake to a sense of utter loss and bottomless despair. Once more I have clutched and missed and forgotten. It is gone from me. The imagination of my heart is left unto me desolate. Sometimes indeed when a waking bird—by preference a mavis—sings outside my window, for a little while after I swim upward out of the ocean of sleep, it seems that I might possibly remember one stanza of the deathless words; or even by chance recapture, like the brown speckled thrush, that "first fine careless rapture" of the adorable refrain.

Even when I arise and walk out in the dawn, as is my custom winter and summer, still I have visions of this book of mine, of which I now remember that the mystic name is "The Book Sealed." Sometimes in these dreams of the morning, as I walk abroad, I find my hands upon the clasps. I touch the binding wax of the seals. When the first rosy fingers of the dawn point upward to the zenith with the sunlight behind them, sanguine like a maid's hand held before a lamp, I catch a farewell glimpse of the hidden pages.

Tales, not poems, are written upon them now. I hear the voices of "Them Ones," as Irish folk impressively say of the Little People, telling me tales out of the Book Sealed, tales which in the very hearing make a man blush hotly and thrill with hopes mysterious. Such stories as they are! The romances of high young blood, of maidens' winsome purity and frank disdain, of strong men who take their lives in hand and hurl themselves upon the push of pikes. And though I cannot grasp more than a hint of the plot, yet as my feet swish through the dewy swathes of the hyacinths or crisp along the frost-bitten snow, a wild thought quickens within me into a belief, that one day I shall hear them all, and tell these tales for my very own so that the world must listen.

But as the rosy fingers of the morn melt and the broad day fares forth, the vision fades, and I who saw and heard must go and sit down to my plain saltless tale. Once I wrote a book, every word of it, in the open air. It was full of the sweet things of the country, so at least as they seemed to me. I saw the hens nestle sleepily in the holes of the bank-side where the dry dust is, and so I wrote it down. I heard the rain drum on the broad leaves over my head, and I wrote that down also. Day after day I rose and wrote in the dawn, and sometimes I seemed to recapture a leaf or a passing glance of a chapter-heading out of the Book Sealed. It came back to me how the girls were kissed and love was made in the days when the Book Sealed was the Book Open, and when I cared not a jot for anything that was written therein. So as well as I could I wrote these things down in the red dawn. And so till the book was done.

Then the day comes when the book is printed and bound, and when the critics write of it after their kind, things good and things evil. But I that have gathered the fairy gold dare not for my life look again within, lest it should be even as they say, and I should find but withered leaves therein. For the sake of the vision of the breaking day and the incommunicable hope, I shall look no more upon it. But ever with the eternal human expectation, I rise and wait the morning and the final opening of the "Book Sealed."

S.R. CROCKETT.

NOTE.

I am deeply in the debt of my friend, Mr. Andrew Lang, for the ballad of 'Kenmure' which he has written to grace my bare boards and spice the plain fare here set out in honour of the ancient Free Province.

BOOK FIRST

ADVENTURES

Lo, in the dance the wine-drenched coronal
From shoulder white and golden hair doth fall!
A-nigh his breast each youth doth hold an head,
Twin flushing cheeks and locks unfilleted;
Swifter and swifter doth the revel move
Athwart the dim recesses of the grove ...
Where Aphrodite reigneth in her prime,
And laughter ringeth all the summer time.

There hemlock branches make a languorous gloom,
And heavy-headed poppies drip perfume
In secret arbours set in garden close;
And all the air, one glorious breath of rose,
Shakes not a dainty petal from the trees,
Nor stirs a ripple on the Cyprian seas.

"The Choice of Herakles."

I

THE MINISTER OF DOUR

This window looketh towards the west,
  And o'er the meadows grey
Glimmer the snows that coldly crest
  The hills of Galloway.

The winter broods on all between—
  In every furrow lies;
Nor is there aught of summer green,
  Nor blue of summer skies.

Athwart the dark grey rain-clouds flash
  The seabird's sweeping wings,
And through the stark and ghostly ash
  The wind of winter sings.

The purple woods are dim with rain,
* The cornfields dank and bare;*
And eyes that look for golden grain
* Find only stubble there.*

And while I write, behold the night
* Comes slowly blotting all,*
And o'er grey waste and meadow bright
* The gloaming shadows fall.*

"*From Two Windows.*"

The wide frith lay under the manse windows of the parish of Dour. The village of Dour straggled, a score of white-washed cottages, along four hundred yards of rocky shore. There was a little port, to attempt which in a south-west wind was to risk an abrupt change of condition. This was what made half of the men in the parish of Dour God-fearing men. The other half feared the minister.

Abraham Ligartwood was the minister. He also feared God exceedingly, but he made up for it by not regarding man in the slightest. The manse of Dour was conspicuously set like a watch-tower on a hill—or like a baron's castle above the huts of his retainers. The fishermen out on the water made it their lighthouse. The lamp burned in the minister's study half the night, and was alight long ere the winter sun had reached the horizon.

Abraham Ligartwood would have been a better man had he been less painfully good. When he came to the parish of Dour he found that he had to succeed a man who had allowed his people to run wild. Dour was a garden filled with the degenerate fruit of a strange vine.

The minister said so in the pulpit. Dour smiled complacently, and considered that its hoary wickednesses would beat the minister in the long-run. But Dour did not at that time know the minister. It was the day of the free-traders. The traffic with the Isle of Man, whence the hardy fishermen ran their cargoes of Holland gin and ankers of French brandy, put good gear on the back of many a burgher's wife, and porridge into the belly of many a fisherman's bairn.

The new minister found all this out when he came. He did not greatly object. It was, he said, no part of his business to collect King George's dues. But he did object when the running of a vessel's cargo became the signal for half his parishioners settling themselves to a fortnight of black, solemn, evil-hearted drinking. He said that he would break up these colloguings. He would not have half the wives in the parish coming to his kirk with black eyes upon the Lord's Sabbath day.

The parish of Dour laughed. But the parish of Dour was to get news of the minister, for Abraham Ligartwood was not a man to trifle with.

One night there was a fine cargo cleanly run at Port Saint Johnston, the village next to Dour. It was got as safely off. The "lingtowmen" went out, and there was the jangling of hooked chains along all the shores; then the troll of the smugglers' song as the cavalcade struck inwards through the low shore-hills for the main free-trade route to Edinburgh and Glasgow. The king's preventive men had notice, and came down as usual three hours late. Then they seized ten casks of the best Bordeaux, which had been left for the purpose on the sand. They were able and intelligent officers—in especial the latter. And they had an acute perception of the fact that if their bread was to be buttered on both sides, it were indeed well not to let it fall.

This cargo-running and seizures were all according to rule, and the minister of Dour had nothing to say. But at night seventeen of his kirk members in good standing and fourteen adherents met at the Back Spital of Port Dour to drink prosperity to the cargo which had been safely run. There was an elder in the chair, and six unbroached casks on a board in the corner.

There was among those who assembled some word of scoffing merriment at the expense of the minister. Abraham Ligartwood had preached a sermon on the Sabbath before, which each man, as the custom was, took home and applied to his neighbour.

"Ay man, Mains, did ye hear what the minister said aboot ye? O man, he was sair on ye!"

"Hoot na, Portmark, it was yersel' he was hittin' at, and the black e'e ye gied Kirsty six weeks syne."

But when the first keg was on the table, and the men, each with his pint-stoup before him, had seated themselves round, there came a knocking at the door—loud, insistent, imperious. Each man ran his hand down his side to the loaded whip or jockteleg (the smuggler's sheath-knife) which he carried with him.

But no man was in haste to open the door. The red coats of King George's troopers might be on the other side. For no mere gauger or preventive man would have the assurance to come chapping on Portmark's door in that fashion.

"Open the door in the name of Most High God!" cried a loud, solemn voice they all knew. The seventeen men and an elder quaked through all their inches; but none moved. Writs from the authority mentioned did not run in the parish of Dour.

The fourteen adherents fled underneath the table like chickens in a storm.

"Then will I open it in my own name!" Whereon followed a crash, and the two halves of the kitchen door sprang asunder with great and sudden noise. Abraham Ligartwood came in.

The men sat awed, each man wishful to creep behind his neighbour.

The minister's breadth of shoulder filled up the doorway completely, so that there was not room for a child to pass. He carried a mighty staff in his hand, and his dark hair shone through the powder which was upon it. His glance swept the gathering. His eye glowed with a sparkle of such fiery wrath that not a man of all the seventeen and an elder, was unafraid. Yet not of his violence, but rather of the lightnings of his words. And above all, of his power to loose and to bind. It is a mistaken belief that priestdom died when they spelled it Presbytery.

The comprehensive nature of the anathema that followed—spoken from the advantage of the doorway, with personal applications to the seventeen individuals and the elder—cannot now be recalled; but scraps of that address are circulated to this day, mostly spoken under the breath of the narrator.

"And you, Portmark," the minister is reported to have said, "with your face like the moon in harvest and your girth like a tun of Rhenish, gin ye turn not from your evil ways, within four year ye shall sup with the devil whom ye serve. Have ye never a word to say, ye scorners of the halesome word, ye blaspheming despisers of doctrine? Your children shall yet stand and rebuke you in the gate. Heard ye not my word on the Sabbath in the kirk? Dumb dogs are ye every one! Have ye not a word to say? There was a brave gabble of tongues enough when I came in. Are ye silent before a man? How, then, shall ye stand in That Day?"

The minister paused for a reply. But no answer came.

"And you, Alexander Kippen, puir windlestrae, the Lord shall thresh ye like ill-grown corn in the day of His wrath. Ye are hardly worth the word of rebuke; but for mine office I wad let ye slip quick to hell! The devil takes no care of you, for he is sure of ye!"

The minister advanced, and with the iron-pointed shod of his staff drove in the bung of the first keg. Then there arose a groan from the seventeen men who sat about. Some of them stood up on their feet. But the minister turned on them with such fearsome words, laying the ban of anathema on them, that their hearts became as water and they sat down. The good spirit gurgled and ran, and deep within them the seventeen men groaned for the pity of it.

Thus the minister broke up the black drinkings. And the opinion of the parish was with him in all, except as to the spilling of the liquor. Rebuke and threatening were within his right, but to pour out the spirit was a waste even in a minister.

"It is the destruction of God's good creature!" said the parish of Dour.

But the minister held on his way. The communion followed after, and Abraham Ligartwood had, as was usual, three days of humiliation and prayer beforehand. Then he set himself to "fence the tables." He stated clearly who had a right to come forward to the table of the Lord, and who were to be debarred. He explained personally and exactly why it was that each defaulter had no right there. As he went on, the congregation, one after another, rose astonished and terrified and went out, till Abraham Ligartwood was left alone with the elements of communion. Every elder and member had left the building, so effective had been the minister's rebuke.

At this the parish of Dour seethed with rebellion. Secret cabals in corners arose, to be scattered like smoke-drift by the whisper that the minister was coming. Deputations were chosen, and started for the manse full of courage and hardihood. Portmark, as the man who smarted sorest, generally headed them; and by the aid of square wide-mouthed bottles of Hollands, it was possible to get the members as far as the foot of the manse loaning. But beyond that they would not follow Portmark's leading, nor indeed that of any man. The footfall of the minister of Dour as he paced alone in his study chilled them to the bone.

They told one another on the way home how Ganger Patie, of the black blood of the gypsy Marshalls, finding his occupation gone, cursed the minister on Glen Morrison brae; but broke neck-bone by the sudden fright of his horse and his own drunkenness at the foot of the same brae on his home-coming. They said that the minister had prophesied that in the spot where Ganger Patie had cursed the messenger of God, even there God would enter into judgment with him. And they told how the fair whitethorn hedge was blasted for ten yards about the spot where the Death Angel had waited for the blasphemer. There were four men who were willing to give warrandice that their horses had turned with them and refused to pass the place.

So the parish was exceedingly careful of its words to the minister. It left him severely alone. He even made his own porridge in the wide-sounding kitchen of the gabled manse, on the hill above the harbour. He rang with his own hands the kirk-bell on the Sabbath morn. But none came near the preachings. There was no child baptized in the parish of Dour; and no wholesome diets of catechising, where old and young might learn the Way more perfectly.

Mr. Ligartwood's brethren spoke to him and pled with him to use milder courses; but all in vain. In those days the Pope was not so autocratic in Rome as a minister in his own parish.

"They left me of their own accord, and of their own accord shall they return," said Abraham Ligartwood.

But in the fall of the year the White Death came to Dour. They say that it came from the blasted town of Kirk Oswald, where the plague had been all the summer. The men of the landward parishes set a watch on all that came out of the accursed streets. But in the night-time men with laden horses ran the blockade, for the prices to be obtained within were like those in a besieged city.

Some said that it was the farmer of Portmark who had done this thing once too often. At least it is sure that it was to his house that the Death first came in the parish of Dour. At the sound of the shrill crying, of which they every one knew the meaning, men dropped their tools in the field and fled to the hills. It was like the Day of Judgment. The household servants disappeared. Hired men and field-workers dispersed like the wave from a stone in a pool, carrying infection with them. Men fell over at their own doors with the rattle in their throats, and there lay, none daring to touch them. In Kirk Oswald town the grass grew in the vennels and along the High Street. In Dour the horses starved in the stables, the cattle in the byres.

Then came Abraham Ligartwood out of the manse of Dour. He went down to the farm towns and into the village huts and lifted the dead. He harnessed the horse in the cart, and swathed the body in sheets. He dug the graves, and laid the corpse in the kindly soil. He nursed the sick. He organised help everywhere. He went from house to stricken house with the high assured words of a messenger fresh from God.

He let out the horses to the pasture. He milked the kine, that bellowed after him with the plague of their milk. He had thought and hands for all. His courage shamed the cowards. He quickened the laggards. He stilled the agony of fear that killed three for every one who died of the White Death.

For the first time since the minister came to Dour, the kirk-bell did not ring on Sabbath, for the minister was at the other end of the parish setting a house in order whence three children had been carried. In the kirkyard there was the dull rattle of sods. The burying-party consisted of the roughest rogues in the parish, whom the minister had fetched from their hiding-holes in the hills.

Up the long roads that led to the kirk on its windy height the scanty funerals wended their way. For three weeks they say that in the kirkyard, from dawn to dusk, there was always a grave uncovered or a funeral in sight. There was no burial service in the kirkyard save the rattle of the clods; for now the minister had set the carpenters to work and coffins were being made. But the minister had prayer in all the houses ere the dead was lifted.

Then he went off to lay hot stones to the feet of another, and to get a nurse for yet another. For twenty days he never slept and seldom ate, till the plague was stayed.

The last case was on the 27th of September. Then Abraham Ligartwood himself was stricken in one of the village hovels, and fell forward across a sick man's bed. They carried him to the manse of Dour, and wept as they went. The next day all the men that were alive in the parish of Dour stood about the minister's grave in the kirkyard on the hill. There was none there that could pray. But as they were about to separate, some one, it was never known who, raised the tune of the first Psalm. And the wind wafted to the weeping wives in the cottages of the stricken parish of Dour the sound of the hoarse and broken singing of men. In three weeks the minister had brought the evil parish of Dour into the presence of God.

And these were the words of their singing, while the gravediggers stood with the red earth ready on their spades, but before a clod fell on the minister's grave:—

"That man hath perfect blessedness
  Who walketh not astray
In counsel of ungodly men,
  Nor stands in sinners' way,
Nor sitteth in the scorner's chair;
  But placeth his delight
Upon God's law, and meditates
  On his law day and night."

The new minister who succeeded had an easy time and a willing people. But he can never be to them what Abraham Ligartwood was. They graved on his tomb, and that with good cause, the words, "Here lyes a Man who never feared the face of Man."

The lovers are whispering under thy shade,
  Grey Tower of Dalmeny!
I leave them and wander alone in the glade
  Beneath thee, Dalmeny.
Their thoughts are of all the bright years coming on,
But mine are of days and of dreams that are gone;
They see the fair flowers Spring has thrown on the grass,
And the clouds in the blue light their eyes as they pass;
But my feet are deep dawn in a drift of dead leaves,
And I hear what they hear not—a lone bird that grieves.
What matter? the end is not far for us all,
And spring, through the summer, to winter must fall,
And the lovers' light hearts, e'en as mine, will be laid,
At last, and for ever, low under thy shade,
  Grey Tower of Dalmeny.

GEORGE MILNER.

II

A CRY ACROSS THE BLACK WATER

With Rosemary for remembrance, And Rue, sweet Rue, for you.

It was at the waterfoot of the Ken, and the time of the year was June.

"Boat ahoy!"

The loud, bold cry carried far through the still morning air. The rain had washed down all that was in the sky during the night, so that the hail echoed through a world blue and empty.

Gregory Jeffray, a noble figure of a youth, stood leaning on the arch of his mare's neck, quieting the nervous tremors of Eulalie, that very dainty lady. His tall, alert figure, tight-reined and manly, was brought out by his riding-dress. His pose against the neck of the beautiful beast, from which a moment before he had swung himself, was that of Hadrian's young Antinous.

"Boat ahoy!"

Gregory Jeffray, growing a little impatient, made a trumpet of his hands, and sent the powerful voice, with which one day he meant to thrill listening senates, sounding athwart the dancing ripples of the loch.

On the farther shore was a flat white ferry-boat, looking, as it lay motionless in the river, like a white table chained in the water with its legs in the air. The chain along which it moved plunged into the shallows beside him, and he could see it descending till he lost it in the dusky pool across which the ferry plied. To the north, Loch Ken ran in glistening levels and island-studded reaches to the base of Cairnsmuir.

"Boat ahoy!"

A figure, like a white mark of exclamation moving over green paper, came out of the little low whitewashed cottage opposite, and stood a moment looking across the ferry, with one hand resting on its side and the other held level with the eyes. Then the observer disappeared behind a hedge, to be seen immediately coming down the narrow, deep-rutted lane towards the ferry-boat. When the figure came again in sight of Gregory Jeffray, he had no difficulty in distinguishing a slim girl, clad in white, who came sedately towards him.

When she arrived at the white boat which floated so stilly on the morning glitter of the water, only just stirred by a breeze from the south, she stepped at once on board. Gregory could see her as she took from the corner of the flat, where it stood erect along with other boating gear, something which looked like a short iron hoe. With this she walked to the end of the boat nearest him. She laid the hoe end of the instrument against a chain that ran breast-high along one side of the boat and at the stern plunged diagonally into the water. His mare lifted her feet impatiently, as though the shoreward end of the chain had brought a thrill across the loch from the moving ferry-boat. Turning her back to him, the girl bent her slim young body without an effort; and, as though by the gentlest magic, the ferry-boat drew nearer to him. It did not seem to move; yet gradually the space of blue water between it and the shore on which the whitewashed cottage stood spread and widened. He could hear the gentle clatter of the wavelets against the lip of the landing-drop as the boat came nearer. His mare tossed her head and snuffed at this strange four-footed thing that glided towards them.

Gregory, who loved all women, watched with natural interest the sway and poise of the girlish figure. He heard the click and rattle of the chain as she deftly disengaged her gripper-iron at the farther end, and, turning, walked the deck's length towards him.

She seemed but a young thing to move so large a boat. He forgot to be angry at being kept so long waiting, for of all women, he told himself, he most admired tall girls in simple dresses. His exceptional interest arose from the fact that he had never before seen one manage a ferry-boat.

As he stood on the shore, and the great flat boat moved towards him, he saw that the end of it nearest him was pulled up a couple of feet clear of the water. Still the boat moved noiselessly forward, till he heard it first grate and then ground gently, as the graceful pilot bore her weight upon the iron bar to stay its progress. Gregory specially admired the flex of her arms bent outwardly as she did so. Then she went to the end of the boat, and let down the tilted gangway upon the pebbles at his feet.

Gregory Jeffray instinctively took off his hat as he said to this girl,
"Good-morning! Can I get to the village of Dullarg by this ferry?"

"This is the way to the Dullarg," said the girl, simply and naturally, leaning as she spoke upon her dripping gripper-iron.

Her eyes did not refuse to take in the goodliness of the youth while his attention was for the moment given to his mare.

"Gently, gently, lass!" he said, patting the neck which arched impatiently as she felt the boards hollow beneath her feet. Yet she came obediently enough on deck, arching her fore-feet high and throwing them out in an uncertain and tentative manner.

Then the girl, with a quiet and matter-of-fact acceptance of her duties, placed her iron once more upon the chain, and bent herself to the task with well-accustomed effort of her slender body.

The heart of the young man was stirred within him. True, he might have beheld fifty field-wenches breaking their backs among the harvest sheaves without a pang. This, however, was very different.

"Let me help you," he said.

"It is better that you stand by your horse," she said.

Gregory Jeffray looked disappointed.

"Is it not too hard work for you?" he queried, humbly and with abased eyes.

"No," said the girl. "Ye see, sir, I live with my mother's two sisters at the boathouse. They are very kind to me. They brought me up, though I had neither father nor mother. And what signifies bringing the boat across the Water a time or two?"

Her ready and easy movements told the tale for her. She needed no pity. She asked for none, for which Gregory was rather sorry. He liked to pity people, and then to right their grievances, if it were not very difficult. Of what use otherwise was it to be, what he was called in Galloway, the "Boy Sheriff"? Besides, he was taking a morning ride from the Great House of the Barr, and upon his return to breakfast he desired to have a tale to tell which would rivet attention upon himself.

"And do you do nothing all day, but only take the boat to and fro across the loch?" he asked.

He saw the way clear now, he thought, to matter for an interesting episode—the basis of which should be the delight of a beautiful girl in spending her life in the carrying of desirable young men, riding upon horses, over the shining morning waters of the Ken. They should all look with eyes of wonder upon her; but she, the cold Dian of the lochside, would never return look for look to any of them, save perhaps to Gregory Jeffray. Gregory went about the world finding pictures and making romances for himself. He meant to be a statesman; and, with this purpose in view, it was wholly necessary for him to study the people, and especially, he might have added, the young women of the people. Hitherto he had done this chiefly in his imagination, but here certainly was material attractive to his hand.

"Do you work at nothing else?" he repeated, for the girl was uncomplimentarily intent upon her gripper-iron. How deftly she lifted it just at the right moment, when it was in danger of being caught upon the revolving wheel! How exactly she exerted just the right amount of strength to keep the chain running sweetly upon its cogs! How daintily she stepped back, avoiding the dripping of the water from the linked iron which rose from the bed of the loch, passed under her hand, and dipped diagonally down again into the deeps! Gregory had never seen anything like it, so he told himself.

It was not until he had put his question the third time that the girl answered, "Whiles I take the boat over to the waterfoot when there's a cry across the Black Water."

The young man was mystified.

"'A cry across the Black Water!' What may that be?" he said.

The girl looked at him directly almost for the first time. Was he making fun of her? She wondered. His face seemed earnest enough, and handsome. It was not possible, she concluded.

"Ye'll be a stranger in these parts?" she answered interrogatively, because she was a Scottish girl, and one question for another is good national barter and exchange.

Gregory Jeffray was about to declare his names, titles, and expectations; but he looked at the girl again, and saw something that withheld him.

"Yes," he said, "I am staying for a week or two over at Barr."

The boat grounded on the pebbles, and the girl went to let down the hinged end. It had seemed a very brief passage to Gregory Jeffray. He stood still by his mare, as though he had much more to say.

The girl placed her cleek in the corner, and moved to leave the boat. It piqued the young man to find her so unresponsive. "Tell me what you mean by 'a cry across the Black Water,'" he said.

The girl pointed to the strip of sullen blackness that lay under the willows upon the southern shore.

"That is the Black Water of Dee," she said simply, "and the green point among the trees is the Rhonefoot. Whiles there's a cry from there. Then I go over in the boat, and set them across."

"Not in this boat?" he said, looking at the upturned deal table swinging upon its iron chain.

She smiled at his ignorance.

"That is the boat that goes across the Black Water of Dee," she said, pointing to a small boat which lay under the bank on the left.

"And do you never go anywhere else?" he asked, wondering how she came by her beauty and her manners.

"Only to the kirk on the Sabbaths," she said, "when I can get some one to watch the boat for me."

"I will watch the boat for you!" he said impulsively.

The girl looked distressed. This gay gentleman was making fun of her, assuredly. She did not answer. Would he never go away?

"That is your way," she said, pointing along the track in front. Indeed, there was but one way, and the information was superfluous.

The end of the white, rose-smothered boathouse was towards them. A tall, bowed woman's figure passed quickly round the gable.

"Is that your aunt?" he asked.

"That is my aunt Annie," said the girl; "my aunt Barbara is confined to her bed."

"And what is your name, if I may ask?"

The girl glanced at him. He was certainly not making fun of her now.

"My name is Grace Allen," she said.

They paced together up the path. The bridle rein slipped from his arm, but his hand instinctively caught it, and Eulalie cropped crisply at the grasses on the bank, unregarded of her master.

They did not shake hands when they parted, but their eyes followed each other a long way.

"Where is the money?" said Aunt Barbara from her bed as Grace Allen came in at the open door.

"Dear me!" said the girl, frightened: "I have forgotten to ask him for it!"

"Did I ever see sic a lassie! Rin after him an' get it; haste ye fast."

But Gregory was far out of reach by the time Grace got to the door. The sound of hoofs came from high up the wooded heights.

Gregory Jeffray reached the Barr in time for late breakfast. There was a large house company. The men were prowling discontentedly about, looking under covers or cutting slices from dishes on the sideboard; but the ladies were brightly curious, and eagerly welcomed Gregory. He at least did not rise with a headache and a bad temper every morning. They desired an account of his morning's ride. But on the way home he had changed his mind about telling of his adventure. He said that he had had a pleasant ride. It had been a beautiful morning.

"But have you nothing whatever to tell us?" they asked; for, indeed, they had a right to expect something.

Gregory said nothing. This was not usual, for at other times when he had nothing to tell, it did not cost him much to invent something interesting.

"You are very dull this morning, Sheriff," said the youngest daughter of the house, who, being the baby and pretty, had grown pettishly privileged in speech.

But deep within him Gregory was saying, "What a blessing that I forgot to pay the ferry!"

When he got outside he said to his host, "Is there such a place hereabouts as the Rhonefoot?"

"Why, yes, there is," said Laird Cunningham of Barr. "But why do you ask? I thought a Sheriff would know everything without asking—even an ornamental one on his way to the Premiership."

"Oh, I heard the name," said Gregory. "It struck me as a curious one."

So that evening there came over the river from the Waterfoot of the Rhone the sound of a voice calling. Grace Allen sat thoughtfully looking out of the rose-hung window of the boathouse. Her face was an oval of perfect curve, crowned with a mass of light brown hair, in which were red lights when the sun shone directly upon it. Her skin was clear, pale as ivory, and even exertion hardly brought the latent under-flush of red to the surface.

"There's somebody at the waterfit. Gang, lassie, an' dinna be lettin' them aff withoot their siller this time!" said her aunt Barbara from her bed. Annie Allen was accustomed to say nothing, and she did it now.

The boat to the Rhonefoot was seldom needed, and the oars were not kept in it. They leaned against the end of the cottage, and Grace Allen took them on her shoulder as she went down. She carried them as easily as another girl might carry a parasol.

Again there came the cry from the Rhonefoot, echoing joyously across the river.

Standing well back in the boat, so as to throw up the bow, she pushed off. The water was deep where the boat lay, and it had been drawn half up on the bank. Where Grace dipped her oars into the silent water, the pool was so black that the blade of the oar was lost in the gloom before it got half-way down. Above there was a light wind moaning and rustling in the trees, but it did not stir even a ripple on the dark surface of the pool where the Black Water of Dee meets the brighter Ken.

Grace bent to her oars with a springing *verve* and force which made the tubby little boat draw towards the shore, the whispering lapse of water gliding under its sides all the while. Three lines of wake were marked behind—a vague white turbulence in the middle and two lines of bubbles on either side where the oars had dipped, which flashed a moment and then winked themselves out.

When she reached the Waterfoot, and the boat touched the shore, Grace Allen looked up to see Gregory Jeffray standing alone on the little copse-enclosed triangle of grass. He smiled pleasantly. She had not time to be surprised.

"What did you think of me this morning, running away without paying my fare?" he asked.

It seemed very natural now that he should come. She was glad that he had not brought his horse.

"I thought you would come by again," said Grace Allen, standing up, with one oar over the side ready to pull in or push off.

Gregory extended his hand as though to ask for hers to steady him as he came into the boat. Grace was surprised. No one ever did that at the Rhonefoot, but she thought it might be that he was a stranger and did not understand about boats. She held out her hand. Gregory leapt in beside her in a moment, but did not at once release the hand. She tried to pull it away.

"It is too little a hand to do so much hard work," he said.

Instantly Grace became conscious that it was rough and hard with rowing.
She had not thought of this before. He stooped and kissed it.

"Now," he said, "let me row across for you, and sit in front of me where I can see you. You made me forget all about everything else this morning, and now I must make up for it."

It was a long way across, and evidently Gregory Jeffray was not a good oarsman, for it was dark when Grace Allen went indoors to her aunts. Her heart was bounding within her. Her bosom rose and fell as she breathed quickly and silently through her parted red lips. There was a new thing in her eye.

Every evening thereafter, through all that glorious height of midsummer, there came a crying at the Waterfoot; and every evening Grace Allen went over to the edge of the Rhone wood to answer it. There the boat lay moored to a stone upon the turf, while Gregory and she walked upon the flowery forest carpet, and the dry leaves watched and clashed and muttered above them as the gloaming fell. These were days of rapture, each a doorway into yet fuller and more perfect joy.

Over at the Waterfoot the copses grew close. The green turf was velvet underfoot. The blackbirds fluted in the hazels there. None of them listened to the voice of Gregory Jeffray, or cared for what he said to Grace Allen when she went nightly to meet him over the Black Water.

She rowed back alone, the simple soul that was in her forwandered and mazed with excess of joy. As she set the boat to the shore and came up the bank bearing the oars which were her wings into the world of love under the green alders, the light in the west, lingering clear and pure and cold, shone upon her and added radiances to her eyes.

But Aunt Annie watched her with silent pain. Barbara from her bed spoke sharp and cruel words which Grace Allen listened to not at all.

For as soon as the morning shone bright over the hills and ran on tip-toe up the sparkling ripples of the loch, she looked across the Black Water to the hidden ways where in the evening her love should meet her.

As she went her daily rounds, and the gripper-iron slipped on the wet chain or grew hot in the sun, as she heard the clack of the wheel and the soft slow grind of the boat's broad lip on the pebbles, Grace Allen said over and over to herself, "It is so long, only so long, till he will come."

So all the days she waited in a sweet content. Barbara reproached her; Aunt Annie perilled her soul by lying to shield her; but Grace herself was shut out from shame or fear, from things past or things to come, by faith and joy that at last she had found one whom her soul loved.

And overhead the dry poplar leaves clashed and rustled, telling out to one another that love was a vain thing, and the thrush cried thrice, "Beware." But Grace Allen would not have believed had one risen to her from the dead.

So the great wasteful summer days went by, the glory of the passionate nights of July, the crisper blonde luxuriance of August. Every night there was the calling from the green plot across the Black Water. Every night Aunt Annie wandered, a withered grey ghost, along the hither side of the inky pool, looking for what she could not see and listening for that which she could not hear. Then she would go in to lie gratuitously to Barbara, who told her to her face that she did not believe her.

But in the first chill of mid-September, swift as the dividing of the blue-black thunder-cloud by the winking flame, fell the sword of God, smiting and shattering. It seemed hard that it should fall on the weaker and the more innocent. But then God has plenty of time.

One chilly gloaming there was no calling at the Rhonefoot. Nevertheless Grace rowed over and waited, imagining that all evil had befallen her lover. Within, her aunt Barbara fretted and murmured at her absence, driving her silent sister into involved refuges of lies to shield young Grace Allen, whom her soul loved.

The next day went by as the night had passed, with an awful constriction about her heart, a numbness over all her body; yet Grace did her work as one who dares not stop.

Two serving-men crossed in the ferry-boat, unconcernedly talking over the country news as men do when they meet.

"Did ye hear aboot young Jeffray?" asked the herd from the Mains.

"Whatna Jeffray?" asked, without much show of interest, the ploughman from Drumglass.

"Wi' man, the young lad that the daft folk in Enbra sent here for Sheriff."

"I didna ken he was hereawa'," said the Mains, with a purely perfunctory surprise.

"Ou ay, he has been a feck ower by at the Barr. They say he's gaun to get marriet to the youngest dochter. She's hae a gye fat stockin'-fit, I'se warrant."

"Ye may say sae, or a lawyer wadna come speerin' her," returned him from Drumglass as the boat reached the farther side.

"Guid-e'en to ye, Grace," said they both as they put their pennies down on the little tin plate in the corner.

"She's an awesome still lassie, that," said the Mains, as he took the road down to Parton Raw, where he had trysted with a maid of another sort. "Did ye notice she never said a word to us, neyther 'Thank ye,' nor yet 'Guid-day'? Her een were fair stelled in her head."

"Na, I didna observe," said Drumglass cotman indifferently.

"Some fowk are like swine. They notice nocht that's no pitten intil the trough afore them!" said the Mains indignantly.

So they parted, each to his own errand.

Day swayed and swirled into a strange night of shooting stars and intensest darkness. The soul of Grace Allen wandered in blackest night. Sometimes the earth appeared ready to open and swallow her up. Sometimes she seemed to be wandering by the side of the great pool of the Black Water with her hands full of flowers. There were roses blush-red, like what he had said her cheeks were sometimes. There were velvety pansies, and flowers of strange intoxicating perfume, the like of which she had never seen. But at every few yards she felt that she must fling them all into the black water and fare forth into the darkness to gather more.

Then in her bed she would start up, hearing the hail of a dear voice calling to her from the Rhonefoot. Once she put on her clothes in haste and would have gone forth; but her aunt Annie, waking and startled, a tall, gaunt apparition, came to her.

"Grace Allen," she said, "where are you gangin' at this time o' the nicht?"

"There's somebody at the boat," she said, "waiting. Let me gang, Aunt Annie: they want me; I hear them cry. O Annie, I hear them crying as a bairn cries!"

"Lie doon on yer bed like a clever lass," said her aunt gently. "There's naebody there."

"Or gin there be," said Aunt Barbara from her bed, "e'en let them cry. Is this a time for decent fowk to be gaun play-actin' aboot?"

So the daylight came, and the evening and the morning were the second day. And Grace Allen went about her work with clack of gripper-iron and dip of oar.

Late on in the gloaming of the third day following, Aunt Annie went down to the broad flat boat that lay so still at the water's edge. Something black was knocking dully against it.

Grace had been gone four hours, and it was weary work watching along the shore or going within out of the chill wind to endure Barbara's bitter tongue.

The black thing that knocked was the small boat, broken loose from her moorings and floating helplessly. Annie Allen took a boathook and pulled it to the shore. Except that the boat was half full of flowers, there was nothing and no one inside.

But the world span round and the stars went out when the finder saw the flowers.

When Aunt Annie Allen came to herself, she found the water was rising rapidly. It was up to her ankles. She went indoors and asked for Grace.

"Save us, Ann!" said Barbara; "I thocht she was wi' you. Where hae ye been till this time o' nicht? An' your feet's dreepin' wat. Haud aff the clean floor!"

"But Gracie! Oor lassie Grade! What's come o' Gracie?" wailed the elder woman.

At that instant there came so thrilling a cry from over the dark waters out of the night that the women turned to one another and instinctively caught at each other's hands.

"Leave me, I maun gang," said Aunt Annie. "That's surely Grace."

Her sister gripped her tight.

"Let me gang—let me gang. She's my ain lassie, no yours!" Annie said fiercely, endeavouring to thrust off Barbara's hands as they clutched her like birds' talons from the bed.

"Help me to get up," said Barbara; "I canna be left here. I'll come wi' ye."

So she that had been sick for twelve years arose, like a ghost from the tomb, and with her sister went out to seek for the girl they had lost. They found their way to the boat, reeling together like drunken men. Annie almost lifted her sister in, and then fell herself among the drenched and waterlogged flowers.

With the instinct of old habitude they fell to the oars, Barbara rowing the better and the stronger. They felt the oily swirl of the Dee rising beneath them, and knew that there had been a mighty rain upon the hills.

"The Lord save us!" cried Barbara suddenly. "Look!"

She pointed up the long pool of the Black Water. What she saw no man knows, for Aunt Annie had fainted, and Barbara was never herself after that hour.

Aunt Annie lay like a log across her thwart. But, with the strength of another world, Barbara unshipped the oar of her sister and slipped it upon the thole-pin opposite to her own. Then she turned the head of the boat up the pool of the Black Watery Something white floated dancingly alongside, upborne for a moment on the boiling swirls of the rising water. Barbara dropped her oars, and snatched at it. She held on to some light wet fabric by one hand; with the other she shook her sister.

"Here's oor wee Gracie," she said: "Ann, help me hame wi' her!"

So they brought her home, and laid her all in dripping white upon her white bed. Barbara sat at the bed-head and crooned, having lost her wits. Aunt Annie moved all in a piece, as though she were about to fall headlong.

"White floo'ers for the angels, where Gracie's ga'en to! Annie, woman, dinna ye see them by her body—four great angels, at ilka corner yin?"

Barbara's voice rose and fell, wayward and querulous. There was no other sound in the house, only the water sobbing against the edge of the ferry-boat.

"And the first is like a lion," she went on, in a more even recitative, "and the second is like an ox, and the third has a face like a man, and the fourth is like a flying eagle. An' they're sittin' on ilka bedpost; and they hae sax wings, that meet owre my Gracie, an' they cry withoot ceasing, 'Holy! holy! holy! Woe unto him that causeth one of these little ones to perish! It were better for him that a millstone were hanged about his neck and he were cast into the deeps o' the Black Water!'"

But the neighbours paid no attention to her—for, of course, she was mad.

Then the wise folk came and explained how it had all happened. Here she had been gathering flowers; here she had slipped; and here, again, she had fallen. Nothing could be clearer. There were the flowers. There was the dangerous pool on the Black Water. And there was the body of Grace Allen, a young thing dead in the flower of her days.

"I see them! I see them!" cried Barbara, fixing her eyes on the bed, her voice like a shriek; "they are full of eyes, behind and before, and they see into the heart of man. Their faces are full of anger, and their mouths are open to devour—"

"Wheesh, wheesh, woman! Here's the young Sheriff come doon frae the Barr wi' the Fiscal to tak' evidence."

And Barbara Allen was silent as Gregory Jeffray came in.

To do him justice, when he wrote her the letter that killed—concerning the necessities of his position and career—he had tried to break the parting gently. How should he know all that she knew? It was clearly an ill turn that fate had played him. Indeed, he felt ill-used. So he listened to the Fiscal taking evidence, and in due course departed.

But within an inner pocket he had a letter that was not filed with the documents, but which might have shed clearer light upon when and how Grace Allen slipped and fell, gathering flowers at night above the great pool of the Black Water.

"There is set up a throne in the heavens," chanted mad Barbara Allen as Gregory went out; "and One sits upon it—and my Gracie's there, clothed in white robes, an' a palm in her hand. And you'll be there, young man," she cried after him, "and I'll be there. There's a cry comin' owre the Black Water for you, like the cry that raised me oot o' my bed yestreen. An' ye'll hear it—ye'll hear it, braw young man; ay—and rise up and answer, too!"

But they paid no heed to her—for, of course, she was mad. Neither did Gregory Jeffray hear aught as he went out, but the water lapping against the little boat that was still half full of flowers.

The days went by, and being added together one at a time, they made the years. And the years grew into one decade, and lengthened out towards another.

Aunt Annie was long dead, a white stone over her; but there was no stone over Grace Allen—only a green mound where daisies grew.

Sir Gregory Jeffray came that way. He was a great law-officer of the Crown, and first heir to the next vacant judgeship. This, however, he was thinking of refusing because of the greatness of his private practice.

He had come to shoot at the Barr, and his baggage was at Barmark station. How strange it would be to see the old places again in the gloom of a September evening!

Gregory still loved a new sensation. All was so long past—the bitterness clean gone out of it. The old boathouse had fallen into other hands, and railways had come to carry the traffic beyond the ferry.

As Sir Gregory Jeffray walked from the late train which set him down at the station, he felt curiously at peace. The times of the Long Ago came back not ungratefully to his mind. There had been much pleasure in them. He even thought kindly of the girl with whom he had walked in the glory of a forgotten summer along the hidden ways of the woods. Her last letter, long since destroyed, was not disagreeable to him when he thought of the secret which had been laid to rest so quietly in the pool of the Black Water.

He came to the water's edge. He sent his voice, stronger now than of yore, but without the old ring of boyish hopefulness, across the loch. A moment's silence, the whisper of the night wind, and then from the gloom of the farther side an answering hail—low, clear, and penetrating.

"I am in luck to find them out of bed," said Gregory Jeffray to himself.

He waited and listened. The wind blew chill from the south athwart the ferry. He shivered, and drew his fur-lined travelling-coat about him. He could hear the water lapping against the mighty piers of the railway viaduct above, which, with its gaunt iron spans, like bows bent to send arrows into the heavens, dimly towered between him and the skies.

Now, this is all that men definitely know of the fate of Sir Gregory Jeffray. A surfaceman who lived in the new houses above the landing-place saw him standing there, heard him hailing the Waterfoot of the Dee, to which no boat had plied for years. Maliciously he let the stranger call, and abode to see what should happen.

Yet astonishment held him dumb when again across the dark stream came the crying, thrilling him with an unknown terror, till he clutched the door to make sure of his retreat within. Mastering his fear, he stole nearer till he could hear the oars planted in the iron pins, the push off the shore, and then the measured dip of oars coming towards the stranger across the pool of the Black Water.

"How do they know, I wonder, that I want to be taken to the Rhonefoot?
They are bringing the small boat," he heard him say.

A skiff shot out of the gloom. It was a woman who was rowing. The boat grounded stern on. The watcher saw the man step in and settle himself on the seat.

"What rubbish is this?" Gregory Jeffray cried angrily as he cleared a great armful of flowers off the seat and threw them among his feet.

The oars dipped, and without sound the boat glided out upon the waves of the loch towards the Black Water, into whose oily depths the blades fall silently, and where the water does not lap about the prow. The night grew suddenly very cold. Somewhere in the darkness over the Black Water the watching surfaceman heard some one call three times the name of Gregory Jeffray. It sounded like a young child's voice. And for very fear he ran in and shut the door, well knowing that for twenty years no boat had plied there.

It was noted as a strange thing that, on the same night on which Sir Gregory Jeffray was lost, the last of the Allens of the old ferry-house died in the Crichton Asylum. Barbara Allen was, without doubt, mad to the end, for the burden of her latest cry was, "He kens noo! he kens noo! The Lord our God is a jealous God! Now let Thy servant depart in peace!"

But Gregory Jeffray was never seen again by water or on shore. He had heard the cry across the Black Water.

III

SAINT LUCY OF THE EYES

[*Taken from the Journals of Travel written by Stephen Douglas, sometime of Culsharg in Galloway.*]

I.

O mellow rain upon the clover tops;
  O breath of morning blown o'er meadow-sweet;
Lush apple-blooms from which the wild bee drops
  Inebriate; O hayfield scents, my feet

Scatter abroad some morning in July;
  O wildwood odours of the birch and pine,
And heather breaths from great red hill-tops nigh,
  Than olive sweeter or Sicilian vine;—

Not all of you, nor summer lands of balm—
  Not blest Arabia,
Nor coral isles in seas of tropic calm.
  Such heart's desire into my heart can draw.

II.

O scent of sea on dreaming April morn
  Borne landward on a steady-blowing wind;
O August breeze, o'er leagues of rustling corn,
  Wafts of clear air from uplands left behind,

And outbreathed sweetness of wet wallflower bed,
  O set in mid-May depth of orchard close,
Tender germander blue, geranium red;
  O expressed sweetness of sweet briar-rose;

Too gross, corporeal, absolute are ye,
  Ye help not to define
That subtle fragrance, delicate and free,
  Which like a vesture clothes this Love of mine.

"Heart's Delight."

CHAPTER I

THE WOMAN OF THE RED EYELIDS

It was by Lago d'Istria that I found my pupil. I had come without halt from Scotland to seek him. For the first time I had crossed the Alps, and from the snow-flecked mountain-side, where the dull yellow-white patches remained longest, I saw beneath me the waveless plain of Lombardy.

The land of Lombardy—how the words had run in my dreams! Surely some ancestor of mine had wandered northwards from that gracious plain. On one side of me, at least, I was sib to the vineyards and the chestnut groves. For strange yearnings thrilled me as I beheld white-garlanded cities strung across the plain, the blue lakes grey in the haze, like eyes that look through tears.

Yet hitherto a hill-farm on the moors of Minnigaff had been my abiding-place. There I had played with the collies and the grey rabbits. There I had listened to the whaup and the peewits crying in the night; and save the cold, grey, resonant spaces of Edinburgh, whither I had gone to study, this was all my eyes had yet known. But when Giovanni Turazza, exile from the city of Verona, paused in his reading of the sonorous Italian to rebuke my Scots accent, and continued softly to give me illustrations of the dialects of north and south, something moved within me that sickened me to think of the Lombard plain sleeping in the gracious sunshine—which I might never see.

Yet I saw it. I trod its ways and stood by its still waters. And already they are become my life and my home.

Now, I who write am Stephen Douglas, of the moorland stock of the northern Douglases—kin to Douglaswater, and on the wrong side of the blanket to Drumdarroch himself. It has been the custom that one of the Douglases should in every generation be sent to the college to rear for the kirk.

For the hand of the Douglas has ever been kind to kin; and since patronage came back—in law or out law, the Douglases have managed to put their man into Drumdarroch parish and to have a Douglas in the white manse by the Waterside. And so it is like to be when, as they say, the rights of patron shall again pass away.

Now, I was in process or manufacture for this purpose, though threatening to turn out somewhat over tardy in development to profit by the act of patronage. But the Douglas dourness stood me in good stead, as it has done all the Douglases that ever lived since the greatest of the race charged to the death, with the point of his spear dropped low and the heart of his lord thrown before him, among the Paynim hordes.

The lad to undertake whose tutelage I went abroad was a Fenwick of Allerton in the Border country—the scion of a reputable stock, sometime impoverished by gambling in the times of the Regent, and before that with whistling "Owre the water to Charlie"; but now, by the opening-up of the sea-coal pits, again gathering in the canny siller as none of the Fenwicks had done in the palmiest days of the moss-trooping.

Well I knew when I set out that I had my work before me, and that I should earn my two hundred pounds a year or all were done. For I had but a couple of years more than my pupil to boast myself upon; and he, having grown up on the Continent, chiefly in Latin cities and German watering-places, was vastly superior to me in the knowledge which comes not easily to the lads from the moors, who at all times know better how to loup a moss-hag than how to make a courtly bow.

Yet for all that I did not mean to be far behind any Border Fenwick when it came to making bows. Nor, as it happened, was I when all was done. This confidence was partly owing to full feeding on fine porridge and braxy, but more to that inbred belief of Galloway in itself which the ill-affected and envious nominate its conceit.

Henry Fenwick was abiding in this city of Vico Averso, as I had been informed by his uncle and guardian, for the baths. He had been advised of my coming, and, like the kindly lad that he proved to be, I found him waiting for me when the diligence arrived.

We met with few words on either side, but I think with instant hearty liking. My pupil was tall and dark, his hair a little long, yet not falling to his shoulders—somewhat feminine in type of feature and Italianate in complexion. But the mouth shewed breeding, the eyes kindliness; and, after all, these are the main features. I was especially glad to find myself taller than he by a span of inches.

He took me to the hotel where a room had been ordered for me—not one of the common Italian inns, but a hotel built for the accommodation of foreigners. As we went up the steps, we passed a lady sitting in the shade with a book. She was a large fair woman, with sleepy eyes and a mane of bronzed gold hair. She had been looking at us as we came, I will be bound; but when we passed she became absorbed and unconscious upon her book.

As Henry raised his hat she bowed slightly to him, lifting at the same time her heavy eyelids and glancing at me. I had once seen that look before—in a spectacle of wild beasts when I happened to stand close to a drowsing tigress that twitched an eyelid and flashed a yellow eye at me. In that eye-shot on the verandah of the hotel in Vico Averso, the crossing of glances was like a challenge, and thrilled me as when one is called to fight. I think we hated one another on the spot; yet for the life of me I could not tell why, save that the woman of the tiger's glance had a red edge to her heavy eyelids, and no eyelashes that I could see—which things are not the marks of a good woman, as I take it. Yet there was no real cause for the bitter and sudden dislike, for, as it chanced, she came but little into our adventures. For youth, for the sake of change, turns as readily away from evil as from good.

So eager was I to be down and out of doors, that I had hardly time to make disposition of my goods in the room which had been reserved for me. I threw open the casement. I hung half out of the window, and satisfied myself with looking upon the still, calm blue of Lago d'Orta beneath, flecked with heavy-bodied craft with deep yellow sails. My heart all the while was crying out hungrily, "At last! at last!"

The precipices of hills, coloured like amethysts, fronted us, where the southern Alps threw themselves downwards to the lake-shore. Half-a-dozen hotels with white walls and green blinds clung about the outside of the little town, and specially about the baths, which ever since the time of the Romans had given the place its reputation. Few English people went there, but many Italians, some Austrians, especially women—German men, and cosmopolitan Russians, to whom all outside their native country was a Fatherland.

"Come," said Henry as soon as we had become a little familiar, "let us go to the baths."

Entering a low stone door, we ran up a flight of steps and found ourselves in a circular building of ancient marble. It was to me the strangest sight. We looked down on a great number of people up to their necks in a kind of thick, coffee-coloured fluid, which steamed and gave off strange odours. Men and women were there, old and young. All were clad in full suits of light material, and comported themselves towards each other as in a drawing-room. The sight of so many heads all bobbing about on the coffee-coloured mud, like a hundred John the Baptists on one large charger, was to me exceedingly diverting.

Little tables were floating about on the muddy water, and some pairs in quiet corners played chess and even cards. But there was a constant circulation among the throng. Introductions were effected in form, save that no one shook hands, at least above the water; only the detached heads bowed ceremoniously. It was a new canto of the *Inferno*—the condemned playing dully at human society in the bubbling caldrons of the place of evil shades. Henry proposed to go down and take a bath, but my stomach rose against the fumes and the slimy brown stuff.

"It is not nearly so bad when you are once in!" he said, for he had tried it. But though I had reason to believe that to be true, I had no heart to make the test for myself.

As we came out, Henry made me an introduction to the Lady of the Red Eyelids.

"Madame von Eisenhagen!" So that is your name, thought I; and I wonder what may be your intentions! I had never seen the breed before, but the side of me that was sib to the South seemed to leap to a comprehension.

As Madame and I crossed our glances again, I am sure we both knew that it was to the knife. For Henry Fenwick, being a lad, had laid his boy's heart in her hands. Yet not seriously, but as a boy will when a woman twice his age thinks it worth her while to spread a net for him, flattering him with her eyes.

So for a while we sat on the terrace, and a kind of scentless, spineless whitethorn wept sprays of flowers upon us. We spoke French, in which my pupil, as I found, had greatly the advantage of me, and thought extremely well of himself in consequence. But within me I said, "My friend, wait till I have you a week at Greek!"

And this indeed came to pass, for over the intricacies of that language
I made him presently to sweat consumedly.

Of the matter of our talk there is not much to say. Henry spoke freely and well, Madame interjecting leading questions, and holding him with her eyes. I, on the contrary, spoke little, being occupied with the scenes going on beneath me—the men in the piazza piling the fine grain for the making of macaroni—the changing and chaffering groups about the kerchiefed market-women—the dark-faced, gypsy-like men with beady eyes. The murmur of the conversation came to me only at intervals, like voices in a dream; and sometimes for whole sentences together I lost its meaning completely.

Indeed, I had more pleasure in looking at the houses in Vico Averso, which were tangled together without the semblance of a plan. Each house, or part of a house, struggled upward to occupy its own patch of sky-line, in a hundred different heights and breadths. Each had a scrap of garden clinging to it along the lake-side, in which the green of the magnolias contrasted with the grey aspens and the warmer oleanders. There was a bright and laughing charm about the whole which drew my heart, and I longed to spend a lifetime in these white and foliage-fringed places.

But I found very soon that the face of Vico Averso was her fortune. For the side of our hostel which was turned to a dark and narrow Street of Smells took away my desire to dwell there. There came out clear in my mind the thought and sight of our hill-farm of Culsharg, set on the edge of its miles of heather, the free airs blowing about it, and all the wild birds crying. My mother would be coming to the door to look for my grandfather as he came off the hill from the sheep. A disgust at the bubbling devil's-caldron, a horror of the smiling, monosyllabic Woman of the Red Eyelids, filled my heart. I resolved to battle it out with Henry that very night, and to leave Vico Averso at once. If he would not do so much for me, I knew that I might take the diligence back again the way I came, and report my failure. But, for all that, I did not mean thus lamely to fail or go home with my finger in my mouth.

That night I drew from the lad his heart. He had been here for two months—indeed, ever since his Swiss tutor, Herr Gunther, had departed for Zurich suddenly, having been ignominiously thrashed by his own pupil. I gathered from him that he had intended to perform the like for me, but had given up the idea after seeing me leap from the top of the diligence.

Yet he was not unwilling to be taught that there are better things out under the free sunshine than to dream away good days with a woman like Madame Von Eisenhagen, who after all had perhaps done nothing worse than encourage the lad to philander and to waste his time. Then I cunningly painted the joys of a walking tour. We should take our packs on our backs, only a few pounds' weight; and, our staves in our hands, like student lads of clerkly learning in the ancient times, we should go forth to seek our adventures—a new one every hour, a new roof to sleep under every night, and maids fairer than dreams waving hands to us over every vineyard wall. Thus cunningly I baited my trap.

So had I gone many a time in mine own country, and so I meant to lead my pupil now. Henry Fenwick rose joyously at the thought. Madame had made his service a little hard, and, what is worse, a little monotonous. He was but a boy, and needed not, she thought, the binding distractions which usually accompany such allegiances.

CHAPTER II

THE WORD OF THE LITTLE PEOPLE

Betimes in the morning we were afoot—long before Madame was awake; and having committed our heavier luggage to the care of our Swiss landlord, we set each a knapsack on our backs, and with light foot passed through the market-place among the bright and chattering throng of Italian folk, whose greetings of "*Buone feste, buon principio, e buona fine*" told of the birth of another day of joy for them under the blue of their sky.

Before we were clear of the town, Henry turned, and as he glanced at the green valanced windows of the Hotel Averso he drew a long breath which was not quite a sigh. And this was all his farewell to the allegiance of half a score of weeks. For my part, I was not easy till we swung out of sight along the dusty road, and had skirted the first two or three miles of old wall and vineyard terrace, where the lizards were already flashing and darting in the sun.

But indeed it takes much to chain a young man's fancy, when the road of life runs enticingly before him, dappled with laurel and carpeted with primrose.

It was our vagabond year, and, as I had foretold, a fair maid stood at every door, smiling at us and leading us on. We did not keep long by the dusty road. Presently we turned up byways, over which the prickly-pear and red valerian broke in profuse and unprecise beauty—fleshy-leaved creepers, too, as of a house-leek turned passion-flower, over-crowned all with scarlet blotches of cunningly placed colour.

We wandered into woodland paths and across fields. A peasant or small farmer ran out to stay us. Something was forbidden, it appeared. We were trampling his artichokes or other precious crop. We understood him not over well, nor indeed tried to. But a touchingly insignificant piece of silver induced him to think more kindly of our error, and he showed us a sweet path, by the side of which a brook tinkled down from the cliffs above. It led us into another scene—and, I am of opinion, upon another man's property. For at the door of a low, square-roofed house stood a man with his hands clasped behind him. He frowned, for he had seen his neighbour of the itching palm lead us to his gate and there leave us. And of the silver that lay within that palm he had not partaken.

The sun was broad and high. Here were flats of hay, greyish-green, blue in parts—but with none of that moist and emerald velvet which would have flashed upon the burnside meadows at home. Again by the water we brushed against the asters, which had no business to be growing here in the spring. Among the young wheat the poppies were flaming—red-coat officers of the Sower of Tares, with flaunting feather leading on to the inquisition of fires, when the reapers edge their keen sickles and fall-to, and the tares are separated from the wheat.

For pence judiciously tendered, we had the young Pan himself for leader—an Italian boy of sixteen, fair as a god of Greece. He went before with the most innocent grace in the world, and looked at us over his shoulder. He called his sister to come also, and as a stimulant he held up his penny. But she hung back, smit with sudden maidenly modesty at the sight of two such proper young men; and so her brother danced on without her.

Looking back, we saw that she had called her mother, and now peeped out wistfully from behind the shelter of the skirt maternal. Perhaps she regretted that she had not gone with us, for there, far ahead, was her brother skipping upon his quest. And suddenly there was no interest in the dull farmyard and the cattle. For that is a way of women—to be willing too late.

As we go, we talk with the young Pan—Henry Fenwick freely, I slowly, yet with comprehension greater than speech.

Will Pan sit down and eat with us? we ask.

Surely! There is no doubt whatever that he will, and that gladly. But we must wait till we come to a spring of hill-water, so that we may have the true and only apostolic baptism for our red wine.

There presently we arrive. The place is verily an inspiration. It is a natural well in the shadow of a great rock. Overhead is the virgin cup rudely cut in the stone. A shelf for sitting on while you drink, and the rocky laver brimming with clear and icy water. Little grains of fine white sand dance at the bottom, where from its living source the pure brew wells up. It is indeed a proper place to break bread.

Here, with Pan talking to us in a speech soft as the Italian air, we eat and are refreshed. Pan himself willingly opens his heart, and tells us of the changes that are coming—an Italy free from lagoon to triangle-which is to say, from Venice to Messina. But there is much dying to be done before then. The tears must fall from many mothers' eyes—from his own, who knows? Will he fight? Ay, surely he will fight! And the face of Pan hardens, till one understands how he could have been so cruel one day to the reeds which grew in the river.

But the distance beckons us, and the sun draws himself upward to his strength. We have on us the English itch for change. The breeze comes and goes as we plunge among the groves of Virgilian ilex, and through the interstices of the trees we see on a hill-slope above us thirty great horned oxen, etched black against the sky.

Here Pan leaves us, saying farewell with tears in his woman's eyes; with silver also in his pocket, which, to do him justice, does not comfort him wholly. Before he goes, for love and gratitude he tells us of a rhyme with which to please the children and to cause the good wives to give us a lodging.

At the next village we try its efficacy upon a company by the well—a group with those oriental suggestions which are common to all villages south of the Alps. The effect is instantaneous. The shy maidens draw nearer, the boys gather from their noisy game, the bambinos stretch to us from many a sisterly shoulder. We sit down, a couple of wayfarers, dusty and hot. But no sooner is the rhyme said than, lo! a tin is dipped for our drinking, and the Rebekah of the well herself expects her kiss, nor, spite of a possible knife, is she disappointed. For the rhyme's sake we are friends of the fairies and can put far the evil eye. It is good to entertain us. Thanks be to Pan! We shall offer him a garland of enduring ivy, or it may be half a kid. The cry that was heard over the waters was not true! Pan is not dead. Perhaps he too but sleeps a while, and in the likeness of young goatherds the god of the earlier time, reborn in dew, comes out still to tell his secrets to wandering lads who, asking no favour, go a-wayfaring with strong hearts as in the ancient days.

Round the corner peeps a laughing face. An urchin of surpassing impishness, one who has come too late to hear our password, taunts us in evil words.

"Ha, Giuseppe, beware of the Giant Caranco! Behold, he has the great teeth of the English. At the water-trough this morning I saw him sharpening them to eat thee, thou exceeding plump one! In the bag at his back he carries the bones of sixteen just as fat as thou art!"

And the rascal flees with a cry of pretended fear. So contagious is terror, that more than half our band flees away a dozen paces, halting there upon one foot, balancing our evil and our good.

But we have wiles as well as rhymes, and great in all places of the earth is the fascination of ready money.

"The Giant Caranco! forsooth," we say; "what lack of sense! Does the Giant Caranco know the good word of the Gentle Folk whose song brings luck? Can the Giant Caranco tell the tale that only the fairies know? Has the Giant Caranco those things in his wallet which are loved of lads and maids? Of a surety, no! Was ever such nonsense heard!"

In vain rings the shout of the maligner on the rocks above, as the circle gathers in again closer than ever about us.

"Beware of his thrice-sharpened teeth, Giuseppe! I saw him bite a fair half-moon out of the iron pipe by the fountain trough this morning!" he cries.

It is worse than useless now. Not only does the devil's advocate lack his own halfpenny; but with a swirl of the hand and a cunning jerk at the side, a stone whizzes after this regardless railer upon honest giants. Wails and agony follow. It is a dangerous thing to sit in the scorner's chair, specially when the divinity has the popular acclaim, with store of sweetmeats and *soldi* as well.

Most dangerous of all is it to interfere with a god in the making, for proselytism is hot, and there are divine possibilities.

CHAPTER III

THE STORY OF THE SEVEN DEAD MEN

And the stories! There were many of them. The young faces bent closer as we told the story of Saint Martin dividing his cloak among the beggars. Then came our own Cornish giant-killer, adapted for an Italian audience, dressed to taste in a great brigand hat and a beltful of daggers and pistols. Blunderbore in the Italian manner was a distinguished success. It was Henry who told the tales, but yet I think it was I who had the more abundant praise. For they heard me prompt my Mercurius, and they saw him appeal to me in a difficulty. Obviously, therefore, Henry was the servant of the chief magician, who like a great lord only communicated his pleasure through his steward.

Then with a tale of Venice[1] that was new to them we scared them out of a year's growth—frightening ourselves also, for then we were but young. It was well that the time was not far from high noon. The story told in brief ran thus. It was the story of the "Seven Dead Men."

[Footnote 1: For the origin of this and much else as profitable and pleasant, see Mr. Horatio Brown's *Life on the Lagoons*, the most charming and characteristic of Venetian books.]

There were once six men that went fishing on the lagoons. They brought a little boy, the son of one of them, to remain and cook the polenta. In the night-time he was alone in the cabin, but in the morning the fishermen came in. And if they found that aught was not to their taste, they beat him. But if all was well, they only bade him to wash up the dishes, yet gave him nothing to eat, knowing that he would steal for himself, as the custom of boys is.

But one morning they brought with them from their fishing the body of a dead man—a man of the mainland whom they had found tumbling about in the current of the Brenta. For he had looked out suddenly upon them where the sea and the river strive together, and the water boils up in great smooth, oily dimples that are not wholesome for men to meddle with.

Now, whether these six men had not gone to confession or had not confessed truly, so that the priest's absolution did them no good, the tale ventures not to say. But this at least is sure, that for their sins they set this dead thing that had been a man in the prow of the boat, all in his wet clothes. And for a jest on the little boy they put his hand on his brow, as though the dead were in deep cogitation.

As this story was in the telling, the attention of the children grew keen and even painful. For the moment each was that lonely lad on the islet, where stood the cabin of the Seven Dead Men.

So as the boat came near in the morning light, the boy stood to greet them on the little wooden pier where the men landed their fish to clean, and he called out to the men in the boat—

"Come quickly," he cried; "breakfast is ready—all but the fish to fry."

He saw that one of the men was asleep in the prow; yet, being but a lad, he was only able to count as many as the crows—that is, four. So he did not notice that in the boat there was a man too many. Nor would he have wondered, had he been told of it. For it was not his place to wonder. He was only sleepy, and desired to lie down after the long night alone. Also he hoped that they had had a good catch of fish, so that he would escape being beaten. For indeed he had taken the best of the polenta for himself before the men came—which was as well, for if he had waited till they were finished, there had been but dog's leavings for him. He was a wise boy, this, when it came to eating. Now, eating and philosophy come by nature, as doth also a hungry stomach; but arithmetic and Greek do not come by nature. To which Henry Fenwick presently agreed.

The men went in with a good appetite to their breakfast, and left the dead man sitting alone in the prow with his hand on his brow.

So when they sat down, the boy said—

"Why does not the other man come in? I see him sitting there. Are you not going to bring him in to breakfast also?" (For he wished to show that he had not eaten any of the polenta.)

Then, for a jest upon him, one of the men answered—

"Why, is the man not here? He is indeed a heavy sleeper. You had better go and wake him."

So the little boy went to the door and called, shouting loud, "Why cannot you come to breakfast? It has been ready this hour, and is going cold!"

And when the men within heard that, they thought it the best jest in a month of Sundays, and they laughed loud and strong.

So the boy came in and said—"What ails the man? He will not answer though I have called my best."

"Oh" said they, "he is but a deaf old fool, and has had too much to drink over-night. Go thou and swear bad words at him, and call him beast and fool!"

So the men put wicked words into the boy's mouth, and laughed the more to hear them come from the clean and innocent lips of a lad that knew not their meaning. And perhaps that is the reason of what followed.

So the boy ran in again.

"Come out quickly, one of you," said the lad, "and wake him, for he does not heed me, and I am sure that there is something the matter with him. Mayhap he hath a headache or evil in his stomach."

So they laughed again, hardly being able to eat for laughing, and said—

"It must be cramp of the stomach that is the matter with him. But go out again, and shake him by the leg, and ask him if he means to keep us waiting here till doomsday."

So the boy went out and shook the man as he was bidden.

Then the dead man turned to him, sitting up in the prow as natural as life, and said—

"What do you want with me?"

"Why in the name of the saints do you not come?" said the boy; "the men want to know if they are to wait till doomsday for you."

"Tell them," said the man, "that I am coming as fast as I can. For this is Doomsday!" said he.

The boy ran back into the hut, well pleased. For a moment his voice could not be heard, because of the noisy laughter of the men. Then he said—

"It is all right. He says he is coming."

Then the men thought that the boy was trying in his turn to put a jest on them, and would have beaten him. In a moment, however, they heard something coming slowly up the ladder, so they laughed no more, but all turned very pale and sat still and listened. And only the boy remembered to cross himself.

The footsteps came nearer. The door was pushed stumblingly open, as by one that fumbles and is not sure of his way. Then the man that had been dead and drowned, of whom they had made their sport, came in and sat down at the boy's place, the seventh at the table. Whereupon there was a great silence. None spoke, but all looked; for none, save the boy only, could withdraw his eyes from those of the dead man. Colder and chillier flowed the blood in their veins, till it ceased to flow at all, and froze about their hearts.

Whereat the boy flung himself shrieking into a boat and rowed away by the power of his own saint, Santa Caterina of Siena. He met some fishermen in a sailing boat, but it was the third day before any dared row to the lonely Casa on the mud bank. When they did go, three men climbed up the posts at different sides, for the ladder had fallen away. They went not in, but only looked through the window. They saw indeed six men, who sat round the platter of cold polenta. But the seventh, who sat at the bottom in the boy's place, shone as though he had been on fire, leaning back in his chair as one that laughed and made merry at a jest. But the six were fallen silent and very sober.

So the three men that looked fell back from off the platform into the water as dead men; and had not their companions been active men of Malamocco, they too had been drowned. So there to this day in the lonely Casa of the Seven Dead Men the six are sitting, and the fiery seventh at the table-foot, in the boy's place—until the Day comes that is Doomsday, which is the last day of all.

CHAPTER IV

THE SINFUL VILLAGE OF SPELLINO

This was the story we told, and there was not a face among the audience that did not blanch, and in that village there were undoubtedly some who that night did not sleep.

Now, the success of the story of the Seven Dead Men was great, surprising, embarrassing. For as soon as we ceased the children ran off to their homes to bring their mothers, who also had to hear. So we had to tell as before, without the alteration of a word.

Then home from the meadow pastures where they had been mowing, past the ripening grain, the fathers came, ill-pleased to find the dinner still not ready. Then these in their turn had to be fetched, and the story told from the beginning. Yea, and did we vary so much as the droop of a hair on the wet beard of the drowned man as he tumbled in the swirl of the lagoon where the Brenta meets the tide, a dozen voices corrected us, and we were warned to be careful. A reputation so sudden and tremendous is, at its beginning, somewhat brittle.

The group about the well now included almost every able-bodied person in the village, and several of the cripples, who cried out if any pushed upon them. Into the midst of this inward-bent circle of heads the village priest elbowed his way, a short and rotund father, with a frown on his face which evidently had no right there.

"Story-tellers!" he exclaimed. "There is no need for such in my village.
We grow our own. Thou, Beppo, art enough for a municipality, and thou,
Andrea. But what have we here?"

He paused open-mouthed. He had expected the usual whining, mumping beggar; and lo, here were two well-attired *forestieri* with their packs on their backs and their hats upon their heads. But we stood up, and in due form saluted the father, keeping our hats in our hands till he, pleased at this recognition and deference before his flock, signed to us courteously to put them on again.

After this, nothing would do but we must go with him to his house and share with him a bottle of the noble wine of Montepulciano.

"It is the wine of my brother, who is there in the cure of souls," he said. "Ah, he is a judge of wine, my brother. It is a fine place, not like this beast of a village, inhabited by bad heretics and worse Catholics."

"Bad Protestants—who are they?" I said, for I had been reared in the belief that all Protestants were good—except, perhaps, they were English Episcopalians. Specially all Protestants in the lands of Rome were good by nature.

The priest looked at us with a question in his eye.

"You are of the Church, it may be?" asked he, evidently thinking of our reverence at the well-stoop.

We shook our heads.

"It matters not," said the easy father; "you are, I perceive, good Christians. Not like these people of Spellino, who care neither for priest nor pastor."

"There he goes," said the priest, pointing out of the window at a man in plain and homely black who went by—the sight of whom, as he went, took me back to the village streets of Dullarg when I saw the minister go by. I had a sense that I ought to have been out there with him, instead of sitting in the presbytery of the Pope's priest. But the father thought not of that, and the Montepulciano was certainly most excellent. "A bad, bad village," said the father, looking about him as if in search of something.

"Margherita!" he cried suddenly.

An old woman appeared, dropping a bleared courtesy, unlike her queenly name.

"What have you for dinner, Margherita?

"Enough for one; not enough for three, and they hungry off the road," she said. "If thou, O father, art about to feed the *lazzaroni* of the north and south thou must at least give some notice, and engage another servant!"

"Nay, good Margherita," answered the priest very meekly, "there is enough boiled fowl and risotto of liver and rice to serve half a score of appetites. See to it," he said.

Margherita went grumbling away. What with beggars and leaping dogs, besides children crawling about the steps, it was ill living in such a presbytery—one also which was at any rate so old that no one could keep it clean, though they laboured twenty-four hours in the day—ay, and rose betimes upon the next day.

As the lady said, the place was old. Father Philip told us that it had been the wing of a monastery.

"See," he said, "I will show you."

So saying, he led us through a wide, cool, dusky place, with arched roof and high windows, the walls blotched and peeling, with the steam of many monkish dinners. The doors had been mostly closed up, and only at one side did an open window and archway give glimpses of pillared cloisters and living green. We begged that we might sit out here, which the priest gladly allowed, for the sight of the green grass and the tall white lilies standing amid was a mighty refreshment in the hot noontide. Sunshine flickered through the mulberry and one grey cherry-tree, and sifted down on the grass.

Then the priest told us all the sin of the villagers of Spellino. It was not that a remnant of the Waldenses was allowed to live there. The priest did not object to good Waldensians. But the people of Spellino would neither pay priest nor pastor. They were infidels.

"A bad people, an accursed people!" he repeated. "I have not had my dues for ten years as I ought. I send my agent to collect; and as soon as he appears, every family that is of the religion turns heretic. Not a child can sign the sign of the Cross, not though I baptized every one of them. All the men belong to the church of Pastor Gentinetta, and can repeat his catechism."

The priest paused and shook his head.

"A bad people! a bad people!" he said over and over again. Then he smiled, with some sense of the humour of the thing.

"But there are many ways with bad people," he said; "for when my good friend, Pastor Gentinetta, collects his stipend, and the blue envelopes of the Church are sent round, what a conversion ensues to Holy Church! Lo, there is a crucifix in every house in Spellino, save in one or two of the very faithful, who are so poor that they have nothing to give. Each child blesses himself as he goes in. Each *bambino* has the picture of its patron saint swung about its neck. The men are out at the *festa*, the women not home from confession, and there is not a *soldo* for priest or pastor in all this evil village of Spellino!"

Father Philip paused to chuckle in some admiration at such abounding cleverness in his parish.

"How then do you live, either of you?" I asked, for the matter was certainly curious.

The father looked at us.

"You are going on directly?" he said, in a subdued manner.

"Immediately," we said, "when we have tired out your excellent hospitality."

"Then I shall tell you. The manner of it is this. My friend Gentinetta;—he is my friend, and an excellent one in this world, though it is likely that our paths may not lie together in the next, if all be true that the Pope preaches. We two have a convention, which is private and not to be named. It is permitted to circumvent the wicked, and to drive the reluctant sheep by innocent craft.

"Now, Pastor Gentinetta has the advantage of me during the life of his people. It is indeed a curious thing that these heretics are eager to partake of the untransformed and unblessed sacraments, which are no sacraments. It is the strangest thing! I who preach the truth cannot drive my people with whips of scorpions to the blessed sacraments of Holy Church. They will not go for whip or cord. But these heretics will mourn for days if they be not admitted to their table of communion. It is one of the mysterious things of God. But, after all, it is a lucky thing," soliloquised Father Philip; "for what does my friend do when they come to him for their cards of communion, but turns up his book of stipend and statute dues. Says he—'My friend, such and such dues are wanting. A good Christian cannot sit down at the sacrament without clearing himself with God, and especially with His messenger.' So there he has them, and they pay up, and often make him a present besides. For such threats my rascals would not care one black and rotten fig."

"But how," said I in great astonishment, "does this affect you?"

"Gently and soothly," said the priest. "Wait and ye shall hear. If the pastor has the pull over me in life, when it comes to sickness, and the thieves get the least little look within the Black Doors that only open the one way—I have rather the better of my friend. It is my time then. My fellows indeed care no button to come to holy sacrament. They need to be paid to come. But, grace be to God for His unspeakable mercy, Holy Church and I between us have made them most consumedly afraid of the world that is to come. And with reason!"

Father Philip waited to chuckle.

"But Gentinetta's people have everything so neatly settled for them long before, that they part content without so much as a 'by your leave' or the payment of a death-duty. Not so, however, the true believer. He hath heard of Purgatory and the warmth and comfort thereof. Of the other place, too, he has heard. He may have scorned and mocked in his days of lightsome ease, but down below in the roots of his heart he believes. Oh, yes, he believes and trembles; then he sends for me, and I go!

"'Confession—it is well, my son! extreme unction, the last sacraments of the Church—better and better! But, my son, there is some small matter of tithes and dues standing in my book against thy name. Dost thou wish to go a debtor before the Judge? Alas! how can I give thee quittance of the heavenly dues, when thou hast not cleared thyself of the dues of earth?' Then there is a scramble for the old canvas bag from its hiding-place behind the ingle-nook. A small remembrance to Holy Church and to me, her minister, can do no harm, and may do much good. Follows confession, absolution—and, comforted thus, the soul passes; or bides to turn Protestant the next time that my assessor calls. It matters not; I have the dues."

"But," said I, "we have here two things that are hard to put together. In a time of health, when there is no sickness in the land, thou must go hungry. And when sickness comes, and the pastor's flock are busy with their dying, they will have no time to go to communion. How are these things arranged?"

"Even thus," replied Father Philip. "It is agreed upon that we pool the proceeds and divide fairly, so that our incomes are small but regular. Yet, I beseech thee, tell it not in this municipality, nor yet in the next village; for in the public places we scowl at one another as we pass by, Pastor Gentinetta and I."

"And which is earning the crust now?" said I.

The jovial priest laughed, nodding sagely with his head.

"Gentinetta hath his sacraments on Tuesday, and his addresses to his folk have been full of pleasant warnings. It will be a good time with us."

"And when comes your turn?" cried Henry, who was much interested by this recital.

"There cometh at the end of the barley harvest, by the grace of God, a fat time of sickness, when many dues are paid; and when the addresses from the altar of this Church of Sant Philip are worth the hearing."

The old priest moved the glass of good wine at his elbow, the fellow of the Montepulciano he had set at ours.

"A bad town this Spellino," he muttered; "but I, Father Philip, thank the saints—and Gentinetta, he thanks his mother, for the wit which makes it possible for poor servants of God to live."

The old servant thrust her head within.

"Tonino Scala is very sick," she said, "and calleth for thee!"

The priest nodded, rose from his seat, and took down a thick leather-bound book.

"Lire thirty-six," he said—"it is well. It begins to be my time. This week Gentinetta and his younglings shall have chicken-broth."

So with heartiest goodwill we bade our kind Father Philip adieu, and fared forth upon our way.

CHAPTER V

THE COUNTESS CASTEL DEL MONTE

After leaving Spellino we went downhill. There was a plain beneath, but up on the hillside only the sheep were feeding contentedly, all with their broad-tailed sterns turned to us. The sun was shining on the white diamond-shaped causeway stones which led across a marshy place. We came again to the foot of the hill. It had indeed been no more than a dividing ridge, which we had crossed over by Spellino.

We saw the riband of the road unwind before us. One turn swerved out of sight, and one alone. But round this curve, out of the unseen, there came toward us the trampling of horses. A carriage dashed forward, the coachman's box empty, the reins flying wide among the horses' feet. There was but little time for thought; yet as they passed I caught at their heads, for I was used to horses. Then I hung well back, allowing myself to be jerked forward in great leaps, yet never quite loosing my hold. It was but a chance, yet a better one than it looked.

At the turn of the road towards Spellino I managed to set their heads to the hill, and the steep ascent soon brought the stretching gallop of the horses to a stand-still.

It seemed a necessary thing that there should be a lady inside. I should have been content with any kind of lady, but this one was both fair and young, though neither discomposed nor terrified, as in such cases is the custom.

"I trust Madame is not disarranged," I said in my poor French, as I went from the horses' heads to the carriage and assisted the lady to alight.

"It serves me right for bringing English horses here without a coachman to match," she said in excellent English. "Such international misalliances do not succeed. Italian horses would not have startled at an old beggar in a red coat, and an English coachman would not have thrown down the reins and jumped into the ditch. Ah, here we have our Beppo"—she turned to a flying figure, which came labouring up hill. To him the lady gave the charge of the panting horses, to me her hand.

"I must trouble you for your safe-conduct to the hotel," she said. Now, though her words were English, her manner of speech was not.

By this time Henry had come up, and him I had to present, which was like to prove a difficulty to me, who did not yet know the name of the lady. But she, seeing my embarrassment, took pity on me, saying—

"I am the Countess Castel del Monte," looking at me out of eyes so broadly dark, that they seemed in certain lights violet, like the deeps of the wine-hearted Greek sea.

By this time Beppo had the horses well under control, and at the lady's invitation we all got into the carriage. She desired, she said, that her brother should thank us.

We went upwards, turning suddenly into a lateral valley. Here there was an excellent road, better than the Government highway. We had not driven many miles when we came in sight of a house, which seemed half Italian *palazzo* and half Swiss cottage, yet which had nevertheless an undefined air of England. There were balconies all about it, and long rows of windows.

It did not look like a private house, and Henry and I gazed at it with great curiosity. For me, I had already resolved that if it chanced to be a hotel, we should lodge there that night.

The Countess talked to us all the way, pointing out the objects of interest in the long row of peaks which backed the Val Bergel with their snows and flashing Alpine steeps. I longed to ask a question, but dared not. "Hotel" was what she had said, yet this place had scarcely the look of one. But she afforded us an answer of her own accord.

"You must know that my brother has a fancy of playing at landlord," she said, looking at us in a playful way. "He has built a hostel for the English and the Italians of the Court. It was to be a new Paris, was it not so? And no doubt it would have been, but that the distance was over great. It was indeed almost a Paris in the happy days of one summer. But since then I have been almost the only guest."

"It is marvellously beautiful," I replied. "I would that we might be permitted to become guests as well."

"As to that, my brother will have no objections, I am sure," replied the Countess, "specially if you tell your countrymen on your return to your own country. He counts on the English to get him his money back. The French have no taste for scenery. They care only for theatres and pretty women, and the Italians have no money—alas! poor Castel del Monte!"

I understood that she was referring to her husband, and said hastily—

"Madame is Italian?"

"Who knows?" she returned, with a pretty, indescribable movement of her shoulders. "My father was a Russian of rank. He married an Englishwoman. I was born in Italy, educated in England. I married an Italian of rank at seventeen; at nineteen I found myself a widow, and free to choose the world as my home. Since then I have lived as an Englishwoman expatriated—for she of all human beings is the freest."

I looked at her for explanation. Henry, whose appreciation of women was for the time-being seared by his recent experience of Madame of the Red Eyelids, got out to assist Beppo with the horses. In a little I saw him take the reins. We were going slowly uphill all the time.

"In what way," I said, "is the Englishwoman abroad the freest of all human beings?"

"Because, being English, she is supposed to be a little mad at any rate. Secondly, because she is known to be rich, for all English are rich. And, lastly, because she is recognised to be a woman of sense and discretion, having the wisdom to live out of her own country."

We arrived on the sweep of gravel before the door. I was astonished at the decorations. Upon a flat plateau of small extent, which lay along the edge of a small mountain lake, gravelled paths cut the green sward in every direction. The waters of the lake had been carefully led here and there, in order apparently that they might be crossed by rustic bridges which seemed transplanted from an opera. Little windmills made pretty waterwheels to revolve, which in turn set in motion mechanical toys and models of race-courses in open booths and gaily painted summer-houses.

"You must not laugh," said the Countess gravely, seeing me smile, "for this, you must know, is a mixture of the courts of Italy and Russia among the Alps. It is to my brother a very serious matter. To me it is the Fair of Asnières and the madhouse at Charenton rolled into one."

I remarked that she did the place scant justice.

"Oh," she said, "the place is lovely enough, and in a little while one becomes accustomed to the tomfoolery."

We ascended the steps. At the top stood a small dark man, with a flash in his eyes which I recognised as kin to the glance which Madame the Countess shot from hers, save that the eyes of the man were black as jet.

"These gentlemen," said the Countess, "are English. They are travelling for their pleasure, and one of them stopped my stupid horses when the stupider Beppo let them run away, and jumped himself into the ditch to save his useless skin. You will thank the gentlemen for me, Nicholas."

The small dark man bowed low, yet with a certain reserve.

"You are welcome, messieurs," he said in English, spoken with a very strong foreign accent. "I am greatly in your debt that you have been of service to my sister."

He bowed again to both of us, without in the least distinguishing which of us had done the service, which I thought unfair.

"It is my desire," he went on more freely, as one that falls into a topic upon which he is accustomed to speak, "that English people should be made aware of the beauty of this noble plateau of Promontonio. It is a favourable chance which brings you here. Will you permit me to show you the hotel?"

He paused as though he felt the constraint of the circumstances. "Here, you understand, gentlemen, I am a hotel-keeper. In my own country—that is another matter. I trust, gentlemen, I may receive you some day in my own house in the province of Kasan."

"It will make us but too happy," said I, "if in your capacity as landlord you can permit us to remain a few days in this paradise."

I saw Henry look at me in some astonishment; but his training forbade him to make any reply, and the little noble landlord was too obviously pleased to do more than bow. He rang a bell and called a very distinguished gentleman in a black dress-coat, whose spotless attire made our rough outfit look exceedingly disreputable, and the knapsacks upon our backs no less than criminal. We decided to send at once to Vico Averso for our baggage.

But these very eccentricities riveted the admiration of our distinguished host, for only the mad English would think of tramping through the Val Bergel in the heart of May with a donkey's load on their backs. Herr Gutwein, a mild, spectacled German, and the manager of this cosmopolitan palace, was instructed to show us to the best rooms in the house. From him we learned that the hotel was nearly empty, but that it was being carried on at great loss, in the hope of ultimate success.

We found it indeed an abode of garish luxury. In the great salon, the furniture was crimson velvet and gold. All the chairs were gilt. The very table-legs were gilded. There were clocks chiming and ticking everywhere, no one of them telling the right time. In the bedrooms, which were lofty and spacious, there were beautiful canopies, and the most recent improvements for comfort. The sitting-rooms had glass observatories built out, like swallows' nests plastered against the sides of the house. Blue Vallauris vases were set in the corners and filled with flowers. Turkey carpets of red and blue covered the floor. Marvellous gold-worked tablecloths from Smyrna were on the tables. Everywhere there was a tinge of romance made real—the dream of many luxuries and civilisations transplanted and etherealised among the mountains.

Then, when we had asked the charges for the rooms and found them exceedingly reasonable, we received from the excellent Herr Gutwein much information.

The hotel was the favourite hobby of Count Nicholas. It was the dream of his life that he should make it pay. While he lived in it, he paid tariff for his rooms and all that he had. His sister also did the same, and all her suite. Indeed, the working expenses were at present paid by Madame the Countess of Castel del Monte, who was a half-sister of Count Nicholas, and much younger. The husband of Madame was dead some years. She had been married when no more than a girl to an Italian of thrice her age. He, dying in the second year of their marriage, had left her free to please herself as to what she did with her large fortune. Madame was rich, eccentric, generous; but to men generally more than a little sarcastic and cold.

At dinner that night Count Nicholas took the head of the table, while Dr. Carson, the resident English physician, sat at his left hand, and Madame at his right. I sat next to the Countess, and Henry Fenwick next to the doctor. We made a merry party. The Count opened for us a bottle of Forzato and another of Sassella, of the quaint, untranslatable bouquet which will not bear transportation over the seas, and to taste which you must go to the Swiss confines of the Valtellina.

"Lucia," said Count Nicholas, "you will join me in a bottle of the Straw wine in honour of the stopping of the horses; and you will drink to the health of these gentlemen who are with us, to whom we owe so much." Afterwards we drank to Madame, to the Count himself, and to the interests of science in the person of the doctor. Then finally we pledged the common good of the hotel and kursaal of the Promontonio.

The Countess was dressed in some rose-coloured fabric, thickly draped with black lace, through whose folds the faint pink blush struggled upward with some suggestion of rose fragrance, so sheathed was she in close-fitting drapery. She looked still a very girl, though there was the slower grace of womanhood in the lissom turn of her figure, slender and *svelte*. Her blue-black hair had purple lights in it. And her great dark violet eyes were soft as La Vallière's. I know not why, but to myself I called her from that moment, "My Lady of the Violet Crown." There was a passion-flower in her hair, and on her pale face her lips, perfectly shaped, lay like the twin petals of a geranium flower fallen a little apart.

Dinner was over. The lingering lights of May were shining through the hill gaps, glorifying the scant woods and the little mountain lake. Henry Fenwick and the Count were soon deep in shooting and breechloaders. Presently they disappeared in the direction of the Count's rooms to examine some new and beautiful specimens more at their leisure.

In an hour Henry came rushing back to us in great excitement.

"I have written for all my things from Lago d'Istria," he said, "and I am getting my guns from home. There is some good shooting, the Count says. Do you object to us staying here a little time?"

I did not contradict him, for indeed such a new-born desire to abide in one place was at that moment very much to my mind. And though I could not conceive what, save rabbits, there could be to shoot in May on a sub-Alpine hillside, I took care not to say a word which might damp my pupil's excellent enthusiasms.

CHAPTER VI

LOVE ME A LITTLE—NOT TOO MUCH

I stood by the wooden pillars of the wide piazza and watched the stars come out. Presently a door opened and the Countess appeared. She had a black shawl of soft lace about her head, which came round her shoulders and outlined her figure.

I knew that this must be that mantilla of Spain of which I had read, and which I had been led to conceive of as a clumsy and beauty-concealing garment, like the *yashmak* of the Turks. But the goodliness of the picture was such that in my own country I had never seen green nor grey which set any maid one-half so well.

"Let us walk by the lake," she said, "and listen to the night."

So quite naturally I offered her my arm, and she took it as though it were a nothing hardly to be perceived. Yet in Galloway of the hills it would have taken me weeks even to conceive myself offering an arm to a beautiful woman. Here such things were in the air. Nevertheless was my heart beating wildly within me, like a bird's wings that must perforce pulsate faster in a rarer atmosphere. So I held my arm a little wide of my side lest she should feel my heart throbbing. Foolish youth! As though any woman does not know, most of all one who is beautiful. So there on my arm, light and white as the dropped feather of an angel's wing, her hand rested. It was bare, and a diamond shone upon it.

The lake was a steel-grey mirror where it took the light of the sky. But in the shadows it was dark as night. The evening was very still, and only the Thal wind drew upward largely and contentedly.

"Tell me of yourself!" she said, as soon as we had passed from under the shelter of the hotel.

I hesitated, for indeed it seemed a strange thing to speak to so great a lady concerning the little moorland home, of my mother, and all the simple people out there upon the hills of sheep.

The Countess looked up at me, and I saw a light shine in the depths of her eyes.

"You have a mother—tell me of her!" she said.

So I told her in simple words a tale which I had spoken of to no one before—of slights and scorns, for she was a woman, and understood. It came into my mind as I spoke that as soon as I had finished she would leave me; and I slackened my arm that she might the more easily withdraw her hand. But yet I spoke on faithfully, hiding nothing. I told of our poverty, of the struggle with the hill-farm and the backward seasons, of my mother who looked over the moorland with sweet tired eyes as for some one that came not. I spoke of the sheep that had been my care, of the books I had read on the heather, and of all the mystery and the sadness of our life.

Then we fell silent, and the shadows of the sadness I had left behind me seemed to shut out the kindly stars. I would have taken my arm away, but that the Countess drew it nearer to herself, clasping her hands about it, and said softly—

"Tell me more—" and then, after a little pause, she added, "and you may call me Lucia! For have you not saved my life?"

Like a dream the old Edinburgh room, where with Giovanni Turazza I read the Tuscan poets, came to me. An ancient rhyme was in my head, and ere I was aware I murmured—

"Saint Lucy of the Eyes!"

The Countess started as if she had been stung.

"No, not that—not that," she said; "I am not good enough."

There was some meaning in the phrase to her which was not known to me.

"You are good enough to be an angel—I am sure," I said—foolishly, I fear.

There was a little silence, and a waft of scented air like balm—I think the perfume of her hair, or it may have been the roses clambering on the wall. I know not. We were passing some.

"No," she said, very firmly, "not so, nor nearly so—only good enough to desire to be better, and to walk here with you and listen to you telling of your mother."

We walked on thus till we heard the roar of the Trevisa falls, and then turned back, pacing slowly along the shore. The Countess kept her head hid beneath the mantilla, but swayed a little towards me as though listening. And I spoke out my heart to her as I had never done before. Many of the things I said to her then, caused me to blush at the remembrance of them for many days after. But under the hush of night, with her hands pressing on my arm, the perfume of flowers in the air, and a warm woman's heart beating so near mine, it is small wonder that I was not quite myself. At last, all too soon, we came to the door, and the Countess stood to say good-night.

"Good-night!" she said, giving me her hand and looking up, yet staying me with her great eyes; "good-night, friend of mine! You saved my life to-day, or at least I hold it so. It is not much to save, and I did not value it highly, but you were not to know that. You have told me much, and I think I know more. You are young. Twenty-three is childhood. I am twenty-six, and ages older than you. Remember, you are not to fall in love with me. You have never been in love, I know. You do not know what it is. So you must not grow to love me—or, at least, not too much. Then you will be ready when the True Love that waits somewhere comes your way."

She left me standing without a word. She ran up the steps swiftly. On the topmost she poised a moment, as a bird does for flight.

"Good-night, Douglas!" she said. "Stephen is a name too common for you—I shall call you Douglas. Remember, you must love me a little—but not too much."

I stood dull and stupid, in a maze of whirling thought. My great lady had suddenly grown human, but human of a kind that I had had no conception of. Only this morning I had been opening the stores of very chill wisdom to my pupil, Henry Fenwick of Allerton. Yet here, long ere night was at its zenith, was I, standing amazed, trying under the stars to remember exactly what a woman had said, and how she looked when she said it.

"To love her a little—yet not to love her too much."

That was the difficult task she had set me. How to perform I knew not.

At the top of the steps I met Henry.

"Do you think that we need go on to-morrow morning?" he said. "Do you not think we are in a very good quarter of the world, and that we might do worse than stop a while?"

"If you wish it, I have no objections," I said, with due caution.

"Thank you!" he said, and ran off to give some further directions about his guns.

CHAPTER VII

THE NEW DAY

It need not be wondered at that during the night I slept little. It seemed such a strange thing which had happened to me. That a great lady should lean upon my arm—a lady of whom before that day I had never heard—seemed impossible to my slow-moving Scots intelligence.

I sat most of the night by my window, from which I looked down the valley. The moonlight was filling it. The stars tingled keen and frosty above. Lucent haze of colourless pearl-grey filled the chasm. On the horizon there was a flush of rose, in the midst of which hung a snowy peak like a wave arrested when it curves to break, and on the upmost surge of white winked a star.

I opened the casement and flung it back. The cool, icy air of night took hold on me. I listened. There came from below the far sound of falling waters. Nearer at hand a goat bleated keenly. A dull, muffled sound, vast and mysterious, rose slumberously. I remembered that I was near to the great Alps. Without doubt it was the rumble of an avalanche.

But more than all these things,—under this roof, closed within the white curtains, was the woman who with her well-deep, serene eyes had looked into my life.

"To-morrow and to-morrow and to-morrow!" I said to myself, seeing the possibilities waver and thicken before me. So I went to my bed, leaving the window open, and after a time slept.

But very early I was astir. The lake lay asleep. The shadows in its depths dreamed on untroubled. There was not the lapse of a wavelet on the shore. The stars diminished to pin-points, and wistfully withdrew themselves into the coming mystery of blue. Behind the eastern mountains the sun rose—not yet on us who were in the valley, but flooding the world overhead with intense light. On the second floor a casement opened and a blind was drawn aside. There was nothing more—a serving-maid, belike. But my heart beat tumultuously.

Nova dies indeed, but I fear me not *nova quies*. But when ever to a man was love a synonym for quietness? Quietness is rest. Rest is embryonic sleep. Sleep is death's brother. But, contrariwise, love to a man is life—new life. Life is energy—the opening of new possibilities, the breaking of ancient habitudes. Sulky self-satisfactions are hunted from their lair. Sloth is banished, selfishness done violence to with swiftest poniard-stroke.

Again, even to a passionate woman love is rest. That low sigh which comes from her when, after weary waiting, at last her lips prove what she has long expected, is the sigh for rest achieved. There is indeed nothing that she does not know. But, for her, knowledge is not enough—she desires possession. The poorest man is glorified when she takes him to her heart. She desires no longer to doubt and fret—only to rest and to be quiet. A woman's love when she is true is like a heaven of Sabbaths. A man's, at his best, like a Monday morn when the work of day and week begins. For love, to a true man, is above all things a call to work. And this is more than enough of theory.

Once I was in a manufacturing city when the horns of the factories blew, and in every street there was the noise of footsteps moving to the work of the day. It struck me as infinitely cheerful. All these many men had the best of reasons for working. Behind them, as they came out into the chill morning air, they shut-to the doors upon wife and children. Why should they not work? Why should they desire to be idle? Had I, methought, such reasons and pledges for work, I should never be idle, and therefore never unhappy. For me, I choose a Monday morning of work with the whistles blowing, and men shutting their doors behind them. For that is what I mean by love.

All this came back to me as I walked alone by the lake while the day was breaking behind the mountains.

As though she had heard the trumpet of my heart calling her, she came. I did not see her till she was near me on the gravel path which leads to the châlet by the lake. There was a book of devotion in her hand. It was marked with a cross. I had forgotten my prayers that morning till I saw this.

Yet I hardly felt rebuked, for it was morning and the day was before me. With so much that was new, the old could well wait a little. For which I had bitterly to repent.

She looked beyond conception lovely as she came towards me. Taller than I had thought, for I had not seen her—you must remember—since. It seemed to me that in the night she had been recreated, and came forth fresh as Eve from the Eden sleep. Her eyelashes were so long that they swept her cheeks; and her eyes, that I had thought to be violet, had now the sparkle in them which you may see in the depths of the southern sea just where the sapphire changes into amethyst.

Did we say good-morning? I forget, and it matters little. We were walking together. How light the air was!—cool and rapturous like snow-chilled wine that is drunk beneath the rose at thirsty Teheran. The ground on which we trod, too, how strangely elastic! The pine-trees give out how good a smell! Is my heart beating at all, or only so fine and quick that I cannot count its pulsings?

What is she saying—this lady of mine? I am not speaking aloud—only thinking. Cannot I think?

She told me, I believe, why she had come out. I have forgotten why. It was her custom thus to walk in the prime. She had still the mantilla over her head, which, as soon as the sun looked over the eastern crest of the mountains, she let drop on her shoulders and so walked bareheaded, with her head carried a trifle to the side and thrown back, so that her little rounded chin was in the air.

"I have thought," she was saying when I came to myself, "all the night of what you told me of your home on the hills. It must be happiness of the greatest and most perfect, to be alone there with the voices of nature—the birds crying over the heather and the cattle in the fields."

"Good enough," I said, "it is for us moorland folk who know nothing better than each other's society—the bleating sheep to take us out upon the hills and the lamp-light streaming through the door as we return homewards."

"There is nothing better in this world!" said the Countess with emphasis.

But just then I was not at all of that mind.

"Ah, you think so," said I, "because you do not know the hardness of the life and its weary sameness. It is better to be free to wander where you will, in this old land of enchantments, where each morning brings a new joy and every sun a clear sky."

"You are young—young," she said, shaking her head musingly, "and you do not know. I am old. I have tried many ways of life, and I know."

It angered me thus to hear her speak of being old. It seemed to put her far from me I remembered afterwards that I spoke with some sharpness, like a petulant boy.

"You are not so much older than I, and a great lady cannot know of the hardness of the life of those who have to earn their daily bread."

She smiled in an infinitely patient way behind her eyelashes.

"Douglas," she said, "I have earned my living for more years than the difference of age that is between us."

I looked at her in amazement, but she went on—

"In my brother's country, which is Russia, we are not secure of what is our own, even for a day. We may well pray there for our daily bread. In Russia we learn the meaning of the Lord's Prayer."

"But have you not," I asked, "great possessions in Italy?"

"I have," the Countess said, "an estate here that is my own, and many anxieties therewith. Also I have, at present, the command of wealth—which I have never yet seen bring happiness. But for all, I would that I dwelt on the wide moors and baked my own bread."

I did not contradict her, seeing that her heart was set on such things; nevertheless, I knew better than she.

"You do not believe!" she said suddenly, for I think from the first she read my heart like a printed book. "You do not understand! Well, I do not ask you to believe. You do not know me yet, though I know you. Some day you will have proof!"

"I believe everything you tell me," I answered fervently.

"Remember," she said, lifting a finger at me—"only enough and not too much. Tell me what is your idea of the place where I could be happy."

This I could answer, for I had thought of it.

"In a town of clear rivers and marble palaces," I answered, "where there are brave knights to escort fair ladies and save them from harm. In a city where to be a woman is to be honoured, and to be young is to be loved."

"And you, young seer, that are of the moorland and the heather," she said, "where would you be in such a city?"

"As for me," I said, "I would stand far off and watch you as you passed by."

"Ah, Messer Dante Alighieri, do not make a mistake. I am no Beatrice. I love not chill aloofness. I am but Lucia, here to-day and gone to-morrow. But rather than all rhapsodies, I would that you were just my friend, and no further off than where I can reach you my hand and you can take it."

So saying, because we came to the little bridge where the pines meet overhead, she reached me her hand at the word; and as it lay in mine I stooped and kissed it, which seemed the most natural thing in the world to do.

She looked at me earnestly, and I thought there was a reproachful pity in her eyes.

"Friend of mine, you will keep your promise," she said. I knew well enough what promise it was that she meant.

"Fear not," I replied; "I promise and I keep."

Yet all the while my heart was busy planning how through all the future
I might abide near by her side.

We turned and walked slowly back. The hotel stood clear and sharp in the morning sunshine, and a light wind was making the little waves plash on the pebbles with a pleasant clapping sound.

"See," she said, "here is my brother coming to meet us. Tell me if you have been happy this morning?"

"Oh," I said quickly, "happy!—you know that without needing to be told."

"No matter what I know," the Countess said, with a certain petulance, swift and lovable—"tell it me."

So I said obediently, yet as one that means his words to the full—

"I have been happier than ever I thought to be this morning!"

"Lucia!" she said softly—"say Lucia!"

"Lucia!" I answered to her will; yet I thought she did not well to try me so hard.

Then her brother came up briskly and heartily, like one who had been a-foot many hours, asking us how we did.

CHAPTER VIII

THE CRIMSON SHAWL

Henry Fenwick and the Count went shooting. He came and asked my leave as one who is uncertain of an answer. And I gave it guiltily, saying to myself that anything which took his mind off Madame Von Eisenhagen was certainly good. But there leaped in my heart a great hope that, in what remained of the day, I might again see the Countess.

I was grievously disappointed. For though I lounged all the afternoon in the pleasant spaces by the lake, only the servants, of the great empty hotel passed at rare intervals. Of Lucia I saw nothing, till the Count and Henry passed in with their guns and found me with my book.

"Have you been alone all the afternoon?" they said, innocently enough. And it was some consolation to answer "Yes," and so to receive their sympathy.

Henry came again to me after dinner. The Count was going over the hills to the Forno glacier, and had asked him; but he would not go unless I wished it. I bade him take my blessing and depart, and again he thanked me.

There was that night a band of thirty excellent performers to discourse music to the guests at the table—being, as the saw says, us four and no more. But the Count was greatly at his ease, and told us tales of the forests of Russia, of wolf-hunts, and of other hunts when the wolves were the hunters—tales to make the blood run cold, yet not amiss being recounted over a bottle of Forzato in the bright dining-room. For, though it was the beginning of May, the fire was sparkling and roaring upwards to dispel the chill which fell with the evening in these high regions.

There is talk of mountaineering and of the English madness for it. The Count and Henry Fenwick are on a side. Henry has been over long by himself on the Continent. He is at present all for sport. Every day he must kill something, that he may have something to show. The Countess is for the hills, as I am, and the *élan* of going ever upward. So we fall to talk about the mountains that are about us, and the Count says that it is an impossibility to climb them at this season of the year. Avalanches are frequent, and the cliffs are slippery with the daily sun-thaw congealing in thin sheets upon the rocks. He tells us that there is one peak immediately behind the hotel which yet remains unclimbed. It is the Piz Langrev, and it rises like a tower. No man could climb that mural precipice and live.

I tell them that I have never climbed in this country; but that I do not believe that there is a peak in the world which cannot in some fashion or another be surmounted—time, money, and pluck being provided wherewith to do it.

"You have a fine chance, my friend," says the Count kindly, "for you will be canonised by the guides if you find a way up the front of the Langrev. They would at once clap on a tariff which would make their fortunes, in order to tempt your wise countrymen, who are willing to pay vast sums to have the risk of breaking their necks, yet who will not invest in the best property in Switzerland when it is offered to them for a song."

The Count is a little sore about his venture and its ill success.

The Countess, who sits opposite to me to-night, looks across and says, "I am sure that the peak can be climbed. If Mr. Douglas says so, it can."

"I thank you, Madame," I say, bowing across at her.

Whereat the other two exclaim. It is (they say) but an attempt on my part to claim credit with a lady, who is naturally on the side of the adventurous. The thing is impossible.

"Countess," say I, piqued by their insistency, "if you will give me a favour to be my *drapeau de guerre*, in twenty-four hours I shall plant your colours on the battlements of the Piz Langrev."

Certainly the Forzato had been excellent.

The Countess Lucia handed a crimson shawl, which had fallen back from her shoulders, and which now hung over the back of her chair, across the table to me.

"They are my colours!" she said, with a light in her eye as though she had been royalty itself.

Now, I had studied the Piz Langrev that afternoon, and I was sure it could be done. I had climbed the worst precipices in the Dungeon of Buchan, and looked into the nest of the eagle on the Clints of Craignaw. It was not likely that I would come to any harm so long as there was a foothold or an armhold on the face of the cliff. At least, my idiotic pique had now pledged me to the attempt, as well as my pride, for above all things I desired to stand well in the eyes of the Countess.

But when we had risen from table, and in the evening light took our walk, she repented her of the giving of the gage, and said that the danger was too great. I must forget it—how could she bear the anxiety of waiting below while I was climbing the rocks of the Piz Langrev? It pleased me to hear her say so, but for all that my mind was not turned away from my endeavour.

It was a foolish thing that I had undertaken, but it sprang upon me in the way of talk. So many follies are committed because we men fear to go back upon our word. The privilege of woman works the other way. Which is as well, for the world would come to a speedy end if men and women were to be fools according to the same follies.

The Countess was quieter to-night. Perhaps she felt that her encouragement had led me into some danger. Yet she had that sense of the binding nature of the "passed word," which is perhaps strongest in women who are by nature and education cosmopolitan. She did not any more persuade me against my attempt, and soon went within. She had said little, and we had walked along together for the most part silent. Methought the stars were not so bright to-night, and the glamour had gone from the bridge under which the water was dashing white.

I also returned, for I had my arrangements to make for the expedition. The weather did not look very promising, for the Thal wind was bringing the heavy mist-spume pouring over the throat of the pass, and driving past the hotel in thin hissing wisps on a chill breeze. However, even in May the frost was keen at night, and to-morrow might be a day after the climber's heart.

I sought the manager in his sanctum of polished wood—a *comptoir* where there was little to count. Managers were a fleeting race in the Kursaal Promontonio. The Count was a kind master. But he was a Russian, and a taskmaster like those of Egypt, in that he expected his managers to make the bricks of dividends without the straw of visitors. With him I covenanted to be roused at midnight.

Herr Gutwein was somewhat unwilling. He had not so many visitors that he could afford to expend one on the cliffs of the Piz Langrev.

I looked out on the lake and the mountains from the window of my room before I turned in. They did not look encouraging.

Hardly, it seemed, had my head touched the pillow, when "clang, clang" went some one on my door. "It is half-past twelve, Herr, and time to get up!"

I saw the frost-flowers on the window-pane, and shivered. Yet there was the laughter of Henry and the Count to be faced; and, above all, I had passed my word to Lucia.

"Well, I suppose I may as well get up and take a look at the thing, any way. Perhaps it may be snowing," I said, with a devout hope that the blinds of mist or storm might be drawn down close about the mountains.

But, pushing aside the green window-blind, I saw all the stars twinkling; and the broad moon, a little worm-eaten about the upper edge, was flinging a pale light over the Forno glacier and the thick pines that hide Lake Cavaloccia.

"Ah, it is cold!" I flung open the hot-air register, but the fires were out and the engineer asleep, for a draft of icy wind came up—direct from the snowfields. I slammed it down, for the mercury in my thermometer was falling so rapidly that I seemed to hear it tap-tapping on the bottom of the scale.

Below there was a sleepy porter, who with the utmost gruffness produced some lukewarm coffee, with stale, dry slices of over-night bread, and flavoured the whole with an evil-smelling lamp.

"Shriekingly cold, Herr; yes, it is so in here!" he said in answer to my complaints. "Yes—but, it is warm to what it will be up there outside."

The pack was donned. The double stockings, the fingerless woollen gloves were put on, and the earflaps of the cap were drawn down. The door was opened quietly, and the chill outer air met us like a wall.

"A good journey, my Herr!" said the porter, a mocking accent in his voice—the rascal.

I strode from under the dark shadow of the hotel, wondering if Lucia was asleep behind her curtains over the porch.

CHAPTER IX

THE PIZ LANGREV

Past the waterfall and over the bridge—our bridge—ran the path. As I turned my face to the mountain, there was a strange constricted feeling about one corner of my mouth, to which I put up a mittened hand. A small icicle fell tinkling down. My feet were now beginning to get a little warm, but I felt uncertain whether my ears were hot or cold. There was a strange unattached feeling about them. Had I not been reading somewhere of a mountaineer who had some such feeling? He put his hand to his ear and broke off a piece as one breaks a bit of biscuit. A horrid thought, but one which assuredly stimulates attention.

Then I took off one glove and rubbed the ear vigorously with the warm palm of my hand. There was a tingling glow, as though some one were striking lucifer matches all along the rim; soon there was no doubt that the circulation was effectually restored. *En avant!* Ears are useless things at the best.

I kept my head down, climbing steadily. But with the tail of my eye I could see that the hills had a sprinkling of snow—the legacy of the Thal wind which last night brought the moisture up the valley. Only the crags of the Piz Langrev were black above me, with a few white streaks in the crevices where the snow lies all the year. The cliffs were too steep for the snow to lie upon them, the season too far advanced for it to remain on the lower slopes.

The moon was lying over on her back, and the stars tingled through the frosty air. The lake lay black beneath on a grey world, plain as a blot of ink on a boy's copybook.

Yet I had only been climbing among the rocks a very few moments when every nerve was thrilling with warmth and all the arteries of the body were filled with a rushing tide of jubilant life. "This is noble!" I said to myself, as if I had never had a thought of retreat. A glow of heat came through my woollen gloves from the black rocks up which I climbed.

But I had gradually been getting out of the clear path on the face of the rocks into a kind of gully. I did not like the look of the place. There was a ground and polished look about the rocks at the sides which did not please me. I have seen the like among the Clints of Minnigaff, where the spouts of shingle make their way over the cliff. In the cleft was a kind of curious snow, dry like sand, creaking and binding together under foot—amazingly like pounded ice.

In the twinkling of an eye I had proof that I was right. There was a kind of slushy roaring above, a sharp crack or two as of some monster whip, and a sudden gust filled the gully. There was just time for me to throw myself sideways into a convenient cleft, and to draw feet up as close to chin as possible, when that hollow which had seemed my path, and high up the ravine on either side, was filled with tumbling, hissing snow, while the rocks on either side echoed with the musketry spatter of stones and ice-pellets.

I felt something cold on my temple. As the glove came down from touching it, there was a stain on the wool. A button of ice, no larger than a shilling, spinning on its edge, had neatly clipped a farthing's-worth out of the skin—as neatly as the house-surgeon of an hospital could do it.

At this point the story of a good Highland minister came up in my mind inopportunely, as these things will. He was endeavouring to steer a boat-load of city young ladies to a landing-place. A squall was bursting; the harbour was difficult. One of the girls annoyed him by jumping up and calling anxiously, "O, where are we going to? Where are we going to?" "If you do not sit down and keep still, my young leddy," said the minister-pilot succinctly, "that will verra greatly depend on how you was brocht up!"

The place at which I remembered this might have been a fine place for an observatory. It was not so convenient for reminiscence. Here the path ended. I was as far as Turn Back. I therefore tried more round to the right. The rocks were so slippery with the melted snow of yesterday that the nails in my boots refused to grip. But presently there, remained only a snow-slope, and a final pull up a great white-fringed bastion of rock. Here was the summit; and even as I reached it, over the Bernina the morning was breaking clear.

I took from my back the pine-branch which had been such a difficulty to me in the narrow places of the ascent; and with the first ray of the morning sun, from the summit of Langrev the pennon of the Countess Lucia streamed out. I thought of Manager Gutwein down there on the look-out, and I rejoiced that I had pledged him to secrecy.

Gutwein—there was a sound as of cakes and ale in the very name.

A little way beneath the summit, where the Thal wind does not vex, I sat me down on the sunny eastern side to consult with the Gutwein breakfast. A bottle of cold tea—"Hum," said I; "that may keep till I get farther down. It will be useful in case of emergency—there is nothing like cold tea in an emergency. *Imprimis*, half a bottle of Forzato—our old Straw wine. How thoughtless of Gutwein! He ought to have remembered that that particular sort does not keep. We had better take it now!" There was also half a chicken, some clove-scented Graubündenfleisch, four large white rolls, crisp as an Engadine cook can make them, half a pound of butter in each—O excellent Gutwein—O great and judicious Gutwein!

But no more—for the sun was climbing the sky, and I must go down with a rush to be in time for the late breakfast of the hotel.

The rocks came first—no easy matter with the sun on them for half an hour; but they at last were successfully negotiated. Then came the long snow-slope. This we went down all sails set. I hear that the process is named glissading in this country. It is called hunker-sliding in Scotland among the Galloway hills—a favourite occupation of politicians. It added to the flavour that we might very probably finish all standing in a crevasse. Snow rushed past, flew up one's nose and froze there. It did not behave itself thus when we slid down Craig Ronald and whizzed out upon the smooth breast of Loch Grannoch. I was reflecting on this unwarrantable behaviour of the snow, when there came a bump, a somersault, a slide, a scramble. "Dear me!" I say; "how did this happen?" Ears, eyes, mouth, nose were full of fine powdered snow—also, there were tons down one's back. Cold as charity, but no great harm done.

The table was set for the *déjeuner* in the dining-room of the hotel. The Count was standing rubbing his hands. Henry, who had been shooting at a mark, came in smelling of gun-oil; and after a little pause of waiting came the Countess.

"Where," said the Count, "is our Alpinist?" Henry had not seen him that day. He was no doubt somewhere about. But Herr Gutwein smiled, and also the waiter. They knew something. There was a crying at the door. The porter, full of noisy admiration, rang the great bell as for an arrival. Gutwein disappeared. The Count followed, then came Lucia and Henry. At that moment I arrived, outwardly calm, with my clothes carefully dusted from travel-stains, all the equipment of the ascent left in the wayside châlet by the bridge. I gave an easy good-morning to the group, taking off my hat to Madame. The Count cried disdainfully that I was a slug-a-bed. Henry asked with obvious sarcasm if I had not been up the Piz Langrev. The Countess held out her hand in an uncertain way. Certainly I must have been very young, for all this gave me intense pleasure. Especially did my heart leap when I took the Countess to the window a little to the right, and, pointing with one hand upwards, put the Count's binocular into her hands. The sun of the mid-noon was shining on a black speck floating from the topmost cliff of the Piz Langrev. As she looked she flung out her hand to me, still continuing to gaze with the glass held in the other. She saw her own scarlet favour flying from the pine-branch. That cry of wonder and delight was better to me than the Victoria Cross. I was young then. It is so good to be young, and better to be in love.

CHAPTER X

THE PURPLE CHÂLET

Our life at the Kursaal Promontonio was full of change and adventure. For adventures are to the adventurous. In the morning we read quietly together, Henry and I, beginning as soon as the sun touched our balcony, and continuing three or four hours, with only such intermission as the boiling of our spirit-lamp and the making of cups of tea afforded to the steady work of the morning.

Then at breakfast-time the work of the day was over. We were ready to make the most of the long hours of sunshine which remained. Sometimes we rowed with Lucia and her brother on the lake, dreaming under the headlands and letting the boat drift among the pictured images of the mountains.

Oftener the Count and Henry would go to their shooting, or away on some of the long walks which they took in company.

One evening it happened that M. Bourget, the architect of the hotel, a bright young Belgian, was at dinner with us, and the conversation turned upon the illiberal policy of the new Belgian Government. Most of the guests at table were landowners and extreme reactionaries. The conversation took that insufferably brutal tone of repression at all hazards which is the first thought of the governing classes of a despotic country, when alarmed by the spread of liberal opinions.

I could see that both the Count and Lucia put a strong restraint upon themselves, for I knew that their sympathies were with the oppressed of their own nation. But the excitement of M. Bourget was painful to see. He could speak but little English (for out of compliment to us the Count and the others were speaking English); and though on several occasions he attempted to tell the company that matters in his country were not as they were being represented, he had not sufficient words to express his meaning, and so subsided into a dogged silence.

My own acquaintance with the political movements in Europe was not sufficient to enable me to claim any special knowledge; but I knew the facts of the Belgian dispute well enough, and I made a point of putting them clearly before the company. As I did so, I saw the Count lean towards me, his face whiter than usual and his eyes dark and intense. The Countess, too, listened very intently; but the architect could not keep his seat.

As soon as I had finished he rose, and, coming round to where I sat, offered me his hand.

"You have spoken well," he said; "you are my brother. You have said what I was not able to say myself."

On the next day the architect, to show his friendship, offered to take us all over a châlet which had been built on the cliffs above the Kursaal, of which very strange tales had gone abroad. The Count and Henry had not come back from one of their expeditions, so that only the Countess Lucia and myself accompanied M. Bourget.

As we went he told us a strange story. The châlet was built and furnished to the order of a German countess from Mannheim, who, having lost her husband, conceived that the light of her life had gone out, and so determined to dwell in an atmosphere of eternal gloom.

To the outer view there was nothing extraordinary about the place—a châlet in the Swiss-Italian taste, with wooden balconies and steep outside stairs.

M. Bourget threw open the outer door, to which we ascended by a wide staircase. We entered, and found ourselves in a very dark hall. All the woodwork was black as ebony, with silver lines on the panels. The floor was polished work of parquetry, but black also. The roof was of black wood. The house seemed to be a great coffin. Next we went into a richly furnished dining-room. There were small windows at both ends. The hangings here were again of the deepest purple—so dark as almost to be black. The chairs were upholstered in the same material. All the woodwork was ebony. The carpet was of thick folds of black pile on which the feet fell noiselessly. M. Bourget flung open the windows and let in some air, for it was close and breathless inside. I could feel the Countess shudder as my hand sought and found hers.

So we passed through room after room, each as funereal as the other, till we came to the last of all. It was to be the bedroom of the German widow. M. Bourget, with the instinct of his nation, had arranged a little *coup de théâtre*. He flung open the door suddenly as we stood in one of the gloomy, black-hung rooms. Instantly our eyes were almost dazzled. This furthest room was hung with pure white. The carpet was white; the walls and roof white as milk. All the furniture was painted white. The act of stepping from the blackness of the tomb into this cold, chill whiteness gave me a sense of horror for which I could not account. It was like the horror of whiteness which sometimes comes to me in feverish dreams.

But I was not prepared for its effects upon the Countess.

She turned suddenly and clung to my arm, trembling violently.

"O take me away from this place!" she said earnestly.

M. Bourget was troubled and anxious, but I whispered that it was only the closeness of the rooms which made Madame feel a little faint. So we got her out quickly into the cool bright sunshine of the Alpine pastures. The Countess Lucia recovered rapidly, but it was a long while before the colour came back to her cheeks.

"That terrible, terrible place!" she said again and again. "I felt as though I were buried alive—shrouded in white, coffined in mort-cloths!"

CHAPTER XI

THE WHITE OWL

To distract her mind I told her tales of the grey city of the North where I had been colleged. I told of the bleak and biting winds which cut their way to the marrow of the bones. I described the students rich and poor, but mostly poor, swarming into the gaunt quadrangles, reading eagerly in the library, hasting grimly to be wise, posting hotfoot to distinction or to death. She listened with eyes intent. "We have something like that in Russia," she said; "but then, as soon as these students of ours become a little wise, they are cut off, or buried in Siberia." But I think that, with all her English speech and descent, Lucia never fully understood that these students of ours were wholly free to come or go, talk folly or learn sense, say and do good and evil, according to the freedom of their own wills. I told of our debating societies, where in the course of one debate there is often enough treason talked to justify Siberia—and yet, after all, the subject under discussion would only be, "Is the present Government worthy of the confidence of the country?"

"And then what happens? What does the Government say?" asked Lucia.

"Ah, Countess!" I said, "in my country the Government does not care to know what does not concern it. It sits aloft and aloof. The Government does not care for the chatter of all the young fools in its universities."

So in the tranced seclusion of this Alpine valley the summer of the year went by. The flowers carpeted the meadows, merging from pink and blue to crimson and russet, till with the first snow the Countess and her brother announced their intention of taking flight—she to the Court of the South, and he to his estates in the North.

The night before her departure we walked together by the lake. She was charmingly arrayed in a scarlet cloak lined with soft brown fur; and I thought—for I was but three-and-twenty—that the turned-up collar threw out her chin in an adorable manner. She looked like a girl. And indeed, as it proved, for that night she was a girl.

At first she seemed a little sad, and when I spoke of seeing her again at the Court of the South she remained silent, so that I thought she feared the trouble of having us on her hands there. So in a moment I chilled, and would have taken my hand from hers, had she permitted it. But suddenly, in a place where there are sands and pebbly beaches by the lakeside, she turned and drew me nearer to her, holding me meantime by the hand.

"You will not go and forget?" she said. "I have many things to forget. I want to remember this—this good year and this fair place and you. But you, with your youth and your innocent Scotland—you will go and forget. Perhaps you already long to go back thither."

I desired to tell her that I had never been so happy in my life. I might have told her that and more, but in her fierce directness she would not permit me.

"There is a maid who sits in one of the tall grey houses of which you speak, or among the moorland farms—sits and waits for you, and you write to her. You are always writing—writing. It is to that girl. You will pass away and think no more of Lucia!"

And I—what could or did I reply? I think that I did the best, for I made no answer at all, but only drew her so close to me that the adorable chin, being thrown out farther than ever, rested for an instant on my shoulder.

"Lucia," I said to her—"not Countess any more—little Saint Lucy of the Eyes, hear me. I am but a poor moorland lad, with little skill to speak of love; but with my heart I love you even thus—and thus—and thus."

And I think that she believed, for it comes natural to Galloway to make love well.

In the same moment we heard the sound of voices, and there were Henry and the Count walking to and fro on the terrace above us in the blessed dark, prosing of guns and battues and shooting.

Lucia trembled and drew away from me, but I put my finger to her lip and drew her nearer the wall, where the creepers had turned into a glorious wine-red. There we stood hushed, not daring to move; but holding close the one to the other as the feet of the promenaders waxed and waned above us. Their talk of birds and beasts came in wafts of boredom to us, thus standing hand in hand.

I shivered a little, whereat the Countess, putting a hand behind me, drew a fold of her great scarlet cloak round me protectingly as a mother might. So, with her mouth almost in my ear, she whispered, "This is delightful—is it not so? Pray, just hearken to Nicholas: 'With that I fired.' 'Then we tried the covert.' 'The lock jammed.' 'Forty-four brace.' Listen to the huntsmen! Shall we startle them with the horn, tra-la?" And she thrilled with laughter in my ear there in the blissful dark, till I had to put that over her mouth which silenced her.

"Hush, Lucy, they will hear! Be sage, littlest," I said in Italian, like one who orders, for (as I have said) Galloway even at twenty-three is no dullard in the things of love.

"Poor Nicholas!" she said again.

"Nay, poor Henry, say rather!" said I, as the footsteps drew away to the verge of the terrace, waxing fine and thin as they went farther from us.

"Hear me," said she. "I had better tell you now. Nicholas wishes me greatly to marry one high in power in our own country—one whose influence would permit him to go back to his home in Russia and live as a prince as before."

"But you will not—you cannot—" I began to say to her.

"Hush!" she said, laughing a little in my ear. "I certainly shall if you cry out like that"—for the footsteps were drawing nearer again. We leaned closer together against the parapet in the little niche where the creepers grew. And the dark grew more fragrant. She drew the great cloak about us both, round my head also. Her own was close to mine, and the touch of her hair thrilled me, quickening yet more the racing of my heart, and making me light-headed like unaccustomed wine.

"Countess!" I said, searching for words to thrill her heart as mine was thrilled already.

"Monsieur!" she replied, and drew away the cloak a little, making to leave me, but not as one that really intends to go.

"Lucia," I said hastily, "dear Lucy—"

"Ah!" she said, and drew the cloak about us again.

And what we said after that, is no matter to any.

But we forgot, marvel at it who will, to hearken to the footsteps that came and went. They were to us meaningless as the lapse of the waves on the shore, pattering an accompaniment above the soft sibilance of our whispered talk, making our converse sweeter.

Yet we had done well to listen a little.

"... I think it went in there," said the voice of the Count, very near to us and just above our heads. "I judge it was a white owl."

"I shall try to get it for the Countess!" said Henry.

Then I heard the most unmistakable, and upon occasion also the most thrilling, of sounds—the clicking of a well-oiled lock. My heart leapt within me—no longer flying in swift, light fashion like footsteps running, but bounding madly in great leaps.

Silently I swept the Countess behind me into the recess of the niche, forcing her down upon the stone seat, and bending my body like a shield over her.

In a moment Henry's piece crashed close at my ear, a keen pain ran like molten lead down my arm; and, spite of my hand upon her lips, Lucia gave a little cry. "I think I got it that time!" I heard Henry's voice say. "Count, run round and see. I shall go this way."

"Run, Lucy," I whispered, "they are coming. They must not find you."

"But you are hurt?" she said anxiously.

"No," I said, lying to her, as a man does so easily to a woman. "I am not at all hurt. Have I hurt you?"

For I had thrust her behind me with all my might.

"I cannot tell yet whether you have hurt me or not," she said. "You men of the North are too strong!"

"But they come. Run, Lucy, beloved!" I said.

CHAPTER XII

A NIGHT ASSAULT

And she melted into the night, swiftly as a bird goes. Then I became aware of flying footsteps. It seemed that I had better not be found there, lest I should compromise the Countess with her brother, and find myself with a duel upon my hands in addition to my other embarrassments. So I set my toes upon the little projections of the stone parapet, taking advantage of the hooks which confined the creepers, and clutching desperately with my hands, so that I scrambled to the top just as the Count and Henry met below.

"Strike a light, Count," I heard Henry say; "I am sure I hit something. I heard a cry."

A light flamed up. There was the rustling noise of the broad leaves of the creeper being pushed aside.

"Here is blood!" cried Henry. "I was sure I hit something that time!"

His tone was triumphant.

"I tell you what it is, Monsieur," said the calm voice of the Count: "if you go through the world banging off shots on the chance of shooting white owls which you do not see, you are indeed likely to hit something. But whether you will like it after it is hit, is another matter."

Then I went indoors, for my arm was paining me. In my own room I eagerly examined the wound. It was but slight. A pellet or two had grazed my arm and ploughed their way along the thickness of the skin, but none had entered deeply. So I wrapped my arm in a little lint and some old linen, and went to bed.

I did not again see the Countess till noon on the morrow, when her carriage was at the door and she tripped down the steps to enter.

The Count stood by it, holding the door for her to enter—I midway down the broad flight of steps.

"Good-bye," she said, holding out her hand, from which she deftly drew the glove. "We shall meet again."

"God grant it! I live for that!" said I, so low that the Count did not hear, as I bent to kiss her hand. For in these months I had learned many things.

At this moment Henry came up to say farewell, and he shook her hand with boyish affectation of the true British indifference, which at that time it was the correct thing for Englishmen to assume at parting.

"Nice boy!" said the Countess indulgently, looking up at me. The Count bowed and smiled, and smiled and bowed, till the carriage drove out of sight.

Then in a moment he turned to me with a fierce and frowning countenance.

"And now, Monsieur, I have the honour to ask you to explain all this!"

I stood silent, amazed, aghast. There was in me no speech, nor reason.
Yet I had the sense to be silent, lest I should say something maladroit.

A confidential servant brought a despatch. The Count impatiently flung it open, glanced at it, then read it carefully twice. He seemed much struck with the contents.

"I am summoned to Milan," he said, "and upon the instant. I shall yet overtake my sister. May I ask Monsieur to have the goodness to await me here that I may receive his explanations? I shall return immediately."

"You may depend that I shall wait," I said.

The Count bowed, and sprang upon the horse which his servant had saddled for him.

But the Count did not immediately return, and we waited in vain. No letter came to me. No communication to the manager of the hostel. The Count had simply ridden out of sight over the pass through which the Thal wind brought the fog-spume. He had melted like the mist, and, so far as we were concerned, there was an end. We waited here till the second snow fell, hardened, and formed its sleighing crust.

Then we went, for some society to Henry, over to the mountain village of Bergsdorf, which strings itself along the hillside above the River Inn.

Bergsdorf is no more than a village in itself, but, being the chief place of its neighbourhood, it supports enough municipal and other dignitaries to set up an Imperial Court. Never was such wisdom—never such pompous solemnity. The Burgomeister of Bergsdorf was a great elephant of a man. He went abroad radiating self-importance. He perspired wisdom on the coldest day. The other officials imitated the Burgomeister in so far as their corporeal condition allowed.
The *curé* only was excepted. He was a thin, spare man with an ascetic face and a great talent for languages. One day during service he asked a mother to carry out a crying child, making the request in eight languages. Yet the mother failed to understand till the limping old apparator led her out by the arm.

There is no doubt that the humours of Bergsdorf lightened our spirits and cheered our waiting; for it is my experience that a young man is easily amused with new, bright, and stirring things even when he is in love.

And what amused us most was that excellent sport—now well known to the world, but then practised only in the mountain villages—the species of adventure which has come to be called "tobogganing." I fell heir in a mysterious fashion to a genuine Canadian toboggan, curled and buffalo-robed at the front, flat all the way beneath; and upon this, with Henry on one of the ordinary sleds with runners of steel, we spent many a merry day.

There was a good run down the road to the post village beneath; another, excellent, down a neighbouring pass. But the best run of all started from high up on the hillside, crossed the village street, and undulated down the hillside pastures to the frozen Inn river below—a splendid course of two miles in all. But as a matter of precaution it was strictly forbidden ever to be used—at least in that part of it which crossed the village street. For such projectiles as laden toboggans, passing across the trunk line of the village traffic at an average rate of a mile a minute, were hardly less dangerous than cannon-balls, and of much more erratic flight.

Nevertheless, there was seldom a night when we did not risk all the penalties which existed in the city of Bergsdorf, by defying all powers and regulations whatsoever and running the hill-course in the teeth of danger.

I remember one clear, starlight night with the snow casting up just enough pallid light to see by. Half a dozen of us—Henry and myself, a young Swiss doctor newly diplomaëd, the adventurous advocate of the place, and several others—went up to make our nightly venture. We gave half a minute's law to the first starter, and then followed on. I was placed first, mainly because of the excellence of my Canadian iceship. As I drew away, the snow sped beneath; the exhilarating madness of the ride entered into my blood. I whooped with sheer delight…. There was a curve or two in the road, and at the critical moment, by shifting the weight of my body and just touching the snow with the point of the short iron-shod stick I held in my hand, the toboggan span round the curve with the delicious clean cut of a skate. It seemed only a moment, and already I was approaching the critical part of my journey. The stray oil-lights of the village street began to waver irregularly here and there beneath me. I saw the black gap in the houses through which I must go. I listened for the creaking runners of the great Valtelline wine-sledges which constituted the main danger. All was silent and safe. But just as I drew a long breath, and settled for the delicious rise over the piled snow of the street and the succeeding plunge down to the Inn, a vast bulk heaved itself into the seaway, like some lost monster of a Megatherium retreating to the swamps to couch itself ere morning light.

It was the Burgomeister of Bergsdorf.

"Acht—u—um—m!" I shouted, as one who, on the Scottish links, should cry "Fore!" and be ready to commit murder.

But the vision solemnly held up its hand and cried "Halt!"

"Halt yourself!" I cried, "and get out of the way!" For I was approaching at a speed of nearly a mile a minute. Now, there is but one way of halting a toboggan. It is to run the nose of your machine into a snow-bank, where it will stick. On the contrary, you do not stop. You describe the curve known as a parabola, and skin your own nose on the icy crust of the snow. Then you "halt," in one piece or several, as the case may be.

But I, on this occasion, did not halt in this manner. The mind moves swiftly in emergencies. I reflected that I had a low Canadian toboggan with a soft buffalo-skin over the front. The Burgomeister also had naturally well-padded legs. *Eh bien*—a meeting of these two could do no great harm to either. So I sat low in my seat, and let the toboggan run.

Down I came flying, checked a little at the rise for the crossing of the village street. A mountainous bulk towered above me—a bulk that still and anon cried "Halt!" There was a slight shock and a jar. The stars were eclipsed above me for a moment; something like a large tea-tray passed over my head and fell flat on the snow behind me. Then I scudded down the long descent to the Inn, leaving the village and all its happenings miles behind.

I did not come up the same way. I did not desire to attract immodest attention. Unobtrusively, therefore, I proceeded to leave my toboggan in its accustomed out-house at the back of the Osteria. Then, slipping on another overcoat, I took an innocent stroll along the village street, in the company of the landlord.

There was a great crowd on the corner by the Rathhaus. In the centre was Henry, in the hands of two officers of justice. The Burgomeister, supported by sympathising friends, limped behind. There is no doubt that Henry was exercising English privileges. His captors were unhappy. But I bade him go quietly, and with a look of furious bewilderment he obeyed. Finally we got the hotel-keeper, a staunch friend of ours and of great importance in these parts, to bail him out.

On the morrow there was a deliciously humorous trial. The young advocate was in attendance, and the whole village was called to give evidence. But, curiously enough, I was not summoned. I had been, it seemed, in the hotel changing my clothes. However, I was not missed, for everybody else had something to say. There were excellent plans of the ground, showing where the miscreant assaulted the magistrate. There, plain to be seen, was the mark in the snow where Henry, starting half a minute after me, and observing a vast prostrate bulk on the path, had turned his toboggan into the snow-bank, duly described his parabola, discuticled his nose—in fact, fulfilled the programme to the letter. Clearly, then, he could not have been the aggressor. The villain has remained, up to the publication of this veracious chronicle, unknown. No matter: I am not going back to Bergsdorf.

But something had to be done to vindicate the offended majesty of the law. So they fined Henry seventeen francs for obstructing the police in the discharge of their duty.

"Never mind," said Henry, "that's just eight francs fifty each. I got in two, both right-handers."

And I doubt not but the officers concerned considered that he had got his money's worth.

CHAPTER XIII

CASTEL DEL MONTE

It was March before we found ourselves in the Capital of the South. The Countess was still there, but the Count, her brother, had not appeared, and the explanation to which he referred remained unspoken. Here Lucia was our kind friend and excellent entertainer; but of the tenderness of the Hotel Promontonio it was hard for me to find a trace. The great lady indeed outshone her peers, and took my moorland eyes as well as the regards of others. But I had rather walked by the lake with the scarlet cloak, or stood with her and been shot at for a white owl in the niche of the terrace.

In the last days of the month there came from Henry's uncle and guardian, Wilfred Fenwick, an urgent summons. He was ill, he might be dying, and Henry was to return at once; while I, in anticipation of his return, was to continue in Italy. There was indeed nothing to call me home.

Therefore—and for other reasons—I abode in Italy; and after Henry's departure I made evident progress in the graces of the Countess. Once or twice she allowed me to remain behind for half an hour. On these occasions she would come and throw herself down in a chair by the fire, and permit me to take her hand. But she was weary and silent, full of gloomy thoughts, which in vain I tried to draw from her. Still, I think it comforted her to have me thus sit by her.

One morning, while I was idly leaning upon the bridge, and looking towards the hills with their white marble palaces set amid the beauty of the Italian spring, one touched me on the shoulder. I turned, and lo—Lucia! Not any more the Countess, but Lucia, radiant with brightness, colour in her cheek for the first time since I had seen her in the Court of the South, animation sparkling in her eye.

"So I have found you, faithless one," she said. "I have been seeking for you everywhere."

"And I, have I not been seeking for you all these weeks—and never have found you till now, Lucia!"

I thought she would not notice the name.

"Why, Sir Heather Jock," she returned, "did you not part with me last night at eleven of the clock?"

"Pardon me," I replied, letting the love in my heart woo her through my eyes, and say what I dared not—at least, not here upon the open bridge over which we slowly walked. "Pardon me, it is true that I parted at eleven of the clock last night with Madame the Countess of Castel del Monte. But, on the contrary, this morning I have met Lucia—my little Saint Lucy of the Eyes."

"Who in Galloway taught you to make such speeches?" she said. "It is all too pretty to have been said thus trippingly for the first time."

"Love," I made answer. "Love, the Master, taught me; for never before have I known either a Countess or a Lucia!"

"'Douglas, Douglas, tender and true,' does not your song say?" said she.
"Will you ever be true, Douglas?"

"Lucy, will you ever be cruel? I dare you to say these things to-night when I come to see you. 'Tis easy to dare to say them in the face of the streets."

"Ah, Douglas, you will not see me to-night! I have come to bid you farewell—farewell!" said she, as tragically as she dared, yet so that I alone would hear her. Her eyes darted here and there, noting who came near; and a smile flickered about her mouth as she calculated precisely the breaking strain of my patience, and teased me up to that point. I can easily enough see her elvish intent now, but I did not then.

"I go this afternoon," she said. "I have come to bid you farewell—'Farewell! The anchor's weighed! Remember me!'"

"Is that why you are so happy to-day, because you are going away?" I asked, putting a freezing dignity into my tones.

She nodded girlishly, and I admit, as a critic, adorably.

"Yes," she said, "that is just the reason."

We were now in the Public Gardens, and walking along a more quiet path.

"Good-bye, then," I said, holding out my hand.

"No, indeed!" she said; "I shall not allow you to kiss my hand in public!"

And she put her hands behind her with a small, petulant gesture. "Now, then!" she said defiantly.

With the utmost dignity I replied—"Indeed, I had no intention of kissing your hand, Madame; but I have the honour of wishing you a very good day."

So lifting my hat, I was walking off, when, turning with me, Lucia tripped along by my side. I quickened my pace.

"Stephen," she said, "will you not forgive me for the sake of the old time? It is true I am going away, and that you will not see me again—unless, unless—you will come and visit me at my country house. Stephen, if you do not walk more slowly, I declare I shall run after you down the public promenade!"

I turned and looked at her. With all my heart I tried to be grave and severe, but the mock-demure look on her face caused me weakly to laugh. And then it was good-bye to all my dignity.

"Lucy, I wish you would not tease me," I said, still more weakly.

"Poor Toto! give it bon-bons! It shall not be teased, then," she said.

Before we parted, I had promised to come and see her at her country house within ten days. And so, with a new brightness in her face, Saint Lucy of the Eyes came back to my heart, and came to stay.

It was mid-April when I started for Castel del Monte. It was spring, and I was going to see my love. The land about on either side, as I went, was faintly flushed with peach-blossom shining among the hoary stones. By the cliff edge the spiny cactus threw out strange withered arms. A whitethorn without spike or spine gracefully wept floods of blonde tears.

At a little port by the sea-edge I left the main route, and fared onward up into the mountains. A mule carried my baggage; and the muleteer who guided it looked like a mountebank in a garb rusty like withered leaves. Like withered leaf, too, he danced up the hillside, scaling the long array of steps which led through the olives toward Castel del Monte. Some of his antics amused me, until I saw that none of them amused himself, and that through all the contortions of his face his eyes remained fixed, joyless, tragic.

Castel del Monte sat on the hill-top, eminent, far-beholding. Vine-stakes ran up hill and down dale, all about it. White houses were sprinkled here and there. As we ascended, the sea sank beneath, and the shining dashes of the wave-crests diminished to sparkling pin-points. Then with oriental suddenness the sun went down. Still upward fared the joyless *farceur*, and still upon the soles of my feet, and with my pilgrim staff in my hand, I followed.

Sometimes the sprays of fragrant blossom swept across our faces. Sometimes a man stepped out from the roadside and challenged; but, on receiving a word of salutation from my knave, he returned to his place with a sharp clank of accoutrement.

White blocks of building moved up to us in the equal dusk of the evening, took shape for a moment, and vanished behind us. The summit of the mountain ceased to frown. The strain of climbing was taken from the mechanic movement of the feet. The mule sent a greeting to his kind; and some other white mountain, larger, more broken as to its sky-line, moved in front of us and stayed.

"Castel del Monte!" said the muleteer, wrinkling all the queer puckered leather of his visage in the strong light which streamed out as the great door opened. A most dignified Venetian senator, in the black and radiant linen of the time, came forth to meet me, and with the utmost respect ushered me within. In my campaigning dress and broad-brimmed hat, I felt that my appearance was unworthy of the grandeur of the entrance-hall, of the suits of armour, the vast pictures, and the massive last-century furniture in crimson and gold.

CHAPTER XIV

AN ERROR IN JUDGMENT

I had expected that Lucia would have come to greet me, and that some of the other guests would be moving about the halls. But though the rooms were brightly lit, and servants moving here and there, there abode a hush upon the place strangely out of keeping with my expectation.

In my own room I arrayed me in clothes more fitted to the palace in which I found myself, though, after all was done, their plainness made a poor contrast to the mailed warriors on the pedestals and the scarlet senators in the frames.

There was a rose, fresh as the white briar-blossom in my mother's garden, upon my table. I took it as Lucia's gage, and set it in my coat.

"My lady waits," said the major-domo at the door.

I went down-stairs, conscious by the hearing of the ear that a heart was beating somewhere loudly, mine or another's I could not tell.

A door opened. A rush of warm and gracious air, a benediction of subdued light, and I found myself bending over the hand of the Countess. I had been talking some time before I came to the knowledge that I was saying anything.

Then we went to dinner through the long lit passages, the walls giving back the merry sound of our voices. Still, strangely enough, no other guests appeared. But my wonder was hushed by the gladness on the face of the Countess. We dined in an alcove, screened from the vast dining-room. The table was set for three. As we came in, the Countess murmured a name. An old lady bowed to me, and moved stiffly to a seat without a word. Lucia continued her conversation without a pause, and paid no further heed to the ancient dame, who took her meal with a single-eyed absorption upon her plate.

My wonder increased. Could it be that Lucia and I were alone in this great castle! I cannot tell whether the thought brought me more happiness or discontent. Clearly, I was the only guest. Was I to remain so, or would others join us after dinner? My heart beat faint and tumultuously. At random I answered to Lucia's questionings about my journey. My slow-moving Northern intelligence began to form questions which I must ask. Through the laughing charm of my lady's face and the burning radiance of her eyes, there grew into plainness against the tapestry the sad, pale face of my mother and her clear, consistent eyes. I talked—I answered—I listened—all through a humming chaos. For the teaching of the moorland farm, the ethic of the Sabbath nights lit by a single candle and sanctified by the chanted psalm and the open Book, possessed me. It was the domination of the Puritan base, and most bitterly I resented, while I could not prevent, its hold upon me.

Dinner was over. We took our way into a drawing-room, divided into two parts by a screen which was drawn half-way. In the other half of the great room stood an ancient piano, and to this our ancient lady betook herself.

The Countess sat down in a luxurious chair, and motioned me to sit close by her in another, but one smaller and lower. We talked of many things, circling ever about ourselves. Yet I could not keep the old farm out of my mind—its simple manners, its severe code of morals, its labour and its pain. Also there came another thought, the sense that all this had happened before—the devil's fear that I was not the first who had so sat alone beside the Countess and seen the obsequious movement of these well-trained servants.

"Tell me, Douglas," at last the Countess said, glancing down kindly at me, "why you are so silent and *distrait*. This is our first evening here, and yet you are sad and forgetful, even of me."

What a blind fool I was not to see the innocence and love in her eyes!

"Countess—" I began, and paused uncertain.

"Sir to you!" she returned, making me a little bow in acknowledgment of the title.

"Lucia," I went on, taking no notice of her frivolity, "I thought—I thought—that is, I imagined—that your brother—that others would be here as well as I—"

I got no further. I saw something sweep across her face. Her eyes darkened. Her face paled. The thin curved nostrils whitened at the edges. I paused, astonished at the tempest I had aroused by my faltering stupidities. Why could I not take what the gods gave?

"I see," she said bitterly: "you reproach me with bringing you here as my guest, alone. You think I am bold and abandoned because I dreamed of an Eden here with friendship and truth as dwellers in it. I saw a new and perfect life; and with a word, here in my own house, and before you have been an hour my guest, you insult me—"

"Lucia, Lucia," I pleaded, "I would not insult you for the world—I would not think a thought—speak a word—dishonouring to you for my life—"

"You have—you have—it is all ended—broken!" she said, standing up—"all broken and thrown down!"

She made with her hands the bitter gesture of breaking.

"Listen," she said, while I stood amazed and silent. "I am no girl. I am older than you, and know the world. It is because I dreamed I saw that which I thought truer and purer in you than the conventions of life that I asked you to come here—"

"Lucia, Lucia, my lady, listen to me," I pleaded, trying to take her hand. She put me aside with the single swift, imperious movement which women use when their pride is deeply wounded.

"That lady"—she pointed within to where the silent dame of years was tinkling unconcernedly on the keys—"is my dead husband's mother. Surely she abundantly supplies the proprieties. And now you—you whom I thought I could trust, spoil my year—spoil my life, slay in a moment my love with reproach and scorn!"

She walked to the door, turned and said—"You, whom I trusted, have done this!" Then she threw out her hands in an attitude of despair and scorn, and disappeared.

I sat long with my head on my hands, thinking—the world about me in ruins, never to be built up. Then I went up to my room, paused at the wardrobe, changed my black coat to that in which I had arrived, and went softly down-stairs again. The waning moon had just risen late, and threw a weird light over the ranges of buildings, the gateways and towers.

I walked swiftly to the outer gate, and, there leaping a hedge of flowering plants, I fled down the mountain through the vineyards. I went swiftly, eager to escape from Castel del Monte, but in the tangle of walls and fences it was not easy to advance. At the parting of three ways I paused, uncertain in which direction to proceed. Suddenly, without warning, a dark figure stepped from some hidden place. I saw the gleam of something bright. I knew that I was smitten. Waves of white-hot metal ran suddenly in upon my brain, and I knew no more.

When I awoke, my first thought was that I was back again in the room where Lucia and I had talked together. I felt something perfumed and soft like a caress. It seemed like the filmy lace that the Countess wore upon her shoulder. My head lay against it. I heard a voice say, as it had been in my ear, through the murmuring floods of many waters—"My boy! my boy! And I, wicked one that I was, sent you to this!"

All the time she who spoke was busy binding something to the place on my side where the pain burned like white metal. And as she did so she crooned softly over me, saying as before—"My poor boy! my poor boy!" It was like the murmuring of a dove over its nestling. Again and again I was borne away from her and from myself on the floods of great waters. The universe alternately opened out to infinite horrors of vastness, and shrank to pinpoint dimensions to crush me. Through it all I heard my love's voice, and was content to let my head bide just where it lay.

Ever and anon I came to the surface, as a diver does lest he die. I heard myself say—"It was an error in judgment!" … Then after a pause—"nothing but an error in judgment."

And I felt that on which my head rested shake with a little earthquake of hysterical laughter. The strain had been too great, yet I had said the right word.

"Yes," she said softly, "my poor boy, it has been indeed an error in judgment for both of us!"

"But a blessed error, Lucia," I said, answering her when she least expected it.

A dark shape flitted before my dazzled eyes.

The Countess looked up. "Leonardi!" she called, "tell me, has one of your people done this?"

"Nay," said the man, "none of the servants of the Bond nor yet of the Mafia. Pietro the muleteer hath done it of his own evil heart for robbery. Here are the watch and purse!"

"And the murderer—where is he?" said again Lucia. "Let him be brought!"

"He has had an accident, Excellency. He is dead," said Leonardi simply.

Then they took me up very softly, and bore me to the door from which I had fled forth. Lucia walked with me. In the dusk of the leaves, while the bearers were fumbling with the inner doors, which would swing in their faces, Lucia put her hot lips to my hand, which she had held kindly in hers all the way.

"Pardon me, Douglas," she said, and there was a break in her voice. I felt the ocean of tears rising about me, and feared that I could not find the words fittingly to answer. For the pain had made me weak.

"Nay," I said at last, just over my breath, "it was my folly. Forgive me, little Saint Lucy of the Eyes! It was—it was—what was it that it was?—I have forgotten—"

"An error in judgment!" said Saint Lucy of the Eyes, and forgave me, though I cannot remember more about it.

I suppose I could take the title if I chose, for these things are easily arranged in Italy; but Lucia and I think it will keep for the second Stephen Douglas.

IV

UNDER THE RED TERROR

What of the night, O Antwerp bells,
  Over the city swinging,
Plaintive and sad, O kingly bells,
  In the winter midnight ringing?

And the winds in the belfry moan
From the sand-dunes waste and lone,
  And these are the words they say,
  The turreted bells and they—

  "Calamtout, Krabbendyk, Calloo,"
  Say the noisy, turbulent crew;
  "Jabbeké, Chaam, Waterloo;
  Hoggerhaed, Sandvaet, Lilloo,
  We are weary, a-weary of you!
  We sigh for the hills of snow,
  For the hills where the hunters go,
  For the Matterhorn, Wetterhorn, Dom,
    For the Dom! Dom! Dom!
  For the summer sun and the rustling corn,
  And the pleasant vales of the Rhineland valley."

"*The Bells of Antwerp.*"

I am writing this for my friend in Scotland, whose strange name I cannot spell. He wishes to, put it in the story-book he is writing. But his book is mostly lies. This is truth. I saw these things, and I write them down now because of the love I have for him, the young Herr who saved my brother's life among the black men in Egypt. Did I tell how our Fritz went away to be Gordon's man in the Soudan of Africa, and how he wrote to our father and the mother at home in the village—"I am a great man and the intendant of a military station, and have soldiers under me, and he who is our general is hardly a man. He has no fear, and death is to him as life"? So this young Herr, whom I love the same as my own brother, met Fritz when there was not the thickness of a Wurst-skin between him and the torture that makes men blanch for thinking on, and I will now tell you the story of how he saved him. It was—

But the Herr has come in, and says that I am a "dumbhead," also condemned, and many other things, because, he says, I can never tell anything that I begin to tell straightforwardly like a street in Berlin. He says my talk is crooked like the "Philosophers' Way" after one passes the red sawdust of the Hirsch-Gasse, where the youngsters "drum" and "drum" all the Tuesdays and the Fridays, like the donkeys that they are. I am to talk (he says violently) about Paris and the terrible time I saw there in the war of Seventy.

Ah! the time when there was a death at every door, the time which Heidelberg and mine own Thurm village will not forget—that made grey the hairs of Jacob Oertler, the head-waiter, those sixty days he was in Paris, when men's blood was spilt like water, when the women and the children fell and were burned in the burning houses, or died shrieking on the bayonet point. There is no hell that the Pfaffs tell of, like the streets of Paris in the early summer of Seventy-one. But it is necessary that I make a beginning, else I shall never make an ending, as Madame Hegelmann Wittwe, of the Prinz Karl, says when there are many guests, and we have to rise after two hours' sleep as if we were still on campaign. But again I am interrupted and turned aside.

Comes now the young Herr, and he has his supper, for ever since he came to the Prinz Karl he takes his dinner in the midst of the day as a man should.

"Ouch," he says, "it makes one too gross to eat in the evening."

So the Herr takes his dinner at midday like a good German; and when there is supper he will always have old Jacob to tell him tales, in which he says that there is no beginning, no era, nor Hegira, no Anno Domini, but only the war of Seventy. But he is a hard-hearted young Kerl, and will of necessity have his jesting. Only yesterday he said—

"Jacob, Jacob, this duck he must have been in the war of Siebenzig; for, begomme, he is tough enough. Ah, yes, Jacob, he is certainly a veteran. I have broken my teeth over his Iron Cross." But if he had been where I have been, he would know that it is not good jesting about the Iron Cross.

Last night the young Herr, he did not come home for supper at all. But instead of him there came an Officier clanging spurs and twisting at seven hairs upon his upper lip. The bracing-board on his back was tight as a drum. The corners stretched the cloth of his uniform till they nearly cut through.

He was but a boy, and his shoulder-straps were not ten days old; but old Jacob Oertler's heels came together with a click that would have been loud, but that he wore waiter's slippers instead of the field-shoes of the soldier.

The Officier looked at me, for I stood at attention.

"Soldier?" said he. And he spoke sharply, as all the babe-officers strive to do.

I bowed, but my bow was not that of the Oberkellner of the Prinz Karl that I am now.

"Of the war?" he asked again.

"Of three wars!" I answered, standing up straight that he might see the Iron Cross I wear under my dress-coat, which the Emperor set there.

"Name and regiment?" he said quickly, for he had learned the way of it, and was pleased that I called him Hauptmann.

"Jacob Oertler, formerly of the Berlin Husaren, and after of the Intelligence Department."

"So," he said, "you speak French, then?"

"Sir," said I, "I was twenty years in France. I was born in Elsass. I was also in Paris during the siege."

Thus we might have talked for long enough, but suddenly his face darkened and he lifted his eyes from the Cross. He had remembered his message.

"Does the tall English Herr live here, who goes to Professor Müller's each day in the Anlage? Is he at this time within? I have a cartel for him."

Then I told him that the English Herr was no Schläger-player, though like the lion for bravery in fighting, as my brother had been witness.

"But what is the cause of quarrel?" I asked.

"The cause," he said, "is only that particular great donkey, Hellmuth. He came swaggering to-night along the New Neckar-Bridge as full of beer as the Heidelberg tun is empty of it. He met your Herr under the lamps where there were many students of the corps. Now, Hellmuth is a beast of the Rhine corps, so he thought he might gain some cheap glory by pushing rudely against the tall Englander as he passed.

"'Pardon!' said the Englishman, lifting his hat, for he is a gentleman, and of his manner, when insulted, noble. Hellmuth is but a Rhine brute—though my cousin, for my sins.

"So Hellmuth went to the end of the Bridge, and, turning with his corps-brothers to back him, he pushed the second time against your Herr, and stepped back so that all might laugh as he took off his cap to mock the Englishman's bow and curious way of saying 'Pardon!'

"But the Englander took him momently by the collar, and by some art of the light hand turned him over his foot into the gutter, which ran brimming full of half-melted snow. The light was bright, for, as I tell you, it was underneath the lamps at the bridge-end. The moon also happened to come out from behind a wrack of cloud, and all the men on the bridge saw—and the girls with them also—so that you could hear the laughing at the Molkenkur, till the burghers put their red night-caps out of their windows to know what had happened to the wild Kerls of the *cafés*."

"But surely that is no cause for a challenge, Excellenz?" said I. "How can an officer of the Kaiser bring such a challenge?"

"Ach!" he said, shrugging his shoulders, "is not a fight a fight, cause or no cause? Moreover, is not Hellmuth after all the son of my mother's sister, though but a Rhineland donkey, and void of sense?"

So I showed him up to the room of the English Herr, and went away again, though not so far but that I could hear their voices.

It was the officer whom I heard speaking first. He spoke loudly, and as I say, having been of the Intelligence Department, I did not go too far away.

"You have my friend insulted, and you must immediately satisfaction make!" said the young Officier.

"That will I gladly do, if your friend will deign to come up here. There are more ways of fighting than getting into a feather-bed and cutting at the corners." So our young Englander spoke, with his high voice, piping and clipping his words as all the English do.

"Sir," said the officer, with some heat, "I bring you a cartel, and I am an officer of the Kaiser. What is your answer?"

"Then, Herr Hauptmann," said the Englishman, "since you are a soldier, you and I know what fighting is, and that snipping and snicking at noses is no fighting. Tell your friend to come up here and have a turn with the two-ounce gloves, and I shall be happy to give him all the satisfaction he wants. Otherwise I will only fight him with pistols, and to the death also. If he will not fight in my way, I shall beat him with a cane for having insulted me, whenever I meet him."

With that the officer came down to me, and he said, "It is as you thought. The Englishman will not fight with the Schläger, but he has more steel in his veins than a dozen of Hellmuths. Thunderweather, I shall fight Hellmuth myself to-morrow morning, if it be that he burns so greatly to be led away. Once before I gave him a scar of heavenly beauty!"

So he clanked off in the ten days' glory of his spurs. I have seen many such as he stiff on the slope of Spichern and in the woods beneath St. Germain. Yet he was a Kerl of mettle, and will make a brave soldier and upstanding officer.

But the Herr has again come in and he says that all this is a particular kind of nonsense which, because I write also for ladies, I shall not mention. I am not sure, also, what English words it is proper to put on paper. The Herr says that he will tear every word up that I have written, which would be a sad waste of the Frau Wittwe's paper and ink. He says, this hot Junker, that in all my writing there is yet no word of Paris or the days of the Commune, which is true. He also says that my head is the head of a calf, and, indeed, of several other animals that are but ill-considered in England.

So I will be brief.

In Seventy, therefore, I fought in the field and scouted with the
Uhlans. Ah, I could tell the stories! Those were the days. It is a
mistake to think that the country-people hated us, or tried to kill us.
On the contrary, if I might tell it, many of the young maids—

Ach, bitte, Herr—of a surety I will proceed and tell of Paris. I am aware that it is not to be expected that the English should care to hear of the doings of the Reiters of the black-and-white pennon in the matter of the maids.

But in Seventy-one, during the siege and the terrible days of the
Commune, I was in Paris, what you call a spy. It was the order of the
Chancellor—our man of blood-and-iron. Therefore it was right and not
ignoble that I should be a spy.

For I have served my country in more terrible places than the field of
Weissenburg or the hill of Spichern.

Ja wohl! there were few Prussians who could be taken for Frenchmen, in Paris during those months when suspicion was everywhere. Yet in Paris I was, all through the days of the investiture. More, I was chief of domestic service at the Hôtel de Ville, and my letters went through the balloon-post to England, and thence back to Versailles, where my brothers were and the Kaiser whom in three wars I have served. For I am Prussian in heart and by begetting, though born in Elsass.

So daily I waited on Trochu, as I had also waited on Jules Favre when he dined, and all the while the mob shouted for the blood of spies without. But I was Jules Lemaire from the Midi, a stupid provincial with the rolling accent, come to Paris to earn money and see the life. Not for nothing had I gone to school at Clermont-Ferrand.

But once I was nearly discovered and torn to pieces. The sweat breaks cold even now to think upon it. It was a March morning very early, soon after the light came stealing up the river from behind Notre-Dame. A bitter wind was sweeping the bare, barked, hacked trees on the Champs Élysées. It happened that I went every morning to the Halles to make the market for the day—such as was to be had. And, of course, we at the Hôtel de Ville had our pick of the best before any other was permitted to buy. So I went daily as Monsieur Jules Lemaire from the Hôtel de Ville. And please to take off your *képis, canaille* of the markets.

Suddenly I saw riding towards me a Prussian hussar of my old regiment. He rode alone, but presently I spied two others behind him. The first was that same sergeant Strauss who had knocked me about so grievously when first I joined the colours. At that time I hated the sight of him, but now it was the best I could do to keep down the German "Hoch!" which rose to the top of my throat and stopped there all of a lump.

Listen! The *gamins* and *vauriens* of the quarters—louts and cruel rabble—were running after him—yes, screaming all about him. There were groups of National Guards looking for their regiments, or marauding to pick up what they could lay their hands on, for it was a great time for patriotism. But Strauss of the Blaue Husaren, he sat his horse stiff and steady as at parade, and looked out under his eyebrows while the mob howled and surged. Himmel! It made me proud. Ach, Gott! but the old badger-grey Strauss sat steady, and rode his horse at a walk—easy, cool as if he were going up Unter den Linden on Mayday under the eyes of the pretty girls. Not that ever old Strauss cared as much for maids' eyes as I would have done—ah me, in Siebenzig!

Then came two men behind him, looking quickly up the side-streets, with carbines ready across their saddles. And so they rode, these three, like true Prussians every one. And I swear it took Jacob Oertler, that was Jules of the Midi, all his possible to keep from crying out; but he could not for his life keep down the sobs. However, the Frenchmen thought that he wept to see the disgrace of Paris. So that, and nothing else, saved him.

When Strauss and his two stayed a moment to consult as to the way, the crowd of noisy whelps pressed upon them, snarling and showing their teeth. Then Strauss and his men grimly fitted a cartridge into each carbine. Seeing which, it was enough for these very faint-heart patriots. They turned and ran, and with them ran Jules of the Midi that waited at the Hôtel de Ville. He ran as fast as the best of them; and so no man took me for a German that day or any other day that I was in Paris.

Then, after this deliverance, I went on to the Halles. The streets were more ploughed with shells than a German field when the teams go to and fro in the spring.

There were two men with me in the uniform of the Hôtel de Ville, to carry the provisions. For already the new marketings were beginning to come in by the Porte Maillot at Neuilly.

As ever, when we came to the market-stalls, it was "Give place to the Hôtel de Ville!" While I made my purchases, an old man came up to the butcher-fellow who was serving, and asked him civilly for a piece of the indifferent beef he was cutting for me. The rascal, a beast of Burgundy, dazed with absinthe and pig by nature, answered foully after his kind. The old man was very old, but his face was that of a man of war. He lifted his stick as though to strike, for he had a beautiful young girl on his arm. But I saw the lip of the Burgundian butcher draw up over his teeth like a snarling dog, and his hand shorten on his knife.

"Have politeness," I said sharply to the rascal, "or I will on my return report you to the General, and have you fusiladed!"

This made him afraid, for indeed the thing was commonly done at that time.

The old man smiled and held out his hand to me. He said—

"My friend, some day I may be able to repay you, but not now."

Yet I had interfered as much for the sake of the lady's eyes as for the sake of the old man's grey hairs. Besides, the butcher was but a pig of a Burgundian who daily maligned the Prussians with words like pig's offal.

Then we went back along the shell-battered streets, empty of carriages, for all the horses had been eaten, some as beef and some as plain horse.

"Monsieur the Commissary," said one of the porters, "do you know that the old man to whom you spoke, with the young lady, is le Père Félix, whom all the patriots of Paris call the 'Deliverer of Forty-eight'?"

I knew it not, nor cared. I am a Prussian, though born in Elsass.

So in Paris the days passed on. In our Hôtel de Ville the officials of the Provisional Government became more and more uneasy. The gentlemen of the National Guard took matters in their own hands, and would neither disband nor work. They sulked about the brows of Montmartre, where they had taken their cannon. My word, they were dirty patriots! I saw them every day as I went by to the Halles, lounging against the walls—linesmen among them, too, absent from duty without leave. They sat on the kerb-stone leaning their guns against the placard-studded wall. Some of them had loaves stuck on the points of their bayonets—dirty scoundrels all!

Then came the flight of one set of masters and the entry of another. But even the Commune and the unknown young men who came to the Hôtel de Ville made no change to Jules, the head waiter from the Midi. He made ready the *déjeuner* as usual, and the gentlemen of the red sash were just as fond of the calves' flesh and the red wine as the brutal *bourgeoisie* of Thiers' Republic or the aristocrats of the *règime* of Buonaparte. It was quite equal.

It was only a little easier to send my weekly report to my Prince and Chancellor out at Saint Denis. That was all. For if the gentlemen who went talked little and lined their pockets exceedingly well, these new masters of mine both talked much and drank much. It was no longer the Commune, but the Proscription. I knew what the end of these things would be, but I gave no offence to any, for that was not my business. Indeed, what mattered it if all these Frenchmen cut each other's throats? There were just so many the fewer to breed soldiers to fight against the Fatherland, in the war of revenge of which they are always talking.

So the days went on, and there were ever more days behind them—east-windy, bleak days, such as we have in Pomerania and in Prussia, but seldom in Paris. The city was even then, with the red flag floating overhead, beautiful for situation—the sky clear save for the little puffs of smoke from the bombs when they shelled the forts, and Valerien growled in reply.

The constant rattle of musketry came from the direction of Versailles. It was late one afternoon that I went towards the Halles, and as I went I saw a company of the Guard National, tramping northward to the Buttes Montmartre where the cannons were. In their midst was a man with white hair at whom I looked—the same whom we had seen at the market-stalls. He marched bareheaded, and a pair of the scoundrels held him, one at either sleeve.

Behind him came his daughter, weeping bitterly but silently, and with the salt water fairly dripping upon her plain black dress.

"What is this?" I asked, thinking that the cordon of the Public Safety would pass me, and that I might perhaps benefit my friend of the white locks.

"Who may you be that asks so boldly?" said one of the soldiers sneeringly.

They were ill-conditioned, white-livered hounds.

"Jules the garçon—Jules of the white apron!" cried one who knew me.
"Know you not that he is now Dictator? *Vive* the Dictator Jules, Emperor-of 'Encore-un-Bock'!"

So they mocked me, and I dared not try them further, for we came upon another crowd of them with a poor frightened man in the centre. He was crying out—"For me, I am a man of peace—gentlemen, I am no spy. I have lived all my life in the Rue Scribe." But one after another struck at him, some with the butt-end of their rifles, some with their bayonets, those behind with the heels of their boots—till that which had been a man when I stood on one side of the street, was something which would not bear looking upon by the time that I had passed to the other. For these horrors were the commonest things done under the rule of Hell—which was the rule of the Commune. Then I desired greatly to have done my commission and to be rid of Paris.

In a little the Nationals were thirsty. Ho, a wine-shop! There was one with the shutters up, probably a beast of a German—or a Jew. It is the same thing. So with the still bloody butts of their *chassepots* they made an entrance. They found nothing, however, but a few empty bottles and stove-in barrels. This so annoyed them that they wrought wholesale destruction, breaking with their guns and with their feet everything that was breakable.

So in time we came to the Prison of Mazas, which in ordinary times would have been strongly guarded; but now, save for a few National Guards loafing about, it was deserted—the criminals all being liberated and set plundering and fighting—the hostages all fusiladed.

When we arrived at the gate, there came out a finely dressed, personable man in a frock-coat, with a red ribbon in his button-hole. The officer in charge of the motley crew reported that he held a prisoner, the citizen commonly called Père Félix.

"Père Félix?" said the man in the frock-coat, "and who might he be?"

"A member of the Revolutionary Government of Forty-eight," said the old man with dignity, speaking from the midst of his captors; "a revolutionary and Republican before you were born, M. Raoul Regnault!"

"Ah, good father, but this is not Forty-eight! It is Seventy-one!" said the man on the steps, with a supercilious air. "I tell you as a matter of information!"

"You had better shoot him and have the matter over!" he added, turning away with his cane swinging in his hand.

Then, with a swirl of his sword, the officer marshalled us all into the courtyard—for I had followed to see the end. I could not help myself.

It was a great, bare, barren quadrangle of brick, the yard of Mazas where the prisoners exercise. The walls rose sheer for twenty feet. The doorway stood open into it, and every moment or two another company of Communists would arrive with a gang of prisoners. These were rudely pushed to the upper end, where, unbound, free to move in every direction, they were fired at promiscuously by all the ragged battalions—men, women, and even children shooting guns and pistols at them, as at the puppet-shows of Asnières and Neuilly.

The prisoners were some of them running to and fro, pitifully trying between the grim brick walls to find a way of escape. Some set their bare feet in the niches of the brick and strove to climb over. Some lay prone on their faces, either shot dead or waiting for the guards to come round (as they did every five or ten minutes) to finish the wounded by blowing in the back of their heads with a charge held so close that it singed the scalp.

As I stood and looked at this horrible shooting match, a human shambles, suddenly I was seized and pushed along, with the young girl beside me, towards the wall. Horror took possession of me. "I am Chief Servitor at the Hôtel de Ville," I cried. "Let me go! It will be the worse for you!"

"There is no more any Hôtel de Ville!" cried one. "See it blaze."

"Accompany gladly the house wherein thou hast eaten many good dinners!
Go to the Fire, ingrate!" cried another of my captors.

So for very shame, and because the young maid was silent, I had to cease my crying. They erected us like targets against the brick wall, and I set to my prayers. But when they had retired from us and were preparing themselves to fire, I had the grace to put the young girl behind me. For I said, if I must die, there is no need that the young maid should also die—at least, not till I am dead. I heard the bullets spit against the wall, fired by those farthest away; but those in front were only preparing.

Then at that moment something seemed to retard them, for instead of making an end to us, they turned about and listened uncertainly.

Outside on the street, there came a great flurry of cheering people, crying like folk that weep for joy—"Vive la ligne! Vive la ligne! The soldiers of the Line! The soldiers of the Line!"

The door was burst from its hinges. The wide outer gate was filled with soldiers in dusty uniforms. The Versaillists were in the city.

"Vive la ligne!" cried the watchers on the house-tops. "Vive la ligne!" cried we, that were set like human targets against the wall. "Vive la ligne!" cried the poor wounded, staggering up on an elbow to wave a hand to the men that came to Mazas in the nick of time.

Then there was a slaughter indeed. The Communists fought like tigers, asking no quarter. They were shot down by squads, regularly and with ceremony. And we in our turn snatched their own rifles and revolvers and shot them down also.... *Coming, Frau Wittwe! So fort!* ...

* * * * *

And the rest—well, the rest is, that I have a wife and seven beautiful children. Yes, "The girl I left behind me," as your song sings. Ah, a joke. But the seven children are no joke, young Kerl, as you may one day find.

And why am I Oberkellner at the Prinz Karl in Heidelberg? Ah, gentlemen, I see you do not know. In the winter it is as you see it; but all the summer and autumn—what with Americans and English, it is better to be Oberkellner to Madame the Frau Wittwe than to be Prince of Kennenlippeschönberghartenau!

V

THE CASE OF JOHN ARNISTON'S CONSCIENCE

Hail, World adored! to thee three times all hail!
 We at thy mighty shrine—profane, obscure
 With clenchèd hands beat at thy cruel door,
O hear, awake, and let us in, O Baal!

Low at thy brazen gates ourselves we fling—
  Hear us, even us, thy bondmen firm and sure,
  Our kin, our souls, our very God abjure!
Art thou asleep, or dead, or journeying?

Bear us, O Ashtoreth, O Baal, that we
  In mystic mazes may a moment gleam,
  May touch and twine with hot hearts pulsing free
Among thy groves by the Orontes stream.

Open and make us, ere our sick hearts fail,
  Hewers of wood within thy courts, O Baal!

"*Pro Fano.*"

John Arniston's heart beat fast and high as he went homeward through the London streets. It had come at last. The blossom of love's passion-flower had been laid within his grasp. The eyes in whose light he had sunned himself for months had leaped suddenly into a sweet and passionate flame. He had seen the sun of a woman's wondrous beauty, and long followed it afar. Miriam Gale was the success of the season. It was understood that she had the entire unattached British peerage at her feet. Nevertheless, her head had touched John Arniston's shoulder to-night. He had kissed her hair. "A queen's crown of yellow gold," was what he said to himself as he walked along, the evening traffic of the Strand humming and surging about him. Because her lips had rested a moment on his, he walked light-headed as one who for the first time "tastes love's thrice-repured nectar."

He tried to remember how it happened, and in what order—so much within an hour.

He had gone in the short and dark London afternoon into her drawing-room. Something had detained him—a look, the pressure of a hand, a moment's lingering in a glance—he could not remember which. Then the crowd of gilded youth ebbed reluctantly away. There was long silence after they had gone, as Miriam Gale and he sat looking at each other in the ruddy firelight. Nor did their eyes sever till with sudden unanimous impulse they clave to one another. Then the fountains of the deep were broken up, and the deluge overwhelmed their souls.

What happened after that? Something Miriam was saying about some one named Reginald. Her voice was low and earnest, thrillingly sweet. How full of charm the infantile tremble that came into it as she looked entreatingly at him! He listened to its tones, and it was long before he troubled to follow the meaning. She was telling him something of an early and foolish marriage—of a life of pain and cruelty, of a new life and sphere of action, all leading up to the true and only love of her life. Well, what of that? He had always understood she had been married before. Enwoven in the mesh-net of her scented hair, her soft cheek warm and wet against his, all this talk seemed infinitely detached—the insignificant problems of a former existence, long solved, prehistoric, without interest. Then he spoke. He remembered well what he had said. It was that to-morrow they twain, drawing apart from all the evil tongues of the world, were to begin the old walk along the Sure Way of Happiness. The world was not for them. A better life was to be theirs. They would wander through noble and high-set cities. Italy, beloved of lovers, waited for them. Her stone-pines beckoned to them. There he would tell her about great histories, and of the lives of the knights and ladies who dwelt in the cities set on the hills.

"I am so ignorant," Miriam Gale had said, pushing his head back that she might look at his whole face at once. "I am almost afraid of you—but I love you, and I shall learn all these things."

It was all inconceivable and strange. The glamour of love mingled with the soft, fitful firelight reflected in Miriam's eyes, till they twain seemed the only realities. So that when she began to speak of her husband, it seemed at first no more to John Arniston than if she had told him that her shoeblack was yet alive. He and she had no past; only a future, instant and immediate, waiting for them to-morrow.

How many times did they not move apart after a last farewell? John Arniston could not tell, though to content himself he tried to count. Then, their eyes drawing them together again, they had stood silent in the long pause when the life throbs to and fro and the heart thunders in the ears. At last, with "To-morrow!" for an iterated watchword between them, they parted, and John Arniston found himself in the street. It was the full rush of the traffic of London; but to him it was all strangely silent. Everything ran noiselessly to-night. Newsboys mouthed the latest horror, and John Arniston never heard them. Mechanically he avoided the passers-by, but it was with no belief in their reality. To him they were but phantom shapes walking in a dream. His world was behind him—and before. The fragrance of the bliss of dreams was on his lips. His heart bounded with the thought of that "To-morrow" which they had promised to one another. The white Italian cities which he had visited alone gleamed whiter than ever before him. Was it possible that he should sit in the great square of St. Mark's with Miriam Gale by his side, the sun making a patchwork of gold and blue among the pinnacles of the Church of the Evangelist? There, too, he saw, as he walked, the Lido shore, and the long sickle sweep of the beach. The Adriatic slumbrously tossed up its toy surges, and lo! a tall girl in white walked hand-in-hand with him. He caught his breath. He had just realised that it was all to begin to-morrow. Then again he saw that glimmering white figure throw itself down in an agony of parting into the low chair, kneeling beside which his life began.

But stop—what was it after all that Miriam had been saying? Something about her husband? Had he heard aright—that he was still alive, only dead to her?—"Dead for many years," was her word. After all, it was no matter. Nothing mattered any more. His goddess had stepped down to him with open arms. He had heard the beating of her heart. She was a breathing, loving woman.

"To-morrow and to-morrow and to-morrow." It seemed so far away. And were there indeed other skies, blue and clear, in Italy, in which the sun shone? It seemed hard to believe with the fog of London, yellow and thick like bad pea-soup, taking him stringently in the throat.

How he found his way back to his room, walking thus in a maze, he never could recall. As the door clicked and he turned towards the fireplace, his eye fell upon a brown-paper parcel lying on the table. John Arniston opened it out in an absent way, his mind and fancy still abiding by the low chair in Miriam's room. What he saw smote him suddenly pale. He laid his hand on the mantelpiece to keep from falling. It was nothing more than a plain, thick quarto volume, covered with a worn overcoat of undressed calf-skin. At the angle of the back and on one side the rough hair was worn thin, and the skin showed through. His mother had done that, reaching it down for his father to "take the book"[2] in the old house at home. John Arniston sat down on the easy-chair with the half-unwrapped parcel on his knee. His eye read the pages without a letter printing itself on his retina. It was a book within a book, and without also, which he read. He read the tale of the smooth places on the side. No one in the world but himself could know what he read. He saw this book, his father's great house Bible, lying above a certain grey head, in the white square hole in the wall. Beneath it was a copy of the *Drumfern Standard*, and on the top a psalm-book in which were his mother's spectacles, put there when she took them off after reading her afternoon portion.

[Footnote 2: Engage in family worship.]

He opened the book at random: "*And God spake all these words saying* … THOU SHALT NOT—" The tremendous sentence smote him fairly on the face. He threw his head violently back so that he might not read any further. The book slipped between his knees and fell heavily on the floor.

But the words which had caught his eye, "THOU SHALT NOT—" were printed in fire on the ceiling, or on his brain—he did not know which. He got up quickly, put on his hat, and went out again into the bitter night. He turned down to the left and paced the Thames Embankment. The fog was thicker than ever. Unseen watercraft with horns and steam-roarers grunted like hogs in the river. But in John Arniston's brain there was a conflict of terrible passion.

After all, it was but folklore, he said to himself. Nothing more than that. Every one knew it. All intelligent people were nowadays of one religion. The thing was manifestly absurd—the Hebrew fetich was dead—dead as Mumbo Jumbo. "Thank God!" he added inconsequently. He walked faster and faster, and on more than one occasion he brushed hurriedly against some of the brutal frequenters of that part of the world on foggy evenings. A rough lout growled belligerently at him, but shrank from the gladsome light of battle which leaped instantly into John Arniston's eye. To strike some one would have been a comfort to him at that moment.

Well, it was done with. The effete morality of a printed book was no tie upon him. The New Freedom was his—the freedom to do as he would and possess what he desired. Yet after all it was an old religion, this of John's. It has had many names; but it has never wanted priests to preach and devotees to practise its very agreeable tenets.

John Arniston stamped with his foot as he came to this decision. The fog was clearing off the river. It was no more than a mere scum on the water. There was a rift above, straight up to the stars.

"AND GOD SPAKE ALL THESE WORDS—."

"No," he said, over and over, "I shall not give her up. It is preposterous. Yet my father believed it. He died with his hand on the old Bible, his finger in the leaves—my mother—"

"AND GOD SPAKE ALL THESE WORDS—." The sentence seemed to flash through the rift over the shot-tower—to tingle down from the stars.

There are no true perverts. When man strips him to the bare buff, he is of the complexion his mother bestowed upon him. When his life's card-castle, laboriously piled, tumbles ignominious, he is again of his mother's religion.

"AND GOD—."

John Arniston stepped to the edge of the parapet. He looked over into the slow, swirling black water. It was a quick way that—but no—it was not to be his way. He looked at his watch. It was time to go to the office. He had an article to do. As well do that as anything. But first he would write a letter to her.

Shut in his room, his hand flying swiftly lest it should turn back in spite of him, John Arniston wrote a letter to Miriam Gale—a letter that was all one lie. He could not tell her the true reason why he would not go on the morrow. Who was he, that he should put himself in the attitude of being holier than Miriam Gale? It was certainly not because he did not wish to go—or that he thought it wrong. Simply, his father's calf-skin Bible barred the way, and he could no more pass over it than he could have trampled over his mother's body to his desire.

It was done. The letter was written. What was the particular excuse, invented fiercely at the moment, there is no use writing down here to cumber the page. John Arniston cheerfully gave himself over to the recording angel. Yet the ninth commandment is of equal interpretation, though it may be somewhat less clearly and tersely expressed than the seventh.

He went out and posted his note at a pillar-box in a quiet street with his own hand. The postman had just finished clearing when John came to thrust in the letter to Miriam Gale. The envelope slid into an empty receiver as the postman clicked the key. He turned to John with a look which said—"Too late that time, sir!" But John never so much as noticed that there was a postman by his side, who shouldered his bags with an air of official detachment. John Arniston went back to his room, and while he waited for a book of reference (for articles must be written so long as the pillars of the firmament stand) he lifted an evening paper which lay on the table. He ran his eye by instinct over the displayed cross headings. His eye caught a name. "Found Drowned at Battersea Bridge—Reginald Gale."

"Reginald Gale," said John to himself—"where did I hear that name?"

Like a flash, every word that Miriam had told him about her worthless husband—his treatment of her, his desertion within a few days of her marriage—stood plain before him as if he had been reading the thing in proof…. Miriam Gale was a free woman.

And his pitiable lying letter? It was posted—lurking in the pillar-box round the corner, waiting to speed on its way to break the heart of the girl, who had been willing to risk all, and count the world well lost for the sake of him.

He seized his hat and ran down-stairs, taking the steps half a dozen at a time. He met the boy coming up with the book. He passed as if he had stepped over the top of him. The boy turned and gazed open-mouthed. The gentlemen at the office were all of them funny upon occasion, but John Arniston had never had the symptoms before.

"He's got a crisis!" said the boy to himself, clutching at an explanation he had heard once given in the sub-editor's room.

For an hour John Arniston paced to and fro before that pillar-box, timing the passing policeman, praying that the postman who came to clear it might prove corruptible.

Would he never come? It appeared upon the white enamelled plate that the box was to be cleared in an hour. But he seemed to have waited seven hours in hell already. The policeman gazed at him suspiciously. A long row of jewellers' shops was just round the corner, and he might be a professional man of standing—in spite of the fur-collar of his coat—with an immediate interest in jewellery.

The postman came at last. He was a young, alert, beardless man, who whistled as he came. John Arniston was instantly beside him as he stooped to unlock the little iron door.

"See here," he said eagerly, in a low voice, "I have made a mistake in posting a letter. Two lives depend on it. I'll give you twenty pounds in notes into your hand now, if you let me take back the letter at the bottom of that pillar!"

"Sorry—can't do it, sir—more than my place is worth. Besides, how do I know that you put in that letter? It may be a jewel letter from one of them coves over there!"

And he jerked his thumb over his shoulder.

John Arniston could meet that argument.

"You can feel it," he said; "try if there is anything in it, coin or jewels—you could tell, couldn't you?"

The man laughed.

"Might be notes, sir, like them in your hand—couldn't do it, indeed, sir."

The devil leaped in the hot Scots blood of John Arniston.

He caught the kneeling servant of Her Majesty's noblest monopoly by the throat, as he paused smiling with the door of the pillar-box open and the light of the street-lamp falling on the single letter which lay within. The clutch was no light one, and the man's life gurgled in his throat.

John Arniston snatched the letter, glanced once at the address. It was his own. There was, indeed, no other. Hurriedly he thrust the four notes into the hand of the half-choked postman. Then he turned and ran, for the windows of many tall houses were spying upon him. He dived here and there among archways and passages, manoeuvred through the purlieus of the market, and so back into the offices of his paper.

"And where is that *Dictionary of National Biography*?" asked John Arniston of the boy. The precious letter for which he had risked penal servitude and the cat in the prisons of his country for robbery of the Imperial mails (accompanied with violence), was blazing on the fire. Then, with professional readiness, John Arniston wrote a column and a half upon the modern lessons to be drawn from the fact that Queen Anne was dead. It was off-day at the paper, Parliament was not sitting, and the columns opposite the publishers' advertisements needed filling, or these gentlemen would grumble. The paper had a genuine, if somewhat spasmodic, attachment to letters. And from this John Arniston derived a considerable part of his income.

When he went back to his room he found that his landlady had been in attending to the fire. She had also lifted the fallen Bible, on which he could now look with some complacency—so strange a thing is the conscience.

On the worn hair covering of the old Bible lay a letter. It was from Miriam—a letter written as hastily as his own had been, with pitiful tremblings, and watered with tears. It told him, through a maze of burning love, among other things that she had been a wicked woman to listen to his words —and that while her husband lived she must never see him again. In time, doubtless, he would find some one worthier, some one who would not wreck his life, as for one mad half-hour his despairing Miriam had been willing to do. Finally, he would forgive her and forget her. But she was his own—he was to remember that.

In half an hour John Arniston was at the mortuary. Of course, he found a pressman there with a notebook before him. With him he arranged what should be said the next morning, and how the inquest should be reported. There was no doubt about the identity, and John Arniston soon possessed the proofs of it. But, after all, there was no need that the British public should know more than it already knew, or that the name of Miriam Gale should be connected with the drowned wretch, whose soddenly friendly leer struck John Arniston cold, as though he also had been in the Thames water that night.

So all through the darkness he paced in front of the house of the Beloved. His letter to her, written on leaves of his notebook, in place of that which he had destroyed, went in with the morning's milk. In half an hour after he was with her. And when he came out again he had seen a wonderful thing—a beautiful woman to whom emotion was life, and the expression of it second nature, running through the gamut of twenty moods in a quarter of an hour. At the end, John departed in search of a licence and a church. And Miriam Gale put her considering finger to her lip, and said, "Let me see—which dresses shall I take?"

The highway robbery was never heard of. The excellent plaster which John Arniston left in the hand of the official had salved effectively the rude constriction of his throat, where John's right hand had closed upon it.

* * * * *

It was even better to sit with Miriam Arniston in reality in the great sun-lit square of St. Mark's than it had been in fantasy with Miriam Gale.

The only disappointment was, that the pigeons of the Square were certainly fatter and greedier than the pictured cloud of doves, which in his day-dream he had seen flash the under-side of their wings at his love as they checked themselves to alight at her feet.

But on Lido side there was no such rift in the lute's perfection. The sands, the wheeling sea-birds, the tall girl in white whose hand he held—all these were even as he had imagined them. Thither they came every day, passing along the straight dusty avenue, and then wandering for hours picking shells. They talked only when the mood took them, and in the pauses they listened idly to the slumbrous pulsations of Adria. John Arniston had lied at large in the letter he had written to his love. He had assaulted a man who righteously withstood him in the discharge of his duty, in order to steal that letter back again. Yet his conscience was wholly void of offence in the matter. The heavens smiled upon his bride and himself. There was now no stern voice to break through upon his blissful self-approval.

Why there should be this favouritism among the commandments, was not clear to John. Indeed, the thing did not trouble him. He was no casuist. He only knew that the way was clear to Miriam Gale, and he went to her the swiftest way.

But there were, for all that, the elements of a very pretty dilemma in the psychology of morals in the case of Miriam Gale and John Arniston. True, the calf-skin Bible said when it was consulted, "The letter killeth, but the spirit maketh alive."

But, after all, that might prove upon examination to have nothing to do with the matter.

VI

THE GLISTERING BEACHES

For wafts of unforgotten music come,
  All unawares, into my lonely room,
    To thrill me with the memories of the past—
Sometimes a tender voice from out the gloom,
  A light hand on the keys, a shadow cast
    Upon a learned tome
That blurs somewhat Alpha and Omega,
  A touch upon my shoulder, a pale face,
  Upon whose perfect curves the firelight plays,
Or love-lit eyes, the sweetest e'er I saw.

"Memory Harvest."

It was clear morning upon Suliscanna. That lonely rock ran hundreds of feet up into the heavens, and pointed downwards also to the deepest part of the blue. Simeon and Anna were content.

Or, rather, I ought to say Anna and Simeon, and that for a reason which will appear. Simeon was the son of the keeper of the temporary light upon Suliscanna, Anna the daughter of the contractor for the new lighthouse, which had already begun to grow like a tall-shafted tree on its rock foundation at Easdaile Point. Suliscanna was not a large island—in fact, only a mile across the top; but it was quite six or eight in circumference when one followed the ins and outs of the rocky shore. Tremendous cliffs rose to the south and west facing the Atlantic, pierced with caves into which the surf thundered or grumbled, according as the uneasy giant at the bottom of the sea was having a quiet night of it or the contrary. Grassy and bare was the top of the island. There was not a single tree upon it; and, besides the men's construction huts, only a house or two, so white that each shone as far by day as the lighthouse by night.

There was often enough little to do on Suliscanna. At such times, after standing a long time with hands in their pockets, the inhabitants used to have a happy inspiration: "Ha, let us go and whitewash the cottages!" So this peculiarity gave the island an undeniably cheerful appearance, and the passing ships justly envied the residents.

Simeon and Anna were playmates. That is, Anna played with Simeon when she wanted him.

"Go and knit your sampler, girl!" Simeon was saying to-day. "What do girls know about boats or birds?"

He was in a bad humour, for Anna had been unbearable in her exactions.

"Very well," replied Anna, tossing her hair; "I can get the key of the boat and you can't. I shall take Donald out with me."

Now, Donald was the second lighthouse-keeper, detested of Simeon. He was grown-up and contemptuous. Also he had whiskers—horrid ugly things, doubtless, but whiskers. So he surrendered at discretion.

"Go and get the key, then, and we will go round to the white beaches.
I'll bring the provisions."

He would have died any moderately painless death rather than say, "The oatcake and water-keg."

So in a little they met again at the Boat Cove which Providence had placed at the single inlet upon the practicable side of Suliscanna, which could not be seen from either the Laggan Light or the construction cottages. Only the lighter that brought the hewn granite could spy upon it.

"Mind you sneak past your father, Anna!" cried Simeon, afar off.

His voice carried clear and lively. But yet higher and clearer rose the reply, spoken slowly to let each word sink well in.

"Teach-your-grandmother-to-suck-eggs—ducks' eggs!"

What the private sting of the discriminative, only Simeon knew. And evidently he did know very well, for he kicked viciously at a dog belonging to Donald the second keeper—a brute of a dog it was; but, missing the too-well-accustomed cur, he stubbed his toe. He then repeated the multiplication table. For he was an admirable boy and careful of his language.

But, nevertheless, he got the provision out with care and promptitude.

"Where are you taking all that cake?" said his mother, who came from Ayrshire and wanted a reason for everything. In the north there is no need for reasons. There everything is either a judgment or a dispensation, according to whether it happens to your neighbour or yourself.

"I am no' coming hame for ony dinner," said Simeon, who adopted a modified dialect to suit his mother. With his father he spoke English only, in a curious sing-song tone but excellent of accent.

Mrs. Lauder—Simeon's mother, that is—accepted the explanation without remark, and Simeon passed out of her department.

"Mind ye are no' to gang intil the boat!" she cried after him; but
Simeon was apparently too far away to hear.

He looked cautiously up the side of the Laggan Light to see that his father was still polishing at his morning brasses and reflectors along with Donald. Then he ran very swiftly through a little storehouse, and took down a musket from the wall. A powder-flask and some shot completed his outfit; and with a prayer that his father might not see him, Simeon sped to the trysting-stone. As it happened, his father was oblivious and the pilfered gun unseen.

Anna's experience had been quite different. Her procedure was much simpler. She found her father sitting in his office, constructed of rough boards. He frowned continuously at plans of dovetailed stones, and rubbed his head at the side till he was rapidly rubbing it bare.

Anna came in and looked about her.

"Give me the key of the boat," she said without preface. She used from habit, even to her father, the imperative mood affirmative.

Mr. Warburton looked up, smoothed his brow, and began to ask, "What are you going to do—?" But in the midst of his question he thought better of it, acknowledging its uselessness; and, reaching into a little press by his side, he took down a key and handed it to Anna without comment. Anna said only, "Thank you, father." For we should be polite to our parents when they do as we wish them.

She stood a moment looking back at the bowed figure, which, upon her departure, had resumed the perplexed frown as though it had been a mask. Then she walked briskly down to the boathouse.

Upon the eastern side of Suliscanna there is a beach. It is a rough beach, but landing is just possible. There are cunning little spits of sand in the angles of the stone reaches, and by good steering between the boulders it is just possible to make boat's-way ashore.

"Row!" said Anna, after they had pushed the boat off, and began to feel the hoist of the swell. "I will steer."

Simeon obediently took the oars and fell to it. So close in did Anna steer to one point, that, raising her hand, she pulled a few heads of pale sea-pink from a dry cleft as they drew past into the open water and began to climb green and hissing mountains.

Then Anna opened her plans to Simeon.

"Listen!" she said. "I have been reading in a book of my father's about this place, and there was a strange great bird once on Suliscanna. It has been lost for years, so the book says; and if we could get it, it would be worth a hundred pounds. We are going to seek it."

"That is nonsense," said Simeon, "for you can get a goose here for sixpence, and there is no bird so big that it would be worth the half of a hundred pounds."

"Goose yourself, boy," said Anna tauntingly. "I did not mean to eat, great stupid thing!"

"What did you mean, then?" returned Simeon.

"You island boy, I mean to put in wise folks' museums—where they put all sorts of strange things. I have seen one in London."

"Seen a bird worth a hundred pounds?" Simeon was not taking Anna's statements on trust any more.

"No, silly—not the bird, but the museum."

"Um—you can tell that to Donald; I know better than to believe."

"Ah, but this is true," said Anna, without anger at the aspersion on her habitual truthfulness. "I tell you it is true. You would not believe about the machine-boat that runs by steam, with the smoke coming from it like the spout of our kettle, till I showed you the picture of it in father's book."

"I have seen the lion and the unicorn fighting for the crown. There are lies in pictures as well as in books!" said Simeon, stating a great truth.

"But this bird is called the Great Auk—did you never hear your father tell about that?"

Simeon's face still expressed no small doubt of Anna's good faith. The words conveyed to him no more meaning than if she had said the Great Mogul.

Then Anna remembered.

"It is called in Scotland the Gare Fowl!"

Simeon was on fire in a moment. He stopped rowing and started up.

"I have heard of it," he said. "I know all that there is to know. It was chased somewhere on the northern islands and shot at, and one of them was killed. But did it ever come here?"

"I have father's book with me, and you shall see!" Being prepared for scepticism, Anna did not come empty-handed. She pulled a finely bound book out of a satchel-pocket that swung at her side. "See here," she said; and then she read: "'After their ill-usage at the islands of Orkney, the Gare Fowl were seen several times by fishermen in the neighbourhood of the Glistering Beaches on the lonely and uninhabited island of Suliscanna. It is supposed that a stray bird may occasionally visit that rock to this day.'"

Simeon's eyes almost started from his head.

"Worth a hundred pounds!" he said over and over as if to himself.

Anna, who knew the ways of this most doubting of Thomases, pulled a piece of paper from her satchel and passed it to him to read. It related at some length the sale in a London auction-room of a stuffed Great Auk in imperfect condition for one hundred and fifty pounds.

"That would be pounds sterling!" said Simeon, who was thinking. He had a suspicion that there might be some quirk about pounds "Scots," and was trying to explain things clearly to himself.

"Now, we are going to the Glistering Beaches to look for the Great Auk!" said Anna as a climax to the great announcement.

The water lappered pleasantly beneath the boat as Simeon deftly drew it over the sea. There is hardly any pleasure like good oarsmanship. In rowing, the human machine works more cleanly and completely than at any other work. Before the children rose two rocky islands, with an opening between, like a birthday cake that has been badly cut in the centre and has had the halves moved a little way apart. This was Stack Canna.

"Do you think that there would be any chance here?" said Anna. The splendour of the adventure was taking possession of her mind.

"Of course there would; but the best chance of all will be at the caves of Rona Wester, for that is near the Glistering Beaches, and the birds would be sure to go there if the people went to seek them at the Beaches."

"Has any one been there?" asked Anna.

"Fishers have looked into them from the sea. No one has been in!" said
Simeon briefly.

The tops of the Stack of Canna were curiously white, and Simeon watched the effect over his shoulder as he rowed.

"Look at the Stack," he said, and the eyes of his companion followed his.

"Is it snow?" she asked.

"No; birds—thousands of them. They are nesting. Let us land and get a boat-load to take back."

But Anna declared that it must not be so. They had come out to hunt the
Great Auk, and no meaner bird would they pursue that day.

Nevertheless, they landed, and made spectacles of themselves by groping in the clay soil on the top of the Stack for Petrels' eggs. But they could not dig far enough without spades to get many, and when they did get to the nest, it was hardly worth taking for the sake of the one white egg and the little splattering, oily inmate.

Yet on the wild sea-cinctured Stack, and in that young fresh morning, the children tasted the joy of life; and only the fascinating vision of the unknown habitant of the Glistering Beaches had power to wile them away.

But there before them, a mile and a half round the point of Stack, lay the Beaches. On either side of the smooth sweep of the sands rose mighty cliffs, black as the eye of the midnight and scarred with clefts like battered fortresses. Then at the Beaches themselves, the cliff wall fell back a hundred yards and left room for the daintiest edging of white sand, shining like coral, crumbled down from the pure granite—which at this point had not been overflowed like the rest of the island of Suliscanna by the black lava.

Such a place for play there was not anywhere—neither on Suliscanna nor on any other of the outer Atlantic isles. Low down, by the surf's edge, the wet sands of the Glistering Beaches were delicious for the bare feet to run and be brave and cool upon. The sickle sweep of the bay cut off the Western rollers, and it was almost always calm in there. Only the sea-birds clashed and clanged overhead, and made the eye dizzy to watch their twinkling gyrations.

Then on the greensward there was the smoothest turf, a band of it only—not coarse grass with stalks far apart, as it is on most sea-beaches; but smooth and short as though it had been cropped by a thousand woolly generations. "Such a place!" they both cried. And Anna, who had never been here before, clapped her hands in delight.

"This is like heaven!" she sighed, as the prow of the boat grated refreshingly on the sand, and Simeon sprang over with a splash, standing to his mid-thigh in the salt water to pull the boat ashore.

Then Simeon and Anna ran races on the smooth turf. They examined carefully the heaped mounds of shells, mostly broken, for the "legs of mutton" that meant to them love and long life and prosperity. They chose out for luck also the smooth little rose-tinted valves, more exquisite than the fairest lady's finger-nails.

Next they found the spring welling up from an over-flow mound which it had built for itself in the ages it had run untended. Little throbbing grains of sand dimpled in it, and the mound was green to the top; so that Simeon and Anna could sit, one on one side and the other upon the other, and with a farle of cake eat and drink, passing from hand to hand alternate, talking all the time.

It was a divine meal.

"This is better than having to go to church!" said Anna.

Simeon stared at her. This was not the Sabbath or a Fast-day. What a day, then, to be speaking about church-going! It was bad enough to have to face the matter when it came.

"I wonder what we should do if the Great Auk were suddenly to fly out of the rocks up there, and fall splash into the sea," he said, to change the subject.

"The Great Auk does not fly," said positive Anna, who had been reading up.

"What does it do, then?" said Simeon. "No wonder it got killed!"

"It could only waddle and swim," replied Anna.

"Then I could shoot it easy! I always can when the things can't fly, or will stand still enough.—It is not often they will," he added after due consideration.

Many things in creation are exceedingly thoughtless.

Thereupon Simeon took to loading his gun ostentatiously, and Anna moved away. Guns were uncertain things, especially in Simeon's hands, and Anna preferred to examine some of the caves. But when she went to the opening of the nearest, there was something so uncanny, so drippy, so clammy about it, with the little pools of water dimpled with drops from above, and the spume-balls rolled by the wind into the crevices, that she was glad to turn again and fall to gathering the aromatic, hay-scented fennel which nodded on the edges of the grassy slopes.

There was no possibility of getting up or down the cliffs that rose three hundred feet above the Glistering Beaches, for the ledges were hardly enough for the dense population of gannets which squabbled and babbled and elbowed one another on the slippery shelves.

Now and then there would be a fight up there, and white eggs would roll over the edge and splash yellow upon the turf. Wherever the rocks became a little less precipitous, they were fairly lined with the birds and hoary with their whitewash.

After Simeon had charged his gun, the children proceeded to explore the caves, innocently taking each other's hands, and advancing by the light of a candle—which, with flint and steel, they had found in the locker of their boat.

First they had to cross a pool, not deep, but splashy and unpleasant. Then more perilously they made their way along the edges of the water, walking carefully upon the slippery stones, wet with the clammy, contracted breath of the cave. Soon, however, the cavern opened out into a wider and drier place, till they seemed to be fairly under the mass of the island; for the cliffs, rising in three hundred feet of solid rock above their heads, stretched away before them black and grim to the earth's very centre.

Anna cried out, "Oh, I cannot breathe! Let us go back!"

But the undaunted Simeon, determined to establish his masculine superiority once for all, denied her plumply.

"We shall go back none," he said, "till we have finished this candle."

So, clasping more tightly her knight-errant's hand, Anna sighed, and resigned herself for once to the unaccustomed pleasure of doing as she was bid.

Deeper and deeper they went into the cleft of the rocks, stopping sometimes to listen, and hearing nothing but the beating of their own hearts when they did so.

There came sometimes, however, mysterious noises, as though the fairy folks were playing pipes in the stony knolls, of which they had both heard often enough. And also by whiles they heard a thing far more awful—a plunge as of a great sea-beast sinking suddenly into deep water.

"Suppose that it is some sea-monster," said Anna with eyes on fire; for the unwonted darkness had changed her, so that she took readily enough her orders from the less imaginative boy—whereas, under the broad light of day, she never dreamed of doing other than giving them.

Once they had a narrow escape. It happened that Simeon was leading and holding Anna by the hand, for they had been steadily climbing upwards for some time. The footing of the cave was of smooth sand, very restful and pleasing to the feet. Simeon was holding up the candle and looking before him, when suddenly his foot went down into nothing. He would have fallen forward, but that Anna, putting all her force into the pull, drew him back. The candle, however, fell from his hand and rolled unharmed to the edge of a well, where it lay still burning.

Simeon seized it, and the two children, kneeling upon the rocky side, looked over into a deep hole, which seemed, so far as the taper would throw its feeble rays downwards, to be quite fathomless.

But at the bottom something rose and fell with a deep roaring sound, as regular as a beast breathing. It had a most terrifying effect to hear that measured roaring deep in the bowels of the earth, and at each respiration to see the suck of the air blow the candle-flame about.

Anna would willingly have gone back, but stout Simeon was resolved and not to be spoken to.

They circled cautiously about the well, and immediately began to descend. The way now lay over rock, fine and regular to the feet as though it had been built and polished by the pyramid-builders of Egypt. There was more air, also, and the cave seemed to be opening out.

At last they came to a glimmer of daylight and a deep and solemn pool. There was a path high above it, and the pool lay beneath black like ink. But they were evidently approaching the sea, for the roar of the breaking swell could distinctly be heard. The pool narrowed till there appeared to be only a round basin of rock, full of the purest water, and beyond a narrow bank of gravel. Then they saw the eye of the sea shining in, and the edge of a white breaker lashing into the mouth of the cave.

But as they ran down heedlessly, all unawares they came upon a sight which made them shrink back with astonishment. It was something antique and wrinkled that sat or stood, it was difficult to tell which, in the pool of crystal water. It was like a little old man with enormous white eyebrows, wearing a stupendous mask shaped like a beak. The thing turned its head and looked intently at them without moving. Then they saw it was a bird, very large in size, but so forlorn, old, and broken that it could only flutter piteously its little flippers of wings and patiently and pathetically waggle that strange head.

"It is the Great Auk itself—we have found it!" said Anna in a hushed whisper.

"Hold the candle till I kill it with a stone—or, see! with this bit of timber."

"Wait!" said Anna. "It looks so old and feeble!"

"Our hundred pounds," said Simeon.

"It looks exactly like your grandfather," said Anna; "look at his eyebrows! You would not kill your grandfather!"

"Wouldn't I just—for a hundred pounds!" said Simeon briskly, looking for a larger stone.

"Don't let us kill him at all. We have seen the last Great Auk! That is enough. None shall be so great as we."

The grey and ancient fowl seemed to wake to a sense of his danger, just at the time when in fact the danger was over. He hitched himself out of the pool like an ungainly old man using a stick, and solemnly waddled over the little bank of sand till he came to his jumping-off place. Then, without a pause, he went souse into the water.

Simeon and Anna ran round the pool to the shingle-bank and looked after him.

The Great Auk was there, swimming with wonderful agility. He was heading right for the North and the Iceland skerries—where, it may be, he abides in peace to this day, happier than he lived in the cave of the island of Suliscanna.

The children reached home very late that night, and were received with varying gladness; but neither of them told the ignorant grown-up people of Suliscanna that theirs were the eyes that had seen the last Great Auk swim out into the bleak North to find, like Moses, an unknown grave.

BOOK SECOND

INTIMACIES

I

Take cedar, take the creamy card,
 With regal head at angle dight;
And though to snatch the time be hard,
 To all our loves at home we'll write.

II

Strange group! in Bowness' street we stand—
 Nine swains enamoured of our wives,
Each quaintly writing on his hand,
 In haste, as 'twere to save our lives.

III

O wondrous messenger, to fly
 All through the night from post to post!
Thou bearest home a kiss, a sigh—
 And but a halfpenny the cost!

IV

To-morrow when they crack their eggs,
  They'll say beside each matin urn—
"These men are still upon their legs;
  Heaven bless 'em—may they soon return!"

GEORGE MILNER.

I

THE LAST ANDERSON OF DEESIDE

Pleasant is sunshine after rain,
  Pleasant the sun;
To cheer the parchèd land again,
  Pleasant the rain.

Sweetest is joyance after pain,
  Sweetest is joy;
Yet sorest sorrow worketh gain,
  Sorrow is gain.

"*As in the Days of Old.*"

"Weel, he's won awa'!"

"Ay, ay, he is that!"

The minister's funeral was winding slowly out of the little manse loaning. The window-blinds were all down, and their bald whiteness, like sightless eyes looking out of the white-washed walls and the trampled snow, made the Free Church manse of Deeside no cheerful picture that wild New Year's Day. The green gate which had so long hung on one hinge, periodically mended ever since the minister's son broke the other swinging on it the summer of the dry year before he went to college, now swayed forward with a miserably forlorn lurch, as though it too had tried to follow the funeral procession of the man who had shut it carefully the last thing before he went to bed every night for forty years.

Andrew Malcolm, the Glencairn joiner, who was conducting the funeral—if, indeed, Scots funerals can ever be said to be conducted—had given it a too successful push to let the rickety hearse have plenty of sea-room between the granite pillars. It was a long and straggling funeral, silent save for the words that stand at the opening of this tale, which ran up and down the long black files like the irregular fire of skirmishers.

"Ay, man, he's won awa'!"

"Ay, ay, he is that!"

This is the Scottish Lowland "coronach," characteristic and expressive as the wailing of the pipes to the Gael or the keening of women among the wild Eirionach.

"We are layin' the last o' the auld Andersons o' Deeside amang the mools the day," said Saunders M'Quhirr, the farmer of Drumquhat, to his friend Rob Adair of the Mains of Deeside, as they walked sedately together, neither swinging his arms as he would have done on an ordinary day. Saunders had come all the way over Dee Water to follow the far-noted man of God to his rest.

"There's no siccan men noo as the Andersons o' Deeside," said Rob Adair, with a kind of pride and pleasure in his voice. "I'm a dale aulder than you, Saunders, an' I mind weel o' the faither o' him that's gane." (Rob had in full measure the curious South-country disinclination to speak directly of the dead.)

"Ay, an angry man he was that day in the '43 when him that's a cauld corp the day, left the kirk an' manse that his faither had pitten him intil only the year afore. For, of coorse, the lairds o' Deeside were the pawtrons o' the pairish; an' when the auld laird's yae son took it intil his head to be a minister, it was in the nature o' things that he should get the pairish.

"Weel, the laird didna speak to his son for the better part o' twa year; though mony a time he drave by to the Pairish Kirk when his son was haudin' an ootdoor service at the Auld Wa's where the three roads meet. For nae *sicht* could they get on a' Deeside for kirk or manse, because frae the Dullarg to Craig Ronald a' belanged to the laird. The minister sent the wife an' bairns to a sma' hoose in Cairn Edward, an' lodged himsel' amang sic o' the farmers as werena feared for his faither's factor. Na, an' speak to his son the auld man wadna, for the very dourness o' him. Ay, even though the minister wad say to his faither, 'Faither, wull ye no' speak to yer ain son?' no' ae word wad he answer, but pass him as though he hadna seen him, as muckle as to say—'Nae son o' mine!'

"But a week or twa after the minister had lost yon twa nice bairns wi' the scarlet fever, his faither an' him forgathered at the fishin'—whaur he had gane, thinkin' to jook the sair thochts that he carried aboot wi' him, puir man. They were baith keen fishers an' graun' at it. The minister was for liftin' his hat to his faither an' gaun by, but the auld man stood still in the middle o' the fit-pad wi' a gey queer look in his face. 'Wattie!' he said, an' for ae blink the minister thocht that his faither was gaun to greet, a thing that he had never seen him do in a' his life. But the auld man didna greet. 'Wattie,' says he to his son, 'hae ye a huik?'

"Ay, Saunders, that was a' he said, an' the minister juist gied him the huik and some half-dizzen fine flees forbye, an' the twa o' them never said *Disruption* mair as lang as they leeved.

"'Ye had better see the factor aboot pittin' up a meetin'-hoose and a decent dwallin', gin ye hae left kirk and manse!' That was a' that the auld laird ever said, as his son gaed up stream and he down.

"Ay, he's been a sair-tried man in his time, your minister, but he's a' by wi't the day," continued Saunders M'Quhirr, as they trudged behind the hearse.

"Did I ever tell ye, Rob, aboot seem' young Walter—his boy that gaed wrang, ye ken—when I was up in London the year afore last? Na? 'Deed, I telled naebody binna the mistress. It was nae guid story to tell on Deeside!

"Weel, I was up, as ye ken, at Barnet Fair wi' some winter beasts, so I bade a day or twa in London, doin' what sma' business I had, an' seein' the sichts as weel, for it's no' ilka day that a Deeside body finds themsel's i' London.

"Ae nicht wha should come in but a Cairn Edward callant that served his time wi' Maxwell in the *Advertiser* office. He had spoken to me at the show, pleased to see a Gallawa' face, nae doot. And he telled me he was married an' workin' on the *Times*. An' amang ither things back an' forrit, he telled me that the minister o' Deeside's son was here. 'But,' says he, 'I'm feared that he's comin' to nae guid.' I kenned that the laddie hadna been hame to his faither an' his mither for a maitter o' maybe ten year, so I thocht that I wad like to see the lad for his faither's sake. So in a day or twa I got his address frae the reporter lad, an' fand him after a lang seek doon in a gey queer place no' far frae where Tammas Carlyle leeves, near the water-side. I thocht that there was nae ill bits i' London but i' the East-end; but I learned different.

"I gaed up the stair o' a wee brick hoose nearly tumlin' doon wi' its ain wecht—a perfect rickle o' brick—an' chappit. A lass opened the door after a wee, no' that ill-lookin', but toosy aboot the heid an' unco shilpit aboot the face.

"'What do you want?' says she, verra sharp an' clippit in her mainner o' speech.

"'Does Walter Anderson o' Deeside bide here?' I asked, gey an' plain, as ye ken a body has to speak to thae Englishers that barely can understand their ain language.

"'What may you want with him?' says she.

"'I come frae Deeside,' says I—no' that I meaned to lichtly my ain pairish, but I thocht that the lassie micht no' be acquant wi' the name o' Whunnyliggate. 'I come frae Deeside, an' I ken Walter Anderson's faither.'

"'That's no recommend,' says she. 'The mair's the peety,' says I, 'for he's a daicent man.'

"So she took ben my name, that I had nae cause to be ashamed o', an' syne she brocht word that I was to step in. So ben I gaed, an' it wasna a far step, eyther, for it was juist ae bit garret room; an' there on a bed in the corner was the minister's laddie, lookin' nae aulder than when he used to swing on the yett an' chase the hens. At the verra first glint I gat o' him I saw that Death had come to him, and come to bide. His countenance was barely o' this earth—sair disjaskit an' no' manlike ava'—mair like a lassie far gane in a decline; but raised-like too, an' wi' a kind o' defiance in it, as if he was darin' the Almichty to His face. O man, Rob, I hope I may never see the like again."

"Ay, man, Saunders, ay, ay!" said Rob Adair, who, being a more demonstrative man than his friend, had been groping in the tail of his "blacks" for the handkerchief that was in his hat. Then Rob forgot, in the pathos of the story, what he was searching for, and walked for a considerable distance with his hand deep in the pocket of his tail-coat.

The farmer of Drumquhat proceeded on his even way.

"The lassie that I took to be his wife (but I asked nae questions) was awfu' different ben the room wi' him frae what she was wi' me at the door—fleechin' like wi' him to tak' a sup o' soup. An' when I gaed forrit to speak to him on the puir bit bed, she cam' by me like stour, wi' the water happin' off her cheeks, like hail in a simmer thunder-shoo'er."

"Puir bit lassockie!" muttered Rob Adair, who had three daughters of his own at home, as he made another absent-minded and unsuccessful search for his handkerchief. "There's a smurr o' rain beginnin' to fa', I think," he said, apologetically.

"'An' ye're Sandy MacWhurr frae Drumquhat,' says the puir lad on the bed. 'Are your sugar-plums as guid as ever?'

"What a quastion to speer on a dying bed, Saunders!" said Rob.

"'Deed, ye may say it. Weel, frae that he gaed on talkin' aboot hoo Fred Robson an' him stole the hale o' the Drumquhat plooms ae back-end, an' hoo they gat as far as the horse waterin'-place wi' them when the dogs gat after them. He threepit that it was me that set the dogs on, but I never did that, though I didna conter him. He said that Fred an' him made for the seven-fit march dike, but hadna time to mak' ower it. So there they had to sit on the tap o' a thorn-bush in the meadow on their hunkers, wi' the dogs fair loupin' an' yowlin' to get haud o' them. Then I cam' doon mysel' an' garred them turn every pooch inside oot. He minded, too, that I was for hingin' them baith up by the heels, till what they had etten followed what had been in their pooches. A' this he telled juist as he did when he used to come ower to hae a bar wi' the lassies, in the forenichts after he cam' hame frae the college the first year. But the lad was laughin' a' the time in a way I didna like. It wasna natural—something hard an' frae the teeth oot, as ye micht say—maist peetifu' in a callant like him, wi' the deid-licht shinin' already in the blue een o' him."

"D'ye no' mind, Saunders, o' him comin' hame frae the college wi' a hantle o' medals an' prizes?" said Rob Adair, breaking in as if he felt that he must contribute his share to the memories which shortened, if they did not cheer, their road. "His faither was rael prood o' him, though it wasna his way to say muckle. But his mither could talk aboot naething else, an' carriet his picture aboot wi' her a' ower the pairish in her wee black retical basket. Fegs, a gipsy wife gat a saxpence juist for speerin' for a sicht o' it, and cryin', 'Blessings on the laddie's bonny face!'"

"Weel," continued Saunders, imperturbably taking up the thread of his narrative amid the blattering of the snow, "I let the lad rin on i' this way for a while, an' then says I, 'Walter, ye dinna ask after yer faither!'

"'No, I don't,' says he, verra short. 'Nell, gie me the draught.' So wi' that the lassie gied her een a bit quick dab, syne cam' forrit, an' pittin' her airm aneath his heid she gied him a drink. Whatever it was, it quaitened him, an' he lay back tired-like.

"'Weel,' said I, after a wee, 'Walter, gin ye'll no' speer for yer faither, maybe ye'll speer for yer ain mither?'

"Walter Anderson turned his heid to the wa'. 'Oh, my mither! my ain mither!' he said, but I could hardly hear him sayin' it. Then more fiercely than he had yet spoken he turned on me an' said, 'Wha sent ye here to torment me before my time?'

* * * * *

"I saw young Walter juist yince mair in life. I stepped doon to see him the next mornin' when the end was near. He was catchin' and twitchin' at the coverlet, liftin' up his hand an' lookin' at it as though it was somebody else's. It was a black fog outside, an' even in the garret it took him in his throat till he couldna get breath.

"He motioned for me to sit doon beside him. There was nae chair, so I e'en gat doon on my knees. The lass stood white an' quaite at the far side o' the bed. He turned his een on me, blue an' bonnie as a bairn's; but wi' a licht in them that telled he had eaten o' the tree o' knowledge, and that no' seldom.

"'O Sandy,' he whispered, 'what a mess I've made o't, haven't I? You'll see my mither when ye gang back to Deeside. Tell her it's no' been so bad as it has whiles lookit. Tell her I've aye loved her, even at the warst—an'—an' my faither too!' he said, with a kind o' grip in his words.

"'Walter,' says I, 'I'll pit up a prayer, as I'm on my knees onyway.' I'm no' giftit like some, I ken; but, Robert, I prayed for that laddie gaun afore his Maker as I never prayed afore or since. And when I spak' aboot the forgiein' o' sin, the laddie juist steekit his een an' said 'Amen!'

"That nicht as the clock was chappin' twal' the lassie cam' to my door (an' the landlady wasna that weel pleased at bein' raised, eyther), an' she askit me to come an' see Walter, for there was naebody else that had kenned him in his guid days. So I took my stave an' my plaid an' gaed my ways wi' her intil the nicht—a' lichtit up wi' lang raws o' gas-lamps, an' awa' doon by the water-side whaur the tide sweels black aneath the brigs. Man, a big lichtit toun at nicht is far mair lanesome than the Dullarg muir when it's black as pit-mirk. When we got to the puir bit hoosie, we fand that the doctor was there afore us. I had gotten him brocht to Walter the nicht afore. But the lassie was nae sooner within the door than she gied an unco-like cry, an' flang hersel' distrackit on the bed. An' there I saw, atween her white airms and her tangled yellow hair, the face o' Walter Anderson, the son o' the manse o' Deeside, lyin' on the pillow wi' the chin tied up in a napkin!

"Never a sermon like that, Robert Adair!" said Saunders M'Quhirr solemnly, after he had paused a moment.

Saunders and Robert were now turning off the wind-swept muir-road into the sheltered little avenue which led up to the kirk above the white and icebound Dee Water. The aged gravedigger, bent nearly double, met them where the roads parted. A little farther up the newly elected minister of the parish kirk stood at the manse door, in which Walter Anderson had turned the key forty years ago for conscience' sake.

Very black and sombre looked the silent company of mourners who now drew together about the open grave—a fearsome gash on the white spread of the new-fallen snow. There was no religious service at the minister's grave save that of the deepest silence. Ranked round the coffin, which lay on black bars over the grave-mouth, stood the elders, but no one of them ventured to take the posts of honour at the head and the foot. The minister had left not one of his blood with a right to these positions. He was the last Anderson of Deeside.

"Preserve us! wha's yon they're pittin' at the fit o' the grave? Wha can it be ava?" was whispered here and there back in the crowd. "It's Jean Grier's boy, I declare—him that the minister took oot o' the puirhoose, and schuled and colleged baith. Weel, that cowes a'! Saw ye ever the like o' that?"

It was to Rob Adair that this good and worthy thought had come. In him more than in any of his fellow-elders the dead man's spirit lived. He had sat under him all his life, and was sappy with his teaching. Some would have murmured had they had time to complain, but no one ventured to say nay to Rob Adair as he pushed the modest, clear-faced youth into the vacant place.

Still the space at the head of the grave was vacant, and for a long moment the ceremony halted as if waiting for a manifestation. With a swift, sudden startle the coil of black cord, always reserved for the chief mourner, slipped off the coffin-lid and fell heavily into the grave.

"He's there afore his faither," said Saunders M'Quhirr.

So sudden and unexpected was the movement, that, though the fall of the cord was the simplest thing in the world, a visible quiver passed through the bowed ranks of the bearers. "It was his ain boy Wattie come to lay his faither's heid i' the grave!" cried Daft Jess, the parish "natural," in a loud sudden voice from the "thruch" stone near the kirkyaird wall where she stood at gaze.

And there were many there who did not think it impossible.

As the mourners "skailed" slowly away from the kirkyaird in twos and threes, there was wonderment as to who should have the property, for which the late laird and minister had cared so little. There were very various opinions; but one thing was quite universally admitted, that there would be no such easy terms in the matter of rent and arrears as there had been in the time of "him that's awa'." The snow swept down with a biting swirl as the groups scattered and the mourners vanished from each other's sight, diving singly into the eddying drifts as into a great tent of many flapping folds. Grave and quiet is the Scottish funeral, with a kind of simple manfulness as of men in the presence of the King of Terrors, but yet possessing that within them which enables every man of them to await without unworthy fear the Messenger who comes but once. On the whole, not so sad as many things that are called mirthful.

So the last Anderson of Deeside, and the best of all their ancient line, was gathered to his fathers in an equal sleep that snowy January morning. There were two inches of snow in the grave when they laid the coffin in. As Saunders said, "Afore auld Elec could get him happit, his Maister had hidden him like Moses in a windin'-sheet o' His ain." In the morning, when Elec went hirpling into the kirkyaird, he found at the grave-head a bare place which the snow had not covered. Then some remembered that, hurrying by in the rapidly darkening gloaming of the night after the funeral, they had seen some one standing immovable by the minister's grave in the thickly drifting snow. They had wondered why he should stand there on such a bitter night.

There were those who said that it was just the lad Archibald Grier, gone to stand a while by his benefactor's grave.

But Daft Jess was of another opinion.

II

A SCOTTISH SABBATH DAY

"On this day Men consecrate their souls, As did their fathers."

* * * * *

And ah! the sacred morns that crowned the week—
  The path betwixt the mountains and the sea,
    The Sannox water and the wooden bridge,
The little church, the narrow seats—and we
  That through the open window saw the ridge
    Of Fergus, and the peak
Of utmost Cior Mohr—nor held it wrong,
  When vext with platitude and stirless air,
  To watch the mist-wreaths clothe the rock-scarps bare
And in the pauses hear the blackbird's song.

"Memory Harvest."

I. THE BUIK

Walter Carmichael often says in these latter days that his life owed much of its bent to his first days of the week at Drumquhat.

The Sabbath morning broke over the farm like a benediction. It was a time of great stillness and exceeding peace. It was, indeed, generally believed in the parish that Mrs. M'Quhirr had trained her cocks to crow in a fittingly subdued way upon that day. To the boy the Sabbath light seemed brighter. The necessary duties were earlier gone about, in order that perfect quiet might surround the farm during all the hours of the day. As Walter is of opinion that his youthful Sabbaths were so important, it may be well to describe one of them accurately. It will then be obvious that his memory has been playing him tricks, and that he has remembered only those parts of it which tell somewhat to his credit—a common eccentricity of memories.

It is a thousand pities if in this brief chronicle Walter should be represented as a good boy. He was seldom so called by the authorities about Drumquhat. There he was usually referred to as "that loon," "the *hyule*" "Wattie, ye mischéevious boy." For he was a stirring lad, and his restlessness frequently brought him into trouble. He remembers his mother's Bible lessons on the green turn of the loaning by the road, and he is of opinion now that they did him a great deal of good. It is not for an outside historian to contradict him; but it is certain that his mother had to exercise a good deal of patience to induce him to give due attention, and a species of suasion that could hardly be called moral to make him learn his verses and his psalm.

Indeed, to bribe the boy with the promise of a book was the only way of inspiring in him the love of scriptural learning. There was a book-packman who came from Balmathrapple once a month, and by the promise of a new missionary map of the world (with the Protestants in red, floating like cream on the top, and the pagans sunk in hopeless black at the bottom) Wattie could be induced to learn nearly anything. Walter was, however, of opinion that the map was a most imperfect production. He thought that the portion of the world occupied by the Cameronians ought to have been much more prominently charted. This omission he blamed on Ned Kenna the bookman, who was a U.P.

Walter looked for the time when all the world, from great blank Australia to the upper Icy Pole, should become Cameronian. He anticipated an era when the black savages would have to quit eating one another and learn the Shorter Catechism. He chuckled when he thought of them attacking *Effectual Calling*.

But he knew his duty to his fellows very well, and he did it to the best of his ability. It was, when he met a Free Kirk or Established boy, to throw a stone at him; or alternatively, if the heathen chanced to be a girl, to put out his tongue at her. This he did, not from any special sense of superiority, but for the good of their souls.

When Walter awoke, the sun had long been up, and already all sounds of labour, usually so loud, were hushed about the farm. There was a breathless silence, and the boy knew even in his sleep that it was the Sabbath morning. He arose, and unassisted arrayed himself for the day. Then he stole forth, hoping that he would get his porridge before the "buik" came on. Through the little end window he could see his grandfather moving up and down outside, leaning on his staff—his tall, stooped figure very clear against the background of beeches. As he went he looked upward often in self-communion, and sometimes groaned aloud in the instancy of his unspoken prayer. His brow rose like the wall of a fortress. A stray white lock on his bare head stirred in the crisp air.

Wattie was about to omit his prayers in his eagerness for his porridge, but the sight of his grandfather induced him to change his mind. He knelt reverently down, and was so found when his mother came in. She stood for a moment on the threshold, and silently beckoned the good mistress of the house forward to share in the sight. But neither of the women knew how near the boy's prayers came to being entirely omitted that morning. And what is more, they would not have believed it had they been informed of it by the angel Gabriel. For this is the manner of women— the way that mothers are made. The God of faith bless them for it! The man has indeed been driven out of Paradise, but the woman, for whose expulsion we have no direct scriptural authority, certainly carries with her materials for constructing one out of her own generous faith and belief. Often men hammer out a poor best, not because they are anxious to do the good for its own sake, but because they know that some woman expects it of them.

The dwelling-house of Drumquhat was a low one-storied house of a common enough pattern. It stood at one angle of the white fortalice of buildings which surrounded the "yard." Over the kitchen and the "ben the hoose" there was a "laft," where the "boys"[3] slept. The roof of this upper floor was unceiled, and through the crevices the winter snows sifted down upon the sleepers. Yet were there no finer lads, no more sturdy and well set-up men, than the sons of the farmhouse of Drumquhat. Many a morning, ere the eldest son of the house rose from his bed in the black dark to look to the sheep, before lighting his candle he brushed off from the coverlet a full arm-sweep of powdery snow. It was a sign of Walter's emancipation from boyhood when he insisted on leaving his mother's cosy little wall-chamber and climbing up the ladder with the boys to their "laft" under the eaves. Nevertheless, it went with a sudden pang to the mother's heart to think that never more should she go to sleep with her boy clasped in her arms. Such times will come to mothers, and they must abide them in silence. A yet more bitter tragedy is when she realises that another woman is before her in her son's heart.

[Footnote 3: As in Ireland, all the sons of the house are "boys" so long as they remain under the roof-tree, even though they may carry grey heads on their shoulders.]

The whole family of Saunders M'Quhirr was collected every Sabbath morning at the "buik." It was a solemn time. No one was absent, or could be absent for any purpose whatever. The great Bible, clad rough-coated in the hairy hide of a calf, was brought down from the press and laid at the table-end. Saunders sat down before it and bowed his head. In all the house there was a silence that could be felt. It was at this time every Sabbath morning that Walter resolved to be a good boy for the whole week. The psalm was reverently given out, two lines at a time—

"They in the Lord that firmly trust,
  Shall be like Zion hill"—

and sung to the high quavering strains of "Coleshill," garnished with endless quavers and grace-notes.

The chapter was then read with a simple trust and manfulness like that of an ancient patriarch. Once at this portion of the service the most terrible thing that ever happened at Drumquhat took place. Walter had gone to school during the past year, and had been placed in the "sixpenny"; but he had promptly "trapped" his way to the head of the class, and so into the more noble "tenpenny," which he entered before he was six. The operation of "trapping" was simply performed. When a mistake was made in pronunciation, repetition, or spelling, any pupil further down the class held out his hand, snapping the finger and thumb like a pop-gun Nordenfeldt. The master's pointer skimmed rapidly down the line, and if no one in higher position answered, the "trapper," providing always that his emendation was accepted, was instantly promoted to the place of the "trapped." The master's "taws" were a wholesome deterrent of persistent or mistaken trapping; and, in addition, the trapped boys sometimes rectified matters at the back of the school at the play-hour, when fists became a high court of appeal and review.

Walter had many fights—"Can ye fecht?" being the recognised greeting to the new comer at Whinnyliggate school. When this was asked of Walter, he replied modestly that he did not know, whereupon his enemy, without provocation, smote him incontinently on the nose. Him our boy-from-the-heather promptly charged, literally with tooth and nail, overbore to the dust, and, when he held him there, proceeded summarily to disable him for further conflict, as he had often seen Royal do when that mild dog went forth to war. Walter could not at all understand why he was dragged off his assailant by the assembled school, and soundly cuffed for a young savage who fought like the beasts. Wattie knew in his heart that this objection was unreasonable, for whom else had he seen fight besides the beasts? But in due time he learned to fight legitimately enough, and to take his share of the honours of war. Moreover, the reputation of a reserve of savagery did him no harm, and induced many an elder boy who had been "trapped" to forego the pleasure of "warming him after the schule comes oot," which was the formal challenge of Whinnyliggate chivalry.

But this Sabbath morning at the "buik," when the solemnity of the week had culminated, and the portion was being read, Walter detected a quaint antiquity in the pronunciation of a Bible name. His hand shot out, cracking like a pistol, and, while the family waited for the heavens to fall, Walter boldly "trapped" the priest of the household at his own family altar!

Saunders M'Quhirr stopped, and darted one sharp, severe glance at the boy's eager face. But even as he looked, his face mellowed into what his son Alec to this day thinks may have been the ghost of a smile. But this he mentions to no one, for, after all, Saunders is his father.

The book was closed. "Let us pray," Saunders said.

The prayer was not one to be forgotten. There was a yearning refrain in it, a cry for more worthiness in those whom God had so highly favoured. Saunders was allowed to be highly gifted in intercession. But he was also considered to have some strange notions for a God-fearing man.

For instance, he would not permit any of his children to be taught by heart any prayer besides the Lord's Prayer. After repeating that, they were encouraged to ask from God whatever they wanted, and were never reproved, however strange or incongruous their supplications might be. Saunders simply told them that if what they asked was not for their good they would not get it—a fact which, he said, "they had as lief learn sune as syne."

This excellent theory of prayer was certainly productive of curious results. For instance, Alec is recorded in the family archives to have interjected the following petition into his devotions. While saying his own prayers, he had been keeping a keen fraternal eye upon sundry delinquencies of his younger brother. These having become too outrageous, Alec continued without break in his supplications—"And now, Lord, will you please excuse me till I gang an' kick that loon Rab, for he'll no' behave himsel'!" So the spiritual exercises were interrupted, and in Alec's belief the universe waited till discipline allowed the petitionary thread to be taken up.

The "buik" being over, the red farm-cart rattled to the door to convey such of the churchgoers as were not able to walk all the weary miles to the Cameronian kirk in Cairn Edward. The stalwart, long-legged sons cut across a shorter way by the Big Hoose and the Deeside kirk. Both the cart and the walkers passed on the way a good many churches, both Established and Free; but they never so much as looked the road they were on.

This hardly applied to Alec, whose sweetheart (for the time-being) attended the Free kirk at Whinnyliggate. He knew within his own heart that he would have liked to turn in there, and the consciousness of his iniquity gave him an acute sense of the fallen nature of man—at least, till he got out of sight of the spireless rigging of the kirk, and out of hearing of the jow of its bell. Then his spirits rose to think that he had resisted temptation. Also, he dared not for his life have done anything else, for his father's discipline, though kindly, was strict and patriarchal.

And, moreover, there was a lass at the Cameronian kirk, a daughter of the Arkland grieve, whose curls he rather liked to see in the seat before him. He had known her when he went to the neighbouring farm to harvest—for in that lowland district the corn was all cut and led, before it was time to begin it on the scanty upland crop which was gathered into the barns of Drumquhat. Luckily, she sat in a line with the minister; and when she was there, two sermons on end were not too long.

II. THE ROAD TO THE KIRK

The clean red farm-cart rattled into the town of Cairn Edward at five minutes past eleven. The burghers looked up and said, "Hoo is the clock?" Some of them went so far as to correct any discrepancy in their time-keepers, for all the world knew that the Drumquhat cart was not a moment too soon or too late, so long as Saunders had the driving of it. Times had not been too good of late; and for some years—indeed, ever since the imposition of the tax on light-wheeled vehicles—the "tax-cart" had slumbered wheelless in the back of the peat-shed, and the Drumquhat folk had driven a well-cleaned, heavy-wheeled red cart both to kirk and market. But they were respected in spite of their want of that admirable local certificate of character, "He is a respectable man. He keeps a gig." One good man in Whinnyliggate says to this day that he had an excellent upbringing. He was brought up by his parents to fear God and respect the Drumquhat folks!

Walter generally went to church now, ever since his granny had tired of conveying him to the back field overlooking the valley of the Black Water of the Dee, while his mother made herself ready. He was fond of going there to see the tents of the invading army of navvies who were carrying the granite rock-cuttings and heavy embankments of the Portpatrick Railway through the wilds of the Galloway moors. But Mary M'Quhirr struck work one day when the "infant," being hungry for a piece, said calmly, "D'ye no think that we can gang hame? My mither will be awa' to the kirk by noo!"

On the long journey to church, Walter nominally accompanied the cart. Occasionally he seated himself on the clean straw which filled its bottom; but most of the time this was too fatiguing an occupation for him. On the plea of walking up the hills, he ranged about on either side of the highway, scenting the ground like a young collie. He even gathered flowers when his grandfather was not looking, and his mother or his "gran," who were not so sound in the faith, aided and abetted him by concealing them when Saunders looked round. The master sat, of course, on the front of the cart and drove; but occasionally he cast a wary eye around, and if he saw that they were approaching any houses he would stop the cart and make Walter get in. On these occasions he would fail to observe it even if Walter's hands contained a posy of wild-flowers as big as his head. His blindness was remarkable in a man whose eyesight was so good. The women-folk in the cart generally put the proceeds of these forays under the straw or else dropped them quietly overboard before entering Cairn Edward.

The old Cameronian kirk sits on a hill, and is surrounded by trees, a place both bieldy and heartsome. The only thing that the Cameronians seriously felt the want of was a burying-ground round about it. A kirk is never quite commodious and cheery without monuments to read and "thruchs" to sit upon and "ca' the crack." Now, however, they have made a modern church of it, and a steeple has been set down before it, for all the world as if Cleopatra's needle had been added to the front wall of a barn.

But Cairn Edward Cameronian kirk has long been a gate of heaven. To many who in their youth have entered it the words heard there have brought the beginning of a new life and another world. Of old, as the morning psalm went upward in a grand slow surge, there was a sense of hallowed days in the very air. And to this day Walter has a general idea that the mansions of the New Jerusalem are of the barn class of architecture and whitewashed inside, which will not show so much upon the white robes when it rubs off, as it used to do on plain earthly "blacks."

III. A CAMERONIAN DIET OF WORSHIP

There were not many distractions for a boy of active habits and restless tendencies during the long double service of two hours and a bittock in the Cameronian kirk of Cairn Edward. The minister was the Reverend Richard Cameron, the youngest scion of a famous Covenanting family.

He had come to Cairn Edward as a stripling, and he was now looked upon as the future high priest of the sect in succession to his father, at that time minister of the metropolitan temple of the denomination. Tall, erect, with flowing black hair that swept his shoulders, and the exquisitely chiselled face of some marble Apollo, Richard Cameron was, as his name-sake had been, an ideal minister of the Hill Folk. His splendid eyes glowed with still and chastened fire, as he walked with his hands behind him and his head thrown back, up the long aisle from the vestry.

His successor was a much smaller man, well set and dapper, who wore black gloves when preaching, and who seemed to dance a minuet under his spectacles as he walked. Alas! to him also came in due time the sore heart and the bitter draught. They say in Cairn Edward that no man ever left that white church on the wooded knoll south of the town and was happier for the change. The leafy garden where many ministers have written their sermons, has seemed to them a very paradise in after years, and their cry has been, "O why left I my hame?"

But these were happy days for Richard Cameron when he brought his books and his violin to the manse that nestled at the foot of the hill. He came among men strict with a certain staid severity concerning things that they counted material, but yet far more kindly-hearted and charitable than of recent years they have gotten credit for.

Saunders did not object to the minister's violin, being himself partial to a game at the ice, and willing that another man should also have his chosen relaxation. Then, again, when the young man began to realise himself, and lay about him in the pulpit, there were many who would tell how they remembered his father—preaching on one occasion the sermon that "fenced the tables," on the Fast Day before the communion, when the partitions were out and the church crowded to the door. Being oppressed with the heat, he craved the indulgence of the congregation to be allowed to remove his coat; and thereafter in his shirt-sleeves, struck terror into all, by denunciations against heresy and infidelity, against all evil-doing and evil-speaking. It was interesting as a battle-tale how he barred the table of the Lord to "all such as have danced or followed after play-actors, or have behaved themselves unseemly at Kelton Hill or other gathering of the ungodly, or have frequented public-houses beyond what is expedient for lawful entertainment; against all such as swear minced oaths, such as 'losh,' 'gosh,' 'fegs,' 'certes,' 'faith'; and against all such as swear by heaven or earth, or visit their neighbours' houses upon the Lord's Day, saving as may be necessary in coming to the house of the Lord."

The young man could not be expected at once to come up to the high standard of this paternal master-work—which, indeed, proved to be too strong meat for any but a few of the sterner office-bearers, who had never heard their brother-elders' weaknesses so properly handled before. But they had, nevertheless, to go round the people and tell them that what the Doctor had said was to be understood spiritually, and chiefly as a warning to other denominations, else there had been a thin kirk and but one sparse table instead of the usual four or five, on the day of high communion in the Cairn Edward Cameronian kirk.

Now, Walter could be a quiet boy in church for a certain time. He did not very much enjoy the service, except when they sang "Old Hundred" or "Scarborough," when he would throw back his head and warble delightedly with the best. But he listened attentively to the prayers, and tracked the minister over that well-kenned ground. Walter was prepared for his regular stint, but he did not hold with either additions or innovations. He liked to know how far he was on in the prayer, and it was with an exhausted gasp of relief that he caught the curious lowering of the preacher's voice which tells that the "Amen" is within reasonable distance.

The whole congregation was good at that, and hearers began to relax themselves from their standing postures as the minister's shrill pipe rounded the corner and tacked for the harbour; but Walter was always down before them. Once, however, after he had seated himself, he was put to shame by the minister suddenly darting off on a new excursion, having remembered some other needful supplication which he had omitted. Walter never quite regained his confidence in Mr. Cameron after that. He had always thought him a good and Christian man hitherto, but thereafter he was not so sure.

Once, also, when the minister visited the farm of Drumquhat, Walter, being caught by his granny in the very act of escaping, was haled to instant execution with the shine of the soap on his cheeks and hair. But the minister was kind, and did not ask for anything more abstruse than "Man's Chief End." He inquired, however, if the boy had ever seen him before.

"Ou ay," said Walter, confidently; "ye're the man that sat at the back window!"

This was the position of the manse seat, and at the Fast Day service Mr. Cameron usually sat there when a stranger preached. Not the least of Walter's treasures, now in his library, is a dusky little squat book called *The Peep of Day*, with an inscription on it in Mr. Cameron's minute and beautiful backhand: "To Walter Carmichael, from the Man at the Back Window."

The minister was grand. In fact, he usually *was* grand. On this particular Sunday he preached his two discourses with only the interval of a psalm and a prayer; and his second sermon was on the spiritual rights of a Covenanted kirk, as distinguished from the worldly emoluments of an Erastian establishment. Nothing is so popular as to prove to people what they already believe and that day's sermon was long remembered among the Cameronians. It redd up their position so clearly, and settled their precedence with such finality, that Walter, hearing that the Frees had done far wrong in not joining the Church of the Protests and Declarations in the year 1843, resolved to have his school-bag full of good road-metal on the following morning, in order to impress the Copland boys, who were Frees, with a sense of their position.

But as the sermon proceeded on its conclusive way, the bowed ranks of the attentive Hill Folk bent further and further forward, during the long periods of the preacher; and when, at the close of each, they drew in a long, united breath like the sighing of the wind, and leaned back in their seats, Walter's head began to nod over the chapters of First Samuel, which he was spelling out.

David's wars were a great comfort to him during long sermons. Gradually he dropped asleep, and wakened occasionally with a start when his granny nudged him when Saunders happened to look his way.

As the little fellow's mind thus came time and again to the surface, he heard snatches of fiery oratory concerning the Sanquhar Declarations and the Covenants, National and Solemn League, till it seemed to him as though the trump of doom would crash before the minister had finished. And he wished it would! But at last, in sheer desperation, having slept apparently about a week, he rose with his feet upon the seat, and in his clear, childish treble he said, being still dazed with sleep —

"Will that man no' soon be dune?"

It was thus that the movement for short services began in the Cameronian kirk of Cairn Edward. They are an hour and twenty minutes now—a sore declension, as all will admit.

IV. THE THREE M'HAFFIES

Again the red farm-cart rattled out of the town into the silence of the hedges. For the first mile or two, the church-folk returning to the moor-farm might possibly meet and, if they did so, frankly reprove with word or look the "Sunday walkers," who bit shamefacedly, as well they might, the ends of hawthorn twigs, and communed together apparently without saying a word to each other. There were not many pairs of sweethearts among them—any that were, being set down as "regardless Englishry," the spawn of the strange, uncannylike building by the lochside, which the "General" had been intending to finish any time these half-dozen years.

For the most part the walkers were young men with companions of their own sex and age, who were anxious to be considered broad in their views. Times have changed now, for we hear that quite respectable folk, even town-councillors, take their walks openly on Sabbath afternoons. It was otherwise in those days.

But none of their own kind did the Drumquhat folk meet or overtake, till at the bottom rise of the mile-long Whinnyliggate Wood the red cart came up with the three brave little old maids who, leaving a Free kirk at their very door, and an Established over the hill, made their way seven long miles to the true kirk of the persecutions.

It had always been a grief to them that there was no Clavers to make them testify up to the chin in Solway tide, or with a great fiery match between their fingers to burn them to the bone. But what they could they did. They trudged fourteen miles every Sabbath day, with their dresses "fait and snod" and their linen like the very snow, to listen to the gospel preached according to their conscience. They were all the smallest of women, but their hearts were great, and those who knew them hold them far more worthy of honour than the three lairds of the parish.

Of them all only one remains. (Alas, no more!) But their name and honour shall not be forgotten on Deeside while fire burns and water runs, if this biographer can help it. The M'Haffies were all distinguished by their sturdy independence, but Jen M'Haffie was ever the cleverest with her head. The parish minister had once mistaken Jen for a person of limited intelligence; but he altered his opinion after Jen had taken him through-hands upon the Settlement of "Aughty-nine" (1689), when the Cameronians refused to enter into the Church of Scotland as reconstructed by the Revolution Settlement.

The three sisters had a little shop which the two less active tended; while Mary, the business woman of the family, resorted to Cairn Edward every Monday and Thursday with and for a miscellaneous cargo. As she plodded the weary way, she divided herself between conning the sermons of the previous Sabbath, arranging her packages, and anathematising the cuddy. "Ye person—ye awfu' person!" was her severest denunciation.

Billy was a donkey of parts. He knew what houses to call at. It is said that he always brayed when he had to pass the Established kirk manse, in order to express his feelings. But in spite of this Billy was not a true Cameronian. It was always suspected that he could not be much more than Cameronian by marriage—a "tacked-on one," in short. His walk and conversation were by no means so straightforward, as those of one sound in the faith ought to have been. It was easy to tell when Billy and his cart had passed along the road, for his tracks did not go forward, like all other wheel-marks, but meandered hither and thither across the road, as though he had been weaving some intricate web of his own devising. He was called the Whinnyliggate Express, and his record was a mile and a quarter an hour, good going.

Mary herself was generally tugging at him to come on. She pulled Billy, and Billy pulled the cart. But, nevertheless, in the long-run, it was the will of Billy that was the ultimate law. Walter was very glad to have the M'Haffies on the cart, both because he was allowed to walk all the time, and because he hoped to get Mary into a good temper against next Tuesday.

Mary came Drumquhat way twice a week—on Tuesdays and Fridays. As Wattie went to school he met her, and, being allowed by his granny one penny to spend at Mary's cart, he generally occupied most of church time, and all the school hours for a day or two before these red-letter occasions, in deciding what he would buy.

It did not make choice any easier that alternatives were strictly limited. While he was slowly and laboriously making up his mind as to the long-drawn-out merits of four farthing biscuits, the way that "halfpenny Abernethies" melted in the mouth arose before him with irresistible force. And just as he had settled to have these, the thought of the charming explorations after the currants in a couple of "cookies" was really too much for him. Again, the solid and enduring charms of a penny "Jew's roll," into which he could put his lump of butter, often entirely unsettled his mind at the last moment. The consequence was that Wattie had always to make up his mind in the immediate presence of the objects, and by that time neither Billy nor Mary could brook very long delays.

It was important, therefore, on Sabbaths, to propitiate Mary as much as possible, so that she might not cut him short and proceed on her way without supplying his wants, as she had done at least once before. On that occasion she said—

"D'ye think Mary M'Haffie has naething else in the world to do, but stan' still as lang as it pleases you to gaup there! Gin ye canna tell us what ye want, ye can e'en do withoot! Gee up, Billy! Come oot o' the roadside—ye're aye eat-eatin', ye bursen craitur ye!"

III

THE COURTSHIP OF TAMMOCK THACKANRAIP, AYRSHIREMAN

The peats were brought, the fires were set,
  While roared November's gale;
With unbound mirth the neighbours met
  To speed the canty tale.

A bask, dry November night at Drumquhat made us glad to gather in to the goodwife's fire. I had been round the farm looking after the sheep. Billy Beattie, a careless loon, was bringing in the kye. He was whacking them over the rumps with a hazel. I came on him suddenly and changed the direction of the hazel, which pleased my wife when I told her.

"The rackless young vaigabond," said she—"I'll rump him!"

"Bide ye, wife; I attended to that mysel'."

The minister had been over at Drumquhat in the afternoon, and the wife had to tell me what he had said to her, and especially what she had said to him. For my guidwife, when she has a fit of repentance and good intentions, becomes exceedingly anxious—not about her own shortcomings, but about mine. Then she confesses all my sins to the minister. Now, I have telled her a score of times that this is no' bonnie, and me an elder of twenty years' standing. But the minister kens her weakness. We must all bear with the women-folk, even ministers, he says, for he is a married man, an' kens.

"Guidman," she says, as soon as I got my nose by the door-cheek, "it was an awsome peety that ye werena inby this afternoon. The minister was graund on smokin'."

"Ay," said I; "had his brither in Liverpool sent him some guid stuff that had never paid her Majesty's duty, as he did last year?"

"Hoots, haivers; I'll never believe that!" said she, scouring about the kitchen and rubbing the dust out of odd corners that were clean aneuch for the Duke of Buccleuch to take his "fower-oors" off. But that is the way of the wife. They are queer cattle, wives—even the best of them. Some day I shall write a book about them. It will be a book worth buying. But the wife says that when I do, she will write a second volume about men, that will make every married man in the parish sit up. And as for me, I had better take a millstone about my neck and loup into the depths of the mill-dam. That is what she says, and she is a woman of her word. My book on wives is therefore "unavoidably delayed," as Maxwell whiles says of his St. Mungo's letter, and capital reading it is.

"Hoots, haivers!" said the wife again. She cannot bide not being answered. Even if she has a *grooin'* in her back, and remarks "*Ateeshoo-oo!*" ye are bound for the sake of peace to put the question, "What ails ye, guidwife?"

"I'll never believe that the minister smokes. He never has the gliff o' it aboot him when he comes here."

"That's the cunnin' o' the body," said I. "He kens wha he's comin' to see, an' he juist cuittles ye till ye gang aboot the hoose like Pussy Bawdrons that has been strokit afore the fire, wi' your tail wavin' owre your back."

"Think shame o' yoursel', Saunders M'Quhirr—you an elder and a man on in years, to speak that gate."

"Gae wa' wi' ye, Mary M'Quhirr," I said. "Do ye think me sae auld? There was but forty-aught hours and twenty meenits atween oor first scraichs in this warld. That's no' aneuch to set ye up to sic an extent, that ye can afford to gang aboot the hoose castin' up my age to me. There's mony an aulder man lookin' for his second wife."

And with that, before my wife had time to think on a rouser of a reply (I saw it in her eye, but it had not time to come away), Thomas Thackanraip hirpled in. Thomas came from Ayrshire near forty years since, and has been called Tammock the Ayrshireman ever since. He was now a hearty-like man with a cottage of his own, and a cheery way with him that made him a welcome guest at all the neighbouring farmhouses, as he was at ours. The humours of Tammock were often the latest thing in the countryside. He was not in the least averse to a joke against himself, and that, I think, was the reason of a good deal of his popularity. He went generally with his hand in the small of his back, as if he were keeping the machinery in position while he walked. But he had a curious young-like way with him for so old a man, and was for ever _pook-pook_ing at the lasses wherever he went.

"Guid e'en to ye, mistress; hoo's a' at Drumquhat the nicht?" says Tammock.

"Come your ways by, an' tak' a seat by the fire, Tammock; it's no' a kindly nicht for auld banes," says the wife.

"Ay, guidwife, 'deed and I sympathise wi' ye," says Tammock. "It's what we maun a' come to some day."

"Doitered auld body!" exclaimed my wife, "did ye think I was meanin' mysel'?"

"Wha else?" said Tammock, reaching forward to get a light for his pipe from the hearth where a little glowing knot had fallen, puffing out sappy wheezes as it burned. He looked slyly up at the mistress as he did so.

"Tammock," said she, standing with her arms wide set, and her hands on that part of the onstead that appears to have been built for them, "wad hae ye mind that I was but a lassock when ye cam' knoitin' an' hirplin' alang the Ayrshire road frae Dalmellington."

"I mind brawly," said Tammock, drawing bravely away. "Ay, Mary, ye were a strappin' wean. Ye said ye wadna hae me; I mind that weel. That was the way ye fell in wi' Drumquhat, when I gied up thochts o' ye mysel'."

"*You* gie up thochts o' me, Tammock! Was there ever siccan presumption? Ye'll no' speak that way in my hoose. Hoo daur ye? Saunders, hear till him. Wull ye sit there like a puddock on a post, an' listen to this—this Ayrshireman misca' your marriet wife, Alexander M'Quhirr? Shame till ye, man!"

My married wife was well capable of taking care of herself in anything that appertained to the strife of tongues. In the circumstances, therefore, I did not feel called upon to interfere.

"Ye can tak' a note o' the circumstance an' tell the minister the next time he comes owre," said I, dry as a mill-hopper.

She whisked away into the milk-house, taking the door after her as far as it would go with a *flaff* that brought a bowl, which had been set on its edge to dry, whirling off the dresser on to the stone floor.

When the wife came back, she paused before the fragments. We were sitting smoking very peacefully and wondering what was coming.

"Wha whammelt my cheeny bowl?" said Mistress M'Quhirr, in a tone which, had I not been innocent, would have made me take the stable.

"Wha gaed through that door last?" said I.

"The minister," says she.

"Then it maun hae been the minister that broke the bowl. Pit it by for him till he comes. I'm no' gaun to be wracked oot o' hoose an' hame for reckless ministers."

"But wha was't?" she said, still in doubt.

"Juist e'en the waff o' your ain coat-tails, mistress," said Tammock. "I hae seen the day that mair nor bowls whammelt themsel's an' brak' into flinders to be after ye."

And Tammock sighed a sigh and shook his head at the red *greesoch* in the grate.

"Hoots, haivers!" said the mistress. But I could see she was pleased, and wanted Tammock to go on. He was a great man all his days with the women-folk by just such arts. On the contrary, I am for ever getting cracks on the crown for speaking to them as ye would do to a man body. Some folk have the gift and it is worth a hundred a year to them at the least.

"Ay," said Tammock thoughtfully, "ye nearly brak' my heart when I was the grieve at the Folds, an' cam' owre in the forenichts to coort ye. D'ye mind hoo ye used to sit on my knee, and I used to sing,

'My love she's but a lassie yet'?"

"I mind no siccan things," said Mistress M'Quhirr. "Weel do ye ken that when ye cam' aboot the mill I was but a wee toddlin' bairn rinnin' after the dyukes in the yaird. It's like aneuch that I sat on your knee. I hae some mind o' you haudin' your muckle turnip watch to my lug for me to hear it tick."

"Aweel, aweel, Mary," he said placably, "it's like aneuch that was it.
Thae auld times are apt to get a kennin' mixter-maxter in yin's held."

We got little more out of him till once the bairns were shooed off to their beds, and the wife had been in three times at them with the broad of her loof to make them behave themselves. But ultimately Tammock Thackanraip agreed to spend the night with us. I saw that he wanted to open out something by ourselves, after the kitchen was clear and the men off to the stable.

So on the back of nine we took the book, and then drew round the red glow of the fire in the kitchen. It is the only time in the day that the mistress allows me to put my feet on the jambs, which is the only way that a man can get right warmed up, from foundation to rigging, as one might say. In this position we waited for Tammock to begin—or rather I waited, for the wife sat quietly in the corner knitting her stocking.

"I was thinkin' o' takin' a wife gin I could get a guid, faceable-like yin," said Tammock, thumbing the dottle down.

"Ay?" said I, and waited.

"Ye see, I'm no' as young as I yince was, and I need somebody sair."

"But I thocht aye that ye were lookin' at Tibby o' the Hilltap," said the mistress.

"I was," said Thomas sententiously. He stroked his leg with one hand softly, as though it had been a cat's back.

Now, Tibby o' the Hilltap was the farmer's daughter, a belle among the bachelors, but one who had let so many lads pass her by, that she was thought to be in danger of missing a down-setting after all. But Tammock had long been faithful.

"I'll gang nae mair to yon toun," said Tammock.

"Hoots, haivers!" (this was Mistress M'Quhirr's favourite expression); "an' what for no'? What said she, Tammock, to turn you frae the Hilltap?"

"She said what settled me," said Tammock a little sadly. "I'm thinkin' there's nocht left for't but to tak' Bell Mulwhulter, that has been my housekeeper, as ye ken, for twenty year. But gin I do mak' up my mind to that, it'll be a heartbreak that I didna do it twenty year since. It wad hae saved expense."

"'Deed, I'm nane so sure o' that," said the goodwife, listening with one ear cocked to the muffled laughter in the boys' sleeping-room.

"Thae loons are no' asleep yet," said she, lifting an old flat-heeled slipper and disappearing.

There was a sharp *slap-slapping* for a minute, mixed with cries of "Oh, mither, it was Alec!" "No, mither, it was Rob!"

Mary appeared at the door presently, breathing as she did when she had half done with the kirning. She set the slipper in the corner to be ready to her hand in case of further need.

"Na, na, Ayrshireman," she said; "it's maybe time aneuch as it is for you to marry Bell Mulwhulter. It's sma' savin' o' expense to bring up a rachle o' bairns."

"Dod, woman, I never thocht a' that," said Tammock. "It's maybe as weel as it is."

"Ay, better a deal. Let weel alane," said the mistress.

"I doot I'll hae to do that ony way noo," said Tammock.

"But what said Tibby o' the Hilltap to ye, Tammock, that ye gied up thochts o' her sae sudden-like?"

"Na, I can tell that to naebody," he said at last.

"Hoots, haivers!" said the wife, who wanted very much to know. "Ye ken that it'll gang nae farder."

"Aweel," said Tammock, "I'll tell ye."

And this he had intended to do from the first, as we knew, and he knew that we knew it. But the rules of the game had to be observed. There was something of a woman's round-the-corner ways about Tammock all his days, and that was the way he got on so well with them as a general rule—though Tibby o' the Hilltap had given him the go-by, as we were presently to hear.

"The way o't was this," began Tammock, putting a red doit of peat into the bowl of his pipe and squinting down at it with one eye shut to see that it glowed. "I had been payin' my respects to Tibby up at the Hilltap off and on for a year or twa—"

"Maistly on," said my wife. Tammock paid no attention.

"Tibby didna appear to mislike it to ony extent. She was fond o' caa'in' the crack, an' I was wullin' that she should miscaa' me as muckle as she likit—for I'm no' yin o' your crouse, conceity young chaps to be fleyed awa' wi' a gibe frae a lassie."

"Ye never war that a' the days o' ye, Tammock!" said the mistress.

"Ay, ye are beginnin' to mind noo, mistress," said Tammas dryly. "Weel, the nicht afore last I gaed to the Hilltap to see Tibby, an' as usual there was a lad or twa in the kitchen, an' the crack was gaun screevin' roond. But I can tak' my share in that," continued Tammas modestly, "so we fell on to the banter.

"Tibby was knitting at a reid pirnie[4] for her faither; but, of course, I let on that it was for her guidman, and wanted her to tak' the size o' my held so that she micht mak' it richt.

[Footnote 4: Night-cap.]

"'It'll never be on the pow o' an Ayrshire drover,' says she, snell as the north wind.

"'An' what for that?' says I.

"'The yairn 's owre dear,' says Tibby. 'It cost twa baskets o' mushrooms in Dumfries market!'

"'An' what price paid ye for the mushrooms that the airn should be owre dear?' said I.

"'Ou, nocht ava,' says Tibby. 'I juist gat them whaur the Ayrshire drover gat the coo. I fand them in a field!'

"Then everybody _haa-haa_ed with laughing. She had me there, I wull alloo—me that had been a drover," said Tammas Thackanraip.

"But that was naething to discourage ye, Tammock," said I. "That was juist her bit joke."

"I ken—I ken," said Tammock; "but hand a wee—I'm no' dune yet. So after they had dune laughin', I telled them o' the last man that was hangit at the Grassmarket o' Edinburgh. There was three coonts in the dittay against him: first, that he was fand on the king's highway withoot due cause; second, he wan'ered in his speech; and, thirdly, he owned that he cam' frae Gallowa'.

"This kind o' squared the reckoning, but it hadna the success o' the Ayrshireman and the coo, for they a' belonged to Gallowa' that was in the kitchen,"

"'Deed, an' I dinna see muckle joke in that last mysel'," said my wife, who also belonged to Galloway.

"And I'll be bound neither did the poor lad in the Grassmarket!" I put in, edgeways, taking my legs down off the jambs, for the peats had burned up, and enough is as good as a feast.

Then Tammas was silent for a good while, smoking slowly, taking out his pipe whiles and looking at the shank of it in a very curious manner.

I knew that we were coming to the kernel of the story now.

"So the nicht slippit on," continued the narrator, "an' the lads that had to be early up in the morning gaed awa yin by yin, an' I was left my lane wi' Tibby. She was gaun aboot here an' there gey an' brisk, clatterin' dishes an' reddin' corners.

"'Hae a paper an' read us some o' the news, gin ye hae nocht better to say,' said she.

"She threw me a paper across the table that I kenned for Maxwell's by the crunkle o' the sheets.

"I ripit a' my pooches, yin after the ither.

"'I misdoot I maun hae comed awa' withoot my specs, Tibby,' says I at last, when I could come on them nowhere.

"So we talked a bit langer, and she screeved aboot, pittin' things into their places.

"'It's a fine nicht for gettin' hame,' she says, at the hinder end.

"This was, as ye may say, something like a hint, but I was determined to hae it oot wi' her that nicht. An' so I had, though no' in the way I had intended exactly.

"'It *is* a fine nicht,' says I; 'but I ken by the pains in the sma' o' my back that it's gaun to be a storm.'

"Wi' that, as if a bee had stang'd her, Tibby cam' to the ither side o' the table frae whaur I was sittin'—as it micht be there—an' she set her hands on the edge o't wi' the loofs doon (I think I see her noo; she looked awsome bonny), an' says she—

"'Tammas Thackanraip, ye are a decent man, but ye are wasting your time comin' here coortin' me,' she says. 'Gin ye think that Tibby o' the Hilltap is gaun to marry a man wi' his een in his pooch an' a weather-glass in the sma' o' his back, ye're maist notoriously mista'en,' says she."

There was silence in the kitchen after that, so that we could hear the clock ticking time about with my wife's needles.

"So I cam' awa'," at last said Tammock, sadly.

"An' what hae ye dune aboot it?" asked my wife, sympathetically.

"Dune aboot it?" said Tammas; "I juist speered Bell Mulwhulter when I cam' hame."

"An' what said she?" asked the mistress.

"Oh," cried Tammas, "she said it was raither near the eleeventh 'oor, but that she had nae objections that she kenned o'."

IV

THE OLD TORY

> *One man alone,*
> *Amid the general consent of tongues.*
> *For his point's sake bore his point—*
> *Then, unrepenting, died.*

The first time I ever saw the Old Tory, he was scurrying down the street of the Radical village where he lived, with a score of men after him. Clods and stones were flying, and the Old Tory had his hand up to protect his head. Yet ever as he fled, he turned him about to cry an epithet injurious to the good name of some great Radical leader. It was a time when the political atmosphere was prickly with electricity, and men's passions easily flared up—specially the passions of those who had nothing whatever to do with the matter.

The Old Tory was the man to enjoy a time like that. On the day before the election he set a banner on his chimney which he called "the right yellow," which flaunted bravely all day so long as David Armitt, the Old Tory, sat at his door busking salmon hooks, with a loaded blunderbuss at his elbow and grim determination in the cock of one shaggy grey eyebrow.

But at night, when all was quiet under the Dullarg stars, Jamie Wardhaugh and three brave spirits climbed to the rigging of the Old Tory's house, tore down his yellow flag, thrust the staff down the chimney, and set a slate across the aperture.

Then they climbed down and proceeded to complete their ploy. Jamie Wardhaugh proposed that they should tie the yellow flag to the pig's tail in derision of the Old Tory and his Toryism. It was indeed a happy thought, and would make them the talk of the village upon election day. They would set the decorated pig on the dyke to see the Tory candidate's carriage roll past in the early morning.

They were indeed the talk of the village; but, alas! the thing itself did not quite fall out as they had anticipated. For, while they were bent in a cluster within the narrow, slippery quadrangle of the pig-sty, and just as Jamie Wardhaugh sprawled on his knees to catch the slumbering inmate by the hind-leg, they were suddenly hailed in a deep, quiet voice—the voice of the Old Tory.

"Bide ye whaur ye are, lads—ye will do bravely there. I hae Mons Meg on ye, fu' to the bell wi' slugs, and she is the boy to scatter. It was kind o' ye to come and see to the repairing o' my bit hoose an' the comfort o' my bit swine. Ay, kind it was—an' I tak' it weel. Ye see, lads, my wife Meg wull no let me sleep i' the hoose at election times, for Meg is a reid-headed Radical besom—sae I e'en tak' up my quarters i' the t'ither end o' the swine-ree, whaur the auld sow died oot o'."

The men appeared ready to make a break for liberty, but the bell-mouth of Mons Meg deterred them.

"It's a fine nicht for the time o' year, Davit!" at last said Jamie Wardhaugh. "An' a nice bit pig. Ye hae muckle credit o't!"

"Ay," said David Armitt, "'deed, an' ye are richt. It's a sonsy bit swine."

"We'll hae to be sayin' guid-nicht, Davit!" at last said Jamie Wardhaugh, rather limply.

"Na, na, lads. It's but lanesome oot here—an' the morn's election day. We'll e'en see it in thegither. I see that ye hae a swatch o' the guid colour there. That's braw! Noo, there's aneuch o't for us a', Jamie; divide it intil five! Noo, pit ilka yin o' ye a bit in his bonnet!"

One of the others again attempted to run, but he had not got beyond the dyke of the swine-ree when the cold rim of Mons Meg was laid to his ear.

"She's fu' to the muzzle, Wullie," said the Old Tory; "I wadna rin, gin I war you."

Willie did not run. On the contrary, he stood and shook visibly.

"She wad mak' an awfu' scatterment gin she war to gang aff. Ye had better be oot o' her reach. Ye are braw climbers. I saw ye on my riggin' the nicht already. Climb your ways back up again, and stick every man o' ye a bit o' the bonny yellow in your bonnets."

So the four jesters very reluctantly climbed away up to the rigging of David Armitt's house under the lowering threat of Mons Meg's iron jaws.

Then the Old Tory took out his pipe, primed it, lighted it, and sat down to wait for the dawning with grim determination. With one eye he appeared to observe the waxing and waning of his pipe; and with the other, cocked at an angle, he watched the four men on his rigging.

"It's a braw seat, up there, gentlemen. Fine for the breeks. Dinna hotch owre muckle, or ye'll maybe gang doon through, and I'm tellin' ye, ye'll rue it gin ye fa' on oor Meg and disturb her in her mornin' sleep. Hearken till her rowtin' like a coo! Certes, hoo wad ye like to sleep a' yer life ayont that? Ye wad be for takin' to the empty swine-ree that the sow gaed oot o', as weel as me."

So the Old Tory sat with his blunderbuss across his knees, and comforted the men on the roof with reminiscences of the snoring powers of his spouse Meg. But, in spite of the entertaining nature of the conversation, Jamie Wardhaugh and the others were more than usually silent. They sat in a row with their chins upon their knees and the ridiculous yellow favours streaming from their broad blue bonnets.

The morning came slowly. Gib Martin, the tailor, came to his door at ten minutes to six to look out. He had hastily drawn on his trousers, and he came out to spit and see what kind of morning it was; then he was going back to bed again. But he wished to tell the minister that he had been up before five that morning; and, as he was an elder, he did not want to tell a whole lie.

Gib glanced casually at the sky, looked west to the little turret on the kirk to see the clock, and was about to turn in again, when something black against the reddening eastern sky caught his eye.

"Preserve us a', what's yon on Davit Armitt's riggin'?" he cried.

And so surprised was Gib Martin, that he came all the way down the street in three spangs, and that on his stocking-feet, though he was a married man.

But he did not see the Old Tory sitting by the side of the pig-sty—a thing he had cause to be sorry for.

"Save us, Jamie, what are ye doin' sittin' on Davit Armitt's hoose-riggin'? Gin the doited auld Tory brute catches ye—"

"A fine mornin' to ye, tailor," said the Old Tory from the side of the dyke.

The tailor faced about with a sudden pallor.

The muzzle of Mons Meg was set fair upon him, and he felt for the first time in his life that he could not have threaded a needle had his life depended on it.

"Climb up there aside the other four," commanded David Armitt.

"I'm on my stockin'-feet, Davit!" said the tailor.

"It's brave an' dry for the stockin'-feet up on the riggin'," said the Old Tory. "Up wi' ye, lad; ye couldna do better."

And the tailor was beside the others before he knew it, a strand of the bright yellow streaming from the button-hole of his shirt. So one after another the inhabitants of Dullarg came out to wonder, and mounted to wear the badge of slavery; until, when the chariot of the Tory candidate dashed in at twenty minutes to seven on its way to the county town, the rigging of David Armitt's house was crowded with men all decorated with his yellow colours. Never had such a sight been seen in the Radical and Chartist village of Dullarg.

Then the Old Tory leaped to his feet as the horses went prancing by.

"Gie a cheer, boys!" he cried; and as the muzzle of Mons Meg swept down the file, a strange wavering cry arose, that was half a gowl of anger and half a broken-backed cheer.

Then "Bang!" went Mons Meg, and David Armitt took down the street at full speed with sixteen angry men jumping at his tail. But, by good luck, he got upon the back of the Laird's coach, and was borne rapidly out of their sight down the dusty road that led to the county town.

It was the Old Tory's Waterloo. He did not venture back till the time of the bee-killing. Then he came without fear, for he knew he was the only man who could take off the honey from the village hives to the satisfaction of the parish.

The Old Tory kept the secret of his Toryism to the last.

Only the minister caught it as he lay a-dying. He was not penitent, but he wanted to explain matters.

"It's no as they a' think, minister," he said, speaking with difficulty. "I cared nocht aboot it, ae way or the ither. I'm sure I aye wantit to be a douce man like the lave. But Meg was sair, sair to leeve wi'. She fair drave me till't. D'ye think the like o' that wull be ta'en into account, as it were—up yonder?"

The minister assured him that it would, and the Old Tory died in peace.

V

THE GREAT RIGHT-OF-WAY CASE

The Vandal and the Visigoth come here,
 The trampler under foot, and he whose eyes,
 Unblest, behold not where the glory lies;
The wallower in mire, whose sidelong leer

Degrades the wholesome earth—these all come near
 To gaze upon the wonder of the hills,
 And drink the limpid clearness of the rills.
Yet each returns to what he holds most dear,

To change the script and grind the mammon mills
 Unpurified; for what men hither bring,
  That take they hence, and Nature doth appear

As one that spends herself for sodden wills,
 Who pearls of price before the swine doth fling,
  And from the shrine casts out the sacred gear.

Glen Conquhar was a summer resort. Its hillsides had never been barred by the intrusive and peremptory notice-board, a bugbear to ladies strolling book in hand, a cock-shy to the children passing on their way to school. The Conquhar was a swift, clear-running river coursing over its bed of gneiss, well tucked-in on either side by green hayfields, where the grasshopper for ever "burred," and the haymakers stopped with elbows on their rakes to watch the passer-by. The Marquis had never enforced his rights of exclusion in his Highland solitudes. His shooting-lodge of Ben Dhu, which lay half a dozen miles to the north, was tenanted only by himself and a guest or two during the months of September and October. The visitors at the hotel above the Conquhar Water saw now and then a tall figure waiting at the bridge or scanning the hill-side through a pair of deer-stalker glasses. Then the underlings of the establishment would approach and in awe-struck tones whisper the information, "That's the Marquis!" For it is the next thing in these parts to being Providence to be the Marquis of Rannoch.

The hotel of Glen Conquhar was far from the haunts of men. Its quiet was never disturbed by the noise of roysterers. It was the summer home of a number of quiet people from the south—fishing men chiefly, who loved to hear the water rushing about their legs on the edges of the deep salmon-pools of the Conquhar Water. There was Cole, Radical M.P., impulsive and warm-hearted, a London lawyer who had declined, doubtless to his own monetary loss, to put his sense of justice permanently into a blue bag. There was Dr. Percival, the father of all them that cast the angle in Glen Conquhar, who now fished little in these degenerate days, but instead told tales of the great salmon of thirty years ago—fellows tremendous enough to make the spick-and-span rods of these days, with their finicking attachments, crack their joints even to think of holding the monsters. Chiefly and finally there was "Old Royle," who came in March, first of all the fishing clan, and lingered on till November, when nothing but the weathered birch-leaves spun down the flooded glen of the Conquhar. Old Royle regarded the best fishing in the water as his birthright, and every rival as an intruder. He showed this too, for there was no bashfulness about Old Royle. Young men who had just begun to fish consulted him as to where they should begin on the morrow. Old Royle was of opinion that there was not a single fish within at least five miles of the hotel. Indeed, he thought of "taking a trap" in the morning to a certain pool six miles up the water, where he had seen a round half-dozen of beauties only the night before. The young men departed, strapped and gaitered, at cock-crow on the morrow. They fished all day, and caught nothing save and except numerous dead branches in the narrow swirls of the linn. But they lost, in addition to their tempers, the tops of a rod or two caught in the close birch tangles, many casts of flies, and a fly-book which one of them had dropped out of his breast-pocket while in act to disentangle his hook from the underlip of a caving bank. His fly-book and he had descended into the rushing Conquhar together. He clambered out fifty yards below; and as for the fly-book, it was given by a mother-salmon to her young barbarians to play with in the deepest pool between Glendona and Loch Alsh.

When these young men returned, jolly Mr. Forbes, of landlords the most excellent, received them with a merry twinkle in his eye. In the lobby, Old Royle was weighing his "take." He had caught two beautiful fish—one in the pool called "Black Duncan," and the other half a mile farther up. He had had the water to himself all day. These young men passed in to dinner with thoughts too deep for words.

Suddenly the quiet politics of the glen were stirred by the posting of a threatening notice, which appeared on the right across the bridge at the end of the path, along which from time immemorial the ladies of the hotel had been in the habit of straying in pairs, communing of feminine mysteries; or mooning singly with books and water-colour blocks, during the absence of the nominal heads of their houses, who were engaged in casting the fly far up the glen.

Once or twice a surly keeper peremptorily turned back the innocent and law-abiding sex, but always when unaccompanied by the more persistent male. So there was wrath at the *table-d'hôte*. There was indignation in the houses of summer residence scattered up and down the strath. It was the new tenant of the Lodge of Glen Conquhar, or rather his wife, who had done this thing. For the first season for many years the shooting and fishing on the north side of the Conquhar had been let by the Marquis of Rannoch. From the minister's glebe for ten miles up the water these rights extended. They had been leased to the scion of a Black Country family, noble in the second generation by virtue of the paternal tubs and vats. The master was a shy man, dwelling in gaiters and great boots, only to be met with far on the hills, and then passing placidly on with quiet down-looking eyes. Contrariwise, the lady was much in evidence. Her noble proportions and determined eye made the boldest quail. The M.P. thanked Heaven three times a day that he was not her husband. She managed the house and the shooting as well. Among other things, she had resolved that no more should mere hotel-visitors walk to within sight of her windows, and that the path which led up the north side of the glen must be shut up for ever and ever. She procured a painted board from a cunning artificer in the neighbouring town of Portmore, which announced (quite illegally) the pains and penalties which would overtake those who ventured to set foot on the forbidden roadway.

There were enthusiastic mass meetings, tempered with tea and cake, on the lawn. Ladies said impressive things of their ill-treatment; and their several protectors, and even others without any direct and obvious claim, felt indignation upon their several accounts. The correct theory of trespass was announced by a high authority, and the famous prescription of the great judge, Lord Mouthmore, was stated. It ran as follows:—

"When called to account for trespass, make use of the following formula if you wish the law to have no hold over you: 'I claim no right-of-way, and I offer sixpence in lieu of damages,' at the same time offering the money composition to the enemy."

This was thought to be an admirable solution, and all the ladies present resolved to carry sixpences in their pockets when next they went a-walking. One lady so mistrusted her memory that she set down the prescription privately as follows: "I claim no sixpence, and I offer damages in lieu of right-of-way!"

"It is always well to be exact," she said; "memory is so treacherous."

But this short and easy method with those who take their stand on coercion and illegality was scouted by the Radical M.P. He pointed out with the same lucidity and precision with which he would have stated a case to a leading counsel, the facts (first) that the right-of-way was not only claimed, but existed; (second) that the threatening notice was inoperative; (third) that an action lay against any person who attempted to deforce the passage of any individual; (fourth) that the road in question was the only way to kirk and market for a very considerable part of the strath, that therefore the right-of-way was inalienable; and (fifth) that the right could be proved back to the beginning of the century, and, indeed, that it had never been disputed till the advent of Mrs. Nokes. The case was complete. It had only to go before any court in the land to be won with costs against the extruder. The only question was, "Who would bell the cat?" Several ladies of yielding dispositions, who went fully intending to beard the lion, turned meekly back at the word of the velveteen Jack-in-office. For such is the conservative basis of woman, that she cannot believe that the wrong can by any possibility be on the side of the man in possession. If you want to observe the only exception to this attitude, undertake to pilot even the most upright of women through the custom-house.

The situation became acute owing to the indignant feelings of the visitors, now reinforced by the dwellers in the various houses of private entertainment. Indignation meetings increased and abounded. A grand demonstration along the path and under the windows of the lodge was arranged for Sunday after morning church—several clergymen agreeing to take part, on the well-known principle of the better day the better deed. What might have happened no one can say. An action for assault and battery would have been the English way; a selection of slugs and tenpenny nails over the hedge might possibly have been the Irish way; but what actually happened in this law-abiding strath was quite different.

In this parish of Glen Conquhar there was a minister, as there is a minister in every parish in broad Scotland. He was very happy. He had a cow or two of his own on the glebe, and part of it he let to the master of the hotel.

The Reverend Donald Grant of Glen Conquhar was an old man now, but, though a little bowed, he was still strong and hearty, and well able for his meal of meat. He lived high up on the hill, whose heathery sides looked down upon the kirk and riverside glebe. His simplicity of heart and excellence of character endeared him to his parish, as indeed was afterwards inscribed upon enduring marble on the tablet which was placed under the list of benefactions in the little kirk of the strath.

The minister did not often come down from his Mount of the Wide Prospects; and when he did, it was for some definite purpose, which being performed, he straightway returned to his hill-nest.

He had heard nothing of the great Glen Conquhar right-of-way case, when one fine morning he made his way down to the hamlet to see one of his scanty flock, whose church attendance had not been all that could be desired. As he went down the hill he passed within a few feet of the newly painted trespass notice-board; but it was not till his return, with slow steps, a little weary with the uphill road and the heat of the day, that his eyes rested on the glaring white notice. Still more slowly and deliberately he got his glasses out of their shagreen case, mounted their massive silver rims on his nose, and slowly read the legend which intimated that "*Trespassers on this Private Road will be Prosecuted with the utmost Rigour of the Law.*"

Having got to the large BY ORDER at the end, he calmly dismounted the benignant silver spectacles, returned them to the shagreen case, and so to the tail-pocket of his black coat. Then, still more benignantly, he sought about among the roots of the trees till he found the stout branch of a fir broken off in some spring gale, but still tough and able-bodied. With an energy which could hardly have been expected from one of his hoar hairs, the minister climbed part way up the pole, and dealt the obnoxious board such hearty thwacks, first on one side and then on the other, that in a trice it came tumbling down.

As he was picking it up and tucking it beneath his arm, the gamekeeper on the watch in some hidden sentry-box among the leaves came hurrying down.

"Oh, Mr. Grant, Mr. Grant!" he exclaimed in horror, "what are you doing with that board?"—his professional indignation grievously at war with his racial respect for the clerical office.

"'Deed, Dugald, I'm just taking this bit spale boardie hame below my arm. It will make not that ill firewood, and it has no business whatever to be cockin' up there on the corner of my glebe."

The end of the Great Glen Conquhar Right-of-Way Case.

VI

DOMINIE GRIER

A grey, grey world and a grey belief,
True as iron and grey as grief;
Worse worlds there are, worse faiths, in truth,
Than the grey, grey world and the grey belief.

"*The Grey Land.*"

What want ye so late with Dominie Grier? To tell you the tale of my going on foot to the town of Edinburgh that I might preserve pure the doctrine and precept of the parish of Rowantree? Ay, to tell of it I am ready, and with right goodwill. Never a day do I sit under godly Mr. Campbell but I think on my errand, and the sore stroke that the deil and Bauldy Todd gat that day when I first won speech with the Lady Lochwinnoch.

It was langsyne in the black Moderate days, and the Socinians were great in the land. 'Deed ay, it was weary work in these times; let me learn the bairns what I liked in the school, it was never in me to please the Presbytery. But whiles I outmarched them when they came to examine; as, indeed, to the knowledge and admiration of all the parish, I did in the matter of Effectual Calling. It was Maister Calmsough of Clauchaneasy that was putting the question, and rendering the meaning into his own sense as he went along. But he chanced upon James Todd of Todston, a well-learned boy; and, if I may say so, a favourite of mine, with whom I had been at great pains that he should grow up in the faith and wholesome discipline. Thereto I had fed him upon precious Thomas Boston of Ettrick and the works of godly Mr. Erskine, desiring with great desire that one day he might, by my learning and the blessing of Almighty God, even come to wag his head in a pulpit—a thing which, because of the sins of a hot youth, it had never been in my power, though much in my heart, to do.

But concerning the examination. Mr. Calmsough was insisting upon the general mercy of God—which, to my thinking, is at the best a dangerous doctrine, and one that a judicious preacher had best keep his thumb upon. At last he asked Jamie Todd what he thought of the matter; for he was an easy examiner, and would put a question a yard long to be answered with "Yes" and "No"—a fool way of examining, which to me was clear proof of his incapacity.

But James Todd was well learned and withstood him, so that Mr. Calmsough grew angry and roared like a bull. I could only sit quiet in my desk, for upon that day it was not within my right to open my mouth in my own school, since it was in the hands of the Presbytery. So I sat still, resting my confidence upon the Lord and the ready answers of James Todd. And I was not deceived. For though he was but a laddie, the root of the matter was in him, and not a Socinian among them could move him from my teaching concerning Justification and Election.

"Ye may explain it away as ye like, sir," said James Todd, "but me and the Dominie and the Bible has anither way o't!"

"Is it thus that you train your elder scholars to speak to their spiritual advisers, Dominie Grier?" asked Mr. Calmsough, turning on me.

"Out of the mouth of babes and sucklings," said I meekly, for pride in James Todd was just boiling within me, and yet I would not let them see it.

I desired them to depart from the school of Rowantree, thinking that any of my first class in the Bible could have answered them even as did James Todd. I was in the fear of my life that they should light upon mine own son Tam, for he knew no more than how to bait a line and guddle trout; but nevertheless he has done wonderfully well at the pack among the ignorant English, and is, (I deny it not to him) the staff of my declining years. But Tam, though as great a dulbert as there is betwixt Saterness and the Corse o' Slakes, sat up looking so gleg that they passed him by and continued to wrestle with James Todd, who only hung his head and looked stupid, yet had in him, for all that, a very dungeon of lear.

Now, it came to pass, less than three weeks after the examination of my bit school at the Rowantree, that our own minister, Mr. Wakerife, took a chill after heating himself at the hay, and died. He was a canny body, and sound on the doctrine, but without unction or the fervour of the Spirit blowing upon him in the pulpit. Still, he was sound, and in a minister that is aye the main thing.

Now, so great was the regardlessness of the parish, that the honest man was not cold in his coffin before two-three of the farmers with whom the members of the Presbytery were wont to stay when they came to examine, laid their heads together that they might make the parish of Rowantree even as Corseglass, and Deadthraws, and other Valleys of Dry Bones about us.

"There shall be no more fanatics in Rowantree!" said they.

And they had half a gallon over the head of it, which, being John
Grieve's best, they might have partaken of in a better cause.

Now, the worst of them was Bauldy Todd of Todston, the father of my James. It was a great thing, as I have often been told, to hear James and his father at it. James was a quiet and loutish loon so long as he was let alone, and he went about his duties pondering and revolving mighty things in his mind. But when you chanced to start him on the fundamentals, then the Lord give you skill of your weapon, for it was no slight or unskilled dialectician who did you the honour to cross swords with you.

But Bauldy Todd, being a hot, contentious man, could not let his son alone. In the stable and out in the hayfield he was ever on his back, though Jamie was never the lad to cross him or to begin an argument. But his father would rage and try to shout him down—a vain thing with Jamie. For the lad, being well learned in the Scriptures, had the more time to bethink himself while the "goldering" of his father was heard as far as the high Crownrigs. And even as Bauldy paused for breath, James would slip a text under his father's guard, which let the wind out of him like a bladder that is transfixed on a thorn-bush. Then there remained nothing for Bauldy but to run at Jamie to lay on him with a staff—an argument which, taking to his heels, Jamie as easily avoided.

It was my own Jamie who brought me word of the ill-contrived ploy that was in the wind. He told me that his father and Mickle Andrew of Ingliston and the rest of that clan were for starting to see the Lady Lochwinnoch, the patron of the parish, to make interest on behalf of Mr. Calmsough's nephew, as cold and lifeless a moral preacher as was ever put out of the Edinburgh College, which is saying no little, as all will admit.

They were to start, well mounted on their market horses, the next morning at break of day, to ride all the way to Edinburgh. In a moment I saw what I was called upon to do. I left Jamie Todd with a big stick to keep the school in my place, while, with some farles of cake bread in my pocket, I took alone my way to Edinburgh. Ten hours' start I had; and though it be a far cry to the town of Edinburgh and a rough road, still I thought that I should be hardly bestead if I could not walk it in two days. For my heart was sore to think of the want of sound doctrine that was about to fall upon the parish of Rowantree. Indeed, I saw not the end of it, for there was no saying what lengths such a minister and his like-minded elders might not run to. They might even remove me from some of my offices and emoluments. And then who would train the Jamie Todds to give a reason of the faith that was in them before minister and elder?

So all that night I walked on sore-hearted. It was hardly dark, for the season of the year was midsummer, and by the morning I had gone thirty miles. But when I came on the hard "made" road again, I hasted yet more, for I knew that by the hour of eight Bauldy and his farmers would be in the saddle. And I heard as it were the hoofs of the horses ringing behind me—the horses of the enemies of sound doctrine; for the Accuser of the Brethren sees to it that his messengers are well mounted. Yet though I was footsore, and had but a farle of oatcake in my pocket, I went not a warfare on my own charges.

For by the way I encountered a carrier in the first spring-cart that ever I had seen. It was before the day of the taxes. And, seeing the staff in my hand and the splashing of the moor and the peatlands on my knee-breeches, he very obligingly gave me a lift, which took me far on my journey. When he loosed his horse to take up his quarters at an inn for the night I thanked him very cordially for his courtesy, and so fared on my way without pause or rest for sleep. I had in my mind all the time the man I was to propose to the Lady Lochwinnoch.

I had not reached the city when I heard behind me the trampling of horses and the loud voices of men. Louder than all I heard Bauldy Todd's roar. It was as much as I could do to make a spring for the stone-dyke at the side of the road, to drag myself over it, and lie snug till their cavalcade had passed. I could hear them railing upon me as they went by.

"I'll learn him to put notions into my laddie's head!" cried Todd of Todston.

"We'll empty the auld carle's meal-ark, I'se warrant!" said Mickle Andrew.

"Faith, lads, we'll get a decent drinking, caird-playin' minister in young Calmsough—yin that's no' feared o' a guid braid oath!" cried Chryston of Commonel.

And I was trembling in all my limbs lest they should see me. So before I dared rise I heard the clatter of their horses' feet down the road. My heart failed me, for I thought that in an hour they would be in Edinburgh town and have audience of my lady, and so prefer their request before me.

Yet I was not to be daunted, and went limping onward as best I might. Nor had I gone far when, in a beautiful hollow, by the lintels of an inn that had for a sign a burn-trout over the door, I came upon their horses.

"Warm be your wames and dry your thrapples!" quoth I to myself; "an', gin the brew be nappy and the company guid at the Fisher's Tryst, we'll bring back the gospel yet to the holms of the Rowantree, or I am sair mista'en!"

So when I got to my lady's house, speering at every watchman, it was still mirk night. But in the shadow of an archway I sat me down to wait, leaning my breast against the sharp end of my staff lest sleep should overcome me. The hope of recommending the godly man, Mr. Campbell, to my lady kept me from feeling hungered. Yet I was fain in time to set about turning my pockets inside out. In them I searched for crumblings of my cakes, and found a good many, so that I was not that ill off.

As soon as it was day, and I saw that the servants of the house began to stir, I went over and knocked soundly upon the great brass knocker. A man with a cropped black poll and powder sifted among it, came and ordered me away. I asked when my lady would be up.

"Not before ten of the clock," said he.

Now, I knew that this would never do for me, because the farmer bodies would certainly arrive before that, drunk or sober. So I told Crophead that he had better go and tell his mistress that there was one come post-haste all the way from the parish of Rowantree, where her property lay, and that the messenger must instantly speak with her.

But Crophead swore at me, and churlishly bade me begone at that hour of the morning. But since he would have slammed the door on me, I set my staff in the crevice and hoised it open again. Ay, and would have made my oak rung acquaint with the side of his ill-favoured head, too, had not a woman's voice cried down the stair to know the reason of the disturbance.

"It is a great nowt from the country, and he will not go away," said Crophead.

Then I stepped forward into the hall, sending him that withstood me over on his back against the wall. Speaking high and clear as I do to my first class, I said—

"I am Dominie Grier, parish schoolmaster of the parish of Rowantree, madam, and I have come post-haste from that place to speak to her ladyship."

Then I heard a further commotion, as of one shifting furniture, and another voice that spoke rapidly from an inner chamber.

In a little while there came one down the stair and called me to follow. So forthwith I was shown into a room where a lady in a flowered dressing-gown was sitting up in bed eating some fine kind of porridge and cream out of a silver platter.

"Dominie Grier!" said the lady pleasantly, affecting the vulgar dialect, "what has brocht ye so far from home? Have the bairns barred ye oot o' the schule?"

"Na, my lady," I replied, with my best bow; "I come to you in mickle fear lest the grace of God be barred out of the poor parish of Rowantree."

So I opened out to her the whole state of the case; and though at first she seemed to be amused rather than edified, she gave me her promise that young William Campbell, who was presently assistant to the great Dr. Shirmers, of St. John's in the city, should get the kirk of Rowantree. He was not a drop's blood to me, though him and my wife were far-out friends, so that it was not as if I had been asking anything for myself. Yet I thanked her ladyship warmly for her promise in the name of all the godly in the parish of Rowantree, and warned her at the same time of the regardless clan that were seeking to abuse her good-nature. But I need not have troubled, for I was but at the door and Crophead sulkily showing me out, when whom should I meet fair in the teeth but Bauldy Todd and all his fighting tail!

Never were men more taken aback. They stopped dead where they were, when they saw me; and Bauldy, who had one hand in the air, having been laying down the law, as was usual with him, kept it there stiff as if he had been frozen where he stood.

Now I never let on that I saw any of them, but went by them with my briskest town step and my head in the air, whistling like a lintie—

> "The Campbells are coming, aha! aha!
> The Campbells are coming, aha! aha!
> The Campbells are coming to bonnie Loch Leven!
> The Campbells are coming, aha! aha!"

"Deil burn me," cried Bauldy Todd, "but the Dominie has done us!"

"'Deed, he was like to do that ony gate," said Mickie Andrew. "We may as weel gang hame, lads. I ken the Dominie. His tongue wad wile the bird aff the tree. We hae come the day after the fair, boys."

But as for me, I never turned a hair; only kept my nose in the straight of my face, and went by them down the street as though I had been the strength of a regiment marching with pipers, whistling all the time at my refrain—

> "The Campbells are coming to bonnie Loch Leven!
> The Campbells are coming, aha! aha!"

VII

THE PRODIGAL DAUGHTER

Hard is it, O my friends, to gather up
  A whole life's goodness into narrow space—
  A life made Heaven-meet by patient grace,
And handling oft the sacramental cup

Of sorrow, drinking all the bitter drains.
  Her life she kept most sacred from the world;
  Though, Martha-wise, much cumber'd and imperill'd
With service, Mary-like she brought her pains,

And laid them and herself low at the feet,
  The travel-weary, deep-scarr'd feet, of Him
    The incarnate Good, who oft in Galilee

Had borne Himself the burden and the heat—
  Ah! couldst thou bear, thy tender eyes were dim
    With humble tears to think this meant for thee!

A certain man had two daughters. The man was a minister in Galloway—a Cameronian minister in a hill parish in the latest years of last century; consequently he had no living to divide to them. Of the two daughters, one was wise and the other was foolish. So he loved the foolish with all his heart. Also he loved the wise daughter; but her heart was hard because that her sister was preferred before her. The man's name was Eli M'Diarmid, and his daughters' names were Sophia and Elsie. He had been long in the little kirk of Cauldshields. To the manse he had brought his young wife, and from its cheerless four walls he had walked behind her hearse one day nigh twenty years ago. The daughters had been reared here; but, even as enmity had arisen on the tilled slips of garden outside Eden, so there had always been strife between the daughters of the lonely manse—on the one side rebellion and the resentment of restraint, on the other tale-bearing and ferret-eyed spying.

This continued till Elsie M'Diarmid was a well-grown and a comely lass, while her sister Sophia was already sharpening and souring towards the thirties. One day there was a terrible talk in the parish. Elsie, the minister's younger daughter, had run off to Glasgow, and there got married to Alec Saunderson, the dominie's ne'er-do-well son. So to Glasgow the minister went, and came back in three weeks with an extra stoop to his shoulders. But with such a still and patient silence on his face, that no man and (what is more wonderful) no woman durst ask him any further questions. After that, Elsie was no more named in the manse; but the report of her beauty and her waywardness was much in the parish mouth. A year afterwards her sister went from the manse in all the odour of propriety, to be the mistress of one of the large farms of a neighbouring glen. Then the minister gathered himself more than ever close in to his lonely hearth, with only Euphemia Kerr, his wise old housekeeper, once his children's nurse. He went less frequently abroad, and looked more patiently than ever out of his absent grey eyes on the "herds" and small sheep-farmers who made up the bulk of his scanty flock.

The Cameronian kirk of Cauldshields was a survival of the time when the uplands of Galloway were the very home and hive of the "Westlan'" Whigs—of the men who marched to Rullion Green to be slaughtered, sent Claverhouse scurrying to Glasgow from Drumclog, and abjured all earthly monarchs at the cross of Sanquhar.

But now the small farms were already being turned into large, the sheep were dispossessing the plough, and the principle of "led" farms was depopulating the countryside. That is, instead of sonsy farmers' wives and their husbands (the order is not accidental) marshalling their hosts into the family pews on Sabbath, many of the farms were held by wealthy farmers who lived in an entirely different part of the country. These gave up the farmhouse, with its feudality of cothouses, to a taciturn bachelor shepherd or two, who squatted promiscuously in the once voluble kitchen.

The morning of the first Sabbath of February dawned bitterly over the scattered clachan of Cauldshields. It had been snowing since four o'clock on Saturday night, and during those hours no dog had put its nose outside the door. At seven in the morning, had any one been able to see across the street for the driving snow, he would have seen David Grier look out for a moment in his trousers and shirt, take one comprehensive glance, and vanish within. That glance had settled David's church attendance for the day. He was an "Auld Kirk," and a very regular hearer, having been thirty years in the service of the laird; but in the moment that he looked out into the dim white chaos of whirling snow, David had settled it that there would be no carriage down from the "Big House" that day. "The drifts will be sax fit in the howes o' the muir-road," he said, as he settled himself to sleep till midday, with a solid consciousness that he had that day done all that the most exacting could require of him. As his thoughts composed themselves to a continuation of his doze, while remaining deliciously conscious of the wild turmoil outside, David Grier remembered the wayfarer who had got a lift in his cart to Cauldshields the night before. "It was weel for the bit bairn that I fell in wi' her at the Cross Roads," said he, as he stirred his wife in the ribs with his elbow, to tell her it was time to get up and make the fire.

* * * * *

In the manse of Cauldshields the Reverend Eli M'Diarmid's housekeeper was getting him ready for church.

"There'll no' be mony fowk at the kirk the day, gin there be ony ava'; but that's nae raison that ye shouldna gang oot snod," she said, as she brushed him faitly down. "Ye mind hoo Miss Elsie used to say that ye wad gang oot a verra ragman gin she didna look efter ye!" The minister turned his back, and the housekeeper continued, like the wise woman of Tekoa, "Eh, but she was a heartsome bairn, Miss Elsie; an' a bonny—nane like till her in a' the pairish!"

"Oh, woman, can ye not hold your tongue?" said the minister, knocking his hands angrily together.

"Haud my tongue or no haud my tongue, ye're no' gaun withoot yer sermon an' yer plaid, minister," said his helper. So with that she brought the first from the study table and placed it in the leather case which held his bands, and reached the plaid from its nail in the hall. It was not for nothing that she had watched the genesis and growth of that sermon which she placed in the case. Some folk declare that she suggested the text. Nor is this so wholly impossible as it looks, for Cauldshields' housekeeper was a very wise woman indeed.

It was but a step to the kirk door from the manse, but it took the minister nearly twenty minutes to overcome the drifts and get the key turned in the lock—for in these hard times it was no uncommon thing for the minister to be also the doorkeeper of the tabernacle. Then he took hold of the bell-rope, and high above him the notes swung out into the air; for though the storm had now settled, vast drifts remained to tell of the blast of the night. But the gale had engineered well, and as the minister looked over the half mile that separated the kirk from the nearest house of the clachan he knew that not a soul would be able to come to the kirk that day. Yet it never occurred to him to put off the service of the sanctuary. He was quite willing to preach to Euphemia Kerr alone, even so precious a discourse as he carried in his band-case that day.

The minister was his own precentor, as, according to the law and regulation of the kirks of Scotland, he always is in the last resort, however he may choose to delegate his authority. He gave out from his swallow's nest the Twenty-third Psalm, and led it off himself in a powerful and expressive voice, which sounded strangely in the empty church. The tune was taken up from the manse pew, in the dusk under the little gallery, by a quavering, uncertain pipe—as dry and unsympathetic as, contrariwise, the singer was warm-hearted and full of the very sap of human kindness. The minister was so absorbed in his own full-hearted praise that he was scarce conscious that he was almost alone in the chill emptiness of the church. Indeed, a strange feeling stole upon him, that he heard his wife's voice singing the solemn gladness of the last verse along with him, as they had sung it together near forty years ago when she had first come to the hill kirk of Cauldshields.

> "Goodness and mercy all my life
>   Shall surely follow me:
> And in God's house for evermore
>   My dwelling-place shall be."

Then the prayer echoed along the walls, bare like a barn before the harvest. Nevertheless, I doubt not that it went straight to the throne of God as the minister pleaded for the weary and the heavy-laden, the fatherless and the oppressed, for the little children and those on whom the Lord has special pity—"for to Thee, O Lord, more are the children of the desolate than the children of the married wife, saith the Lord." And the minister seemed to hear somewhere a sound of silent weeping, like that which he had hearkened to in the night long ago, when his wife sorrowed by his side and wept in the darkness for the loss of their only man-bairn.

The minister gave out his text. There was silence within, and without the empty church only the whistling sough of the snowdrift. "And when he was yet a great way off, his father saw him, and had compassion, and ran, and fell on his neck and kissed him."

There was a moment's pause, and a strange, unwonted sound came from the manse seat under the dark of the gallery. It was the creak of the housekeeper opening the door of the pew. The minister paused yet a moment in his discourse, his dim eyes vaguely expectant. But what he saw, stilled for ever the unspoken opening of his sermon. A girlish figure came up the aisle, and was almost at the foot of the pulpit-steps before the minister could move. And she carried something tenderly in her arms, as a bairn is carried when it is brought forward for the baptizing.

"My father!" she said.

Nobody knows how the minister got out of the pulpit except Euphemia Kerr, and it is small use asking her; but it is currently reported that it was in such fashion as never minister got out of pulpit before. And, at the door of the manse seat stood Euphemia, the wise woman of Tekoa, her tears falling *pat-pat* like raindrops on the narrow book-board; but with a smile on her face, as who would say, "Now, Lord, let Thy servant depart in peace," when she saw the minister fall on the neck of his well-beloved daughter and kiss her, having compassion on her.

But this is what Sophia M'Diarmid that was, said when she heard of the home-coming of her sister Elsie.

"It was like her brazen face to come back when she had shut every other door. My father never made ony sic wark wi' me that bade wi' him respectable a' my days; but hear ye to me, Mistress Colville, I will never darken their doorstep till the day of my death." So she would not go in.

BOOK THIRD

HISTORIES

I

FENWICK MAJOR'S LITTLE 'UN

A short to-day,
    And no to-morrow:
A winsome wife,
    And a mickle sorrow—
Then done was the May
    Of my love and my life.

"Secrets."

[*Edinburgh student lodgings of usual type.* ROGER CHIRNSIDE, M.A.; *with many books about him, seated at table.* JO BENTLEY *and* "TAD" ANDERSON *squabbling by the fireplace.*]

Loquitur ROGER CHIRNSIDE.

Look here, you fellows, if you can't be quiet, I'll kick you out of this! How on earth is a fellow to get up "headaches" for his final, if you keep making such a mischief of a row? By giving me a fine one for a sample, do you say? I'll take less of your sauce, Master Tad, or you'll get shown out of here mighty quick. Now, not another word out of the heads of you!

[*Chirnside attacks his books again, murmuring intermittently as the others subside for the time.*

CHIRNSIDE. Migraine—artery—decussate—wonder what this other fool says (*rustling leaves*). They all contradict one another, and old Rutherland will never believe you when you tell him so.

[*A new quarrel arises at the upper end of the room between Jo Bentley and Tad.*

CHIRNSIDE (*starting to his feet*). Lay down that book, Bentley! Do you hear? I know Tad is a fool, and needs his calf's head broken. But do it with another book—Calderhead's *Mind and Matter*, or *T. and T.*—anything but that. Take the poker or anything! But lay down that book. Do you hear me, Bentley?

[*The book is laid down.*

CHIRNSIDE (*continuing*). What am I in such a funk about? No, it's not because it is a Bible, though a Bible never makes a good missile. I always keep an *Oliver and Boyd* on purpose—one of the old leather-backed kind that never wears out, even when half the leaves are ripped out for pipe-lights.

[*Tad Anderson asks a question.*

Why am I so stung up about that book? Tell you fellows? Well, I don't mind knocking off a bit and giving you the yarn. That Bible belonged to Fenwick Major. Never heard of Fenwick Major! What blessed ignorant chickens you must be! Where were you brought up?

[*Chirnside slowly lights his pipe before speaking again.*

Well—I entered with Fenwick Major when I came up as a first year's man in Arts. I was green as grass, or as you fellows last year. Not that you know much yet, by the way.

Now, drop that *Medical Ju*, Bentley! Hand me the *Lancet*. It makes good pipe-lights—about all it's good for. Oh—Fenwick Major? Well (*puff-puff-puff*), he came up to college with me. Third-class carriage—our several *maters* at the door weeping—you know the kind of thing. Fenwick's governor prowling about in the background with a tenner in an envelope to stick in through the window. His mother with a new Bible and his name on the first leaf. I had no governor and no blooming tenner. Only my old *mater* told me to spend my bursary as carefully as I could, and not to disgrace my father's memory. Then something took me, and I wanted to go over to the other side of the compartment and look out at the window. Good old lady, mine, as ever they make them. Ever felt that way, fellows?

[*Chirnside's pipe goes out. Jo Bentley and Tad shift their legs uneasily and cross them the other way.*

So we came up. Fenwick Major's name stands next to mine on the University books. You know the style. Get your money all ready. Make out your papers—What is your place of birth? Have you had the small-pox? If so, how often and where? And shove the whole biling across the counter to the fellow with the red head and the uncertain temper. You've been there?

[*Bentley and Tad Anderson nod. They had been there.*

Well, you fellows, Fenwick Major and I got through our first session together. We were lonely, of course, and we chummed some. First go off, we lodged together. But Fenwick had hordes of chips and I had only my bursary, and none too much of that. Fenwick wanted a first floor. I preferred the attic, and thought a sitting-room unnecessary. So we parted. Fenwick Major used to drop in after that, and show me his new suits and the latest thing in sticks—nobby things, with a silver band round them and his name. Then he got a terrier, and learned to be knowing as to bars. I envied, but luckily had no money. Besides, that's all skittles any way, and you've to pay for it sweetly through the nose in the long-run. Now mind me, you fellows!

[*Bentley and Tad mind Chirnside.*

Oh, certainly, I'll get on with my apple-cart and tell you about the book.

Well, the short and the long of it is that Fenwick Major began to go to the dogs, the way you and I have seen a many go. Oh, it's a gay road—room inside, and a penny all the way. But there's always the devil to pay at the far end. I'm not preaching, fellows; only, you take my word for it and keep clear.

Yet, in spite of the dogs, there was no mistake but Fenwick Major could work. His father was a parson—white hair on his shoulders, venerable old boy, all that sort of thing. Had coached Fenwick till he was full as a sheep-tick. So he got two medals that session, and the fellows—his own set—gave him a supper—whisky-toddy, and we'll not go home till morning—that style! But most of them wouldn't even go home when it was morning. They went down to the Royal and tried to break in with sticks—young fools! The bobbies scooped them by couples and ran them in. They were all in court the next day. Most of the fellows gave their right enough names, but they agreed to lie about Fenwick's for his father's sake and his medals. Most of them were colonial medicals anyway. It didn't matter a toss-up to them. So Fenwick went home all right with his two medals. His father met him at the station, proud as Punch. His mother took possession of the medals; and when she thought that Fenwick Major was out of the way, she took them all round the parish in her black reticule basket, velvet cases and all, and showed them to the goodwives.

Fenwick Minor was home from school, and went about like a dog worshipping his big brother. This is all about Fenwick Minor.

But Greenbrae parish and its humble, poor simpletons of folk did not content Fenwick Major long. He went back to Edinburgh, as he told his father, to read during the summer session; and when we came up again in November, Fenwick Major was going it harder than ever.

[*Jo Bentley and Tad Anderson look at each other. They know all about that.*

CHIRNSIDE (*continues*). Then he gave up attending class much, only turning up for examinations. He had fits of grinding like fire at home. Again he would chuck the whole thing, and lounge all day and most of the night about shops in the shady lanes back of the Register. So we knew that Fenwick Major was burning his fingers. Then he cut classes and grinds altogether, and when I met him next, blest if he didn't cut me. That wasn't much, of course, and maybe showed his good taste. But it was only a year since we chummed—and I knew his people, you know.

Fact was, we felt somebody ought to speak to Fenwick—so all the fellows said. But of course, when it came to the point, they pitched on me, and stuck at me till they made me promise.

So I met him and said to him: "Now, look here, Fenwick, this is playing it pretty low down on the old man at home and your mother. Better let up on this drinking and cutting round loose. It's skittles anyway, and will come to no good!" Just as I would say to you fellows.

I think Fenwick Major was first of all a bit staggered at my speaking to him. Later he came to himself, and told me where to go for a meddling young hypocrite.

"Who are you to come preaching to me, any way?" he said.

And I admitted that I was nobody. But I told him all the same that he had better listen to what I said.

"You are playing the fool, and you'll come an awful cropper," I went on. "Not that it matters so much for you, but you've got a father and a mother to think about."

What Fenwick Major said then about his father and mother I am not going to tell you. He had maybe half a dozen "wets" on board, so we won't count him responsible.

But after that Fenwick Major never looked the way I was on. He drank more than ever, till you could see the shakes on him from the other side of the street. And there was the damp, bleached look about his face that you see in some wards up at the Infirmary.

[*Jo Bentley and Tad Anderson nod. Their heads are bent eagerly towards Chirnside.*

But I heard from other fellows that he still tried to work. He would come out of a bad turn. Then he would doctor himself, Turkish-bath himself, diet himself, and go at his books. But, as I am alive, fellows, he had got himself into such a state that what he learned the night before, he had forgotten the next morning. Ay, even the book he had been reading and the subject he was cramming. Talk about no hell, fellows! Don't you believe 'em. I know four knocking about Edinburgh this very moment.

But right at the close of the session we heard that the end had come.
So, at least, we thought. Fenwick Major had married a barmaid or
something like that. "What a fool!" said some. I was only thankful that
I had not to tell his mother.

But his mother was told, and his father came to Edinburgh to find Fenwick Major. He did not find the prodigal son, who was said to have gone to London. At any rate, his father went home, and in a fortnight there was a funeral—two in a month. Mother went first, then the old man. I went down to both, and cursed Fenwick Major and his barmaid with all the curses I knew. And I was a second-year medical at the time.

I never thought to hear more of him. Did not want to. He was lost. He had married a barmaid, and I knew where his father and mother lay under the sod. And my own old *mater* kept flowers on the two graves summer and winter.

One night I was working here late—green tea, towel round my head—oral next morning. There was a knock at the door. The landlady was in bed, so I went. There was a laddie there, bare-legged and with a voice like a rip-saw.

"If ye please, there's a man wants awfu' to see ye at Grant's Land at the back o' the Pleasance."

I took my stick and went out into the night. It was just coming light, and the gas-jets began to look foolish. I stumbled up to the door, and the boy showed me in. It was a poor place—of the poorest. The stair was simply filthy.

But the room into which I was shown was clean, and there on a bed, with the gas and the dawn from the east making a queer light on his face, sat Fenwick Major.

He held out his hand.

"How are you, Chirnside? Kind of you to come. This is the little wife!" was what he said, but I can tell you he looked a lot more.

At the word a girl in black stole silently out of the shadow, in which I had not noticed her.

She had a white, drawn face, and she watched Fenwick Major as a mother watches a sick child that is going to be taken from her up at the hospital.

"I wanted to see you, old chap, before I went—you know. It's a long way to go, and there's no use in hanging back even if I could. But the little wife says she knows the road, and that I won't find it dark. She can't read much, the little wife—education neglected and all that. Precious lot I made of mine, medals and all! But she's a trump. She made a man of me. Worked for me, nursed me. Yes, you did, Sis, and I *shall* say it. It won't hurt me to say it. Nothing will hurt me now, Sis."

"James, do not excite yourself!" said the little wife just then.

I had forgotten his name was James. He was only Fenwick Major to me.

"Now, little wife," he said, "let me tell Chirnside how I've been a bad fellow, but the Little 'Un pulled me through. It was the best day's work I ever did when I married Sis!"

"James!" she said again, warningly.

"Look here, Chirnside," Fenwick went on, "the Little 'Un can't read; but, do you know, she sleeps with my old mother's Bible under her pillow. I can't read either, though you would hardly know it. I lost my sight the year I married (my own fault, of course), and I've been no better than a block ever since. I want you to read me a bit out of the old Book."

"Why didn't you send for a minister, Fenwick?" I said. "He could talk to you better than I can."

"Don't want anybody to speak to me. Little 'Un has done all that. But I want you to read. And, see here, Chirnside, I was a brute beast to you once—quarrelled with you years ago—"

"Don't think of that, Fenwick Major!" I said. "That's all right!"

"Well, I won't," he said; "for what's the use? But Little 'Un said, 'Don't let the sun go down upon your wrath.' 'And no more I will, Little 'Un,' says I. So I sent a boy after you, old man."

Now, you fellows, don't laugh; but there and then I read three or four chapters of the Bible—out of Fenwick's mother's Bible—the one she handed in at the carriage window that morning he and I set off for college. I actually did and this is the Bible.

[*Bentley and Tad Anderson do not laugh.*

When I had finished, I said—"Fenwick, I'm awfully sorry, but fact is—I can't pray."

"Never mind about that, old man!" said he; "Little 'Un can pray!"

And Little 'Un did pray; and I tell you what, fellows, I never heard any such prayer. That little girl was a brick.

Then Fenwick Major put out fingers like pipe-staples, and said—

"Old man, you'll give Little 'Un a hand—after—you know."

I don't know that I said anything. Then he spoke again, and very slowly—

"It's all right, old boy. Sun hasn't gone down on our wrath, has it?"

And even as he smiled and held a hand of both of us, the sun went down.

Little brick, wasn't she? Good little soul as ever was! Three cheers for the little wife, I say. What are you fellows snuffling at there? Why can't you cheer?

II

MAC'S ENTERIC FEVER

Merry are the months when the years go slow,
Shining on ahead of us, like lamps in a row:
Lamps in a row in a briskly moving town.
Merry are the moments ere the night shuts down.

"*Halleval and Haskeval.*"

In those days we took great care of our health. It was about the only thing we had to take care of. So we went to lodge on the topmost floor of a tall Edinburgh land, with only some indifferent slates and the midnight tomcats between us and the stars. The garret story in such a house is, medically speaking, much the healthiest. We have always had strong views about this matter, and we did not let any considerations of expense prevent us taking care of our health.

Also, it is a common mistake to over-eat. Therefore, we students had porridge twice a day, with a herring in between, except when we were saving up for a book. Then we did without the herring. It was a fine diet, wholesome if sparse, and kept us brave and hungry. Hungry dogs hunt best, except retrievers.

In this manner we lived for many years with an excellent lady, who never interfered with our ploys unless we broke a poker or a leaf of the table at least. Then she came in and told us what she thought of us for ten eloquent minutes. After that we went out for a walk, and the landlady gathered up the fragments that remained.

It was a lively place when Mac and I lodged together. Mac was a painter, but he had not yet decided which Academy he would be president of—so that in the meantime Sir Frederick Langton and Sir Simeon Stormcloud could sleep in their beds with some ease of mind.

Our room up near the sky was festooned with dim photographs of immense family tombstones—a perfect graveyard of them, which proved that the relations of Mrs. Christison, our worthy landlady, would have some trouble in getting to bed in anything like time if by chance they should be caught wandering abroad at cock-crow. Mixed with these there were ghastly libels on the human form divine, which Mac had brought home from the students' atelier—ladies and gentlemen who appeared to find it somewhat cold, and had therefore thoughtfully provided themselves with a tight-fitting coat of white-wash. Mac said this was the way that flesh-colour was painted under direct illumination. Well, it might have been. We did not set up for judges. But to an inexperienced eye they looked a great deal more like deceased white-washed persons who had been dug up after some weeks' decent burial. We observed that they appeared to be mildewed in patches, but Mac explained that these were the muscles. This also was possible; but, all the same, we had never seen any ladies or gentlemen who carried their muscles outside, so to speak. Mac said he did this sort of thing because he was applying for admission to the Academy Life Class. We all hoped he would get in, for we had had quite enough of dead people, especially when they were white-washed and resurrected, besides given to wearing their muscles outside.

Mac used, in addition to this provocation, to play jokes on us, because Almond and I were harmless and quiet. Almond was studying engineering because he was going to be a wholesale manufacturer of wheelbarrows. I was an arts student who wrote literary and political articles in the office of a moribund newspaper all night, and wakened in time to go along the street to dine in a theological college.

So Mac used to play off his wicked jokes upon Almond and myself for the reasons stated. He bored a hole through the wall at the head of our bed, and awoke us untimeously in the frosty mornings by squirting mysterious streams of water upon us. He said he had promised Almond's mother to see that he took a bath every morning, and he was going to do it. He anticipated us at our tins of sardines, and when we re-opened them we found all the tails carefully preserved in oil and sawdust. He made disgraceful caricatures of our physiognomies by falsely representing that he wished us to sit for our portraits. He perpetrated drawings upon the backs of our college exercises, mixing them with opprobrious remarks concerning our preceptors, which we did not observe till our attention was called to them upon their return by the preceptors themselves. We bore these things meekly on the whole, for that was our nature—at least mine.

Occasionally the worm turned, and then a good many articles of furniture were overset; and the Misses Hope, who resided beneath us, knocked up through the ceiling with the tongs, whereupon the landlady and her daughter came in armed with the poker and a long-handled broom to promote peace.

But after the affair of the squirt Almond and I took counsel, and Almond said (for Professor Jeeming Flenkin had discovered on the back of a careful drawing of an engine wheel a caricature of himself pointing with index-finger and saying, "Very smutty!") that he would stand this sort of thing no longer.

So we resolved to work a sell on Mac which he would not forget to his dying day. To effect this we took our landlady and our landlady's daughter into the plot, and the matter was practically complete when Mac came home. We heard him whistling up the stairs. The engineer was drawing a cherub in Indian ink. The arts student was reading a text-book of geology. The landlady and her daughter were busy about their work in their own quarters. All was peace.

The key clicked in the lock, and then the whistle stopped as Mac entered.

The landlady met him at the door. She gazed anxiously and maternally at his face. She seemed surprised also, and a trifle agitated.

"Dear me, Maister Mac, what's the maitter? Ye're no' lookin' weel."

Mac was a little surprised, but not alarmed.

"There is nothing the matter, Mrs. Christison," said he lightly.

"Eh, Teena, come here," she cried to her daughter.

Teena came hurriedly at her mother's call. But as she looked upon Mac the fashion of her countenance changed.

"Are you not well?" she said, peering anxiously into the pupils of Mac's eyes.

Such attentions are flattering, and Mac, being a squire of dames, was desirous of making the most of it.

"Well, I was not feeling quite up to the mark, but I daresay it'll pass off," he said diplomatically.

"You must not be working so hard. You will kill yourself one of these days."

For which we hope and trust she may be forgiven, though it is a good deal to hope.

"Where do you feel it most, Mr. Mac?" then inquired Teena tenderly.

Mac is of opinion that, if anywhere, he feels it worst in his head, but his chest is also paining him a little.

"Gang richt awa' in, my laddie," says the landlady, "an' lie doon and rest ye on the sofa, an' I'll be ben the noo wi' something till ye!"

Mac comes in with a slightly scared and conscious expression on his face. Almond and I look up from our work as he enters, though, as it were, only in a casual manner. But what we see arrests our attention, and Almond's jaw drops as he looks from Mac to me, and back again to Mac.

"Good gracious, what's wrang wi' ye, man?" he gasps, in his native tongue.

I get up hastily and go over to the patient. I take him by the arm, pull him sharply to the window and turn him round—an action which he resents.

"I wish to goodness you fellows would not make asses of yourselves," he says, as he flings himself down on the sofa.

Almond and I look at one another as if this fretfulness were one of the worst signs, and we had quite expected it. We say nothing for a little as we sit down to work; but uneasily, as if we have something on our minds. Presently I rise, and, going into the bedroom, motion to Almond as I go. This action is not lost on Mac. I did not mean that it should be. We shut the door and whisper together. Mac comes and shakes the door, which is locked on the inside.

"Come out of that, you fellows," he cries, "and don't be gibbering idiots!"

But for all that he is palpably nervous and uneasy.

"Go away and lie down, like a good fellow," I say soothingly; "it'll be all right—all right."

But Mac is not soothed in the least. Then we whisper some more, and rustle the leaves of a large Quain which lies on the mantelpiece, a legacy from some former medical lodger. After a respectable time we come out without looking at Mac, who peers at us steadily from the sofa. I go directly to the *Scotsman* of the day, and run my finger down the serried columns till I come to the paragraph which gives the mortality for the week. Almond looks over my shoulder the while, and I make a score with my finger-nail under the words "enteric fever." We are sure that Mac does not know what enteric fever is. No more do we, but that does not matter.

We withdraw solemnly one by one, as if we were a procession, with a muttered excuse to Mac that we are going out to see a man. Almond sympathetically and silently brings a dressing-gown to cover his feet. He angrily kicks it across the floor.

"I say, you fellows—" he begins, as we go out.

But we take no heed. The case is too serious. Then we go into the kitchen and discuss it with the landlady.

We do this with solemn pauses, indicative of deep thought. We go back into the sitting-room. Mac has been to look at the paper where my nail scored it. We knew he would, and he is now lying on the sofa rather pale. He even groans a little. The symptoms work handsomely. It is small wonder we are alarmed.

We ring for the landlady, and she comes in hastily and with anxiety depicted on her countenance. She asks him where he feels it worst. Teena runs for Quain, and, being the least suspect of the party, she reads, in a low, hushed tone, an account of the symptoms of enteric fever (previously inserted in manuscript) which would considerably astonish Dr. Quain and the able specialist who contributed the real account of that disease to the volume.

It seems that for the disease specified, castor-oil and a mustard blister, the latter applied very warm between the shoulders, are the appropriate and certain cures. There is nothing that Mac dislikes so much as castor-oil. He would rather die than take it—so he says. But a valuable life, which might be spent in the service of the highest art, must not be permitted to be thus thrown away. So we get the castor-oil in a spoon, and with Teena coaxing and Almond acting on the well-known principle of twenty years' resolute government—down she goes.

Instantly Mac feels a little better, for he can groan easier than before. That is a good sign. The great thing now is to keep up the temperature and induce perspiration. The mustard approaches. The landlady cries from the kitchen to know if he is ready. Teena retires to get more blankets. The patient is put to bed, and in a little the mustard plaster is being applied in the place indicated by Quain. We tell one another what a mercy it is that we have all the requisites in the house. (There is no mustard in the plaster, really—only a few pepper-corns and a little sand scraped from the geological hammer.) But we say aloud that we hope Mac can bear it for twenty minutes, and we speculate on whether it will bring *all* the skin with it when it comes off.

This is too much, and the groaning recommences. The blankets are applied, and in a trice there is no lack of perspiration. But within three minutes Mac shouts that the abominable plaster is burning right down through him. It is all pure mustard, he says. We must have put a live coal in by mistake. We tell him it will be all right—in twenty minutes. It is no use; he is far past advice, and in his insanity he would tear it off and so endanger the success of the treatment. But this cannot be permitted. So Almond sits on the plaster to keep it in its place, while I time the twenty minutes with a stop-watch.

At the end of this period of crisis the patient is pronounced past the worst. But, being in a state of collapse, it becomes necessary to rouse him with a strong stimulant. So, having sent the ladies to a place of safety, we take off the plaster tenderly, and kindly show Mac the oatmeal and the sand. We tell him that there was never anything the matter with him at all. We express a hope that he will find that the castor-oil has done him good. A little castor-oil is an excellent thing at any time. And we also advise him, the next time he feels inclined to work off a sell on us or play any more of his pranks, to have a qualified medical man on the premises. Quain is evidently not good enough. He makes mistakes. We show him the passage.

Then we advise him to put on his clothes, and not make a fool of himself by staying in bed in the middle of the day.

Whereupon, somewhat hurriedly, we retreat to our bedrooms; and, locking the doors, sit down to observe with interest the bolts bending and the hinges manfully resisting, while Mac with a poker in either hand flings himself wildly against them. He says he wants to see us, but we reply that we are engaged.

III

THE COLLEGING OF SIMEON GLEG

Forth from the place of furrows
  To the Town of the Many Towers;
Full many a lad from the ploughtail
  Has gone to strive with the hours,

Leaving the ancient wisdom
  Of tilth and pasturage,
For the empty honour of striving,
  And the emptier name of sage.

"Shadows."

Without blared all the trumpets of the storm. The wind howled and the rain blattered on the manse windows. It was in the upland parish of Blawrinnie, and the minister was preparing his Sabbath's sermon. The study lamp was lit and the window curtains were drawn. Robert Ford Buchanan was the minister of Blawrinnie. He was a young man who had only been placed a year or two, and he had a great idea of the importance of his weekly sermons to the Blawrinnie folk. He also spoke of "My People" in an assured manner when he came up to the Assembly in May:

"I am thinking of giving my people a series of lectures on the Old
Testament, embodying the results of—"

"Hout na, laddie," said good Roger Drumly, who got a D.D. for marrying a professor's sister (and deserved a V.C.), "ye had better stick to the Shorter's Quastions an' preach nae whigmaleeries i' the pairish o' Blawrinnie. Tak' my word for it, they dinna gie a last year's nest-egg for a' the results of creeticism. I was yince helper there mysel', ye maun mind, an' I ken Blawrinnie."

There is no manner of doubt that Dr. Drumly was right. Since he married the professor's sister, he did not speak much himself, except in his sermons, which were inordinately long; but he was a man very much respected, for, as one of his elders said, "Gin he does little guid in the pairish, he is a quate, ceevil man, an' does just as little ill." And this, after all, is chiefly what is expected of a settled and official minister with a manse and glebe in that part of the country. Too much zeal is not thought to become him. It is well enough in a mere U.P.

But the Reverend Robert Ford Buchanan had not so settled on his lees as to accept such a negative view of his duties. He must try to help his people singly and individually, and this he certainly did to the best of his ability. For he neither spent all his time running after Dissenters, as the manner of some is; nor yet did he occupy all his pastoral visits with conversations on the iniquity of Disestablishment, as is others' use and wont. He went in a better way about the matter, in order to prove himself a worthy minister of the parish, taking such a vital interest in all that appertained to it, that no man could take his bishopric from him.

Among other things, he had a Bible-class for the young, in which the hope of the parish of Blawrinnie was instructed as to the number of hands that had had the making of the different prophecies, and upon the allusions to primitive customs in the book of Genesis (which the minister called a "historical synopsis"). There were three lassies attending the class, and three young men who came to walk home with the lassies. Unfortunately, two of the young men wanted to walk home with the same young lass, so that the minister's Bible-class could not always be said to make for peace. As, indeed, the Reverend Doctor Drumly foretold when the thing was started. He had met the professor's sister first at a Bible-class, and was sore upon the subject.

But it was the minister's Bible-class that procured Mr. Ford Buchanan the honour of a visit that night of storm and stress. First of all there was an unwonted stir in the kitchen, audible even in the minister's study, where he stood on one leg, with a foot on a chair, consulting authorities. (He was an unmarried man.)

Elizabeth Milligan, better known as "the minister's Betsy," came and rapped on the door in an undecided way. It was a very interesting authority the minister was consulting, so he only said "Thank you, Elizabeth!" in an absent-minded way and went on reading, rubbing his moustache the while with the unoccupied hand in a way which, had he known it, kept it perpetually thin.

But Betty continued to knock, and finally put her head within the study door.

"It's no' yer parritch yet," she said. "It's but an hour since ye took yer tea. But, if ye please, minister, wad ye be so kind as open the door? There's somebody ringing the front-door bell, an' it's jammed wi' the rain forbye, an' nae wise body gangs and comes that gait ony way, binna yersel'."

"Certainly, certainly, Elizabeth; I will open the door immediately!" said the minister, laying down his book and marking the place with last week's list of psalms and intimations.

Mr. Buchanan went to the seldom-used front door, turned the key, and threw open the portal to see who the visitor might be who rang the manse bell at eight o'clock on such a night. Betsy hung about the outskirts of the hall in a fever of anticipation and alarm. It might be a highwayman—or even a wild U.P. There was no saying.

But when the minister pulled the door wide open, he looked out and saw nothing. Only blackness and tossing leaves were in front of him.

"Who's there?" he cried, peremptorily, in his pulpit voice—which he used when "my people" stood convicted of some exhibition of extreme callousness to impression.

But only the darkness fronted him and the swirl of wind slapped the wet ivy-leaves against the porch.

Then apparently from among his feet a little piping voice replied—

"If ye please, minister, I want to learn Greek and Laitin, an' to gang to the college."

The minister staggered back aghast. He could see no one at all, and this peeping, elfish-like voice, rising amid the storm to his ear out of the darkness, reminded him of the days when he believed in the other world—that is, of course, the world of spirits and churchyard ghosts.

But gradually there grew upon him a general impression of a little figure, broad and squat, standing bareheaded and with cap in hand on his threshold. The minister came to himself, and his habits of hospitality asserted themselves.

"You want to learn Greek and Latin," he said, accustomed to extraordinary requests. "Come in and tell me all about it."

The little, broad figure stepped within the doorway.

"I'm a' wat wi' the rain," again quoth the elfish voice, more genially, "an' I'm no' fit to gang into a gentleman's hoose."

"Come into the dining-room," said the minister kindly.

"'Deed, an' ye'll no," interposed Betsy, who had been coming nearer. "Ye'se juist gang into the study, an' I'll lay doon a bass for ye to stand an' dreep on. Where come ye frae, laddie?"

"I am Tammas Gleg's laddie. My faither disna ken that I hae come to see the minister," said the boy.

"The loon's no' wise!" muttered Betsy. "Could the back door no' hae served ye?—Bringing fowk away through the hoose traikin' to open the front door to you on sic a nicht! Man, ye are a peetifu' object!"

The object addressed looked about him. He was making a circle of wetness on the floor. He was taken imperatively by the coat-sleeve.

"Ye canna gang into the study like that. There wad be nae dryin' the floor. Come into the kitchen, laddie," said Betsy. "Gang yer ways ben, minister, to your ain gate-end, an' the loon'll be wi' ye the noo."

So Betsy, who was accustomed to her own way in the manse of Blawrinnie, drove Tammas Gleg's laddie before her into the kitchen, and the minister went into the study with a kind of junior apostolic meekness. Then he meditatively settled his hard circular collar, which he wore in the interests of Life and Work, but privately hated with a deadly hatred, as his particular form of penance.

It was no very long season that he had to wait, and before he had done more than again lift up his interesting "authority," the door of the study was pushed open and Betsy cried in, "Here he's!" lest there might be any trouble in the identification. And not without some reason. For, strange as was the figure which had stepped into the minister's lobby out of the storm, the vision which now met his eyes was infinitely stranger.

A thick-set body little over four and a half feet high, exceedingly thick and stout, was surmounted with one of the most curious heads the minister had ever seen. He saw a round apple face, eyes of extraordinary brightness, a thin-lipped mouth which seemed to meander half-way round the head as if uncertain where to stop. Betsy had arrayed this "object" in a pink bed-gown of her own, a pair of the minister's trousers turned up nearly to the knee in a roll the thickness of a man's wrist, and one of the minister's new-fangled M.B. waistcoats, through the armholes of which two very long arms escaped, clad as far as the elbows in the sleeves of the pink bed-gown.

Happily the minister was wholly destitute of a sense of humour (and therefore clearly marked for promotion in the Church); and the privation stood him in good stead now. It only struck him as a little irregular to be sitting in the study with a person so attired. But he thought to himself—"After all, he may be one of My People."

"And what can I do for you?" he said kindly, when the Object was seated opposite to him on the very edge of a large arm-chair, the pink arms laid like weapons of warfare upon his knees, and the broad hands warming themselves in a curious unattached manner at the fire.

"Ye see, sir," began the Object, "I am Seemion Gleg, an' I am ettlin' to be a minister."

The Reverend Robert Ford Buchanan started. He came of a Levitical family, and over his head there were a series of portraits of very dignified gentlemen in extensive white neckerchiefs, his forebears and predecessors in honourable office—a knee-breeched, lace-ruffled moderator among them.

It was as if a Prince of the Blood had listened to some rudely democratic speech from a waif of the causeway.

"A minister!" he exclaimed. Then, as a thought flashed across him—"Oh, a Dissenting preacher!" he continued.

This would explain matters.

"Na, na," said Simeon Gleg; "nae Dissenter ava'. I'm for the Kirk itsel'—the Auld Kirk or naething. That was the way my mither brocht me up. An' I want to learn Greek an' Laitin. I hae plenty o' spare time, an' my maister gies me a' the forenichts. I can learn at the peat fire after the ither men are gane to their beds."

"Your master!" said the minister. "Do you mean your teacher?"

"Na, na," said Simeon Gleg; "I mean Maister Golder o' the Glaisters. I serve there as plooman!"

"You!" exclaimed the minister, aghast. "How old may you be?"

"I'm gaun in my nineteenth year," said Simeon. "I'm no' big for my age, I ken; but I can throw ony man that I get grups on, and haud ony beast whatsomever. I can ploo wi' the best an' maw—Weel, I'm no' gaun to brag, but ye can ask Maister Golder—that is an elder o' your ain, an' comes at least twa Sabbaths afore every Communion to hear ye."

"But why do ye want to learn Greek and Latin?" queried the minister.

"Weel, ye see, sir," said Simeon Gleg, leaning forward to poke the manse fire with the toe of his stocking—the minister watching with interest to see if he could do it without burning the wool—"I hae saved twunty pounds, and I thocht o' layin' it oot on the improvement o' my mind. It's a heap o' money, I ken; but, then, my mind needs a feck o' impruvement—if ye but kenned hoo ignorant I am, ye wadna wonder. Ay, ay"—taking, as it were, a survey of the whole ground—"my mind will stand a deal o' impruvement. It's gey rough, whinny grund, and has never been turned owre. But I was thinkin' Enbra wad gie it a rare bit lift. What do ye think o' the professors there? I was hearin' some o' them wasna thocht muckle o'!"

The minister moved a little uneasily in his chair, and settled his circular collar.

"Well," he said, "they are able men—most of them."

He was a cautious minister.

"Dod, an' I'm gled to hear ye sayin' that. It's a relief to my mind," said Simeon Gleg. "I dinna want to fling my twunty pound into the mill-dam."

"But I understood you to say," went on the minister, "that you intended to enter the ministry of the Kirk."

"Ou ay, that's nae dout my ettlin'. But that's a lang gate to gang, an' in the meantime my object in gaun to the college is juist the cultivation o' my mind."

The wondrous apple-faced ploughboy in the red-sleeved bed-gown looked thoughtfully at the palms of his horny hands as he reeled off this sentence. But he had more to say.

"I think Greek and Laitin wull be the best way. Twunty pounds' worth—seven for fees an' the rest for providin'. But my mither says she'll gie me a braxy ham or twa, an' a crock o' butter."

"But what do you know?" asked the minister. "Have you begun the languages?"

Simeon Gleg wrestled a moment with the M.B. waistcoat, and from the inside of it he extricated two books.

"This," he said, "is Melvin's Laitin Exercises, an' I hae the Rudiments at hame. I hae been through them twice. An' this is the Academy Greek Rudiments. O man—I mean, O minister"—he broke out earnestly, "gin ye wad juist gie the letters a bit rin owre. I dinna ken hoo to mak' them soond!"

The minister ran over the Greek letters.

The eyes of Simeon Gleg were upturned in heartfelt thankfulness. His long arms danced convulsively upon his knees. He shot out his red-knotted fingers till they cracked with delight.

"Man, man, an' that's the soond o' them! It's awsome queer! But, O, it's bonny, bonny! There's nocht like the Greek and the Laitin!"

Now, there were many more brilliant ministers in Scotland than the minister of Blawrinnie, but none kindlier; and in a few minutes he had offered to give Simeon Gleg two nights a week in the dead languages. Simeon quivered with the mighty words of thankfulness that rose to his Adam's apple, but which would not come further. He took the minister's hand.

"Oh, sir," he said, "I canna thank ye! I haena words fittin'! Gin I had the Greek and Laitin, I wad ken what to say till ye—"

"Never mind, Simeon; do not say a word. I understand all about it," replied the minister warmly.

Simeon still lingered undecided. He was now standing in the M.B. waistcoat and the pink bed-gown. The sleeves were more obtrusive than ever. The minister was reminded of his official duties. He said tentatively—

"Ah—would you—perhaps you would like me to give you a word of advice, or—ah—perhaps to engage in prayer?"

These were things usually expected in Blawrinnie.

"Na, na!" cried Simeon eagerly. "No' that! But, O minister, ye micht gie thae letters anither skelp owre—aboot *Alfy, Betaw, Gaumaw*!"

The minister took the Greek Rudiments again without a smile, and read the alphabet slowly and with unction, as if it were his first chapter on the Sabbath morning—and a full kirk.

Simeon Gleg stood by, looking up and clasping his hands in ecstasy.

"O Lord," he said, "help me keep mind o' it! It's just like the kingdom o' heaven! Greek an' Laitin's the thing! There's nae mistak', Greek and Laitin's the thing!"

Then on the doorstep he turned, after Betsy had reclad him in his dry clothes and lent him the minister's third best umbrella.

This was Simeon Gleg's good-bye to the minister—

"Twunty pound is a dreadfu' heap o' siller; but, O minister, my mind 'ill stand an awfu' sicht o' impruvement! It'll no' be a penny owre muckle!"

IV

KIT KENNEDY, NE'ER-DO-WELL

"Now I wonder," with a flicker
Of the Old Ford in his eyes
As he watched the snow come thicker,
"Are the angels warm and rosy
When the snow-storms fill the skies,
As in summer when the sun
Makes their cloud-beds warm and cosy?
And I wonder if they're sleeping
Through this bitter winter weather
Or aloft their watches keeping,
As the shepherds told of them,
Hosts and hosts of them together,
Singing o'er the lowly stable,
   In that little Bethlehem!"

"*Ford Bereton.*"

"Kit Kennedy, ye are a lazy ne'er-do-weel—lyin' snorin' there in your bed on the back o' five o'clock. Think shame o' yoursel'!"

And Kit did.

He was informed on an average ten times a day that he was lazy, a skulker, a burden on the world, and especially on the household of his mother's cousin, Mistress MacWalter of Loch Spellanderie. So, being an easy-minded boy, and moderately cheerful, he accepted the fact, and shaped his life accordingly.

"Get up this instant, ye scoondrel!" came again the sharp voice. It was speaking from under three ply of blankets, in the ceiled room beneath. That is why it seemed a trifle more muffled than usual. It even sounded kindly, but Kit Kennedy was not deceived. He knew better than that.

"Gin ye dinna be stirrin', I'll be up to ye wi' a stick!" cried Mistress MacWalter.

It was a greyish, glimmering twilight when Kit Kennedy awoke. It seemed such a short time since he went to bed, that he thought that surely his aunt was calling him up the night before. Kit was not surprised. She had married his uncle, and was capable of anything.

The moon, getting old, and yawning in the middle as if tired of being out so late, set a crumbly horn past the edge of his little skylight. Her straggling, pallid rays fell on something white on Kit's bed. He put out his hand, and it went into a cold wreath of snow up to the wrist.

"Ouch!" said Kit Kennedy.

"I'm comin' to ye," repeated his aunt, "ye lazy, pampered guid-for-naething! Dinna think I canna hear ye grumblin' and speakin' ill words there!"

Yet all he had said was "Ouch!"—in the circumstances, a somewhat natural remark.

Kit took the corner of the scanty coverlet and, with a well-accustomed arm-sweep, sent the whole swirl of snow over the end of his bed, getting across the side at the same time himself. He did not complain. All he said, as he blew upon his hands and slapped them against his sides, was—

"Michty, it'll be cauld at the turnip-pits this mornin'!"

It had been snowing in the night since Kit lay down, and the snow had sifted in through the open tiles of the farmhouse of Loch Spellanderie. That was nothing. It often did that. But sometimes it rained, and that was worse. Yet Kit Kennedy did not much mind even that. He had a cunning arrangement in old umbrellas and corn-sacks that could beat the rain any day. Snow, in his own words, he did not give a "buckie"[5] for.

[Footnote 5: The fruit of the dog-rose is, when large and red, locally called a "buckie."]

Then there was a stirring on the floor, a creaking of the ancient joists. It was Kit putting on his clothes. He always knew where each article lay—dark or shine, it made no matter to him. He had not an embarrassment of apparel. He had a suit for wearing, and his "other clothes." These latter were, however, now too small for him, and so he could not go to the kirk at Duntochar. But his aunt had laid them aside for her son Rob, a growing lad. She was a thoughtful, provident woman.

"Be gettin' doon the stair, my man, and look slippy," cried his aunt, as a parting shot, "and see carefully to the kye. It'll be as weel for ye."

Kit had on his trousers by this time. His waistcoat followed. But before he put on his coat he knelt down to say his prayer. He had promised his mother to say it then. If he put on his coat he was apt to forget, in his haste to get out-of-doors where the beasts were friendly. So between his waistcoat and his coat he prayed. The angels were up at the time, and they heard, and went and told the Father who hears prayer. They said that in a garret at a hill-farm a boy was praying with his knees in a snow-drift—a boy without father or mother.

"Ye lazy guid-for-naething! Gin ye are no' doon the stairs in three meenits, no' a drap o' porridge or a sup o' milk shall ye get the day!"

So Kit got on his feet, and made a queer little shuffling noise with them, to induce his aunt to think that he was bestirring himself. So that is the way he had to finish his prayers—on his feet, shuffling and dancing a break-down. The angels saw, and smiled. But they took it to the Father, just the same as if Kit Kennedy had been in church. All save one, who dropped something that might have been a pearl and might have been a tear. Then he also went within the inner court, and told that which he had seen.

But to Kit there was nothing to grumble about. He was pleased, if any one was. His clogs did not let in the snow. His coat was rough, but warm. If any one was well off, and knew it, it was Kit Kennedy.

So he came down-stairs, if stairs they could be called that were but the rounds of a ladder. His aunt heard him.

"Keep awa' frae the kitchen, ye thievin' loon! There's nocht there for ye—takin' the bairns' meat afore they're up!"

But Kit was not hungry, which, in the circumstances, was as well. Mistress MacWalter had caught him red-handed on one occasion. He was taking a bit of hard oatcake out of the basket of "farles" which swung from the black, smoked beam in the corner. Kit had cause to remember the occasion. Ever since, she had cast it up to him. She was a master at casting up, as her husband knew. But Kit was used to it, and he did not care. A thick stick was all that he cared for, and that only for three minutes; but he minded when Mistress MacWalter abused his mother, who was dead.

Kit Kennedy made for the front door, direct from the foot of the ladder. His aunt raised herself on one elbow in bed, to assure herself that he did not go into the kitchen. She heard the click of the bolt shot back, and the stir of the dogs as Tweed and Tyke rose from the fireside to follow him. There was still a little red gleaming between the bars, and Kit would have liked to go in and warm his toes on the hearthstone. But he knew that his aunt was listening. He was going thirteen, and big for his age, so he wasted no pity on himself, but opened the door and went out. Self-pity is bad at any time. It is fatal at thirteen.

At the door one of the dogs stopped, sniffed the keen frosty air, turned quietly, and went back to the hearthstone. That was Tweed. But Tyke was out rolling in the snow when Kit Kennedy shut the door.

Then his aunt went to sleep. She knew that Kit Kennedy did his work, and that there would be no cause to complain. But she meant to complain all the same. He was a lazy, deceitful hound, an encumbrance, and an interloper among her bairns.

Kit slapped his long arms against his sides. He stood beneath his aunt's window, and crowed so like a cock that Mistress Mac Walter jumped out of her bed.

"Save us!" she said. "What's that beast doin' there at this time in the mornin'?"

She got out of bed to look; but she could see nothing, certainly not Kit. But Kit saw her, as she stood shivering at the window in her night-gear. Kit hoped that her legs were cold. This was his revenge. He was a revengeful boy.

As for himself, he was as warm as toast. The stars tingled above with frost. The moon lay over on her back and yawned still more ungracefully. She seemed more tired than ever.

Kit had an idea. He stopped and cried up at her—

"Get up, ye lazy guid-for-naething! I'll come wi' a stick to ye!"

But the moon did not come down. On the contrary, she made no sign. Kit laughed. He had to stop in the snow to do it. The imitation of his aunt pleased him. He fancied himself climbing up a rung-ladder to the moon, with a broomstick in his hand. He would start that old moon, if he fell down and broke his neck. Kit was hungry now. It was a long time since supper. Porridge is, no doubt, good feeding; but it vanishes away like the morning cloud, and leaves behind it only an aching void. Kit felt the void, but he could not help it. Instead, however, of dwelling upon it, his mind was full of queer thoughts and funny imaginings. It is a strange thing that the thought of rattling on the ribs of a lazy, sleepy moon with a besom-shank pleased him as much as a plate of porridge and as much milk as he could sup to it. But that was the fact.

Kit went next into the stable to get a lantern. The horses were moving about restlessly, but Kit had nothing to do with them. He went in only to get a lantern. It was on the great wooden corn-crib in the corner. Kit lighted it, and pulled down his cap over his ears.

Then he crossed over to the cattle-sheds. The snow was crisp under foot. His feet went through the light drift which had fallen during the night, and crackled frostily upon the older and harder crust. At the barn, Kit paused to put fresh straw in his iron-shod clogs. Fresh straw every morning in the bottom of one's clogs is a great luxury. It keeps the feet warm. Who can afford a new sole of fleecy wool every morning to his shoe? Kit could, for straw is cheap, and even his aunt did not grudge a handful. Not that it would have mattered if she had.

The cattle rattled their chains in a friendly and companionable way as he crossed the yard, Tyke following a little more sedately than before. Kit's first morning job was to fodder the cattle. He went to the hay-mow and carried a great armful of fodder, filling the manger before the bullocks, and giving each a friendly pat as he went by. Great Jock, the bull in the pen by himself in the corner, pushed a moist nose over the bars, and dribbled upon Kit with slobbering affection. Kit put down his head and pretended to run at him, whereat Jock, whom nobody else dared go near, beamed upon him with the solemn affection of "bestial"—his great eyes shining in the light of the lamp with unlovely but genuine affection.

Then came the cows' turn. Kit Kennedy took a milking-pail, which he would have called a luggie, set his knee to Crummie, his favourite, who was munching her fodder, and soon had a warm draught. He pledged her in her own milk, wishing her good health and many happy returns. Then, for his aunt's sake, he carefully wiped the luggie dry, and set it where he had found it. He had got his breakfast—no mean or poor one.

But he did not doubt that he was, as his aunt had said, "a lazy, deceitful, thieving hound."

Kit Kennedy came out of the byre, and trudged away out over the field at the back of the barn, to the sheep in the park. He heard one of them cough as a human being does behind his hand. The lantern threw dancing reflections on the snow. Tyke grovelled and rolled in the light drift, barking loudly. He bit at his own tail. Kit set down the lantern, and fell upon him for a tussle. The two of them had rolled one another into a snowdrift in exactly ten seconds, from which they rose glowing with heat—the heat of young things when the blood runs fast. Tyke, being excited, scoured away wildly, and circled the park at a hand-gallop before his return. But Kit only lifted the lantern and made for the turnip-pits.

The turnip-cutter stood there, with great square mouth black against the sky. That mouth must be filled. Kit went to the end of the barrow-like mound of the turnip-pit. It was covered with snow, so that it hardly showed above the level of the field. Kit threw back the coverings of old sacks and straw which kept the turnips from the frost. There lay the great green-and-yellow globes full of sap. The snow fell upon them from the top of the pit. The frost grasped them without. It was a chilly job to handle them, but Kit did not hesitate a moment.

He filled his arms with them, and went to the turnip-cutter. Soon the *crunch, crunch* of the knives was to be heard as Kit drove round the handle, and afterwards the frosty sound of the square finger-lengths of cut turnip falling into the basket. The sheep had gathered about him, silently for the most part. Tyke sat still and dignified now, guarding the lantern, which the sheep were inclined to butt over. Kit heard the animals knocking against the empty troughs with their hard little trotters, and snuffing about them with their nostrils.

He lifted the heavy basket, heaved it against his breast, and made his way down the long line of troughs. The sheep crowded about him, shoving and elbowing each other like so many human beings, callously and selfishly. His first basket did not go far, as he shovelled it in great handfuls into the troughs, and Kit came back for another. It was tiring work, and the day was dawning grey when he had finished. Then he made the circuit of the field, to assure himself that all was right, and that there were no stragglers lying frozen in corners, or turned *avel*[6] in the lirks of the knowes.

[Footnote 6: A sheep turns *avel* when it so settles itself upon its back in a hollow of the hill that it cannot rise.]

Then he went back to the onstead. The moon had gone down, and the farm-buildings loomed very cold and bleak out of the frost-fog.

Mistress MacWalter was on foot. She had slept nearly two hours, being half-an-hour too long, after wearying herself with raising Kit; and, furthermore, she had risen with a very bad temper. But this was no uncommon occurrence.

She was in the byre with a lantern of her own. She was talking to herself, and "flyting on" the patient cows, who now stood chewing the cuds of their breakfast. She slapped them apart with her stool, applied savagely to their flanks. She even lifted her foot to them, which affronts a self-respecting cow as much as a human being.

In this spirit she greeted Kit when he appeared.

"Where hae ye been, ye careless deevil, ye? A guid mind hae I to gie ye my milking-stool owre yer crown, ye senseless, menseless blastie! What ill-contriving tricks hae ye been at, that ye haena gotten the kye milkit?"

"I hae been feeding the sheep at the pits, aunt," said Kit Kennedy.

"Dinna tell me," cried his aunt; "ye hae been wasting your time at some o' your ploys. What do ye think that John MacWalter, silly man, feeds ye for? He has plenty o' weans o' his ain to provide for withoot meddling wi' the like o' you—careless, useless, fushionless blagyaird that ye are."

Mistress Mac Walter had sat down on her stool to the milking by this time. But her temper was such that she was milking unkindly, and Crummie felt it. Also she had not forgotten, in her slow-moving bovine way, that she had been kicked. So in her turn she lifted her foot and let drive, punctuating a gigantic semi-colon with her cloven hoof just on that part of the person of Mistress MacWalter where it was fitted to take most effect.

Mistress MacWalter found herself on her back, with the milk running all over her. She picked herself up, helped by Kit, who had come to her assistance.

Her words were few, but not at all well ordered. She went to the byre door to get the driving-stick to lay on Crummie. Kit stopped her.

"If you do that, aunt, ye'll pit a' the kye to that o't that they'll no' let doon a drap o' milk this morning—an' the morn's kirning-day."

Mistress Mac Walter knew that the boy was right; but she could only turn, not subdue, her anger. So she turned it on Kit Kennedy, for there was no one else there.

"Ye meddlin' curse," she cried, "it was a' your blame!"

She had the shank of the byre besom in her hand as she spoke. With this she struck at the boy, who ducked his head and hollowed his back in a manner which showed great practice and dexterity. The blow fell obliquely on his coat, making a resounding noise, but doing no great harm.

Then Mistress MacWalter picked up her stool and sat down to another cow. Kit drew in to Crummie, and the twain comforted one another. Kit bore no malice, but he hoped that his aunt would not keep back his porridge. That was what he feared. No other word of good or bad said the Mistress of Loch Spellanderie by the Water of Ken. Kit carried the two great reaming cans of fresh milk into the milkhouse; and as he went out empty-handed, Mistress Mac Walter waited for him, and with a hand both hard and heavy fetched him a ringing blow on the side of the head, which made his teeth clack together and his eyes water.

"Tak' that, ye gangrel loon!" she said.

Kit Kennedy went into the barn with fell purpose in his heart. He set up on end a bag of chaff, which was laid aside to fill a bed. He squared up to it in a deadly way, dancing lightly on his feet, his hands revolving in a most knowing manner.

His left hand shot out, and the sack of chaff went over in the corner.

"Stand up, Mistress MacWalter," said Kit, "an' we'll see wha's the better man."

It was evidently Kit who was the better man, for the sack subsided repeatedly and flaccidly on the hard-beaten earthen floor. So Kit mauled Mistress MacWalter exceeding shamefully, and obtained so many victories over that lady that he quite pleased himself, and in time gat him into such a glow that he forgot all about the tingling on his ear which had so suddenly begun at the milkhouse door.

"After all, she keeps me!" said Kit Kennedy cheerily.

There was an angel up aloft who went into the inner court at that moment and told that Kit Kennedy had forgiven his enemies. He said nothing about the sack. So Kit Kennedy began the day with a clean slate and a ringing ear.

He went to the kitchen door to go in and get his breakfast.

"Gae'way wi' ye! Hoo daur ye come to my door after what yer wark has been this mornin'?" cried Mistress MacWalter as soon as she heard him. "Aff to the schule wi' ye! Ye get neither bite nor sup in my hoose the day."

The three MacWalter children were sitting at the table taking their porridge and milk with horn spoons. The ham was skirling and frizzling in the pan. It gave out a good smell, but that did not cost Kit Kennedy a thought. He knew that that was not for the like of him. He would as soon have thought of wearing a white linen shirt or having the lairdship of a barony, as of getting ham to his breakfast. But after his morning's work, he had a sore heart enough to miss his porridge.

But he knew that it was no use to argue with Mistress MacWalter. So he went outside and walked up and down in the snow. He heard the clatter of dishes as the children, Rob, Jock, and Meysie MacWalter, finished their eating, and Meysie set their bowls one within the other and carried them into the back-kitchen to be ready for the washing. Meysie was nearly ten, and was Kit's very good friend. Jock and Rob, on the other hand, ran races who should have most tales to tell of his misdoings at home, and also at the village school.

"Kit Kennedy, ye scoondrel, come in this meenit an' get the dishes washen afore yer uncle tak's the 'Buik,'"[7] cried Mistress MacWalter, who was a religious woman, and came forward regularly at the half-yearly communion in the kirk of Duntochar. She did not so much grudge Kit his meal of meat, but she had her own theories of punishment. So she called Kit in to wash the dishes from which he had never eaten. Meysie stood beside them, and dried for him, and her little heart was sore. There was something in the bottom of some of them, and this Kit ate quickly and furtively—Meysie keeping a watch that her mother was not coming. The day was now fairly broken, but the sun had not yet risen.

[Footnote 7: Has family worship.]

"Tak' the pot oot an' clean it. Gie the scrapins' to the dogs!" ordered Mistress MacWalter.

Kit obeyed. Tyke and Tweed followed with their tails over their backs. The white wastes glimmered in the grey of the morning. It was rosy where the sun was going to rise behind the great ridge of Ben Arrow, which looked, smoothly covered with snow as it was, exactly like a gigantic turnip-pit. At the back of the milkhouse Kit set down the pot, and with a horn spoon which he took from his pocket he shared the scraping of the pot equally into three parts, dividing it mathematically by lines drawn up from the bottom. It was a good big pot, and there was a good deal of scrapings, which was lucky for both Tweed and Tyke, as well as good for Kit Kennedy.

Now, this is the way that Kit Kennedy—that kinless loon, without father or mother—won his breakfast.

He had hardly finished and licked his spoon, the dogs sitting on their haunches and watching every rise and fall of the horn, when a well-known voice shrilled through the air—

"Kit Kennedy, ye lazy, ungrateful hound, come ben to the "Buik." Ye are no better than the beasts that perish, regairdless baith o' God and man!"

So Kit Kennedy cheerfully went in to prayers and thanksgiving, thinking himself not ill off. He had had his breakfast.

And Tweed and Tyke, the beasts that perish, put their noses into the porridge-pot to see if Kit Kennedy had left anything. There was not so much as a single grain of meal.

THE BACK O' BEYONT

I

O nest, leaf-hidden, Dryad's green alcove,
  Half-islanded by hill-brook's seaward rush,
    My lovers still bower, where none may come but I!
  Where in clear morning prime and high noon hush
    With only some old poet's book I lie!
      Sometimes a lonely dove
Calleth her mate, or droning honey thieves
  Weigh down the bluebell's nodding campanule;
  And ever singeth through the twilight cool
Low voice of water and the stir of leaves.

II

Perfect are August's golden afternoons!
　All the rough way across the fells, a peal
　　Of joy-bells ring, not heard by alien ear.
The jealous brake and close-shut beech conceal
　The sweet bower's queen and mine, albeit I hear
　　Hummed scraps of dear old tunes,
I push the boughs aside, and lo, I look
　Upon a sight to make one more than wise,—
　A true maid's heart, shining from tender eyes,
Rich with love's lore, unlearnt in any book.

"*Memory Harvest.*"

"An' what brings the lang-leggit speldron howkin' an' scrauchlin' owre the Clints o' Drumore an' the Dungeon o' Buchan?" This was a question which none of Roy Campbell's audience felt able to answer. But each grasped his rusty Queen's-arm musket and bell-mouthed horse-pistol with a new determination. The stranger, whoever he might be, was manifestly unsafe. Roy Campbell had kept the intruder under observation for some time through the weather-beaten ship's prospect-glass which he had stayed cumbrously on the edge of a rock. The man was poking about among rocks and *débris* at the foot of one of the cliffs in which the granite hills break westward towards the Atlantic.

Roy Campbell, the watcher, was a grey-headed man, slack in the twist but limber in the joints—distinguished by a constant lowering of the eye and a spasmodic twitching of the corners of the mouth. He was active and nimble, and in moments of excitement much given to spitting Gaelic oaths like a wild-cat. But, spite his half-century of life, he was still the best and the most daring man of a company who had taken daring as their stock-in-trade.

It was in the palmy days of the traffic with the Isle of Man, when that tight little island supplied the best French brandy for the drouthy lairds of half Scotland, also lace for the "keps" and stomachers of their dames, not to speak of the Sabbath silks of the farmer's goodwife, wherein she brawly showed that she had as proper a respect for herself in the house of God as my lady herself.

Solway shore was a lively place in those days, and it was worth something to be in the swim of the traffic; ay, or even to have a snug farmhouse, with perhaps a hidden cellar or two, on the main trade-routes to Glasgow and Edinburgh. Much of the stuff was run by the "Rerrick Nighthawks," gallant lads who looked upon the danger of the business as a token of high spirit, and considered that the revenue laws of the land were simply made to be broken—an opinion in which they were upheld generally by the people of the whole countryside, not excepting even those of the austere and Covenanting sort.

How Roy Campbell had found his way among the Westland Whigs is too long a story to be told—some little trouble connected with the days of the '45, he said. More likely something about a lass. Suffice it that he had drawn himself into hold in a lonely squatter shieling deep among the fastnesses of the Clints o' Drumore. He had built the house with his own hands. It was commonly known to the few who ventured that way as "The Back o' Beyont." In the hills behind the hut, which itself lay high on the brae-face, were many caves, each with its wattling of woven wicker, over which the heather had been sodded, so that in summer and autumn it grew as vigorously as upon the solid hill-side. Here Roy Campbell, late of Glen Dochart, flourished exceedingly, in spite of all the Kennedys of the South.

So it was that from the Clints o' Drumore and from among the scattered boulder-shelters around it, Roy and his men had been watching this intrusive stranger. Suddenly Roy gave a cry, and the prospect-glass shook in his hand. A little after there came the far-away sound of a gun.

"Somebody has let a shot intil him," said Roy, dancing with excitement, "but it has no' been a verra good shot, for he's sittin' on a stane an' rubbin' the croon o' his hat. Have I no telled you till I'm tired tellin' you, that there was no' be no shootin' till there was no fear o' missin'? It is not good to have to shoot; but it iss a verra great deal waur to shoot an' miss. If that's Gavin Stevenson, the muckle nowt, I declare I'll brek his ramshackle blunderbuss owre his thick heid."

Taming for an instant his fury, the old man kept his eye on the distant point of interest, and the others fixed their eyes on him. Suddenly he leapt to his feet, uttering what, by the sound, were very strong words indeed, for they were in the Gaelic, a language in which it is good and mouth-filling to read the imprecatory psalms. When at last his feelings subsided to the point when his English returned to him, he said—

"May I, Roy Campbell, be boiled in my ain still-kettle, distilled through my ain worm, an' drucken by a set o' reckless loons, if that's no my ain Flora that's speakin' till the man himsel'!"

The old man himself seemed much calmed either by the outbreak or by the discovery he had made; but on several of the younger men among his followers the news seemed to have an opposite effect.

* * * * *

At the same moment, high on the hill-side above them, a young woman was talking to a young man. She had walked towards him holding a bell-mouthed musket in her hands. As she approached, the youth rose to his feet with a puzzled expression on his face. But there was no fear in it, only doubt and surprise, slowly fading into admiration. He put his forefinger and the one next it through the hole in his hat, and said calmly, since the young woman seemed to expect him to begin the conversation—

"Did you do this?"

"I took the gun from the man who did. The accident will not happen again!"

It seemed inadequate as an explanation, but there was something in the girl's manner of saying it which seemed to give the young man complete satisfaction. Then the speaker seated herself on a fragment of rock, and set her chin upon her hand. It was a round and rather prominent chin, and the young man, who stood abstractedly twirling his hat, making a pivot of the two fingers which protruded through the hole, thought that he had never seen a chin quite like it. Or perhaps, on second thoughts, was it that dimple at the side of the mouth, in which an arch mockery seemed to be lurking, which struck him more? He resolved to think this out. It seemed now more important than the little matter of the hole in the hat.

"You had better go away," said the young girl suddenly.

"And why?" asked the young man.

"Because my father does not like strangers!" she said.

Again the explanation appeared inadequate, but again the youth was satisfied, finding reason enough for the dislike, mayhap, either in the dimple on the prominent chin, or in the hole by which he twirled his hat.

"Do you come from England?" he asked, referring to her accent.

The girl rose from her seat as she answered—

"Oh, no, I come from the 'Back o' Beyont'! What is your name?"

"My name," said the young man stolidly, "is Hugh Kennedy; and I am coming soon to the 'Back o' Beyont,' father or no father!"

* * * * *

It was a dark night in August, brightening with the uncertain light of a waning moon, which had just risen. High up on a mountain-side a man was hastening along, running with all his might whenever he reached a dozen yards of fairly level ground, desperately clinging at other times with fingers and knees and feet to the niches in the bare slates which formed the slippery roofing of the mountain-side. As he paused for a long moment, the moon turned a scarred and weird face towards him, one-half of it apparently eaten away. Panting, he resumed his course, and the pebbles that he started rattled noisily down the mountain-side. But as he drew near the top of the ridge up which he had been climbing, he became more cautious. He raced no more wildly, and took care that he loosened no more boulders to go trundling and thundering down into the valley. Here he crawled carefully among the bare granite slabs which lay in hideous confusion—the weather-blanched bones of the mountain, each casting an ebony shadow on its neighbour. He looked over the ridge into the gulf through which the streams sped westward towards the Atlantic. A deep glen lay beneath him—over it on the other side a wilderness of rugged screes and sheer precipices. Opposite, to the east, rose the solemn array of the Range of Kells, deep indigo-blue under the gibbous moon. There were the ridges of towering Millfore, the shadowy form of Millyea, to the north, the mountain of the eagle, Ben Yelleray, with his sides gashed and scarred. But the young man's eyes instinctively sought the opener space between the precipices, whence the face of the loch glimmered like steel on which one has breathed, in the scanty moonbeams. Hugh Kennedy had come as he said to seek the Back o' Beyont, and, by his familiarity and readiness, he sought it not for the first time.

Surmounting the ridge, he wormed his way along the sky-line with caution, till, getting his back into a perpendicular cleft down the side of the mountain, he cautiously descended, making no halt until he paused in the shadow of the precipice at the foot of the perilous stairway. A plain surface of benty turf lay before him, bright in the moonlight, dangerous to cross, upon which a few sheep came and went. A little burn from the crevice of the rocks, through which he had descended, cut the green surface irregularly. Into this the daring searcher for hidden treasure descended, and prone on his face pushed his way along, hardly a pennon of heather or a spray of red sorrel swaying with his stealthy passage.

At the end of the grassy level the little burn fell suddenly with a ringing sound into a basin of pure white granite—a drinking-cup with a yard-wide edge of daintiest silver sand. The young man made his way hastily across the water to a little bower beneath the western bank, overhung with birch and fern, half islanded by the swift rush of the mountain streamlet. Here a tiny circle of stones lay on the sand. Hugh Kennedy stooped to examine their position with the most scrupulous care. Five black at intervals, and a white one to the north with a bit of ribbon under it.

"That means," he said, "that the whole crew are out, and they are expecting a cargo from the south. The white stone to the north and the bit ribbon—Flora is waiting, then, at the Seggy Goats."

He strained his eyes forward, but they could see nothing. Far away to the south he heard voices, and a gun cracked. "I'm well off the ridge," he muttered; "they could have marked me down like a foumart as I ran. They'll be fetching a cargo up from the Brig o' Cree," he added, "and it'll be all Snug at the 'Back o' Beyont' before the morning." He listened again, and laughed low to himself, the pleased laugh a lover laughs when things are speeding well with him.

"Maybe," said he, "Roy Campbell may miss something from the 'Back o' Beyont' the morrow's morn, that a score of casks of Isle of Man brandy will not make up for."

So saying, he took his way back through the low, overgrown cavity of the runnel. When he was midway he heard a step coming across the heath, brushing through the "gall"[8] bushes, splashing through the shallow pools. A foot heavily booted crashed through the half-concealed tunnel, not six inches from where the young man lay, a gun was discharged, evidently by the sudden jerk upon the earth, and the air was rent above him by a perfect tornado of vigorous Gaelic—a good language, as has been said, for preaching or swearing.

[Footnote 8: The bog-myrtle is locally called "gall" bushes. It is the most characteristic and delightful of Galloway scents.]

"That's Roy himsel'!" said the young man. "It's a strange chance when a Kennedy comes near to getting his brains knocked out on his own land by the heel of an outlaw Highlander."

Once on the hillside again, he kept an even way over the boulders and stones which cumbered it, with less care than hitherto, as though to protest against the previous indignity of his position. But, Kennedy though he might be, it had been fitter if he had remembered that he was on the No Man's Land of the Dungeon of Buchan, for here, about this time, was a perfect Adullam cave of all the broken and outlaw men south of the Highland border. A challenge came from the hill-side—"Wha's there?" Kennedy dropped like a stone, and a shot rang out, followed immediately by the "scat" of a bullet against the rock behind which he lay concealed.

A tramp of heavy Galloway brogans was heard, and a half-hearted kicking about among the heather bushes, and at last a voice saying discontentedly—

"Gin Roy disna keep Kennedy's liftit beasts in the hollow whaur they should be, he needna blame me gin some o' them gets a shot intil their hurdies."

"My beasts!" said Kennedy to himself, silently chuckling, "mine for a groat!" He was in a mood to find things amusing. So, having won clear of the keen-eyed watcher, the young man made the best of his way with more caution to that northern gateway he had called the Seggy Goats.

There he turned to the right up a little burnside which led into a lirk in the hill, such as would on the border have been called a "hope." As he came well within the dusky-walled basin of the hill-side, some one tall and white glided out to meet him; but at this moment the moon discreetly withdrew herself behind a cloud, mindful, it may be, of her own youth and of Endymion's greeting on the Latmian steep. So the chronicler, willing though he be, is yet unable to say how these two met. He only knows that when the pale light flooded back upon the hillside and cast its reflection into the dim depths of the hope, they were evidently well agreed. "It is true what I told you," he is saying to her, "that my name is Hugh Kennedy, but I did not tell you that I am Kennedy of Bargany, and yours till death!"

"Then," said the girl, "it is fitter that I should return to the 'Back of Beyont' till such time as you and your men come back to burn the thatch about our ears."

The young man smiled and said—"No, Flora, you and I have another road to travel this night. Over there by the halse o' the pass, there stand tethered two good horses that will take us before the morning to the Manse of Balmaclellan, where my cousin, the minister, is waiting, and his mother is expecting you. Come with me, and you shall be Lady of Bargany before morning." He stooped again to take her hand.

"My certes, but ye made braw and sure of me with your horses," she said.
"I have a great mind not to stir a foot."

But the young man laughed, being still well pleased, and giving no heed to her protestations.

* * * * *

So there was a wedding in the early morning at the Manse of the Kells, and a young bride was brought home to Bargany. As for old Roy Campbell, he was made the deputy-keeper of the Forest of Buchan, which was an old Cassilis distinction—and a post that exactly suited his Highland blood. Time and again, however, had his son to intercede with him not to be too severe with those smugglers and gangrel bodies who had come to look upon the fastnesses of the Forest as their own.

"Have ye no fellow-feeling, Roy, for old sake's sake?" Kennedy would ask.

"Feeling? havers!" growled Roy impolitely, for Roy was spoiled. "I'm a chief's man noo, and I'll harbour nae gangrel loons on the lands o' Kennedy."

So the old cateran would depart humming the Galloway rhyme—

"Frae Wigtown to the Toon o' Ayr,
  Portpatrick to the Cruives o' Cree;
Nae man need hope to bide safe there,
  Unless he court wi' Kennedy."

"Body o' MacCallum More," chuckled the deputy-keeper of the Forest of Buchan, "but it was Kennedy that cam' coortin' to the 'Back o' Beyont' that time, whatever, I'm thinkin'!"

VI

NORTH TO THE ARCTIC

At home 'tis sunny September,
  Though here 'tis a waste of snows,
So bleak that I scarce remember
  How the scythe through the cornland goes.

With an aching heart I wander
  Through the cold and curved wreaths,
And dream that I see meander
  Brown burns amid purple heaths:

That I hear the stags on the mountains
  Bray loud in the early morn,
And that scarlet gleams by the fountains
  The red-berried wild-rose thorn.

"It was bad enough in the Free Command," said Constantine, leaning back in his luxurious easy-chair and joining his thin fingers easily before him as though he were measuring the stretch between thumb and middle finger. "But, God knows, it was Paris itself to the hell on earth up at the Yakût Yoort."

It was a strange sentence to hear, sitting thus in the commonplace drawing-room of a London house with the baker's boy ringing the area bell and the last edition of the *Pall Mall* being cried blatantly athwart the street.

But no one could look twice at Constantine Nicolai and remain in the land of the commonplace. I had known him nearly two years, and we had talked much—usually on literary and newspaper topics, seldom of Russia, and never of his experiences. Constantine and I had settled down together as two men will sometimes do, who work together and are drawn by a sympathy of unlikeness which neither can explain. Both of us worked on an evening paper of pronounced views upon moral questions and a fine feeling for a good advertising connection.

We had been sitting dreamily in the late twilight of a gloomy November day. Work was over, and we were free till Monday morning should call us back again to the Strand. We sat silent a long while, till Constantine broke out unexpectedly with the words which startled me.

I looked up with a curiosity which I tried to make neither too apparent nor yet too lukewarm.

"You were speaking of the time you spent in Siberia?" I said, as though we had often discussed it.

"Yes; did I ever tell you how I got away?"

Constantine took out his handkerchief and flicked a speck of dust from his clothes. He was an exception to the rule that revolutionaries care nothing about their persons—Russian ones especially. He said that it was because his mother was an English-woman, and England is a country where they manufacture soap for the world.

"Yes," he continued thoughtfully, "the Free Command was purgatory, but the Yoort was Hell!" Then he paused a moment, and added, "*I* was in the Yoort." He went on—

"There were three of us in the cage which boated us along the rivers. Chained and manacled we were, so that our limbs grew numb and dead under the weight of the iron. All Kazan University men, I as good as an Englishman. The others, Leof and Big Peter, had been students in my class. They looked up to me, for it was from me that they had learned to read Herbert Spencer. They had taught themselves to plot against the White Czar. Yet I had been expatriated because it could not be supposed that I could teach them Spencer without Anarchy."

Constantine paused and smiled at the stupidity of his former rulers.

"Well," he continued, "the two who had plotted to blow up his Majesty were sent to the Free Command. They could come and go largely at their own pleasure—in fact, could do most things except visit their old teacher, who for showing them how to read Spencer was isolated in the Yakût Yoort.' Not that the Yakûts meant to be unkind. They were a weak and cowardly set—cruel only to those who could not possibly harm them. They had the responsibility of my keeping. They were paid for looking after me, therefore it was to their interest to keep me alive. But the less this cost them, the greater gainers were they. They knew also that if, by accident, they starved the donkey for the lack of the last straw, a paternal Government would not make the least trouble.

"At first I was not allowed to go out of their dirty tents or still filthier winter turf-caves, than which the Augean stables were a cleaner place of abode. Within the tent the savages stripped themselves naked. The reek of all abominations mingled with the smoke of seal-oil and burning blubber, and the temperature even on the coldest day climbed steadily away up above a hundred. Sometimes I thought it must be the smell that sent it up. The natives had apparently learned their vices from the Russians and their habits of personal cleanliness from monkeys. For long I was never allowed to leave the Yoort for any purpose, even for a moment, without a couple of savages coming after me with long fish-spears.

"But for all that, much is possible, even in Siberia, to a man who has a little money. By-and-by my hosts began to understand that when the inspector visited us to see me in the flesh, there was money enclosed in the letters (previously carefully edited by the Government official), money which could be exchanged at Bulun Store for raw leaf-tobacco. After this discovery, things went much better. I was allowed a little tent to myself within the enclosure, and close to the great common tent in which the half-dozen families lived, each in its screened cubicle, with its own lamp and common rights on the fire of driftwood and blubber in the centre. This was of course much colder than the great tent, but with skins and a couple of lamps I did not do so badly.

"One day I had a letter stealthily conveyed to me from Big Peter, to say that he and Leof were resolved on escaping. They had a boat, he said, concealed about eight miles up the Lena under some willows on a stagnant backwater. They intended to try for the north as soon as the water opened, and hoped then to go towards the west and Wrangell Island, where they felt pretty sure of being picked up by American sealers by the month of August or September.

"This letter stirred all my soul. I did not believe rightly in their chance. It is seldom, I knew, that whalers come that way, or enter far through the Straits of Behring. Still, undoubtedly, a few did so every year. It was worth risking, any way, for any kind of action was better than that ghastly wearing out of body and fatty degeneration of soul. One or two more letters passed, stimulated by the tobacco-money, and the day of rendezvous was fixed.

"Leof and Big Peter were to make their own way down the river, hiding by day and travelling by night. I was to go straight across country and meet them at the tail of the sixth island above Bulun. So, very quietly, I made my preparations, and laid in a store of frozen meat and fish, together with a fish-spear, which I *cached* due south of my Yoort, never by any chance allowing myself to take a walk towards the north, the direction in which I would finally endeavour to escape. It was very lonely, for I had no one to consult, and no friend to whom to intrust any part of my arrangements. But the suspicion of the Yakûts was now very considerably allayed, for, said they, he is now well fed. A dog in good condition does not go far from home to hunt. He will therefore stay. They knew something about dogs, for they tried their hunting condition by running a finger up and down the spine sharply. If that member was not cut, the dog was in good condition.

"At last, in the dusk of a night in early summer, when the mosquitos were biting with all their first fury and it was still broad day at ten o'clock, I started, walking easily and conspicuously to the south, sitting down occasionally to smoke as though enjoying the night air before turning in, lest any of my hosts should chance to be awake. Once out of sight of the Yoort, I went quickly to my *cache* of provisions, and, shouldering the whole, I turned my face towards the river and the Northern Ocean.

"I had not gone far when I struck the track which led along the riverside in the direction of Bulun. There, to my intense horror, I saw a man sitting still in a Siberian cart within a few hundred yards, apparently waiting for me to descend. I gave myself up for lost, but, nevertheless, made my way down to him. He was a young man with an uncertain face and weak, shifty eyes.

"'Halloo!' I cried, in order to have the first word, 'what will you take to drive me to Maidy, where I wish to fish?'

"'I cannot drive you to Maidy,' he returned, 'for I am carrying provisions to my father, who has the shop in Bulun; but for two roubles I will give you a lift to Wiledóte, where you can cross the river to Maidy in a boat.'

"It was none so evil a chance after all which took me in his way. He was a useless fellow enough, and intolerably conceited. He was for ever asking if I could do this and that, and jeering at me for my incapacity when I disclaimed my ability.

"'You cannot kill a wild goose at thirty paces when it is coming towards you—*plaff*—so fast! You could not shoot as I. Last week I killed thirty ducks with one discharge of my gun.'

"At this point he drove into a ditch, and we were both spilled out on the *tundra*, an unpleasant thing in summer when the peaty ground is one vast sponge. At Maidy we met this young man's father. Here I found that it was a good thing for me that I had been isolated at the Yoort, for had I been in the Free Command I should certainly have been spotted. The wily old merchant knew every prisoner in the Command; but as I had always obtained all my supplies indirectly through Big Peter, my name and appearance were alike unknown to him. He approached me, however, with caution and circumspection, and asked for a drink of *vodka* for the ride which his son had given me.

"'Why should I give thee a drink of *vodka*?' I asked, lest I should seem suspiciously ready to be friendly.

"'Because my son drove you thirteen versts and more.'

"'But I paid your son for all he has done—two roubles, according to bargain. Why should I buy thee *vodka*? Thou art better without *vodka*. *Vodka* will make thee drunk, and thou shalt be brought before the *ispravnik*.'

"The dirty old rascal drew himself up.

"'I, even I, am *ispravnik*, and the horses were mine and the *tarantass* also.'

"'But thy son drove badly and upset us in the ditch.'

"'Then,' whispered the old scoundrel, coming close up with a look of indescribable cunning on his face, 'give my son no *vodka*—give me all the *vodka*.'

"Being glad on any terms to get clear of the precious couple, I gave them both money for their *vodka*, and set off along the backwaters towards the place described by Leof and Big Peter. I found them there before me, and we lost no time in embarking. I found that they had the boat well provendered and equipped. Indeed, the sight of their luxuries tempted us all to excess; but I reminded them that we were still in a country of game, and that we must save all our supplies till we were out in the ocean. The Lena was swollen by the melting snows, and the boat made slow progress, especially as we had to follow the least frequented arms of the vast delta. We found, however, plenty of fish—specially salmon, which were in great quantities wherever, in the blind alleys of the backwaters, we put down the fish-spear. We were not the only animals who rejoiced in the free and open life of the delta archipelago. Often we saw bears swimming far ahead, but none of them came near our boat.

"One night when the others were sleeping I strayed away over the marshy *tundra*, plunging through the hundred yards of black mud and moss where the willow-grouse and the little stint were feeding. I came upon a nest or two of the latter, and paused to suck some of the eggs, one of the birds meanwhile coming quite close, putting its head quaintly to the side as though to watch where its property was going, with a view to future recovery. A little farther along I got on the real *tundra*, and wandered on in the full light of a midnight sun, which coloured all the flat surface of the marshy moorland a deep crimson, and laid deep shadows of purple mist in the great hollow of the Lena river.

"In a little I sat down, and, putting up the collar of my coat—for the air was beginning to bite sharply—I meditated on the chances of our life. It did not seem that we had much more than one chance in a hundred, yet the hundredth chance was indubitably worth the risk—better than inaction, and better than the suicide which would inevitably come with the weakening brain, after another winter such as that we had just passed through.

"Meditating so, I heard a noise behind me, and, turning, found myself almost face to face with a great she-bear, with two cubs of the year running gambolling about her. I had not even so much as a fish-spear with me. With my heart leaping like the piston-rod of an engine, I sat as still as though I had been a pillar of ice carved out of the hummock. The cubs were within twenty paces, and the mother would have passed by but for the roystering youngsters. They came galloping awkwardly up, and nosed all over me, rubbing themselves against my clothes with just such a purring noise as a cat might make. There was no harm in them, but their whining caused the old bear to halt, then abruptly to turn round and come slowly toward me.

"As I sat motionless I saw that she stood on the ground beside me, her nose quite on a level with my face. She came and smelled me over as if uncertain. Then she took a walk all round me. One of the cubs put his long thin snout into the pocket of my fur coat, and nuzzled delightedly among the crumbs. His mother gave him a cuff with her paw which knocked him sprawling three or four paces.

"Having finished her own survey, the bear-mother called away her offspring. The young bear which had first taken the liberty of search, waited till his mother was a few steps off, and then came slyly round and sunk his nose deep in the corresponding pocket on the other side. It was a false move and showed bad judgment. A fish-hook attached itself sharply to his nostril, and he withdrew his head with a howl of pain. The mother turned with an impatient grunt, and I gave myself up for lost. She came back at a great stretching gallop, to where the cub was lying on the snow pawing at his nose. His mother, having turned him over two or three times as if he were a bag of wool, and finding nothing wrong, concluded that he had been stung by a gadfly, or that he was making a fuss about nothing, paying no attention to me whatever. Having finished her inspection, she cuffed him well for his pains, as a troublesome youngster, and disappeared over the *tundra*. I sat there for the matter of an hour, not daring to move lest the lady-bruin might return. Then fearfully and cautiously I found my way back to the boat and my companions.

"Our voyage after this was quiet and uneventful. Siberia is like no other country in the world, except the great Arctic plains which fence in the Pole on the American side. The very loneliness and vastness of the horizon, like the changeless plain of the sea, envelop you. As soon as you are off the main roads, wide, untrodden, untouched, virgin space swallows you up.

"Specially were we safe in that we had chosen to go to the north. Had we fled to the east, we should have been pursued by swift horses; to the west, the telegraph would have stopped us; to the south, the Altai and Himalaya, to say nothing of three thousand miles, barred our way. But no escape had ever been made to the north, and, so far as we knew, no attempt.

"One evening, while I was rowing, bending a back far too weary to be conscious of any additional fatigue, Leof, who happened to be resting, cried out suddenly, 'The Arctic Ocean!' And there, blue and clear, through the narrow entrance of a channel half-filled with drift-ice, lay the mysterious ocean of which we had thought so long. The wind had been due from the north, and therefore in our teeth, so that not till now had we had any chance of sailing. Now, however, we rigged a sail, and, passing over the bar, we felt for the first time the lift of the waves of the Polar Sea.

"Day by day we held on to the eastward, coasting along almost within hail of the lonely shore. Often the ice threatened to close in upon us. Sometimes the growling of the pack churned and crackled only a quarter of a mile out. One night as we lay asleep—it was my watch, but in that great silence I too had fallen asleep—Big Peter waked first, and in his strong emphatic fashion he rose to take the oars. But there before us were three boats' crews within half a mile, all rowing toward us, while a mile out from shore, near the edge of the pack, lay a steamer, blowing off steam through her escape-valves, as though at the end of her day's run.

"As we woke our first thought was, 'Lost!' For we had no expectation that any other vessel save a Russian cruiser could be in these waters. But out from the sternsheets of the leading cutter fluttered the blessed Stars and Stripes. My companions did not know all the happiness that was included in the sight of that ensign. Leof had reached for his case-knife to take his life, and I snatched it from him ere I told him that of all peoples the Americans would never give us up.

"We were taken on board the U.S. search-vessel *Concord*, commissioned to seek for the records of the lost American Polar expedition. There we were treated as princes, or as American citizens, which apparently means the same thing. That is all my yarn. The Czar's arm is long, but it does not reach either London or New York."

"And Leof and Big Peter?" I asked, as Constantine ceased speaking. As though with an effort, he recalled himself.

"Big Peter," he said, "is at St. Louis. He is in the pork trade, is married, and has a large family."

"And Leof?"

"Ah, Leof! he went back to Russia at the time of the former Czar's death, and has not been heard of since."

"And you, Constantine, you will never put your nose in the lion's den again—*you* will never go back to Russia?"

Almost for the first time throughout the long story, Constantine looked me fixedly in the eyes. The strange light of another world, of the fatalist East, looked plainly out of his eyes. Every Russian carries a terrible possibility about with him like a torch of tragic flame, ready to be lighted at any moment.

"That is as may be," he said very slowly; "it is possible that I may go back—at the time of other deaths, *and—also—not—return—any—more.*"

BOOK FOURTH

IDYLLS

I

ACROSS THE MARCH DYKE

I

Far in the deep of Arden wood it lies;
  About it pleasant leaves for ever wave.
    Through charmèd afternoons we wander on,
  And at the sundown reach the seas that lave
    The golden isles of blessèd Avalon.
      When the sweet daylight dies,
  Out of the gloom the ferryman doth glide
    To take us both into a younger day;
    And as the twilight land recedes away,
  My lady draweth closer to my side.

II

Thus to a granary for our winter need
  We bring these gleanings from the harvest field;
    Not the full crop we bring, but only sheaves
  At random ta'en from autumn's golden yield—
    One handful from a forest's fallen leaves;
      Yet shall this grain be seed
  Wherewith to sow the furrows year by year—
    These wither'd leaves of other springs the pledge,
    When thou shalt hear, over our hawthorn hedge
  The mavis to his own mate calling clear.

"*Memory Harvest.*"

There was the brool of war in the valley of Howpaslet. It was a warlike parish. Its strifes were ecclesiastical mainly, barring those of the ice and the channel-stones. The deep voice of the Reverend Doctor Spence Hutchison, minister of the parish, whose lair was on the broomy knowes of Howpaslet beside its ancient kirk, was answered by the keener, more intense tones of the Reverend William Henry Calvin, of the Seceder kirk, whose manse stood defiant on an opposite hill, and dared the neighbourhood to come on. But the neighbourhood never came, except only the Kers. In fact, the neighbourhood mostly went to Dr. Hutchison's, for Howpaslet was a great country of the Moderates. Unto whom, as Mr. Calvin said, be peace in this world, for they have small chance of any in the next—at least not to speak of.

Now, ever since the school-board came to Howpaslet its meetings are the great arena of combat. At the first election Dr. Spence Hutchison had the largest number of votes by a very great deal, and carried two colleagues with him to the top of the poll as part of his personal baggage. He did not always remember to consult them, because he knew that they were put there to vote as he wished them, and for no other purpose. And, being honest and modest men, they had no objections. So Dr. Hutchison was chairman of Howpaslet school-board.

But he reigned not without opposition. The forces of revolution had carried the two minority men, and the Doctor knew that at the first meeting of the board he would be met by William Henry Calvin, minister of the Seceder kirk of the Cowdenknowes, and his argumentative elder, Saunders Ker of Howpaslet Mains—one of a family who had laid aside moss-trooping in order to take with the same hereditary birr to psalm-singing and church politics. They were, moreover, great against paraphrases.

That was a great day when the board was formed. There was a word that the Doctor was to move that the meetings of the school-board be private. So the Kers got word of it and sent round the fiery cross. They gathered outside and roosted on the dyke by dozens, all with long faces and cutty pipes. If the proceedings were to be private they would ding down the parish school. So they said, and the parish believed them.

It is moved by the majority farmer, and seconded by the majority publican (whose names do not matter), that the Reverend Dr. Spence Hutchison, minister of the parish, take the chair. It is moved and seconded that the Reverend William Henry Calvin take the chair—moved by Saunders Ker, seconded by himself. So Dr. Hutchison has the casting vote, and he gives it on the way to the chair.

The school-board is constituted.

"Preserve us! what's that?" say the Kers from the windows where they are listening. They think it is some unfair Erastian advantage.

"Nocht ava'—it's juist a word!" explains to them over his shoulder their oracle Saunders, from where he sits by the side of his minister—a small but indomitable phalanx of two in the rear of the farmer and publican. The schoolroom, being that of the old parochial school, is crowded by the supporters of Church and State. These are, however, more especially supporters of the Church, for at the parliamentary elections they mostly vote for "Auld Wullie" in spite of parish politics and Dr. Spence Hutchison.

"Tak' care o' Auld Willie's tickets!" is the cry when in Howpaslet they put the voting-urns into the van to be carried to the county town buildings for enumeration. It was a Ker who drove, and the Tories suspected him of "losing" the tickets of Auld Wullie's opponent by the way. They say that is the way Auld Wullie got in. But nobody really knows, and everybody is aware that a Tory will say anything of a Ker.

So the schoolroom was crowded with "Establishers," for the Kers would not come within such a tainted building as a parochial school—except to a comic nigger minstrel performance, which in Howpaslet levels and composes all differences. So instead they waited at the windows and listened. One prominent and officious stoop of the Kirk tried to shut a window. But he got a Ker's clicky[9] over his head from without, and sat down discouraged.

[Footnote 9: Shepherd's staff.]

"Wull it come to ocht, think ye?" the Kers asked of each other outside.

"I'm rale dootfu'," was the general opinion; "but we maun juist howp for the best."

So the Kers stood without and hoped for the best—which, being interpreted, was that their champions, the Reverend William Calvin and Saunders Ker of the Mains, would get ill-treated by their opponents inside, and that they, the Kers, might then have a chance of clearing out the school. Every Ker had already picked his man. It has never been decided, though often argued, whether in his introductory prayer Mr. Calvin was justified in putting up the petition that peace might reign. The general feeling was against him at the time.

"But there's three things that needs to be considered," said Saunders Ker: "in the first place, it was within his richt as a minister to pit up what petition he liked; and, in the second, he didna mean it leeterally himsel', for we a' kenned it was his intention to be doon the Doctor's throat in five meenits; an', thirdly, it wad be a bonny queer thing gin thirty-three Kers an' Grahams a' earnestly prayin' the contrar', hadna as muckle influence at a throne o' grace, as ae man that didna mean what he said, even though the name o' him was William Henry Calvin."

Saunders expressed the general feeling of the meeting outside, which was frankly belligerent. They had indeed been beaten at the polls as they had expected, but in an honest tulzie with dickies the parish would hear a different tale.

But there was one element in the meeting that the Kers had taken no notice of. There was but one woman there, and she a girl. In the corner of the schoolroom, on the chairman's right hand, sat Grace Hutchison, daughter of the manse. The minister was a widower, and this was his only daughter. She was nineteen. She kept his house, and turned him out like a new pin. But the parish knew little of her. It called her "the minister's shilpit bit lassie."

Her face was indeed pale, and her dark eyes of a still and serene dignity, like one who walks oft at e'en in the Fairy Glen, and sees deeper into the gloaming than other folk.

Grace Hutchison accompanied her father, and sat in the corner knitting. A slim, girlish figure hardly filled to the full curves of maidenhood, she was yet an element that made for peace. The younger men saw that her lips were red and her eyes had the depth of a mountain tarn. But they had as soon thought of trysting with a ghaist from the kirkyaird, or with the Lady of the Big House, as with Grace Hutchison, the minister's daughter.

So it happened that Grace Hutchison had reached the age of nineteen years, without knowing more of love than she gathered from the seventeenth and eighteenth century books in her father's library. And one may get some curious notions out of Laurence Sterne crossed with Rutherfurd's *Letters* and *The Man of Feeling*.

"It is moved and seconded that the meetings be opened with prayer."

Objected to by Doctor Hutchison, ostensibly on the ground that they are engaged in a purely practical and parochial business, really because it is proposed by Mr. Calvin and seconded by Saunders Ker. Loyalty to the National Zion forbade agreement. Yet even Dr. Hutchison did not see the drift of the motion, but only had a general impression that some advantage for the opposition was intended. So he objected. Then there was a great discussion, famous through the parish, and even heard of as far as Polmont and Crossraguel. William Henry Calvin put the matter on the highest moral and spiritual grounds, and is generally considered, even by the Government party, to have surpassed himself. His final appeal to the chairman as a professing minister of religion was a masterpiece. Following his minister, Saunders Ker put the matter practically in his broadest and most popular Scots. The rare Howpaslet dialect thrilled to the spinal cord of every man that heard it, as it fell marrowy from the lips of Saunders; and when he reached his conclusion, even the ranks of Tuscany could scarce forbear to cheer.

"Ye are men, ye are faithers, near the halewar o' ye—maist o' ye are marriet. Ye mind what ye learned aboot your mither's knee. Ye mind where ye learned the twenty-third psalm on the quiet Sabbath afternoons. Ye dinna want to hae yer ain bairns grow up regairdless o' a' that's guid. Na, ye want them to learn the guid an' comfortable word in the schule as ye did yoursel's. Ye want them to begin wi' the psalm o' Dawvid an' the bit word o' prayer. Can ye ask a blessin' on the wark o' the schule, that hasna been askit on the wark o' the schule-board? Gin ye do, it'll no be the first time or the last that the bairn's hymn an' the bairn's prayer has put to shame baith elder an' minister."

As he sat down, Grace Hutchison looked at her father. The Doctor was conscious of her look, and withdrew his motion. The meetings were opened with prayer in all time coming.

There was a murmur of rejoicing among the Kers outside, and thighs were quietly slapped with delight at the management of the question by the minister and Saunders. It was, with reason, considered masterly.

"Ye see their drift, dinna ye, man?" said one Ker to another. "What, no?—ye surely maun hae been born on a Sabbath. D'ye no see that ilka time the Doctor is awa, eyther aboot his ain affairs or aboot the concerns o' the General Assembly, or when he's no weel, they'll be obleeged to vote either Saunders or oor minister into the chair—for, of coorse, the ither two can pray nane, bein' elders o' the Establishment? An' the chairman has aye the castin' vote!"

"Dod, man, that's graund—heard ye ever the like o' that!"

The Kers rejoiced in first blood, but they kept their strategical theories to themselves, so as not to interfere with the designs of Saunders and Mr. Calvin.

Little else was done that day. A clerk of school-board was appointed—the lawyer factor of the Laird of Howpaslet and a strong member of the State Church.

Mr. Calvin proposed the young Radical lawyer from the next town, but simply for form's sake, and to lull the other side with the semblance of victory.

"The clerk has nae vote," Saunders explained quietly through the window to the nearest Ker. This satisfied the clan, which was a little inclined to murmur.

It was then decided that a new teacher was to be appointed, and applications were to be advertised for. This was really the crux of the situation. The old parochial dominie had retired on a comfortable allowance. The company inside the school wanted him to get the allowance doubled, because he was precentor in the parish kirk, till they heard that it was to come out of the rates. Then they wanted him to have none at all. He should just have saved his siller like other folk. Who would propose to support them with forty-five pounds a year off the rates when they came to retire?—a fresh strong man, too, and well able for his meat, and said to be looking out for his third wife. The idea of giving him forty-five of their pounds to do nothing at all the rest of his life was a preposterous one. Some said they would have voted for the Seceders if they had known what the minister had in his head. But, in spite of the murmurs, the dominie got the money.

The next meeting was to be held on Tuesday fortnight—public intimation whereof having been made, the meeting was closed with the benediction, pronounced by Dr. Hutchison in a non-committal official way to show the Kers that he was not to be coerced into prayer by them.

Applications for the mastership poured in thick and fast. The members of the school-board were appealed to by letter and by private influence. They were treated at the market and buttonholed on the street—all except Saunders and his minister. These two kept their counsel sternly to themselves, knowing that they had no chance of carrying their man unless some mysterious providence should intervene.

Providence did intervene, and that manifestly, only three days before the meeting. After Sabbath service in the parish church, the Reverend Doctor Hutchison went home to the manse complaining of a violent pain in his breast.

His daughter promptly put on mustard, and sent for the doctor. By so doing she probably saved his life. For when the doctor came, he shook his head, and immediately pronounced it lung inflammation of a virulent type. The Doctor protested furiously that he must go to the meeting on Tuesday. He would go, even if he had to be carried. His daughter said nothing, but locked the door and put the key in her pocket, till she got the chance of conveying away every vestige of his clerical clothing out of his reach, locking it where Marget Lamont, his faithful servant, could not find it. Marget would have brought him a rope to hang himself if the Doctor had called for it. Sometimes in his delirium he made the speeches which he had meant to make at the school-board meeting on Tuesday; and sometimes, but more rarely, he opened the meeting with prayer. Grace sat by the side of the bed and moistened his lips. He said it was ridiculous—that he was quite well, and would certainly go to the meeting. Grace said nothing, and gave him a drink. Then he went babbling on.

The meeting was duly held. As the Kers had foretold, Mr. Calvin was voted into the chair unanimously, owing to a feint of Saunders Ker's, who proposed that the publican majority elder take the chair and open the proceedings with prayer—which so frightened that gentleman that he proposed Mr. Calvin before he knew what he was about. It was "more fitting," he said.

Dr. Hutchison fitted him afterwards for this.

At the close of the prayer, which was somewhat long, the Clerk proposed that, owing to the absence of an important member, they should adjourn the meeting till that day three weeks.

Mr. Calvin looked over at the Clerk, who was a broad, hearty, dogmatic man, accustomed to wrestle successfully with tenants about reductions and improvements.

"Mr. Clerk," he said sharply, "it is your business to advise us as to points of law. How many members of this board does it take to make a quorum?"

"Three," said the solicitor promptly.

"Then," answered Mr. Calvin, with great pith and point, "as we are one more than a quorum, we shall proceed to our business. And yours, Mr. Clerk, is to read the minutes of last meeting, and to take note of the proceedings of this. It will be as well for you to understand soon as syne that you have no *locus standi* for speech on this board, unless your opinion is asked for by the chair."

This was an early instance of what was afterwards, in affairs imperial, called the *closure*, a political weapon of some importance. The Kers afterwards observed that they always suspected that "Auld Wullie" (referring to the Prime Minister of the time) studied the reports of the Howpaslet school-board proceedings in the *Bordershire Advertiser*. Indeed, Saunders Ker was known to post one to him every week. So they all knew where the closure came from.

This is how the strongly Auld Kirk parish of Howpaslet came to have a Dissenting teacher in the person of Duncan Rowallan, a young man of great ability, who had just taken a degree at college after passing through Moray House (an ancient ducal palace where excellent dominies are manufactured), at a time when such a double qualification was much less common than it is now.

Duncan Rowallan was admitted by all to be the best man for the position. It was, indeed, a wonder that one who had been so brilliant at college, should apply for so quiet a place as the mastership of the school of Howpaslet. But it was said that Duncan Rowallan came to Howpaslet to study. And study he did. In one way he was rather a disappointment to the Kers, and even to his proposer and seconder. He was not bellicose and he was not political; but, on the other hand, he did his work soundly and thoroughly, and obtained wondrous reports written in the official hand of H.M. Inspector, and signed with a flourish like the tail of a kite. But he shrank from the more active forms of partisanship, and devoted himself to his books.

Yet even in Howpaslet his life was not to be a peaceful one.

The Reverend Doctor Hutchison arose from his bed of sickness with the most fixed of determinations to make it hot for the new dominie. When he lay near the gate of death he had seen a vision, and heaven had been plain to him. He had observed, among other things, that there was but one establishment there, a uniform government in the church triumphant. He took this as a sign that there should be only one on earth. He understood the secession of the fallen angels referred to by Milton to be a type of the Disruption. He made a note of this upon his cuff at the time, resolving to develop it in a later sermon. Then, on rising, he proceeded at once to act upon it by making the young dominie's life a burden to him.

Duncan Rowallan found himself hampered on every hand. He was refused material for the conduct of his school. The new schoolhouse was only built because the Inspector wrote to the board that the grant would be withheld till the alterations were made.

The militant Doctor could not dismiss Duncan Rowallan openly. That, at the time, would have been going too far; but he could, and did, cut down his salary to starvation point, in the hope that he would resign. But Duncan Rowallan had not come to Howpaslet for salary, and his expenses were so few that he lived as comfortably on his pittance as ever he had done. Porridge night and morning is not costly when you use little milk.

So he continued to wander much about the lanes with a book. In the summer he could be met with at all hours of light and dusk. Howpaslet was a land of honeysuckle and clematis. The tendrils clung to every hedge, and the young man wandered forth to breathe the gracious airs. One day in early June he was abroad. It was a Saturday, his day of days. Somehow he could not read that morning, though he had a book in his pocket, for the stillness of early summer (when the buds come out in such numbers that the elements are stilled with the wonder of watching) had broken up. It was a day of rushing wind and sudden onpelts of volleying rain. The branches creaked, and the young green leaves were shred untimeously from the beeches. All the orchards were dappled with flying showers of rosy snow, as the blossoms of the apple and cherry fled before the swirling gusts of cheerful tempest.

Duncan Rowallan was up on the windy braeface above the kirk of Howpaslet, with one hand to his cloth cap, as he held down his head and bored himself into the eye of the wind. Of a sudden he was amazed to see a straw hat, with a flash of scarlet about it, whirl past him, spinning upon its edge. To turn and pursue was the work of a moment. But he did not catch the run-away till it brought up, blown flat against the kirkyard dyke. He returned with it in his hand. A tall slip of a girl stood on the slope, her hair wind-blown and unfilleted—wind-blown also as to her skirts. Duncan knew her. It was the minister's daughter, the only child of the house of his enemy.

They met—he beneath, she above on the whinny braeface. Her hair, usually so smooth, blew out towards him in love-locks and witch-tangles. For the first time in his life Duncan saw a faint colour in the cheeks of the minister's daughter.

The teacher of the village school found himself apologising, he was not quite sure for what. He held the hat out a little awkwardly.

"I found it," he said, not knowing what else to say.

This description of his undignified progress as he rattled down the face of the hill after the whirling hat amused Grace Hutchison, and she laughed a little, which helped things wonderfully.

"But you have lost your own cap," she said, looking at his cropped blond poll without disapproval.

"It does not matter," said Duncan, rubbing it all over with his hand as though the action would render it waterproof.

Now, Grace Hutchison was accustomed to domineer over her father in household matters, such as the care of his person; so it occurred to her that she ought to order this young man to go and look after his cap. But she did not. On the contrary, she took a handkerchief out of her pocket, disentangling it mysteriously from the recesses of flapping skirts.

"Put that over your head till you get your own," she said.

Sober is not always that which sober looks, and it may be that Grace Hutchison had no objections to a little sedate merriment with this young man. It was serious enough down at the manse, in all conscience; and every young man in the parish stood ten yards off when he spoke to Miss Hutchison. She had not been at a party since she left the Ministers' Daughters' College two years ago, and then all the young men were carefully selected and edited by the lady principal. And Grace Hutchison was nineteen. Think of that, maids of the many invitations!

The young master's attempts to tie the handkerchief were ludicrous in the extreme. One corner kept falling over and flicking into his eye, so that he seemed to be persistently winking at her with that eyelid, a proceeding which would certainly not have been allowed at the parties of the Ministers' Daughters' College with the consent of the authorities—at least not in Grace's time.

"Oh, how stupid you are!" said Grace, putting a pin into her mouth to be ready; "let me do it."

She spoke just as if she had been getting her father ready for church.

She settled the handkerchief about Duncan Rowallan's head with one or two little tugs to the side. Then she took the pin out of her mouth and pinned it beneath his chin, in a way mightily practical, which the youth admired.

"Now, then," she said, stepping back to put on her own hat, fastening it with a dangerous-looking weapon of war shaped like a stiletto, thrust most recklessly in.

The two young people stood in the lee of the plantation on the corner of the glebe, which had been planted by Dr. Hutchison's predecessor, an old bachelor whose part in life had been to plant trees for other people to make love under.

But there was no love made that day—only a little talk on equal terms concerning Edinburgh and Professor Ramage's, where on an eve of tea and philosophy it was conceivable that they might have met. Only, as a matter of fact they did not. But at least there were a great many wonderful things which might have happened. And the time flew.

But in the mid-stream of interest Grace Hutchison recollected herself.

"It is time for my father's lunch. I must go in," she said.

And she went. She had forgotten her duties for more than half an hour.

But even as she went, she turned and said simply, "You may keep the handkerchief till you find your cap."

"Thank you," said Duncan, watching her so soberly that the white cap on his head did not look ridiculous—at least not to Grace.

As soon as she was out of sight he took off the handkerchief carefully, and put it, pin and all, into the leather case in his inner pocket where he had been accustomed to keep his matriculation card.

He looked down at the kirkyard wall over which his cap had flown.

"Oh, hang the cap!" he said; "what's about a cap, any way?"

Now, this was a most senseless observation, for the cap was a good cap and a new cap, and had cost him one shilling and sixpence at the hat-shop up three stairs at the corner of the Bridges.

* * * * *

The next evening Duncan Rowallan stood by his own door. Deaf old Mary Haig, his housekeeper, was clacking the pots together in the kitchen and grumbling steadily to herself. Duncan drew the door to, and went up by the side of his garden, past the straw-built sheds of his bees, a legacy from a former occupant, into the cool breathing twilight of the fields.

He sauntered slowly up the dykeside with his hands behind his back. He was friends with all the world. It was true that the school-board had met that day and his salary had been still further reduced, so that it was now thought that for very pride he would leave. In his interests the Kers had assaulted and battered four fellow-Christians of the contrary opinion, and the Reverend William Henry Calvin had shaken his fist in the stern face of Dr. Hutchison as he defied him at the school-board meeting. But Duncan only smiled and set his lips a little more firmly. He did not mean to let himself be driven out—at least not yet.

Up by the little wood there was a favourite spot from which the whole village could be seen from under the leaves. It was a patch of firs on the edge of the glebe, a useless rocky place let alone even by the cows. Against the rough bark of a fir-tree Duncan had fastened a piece of plank in order to form a rude seat.

As soon as he reached his favourite thinking stance, he forgot all about ecclesiastical politics and the strifes of the Kers with the minister. He stood alone in the wonder of the sunset. It glowed to the zenith. But, as very frequently in his own water-colours, the colour had run down to the horizon and flamed intensest crimson in the Nick of Benarick. Broader and broader mounted the scarlet flame, till he seemed in that still place to hear the sun's corona crackle, as observers think they do when watching a great eclipse. The set of the sun affected him like a still morning—that most mysterious thing in nature. He missed, indeed, the diffused elation of the dawn; but it was infinitely sweet to hear in that still place the softened sounds of the sweet village life—for Howpaslet was a Paradise to those to whom its politics were naught. He saw the blue smoke go up from the supper fires into the windless air in pillars of cloud, then halt, and slowly dissipate into lawny haze.

The cries of the playing children, the belated smith ringing the evening chimes on his anvil in the smithy, the tits chirping among the firs, the crackle of the rough scales on the red boughs of the Scotch fir above him as they cooled—all fed his soul as though Peter's sheet had been let down, and there was nothing common or unclean on all the earth.

"I beg your pardon—will you speak to me?"

The words stole upon him as from another sphere, startling him into dropping his book. Duncan looked round. Some one was standing by the rough stone dyke within a dozen yards of his summer-seat. It was Grace Hutchison.

Duncan went towards the dyke, taking off his cap as he went—a new cap.

So they stood there, the wall of rough hill-stones between them, but looking into one another's eyes.

There was no merriment now in the eyes that met his, no word of the return of handkerchief or any maidenly coquetry. The mood of the day of blowing leaves had passed away. She had a shawl over her head, drawn close about her shoulders. Underneath it her eyes were like night. But her lips showed on her pale face like a geranium growing alone and looking westward in the twilight.

"You will pardon me, Mr. Rowallan," she said, "if I have startled you. I am grieved for what is happening—more sorry than I can say—my father thinks that it is his duty, but—"

Duncan Rowallan did not suffer her to go on.

"Pray do not say a word about the matter, Miss Hutchison; believe that I do not mind at all. I know well the conscientiousness of your father, and he is quite right to carry out his duty."

"He has no quarrel against you," said Grace.

"Only against my office," said Duncan; "poor office! If it were not for the peace of this countryside up here against the skies, I should go at once and be no barrier to the unanimity of the parish."

She seemed to draw a long breath as his words came to her across the stone dyke.

"Ah," she said, "I hope that you will not go; for if Howpaslet did not quarrel about you, it would just be something else. But I am sorry you should be annoyed by our bickerings."

"No one could be less annoyed," said Duncan, smiling; "so perhaps it is to save some more sensitive person from suffering, that I have been sent here."

They were very near to each other, these two young people, though the dyke was between them. They leaned their elbows on it, turning together and looking down the valley. A scent that was not the scent of flowers stole on Duncan Rowallan's senses, quickening his pulses, and making him breathe faster to take it in. He was very near the dark, bird-like head from which the June wind had blown the love-locks. A balmy breath surrounded him like a halo—the witchery of youth's attraction, which is as old as Eden, ambient as the air.

Grace Hutchison may have felt it too, for she shuddered slightly, and drew her shawl closer about her shoulders.

"My father—" she began, and paused.

"Please do not talk of these things," said Duncan, the heart within him thrilling to the hinted womanhood which came to him upon the balmy breath; "I do not care for anything if you are not mine enemy."

"I—your enemy!" she said softly, with a pause between the words; "oh no, not that."

Her hand fell from the folds of her shawl and lay across the dyke. It looked a lonely thing, and Duncan Rowallan was sure that it trembled, so he took it in his. There it fluttered a little and then lay still, as a taken bird that knows it cannot escape. The dyke was between them, but they drew very near to it on either side.

Then at the same moment each drew a deep breath, and one looked at the other as if expecting speech. Yet neither spoke, and after a slow dwelling of questioning eyes, each on each, as if in a kind of reproach they looked suddenly away again.

The sunset glow deepened into rich crimson. The valleys into which they looked down from the high corner of the field were lakes of fathomless sapphire. The light smoky haze on the ridges was infinitely varied in tone, and caused the distance to fall back, crest behind crest, in illimitable perspective.

Still they did not speak, but their hearts beat so loudly that they answered each other. The stone dyke was between. Grace Hutchinson took back her hand.

Opportunity stood on tip-toe. The full tide of Duncan Rowallan's affairs lipped the watershed, the stone dyke only standing between.

He turned towards her. Far away a sheep bleated. The sound came to Duncan scornfully, as though a wicked elf had laughed at his indecision.

He put out his hands across the rough stones to take her hand again. He touched her warm shoulders instead beneath the shawl. He drew her to him. Into the deep eyes luminous with blackness he looked as into the mirror of his fate. Now, what happened just then is a mystery, and I cannot explain it. Neither can Grace nor Duncan. They have gone many times to the very place to find out exactly how it all happened, but without success. Where they have failed, can I succeed?

I can only tell what did happen.

Duncan Rowallan seemed to rise into another world, as in his childhood he had often dreamed of doing, looking up and up into the fleecy waves of the highest cloudlets. Her lips beckoned to him in the gloaming, like a red flower whose petals have fallen a little apart. It came at last.

For the dyke proved too narrow, and in one swift electric touch their old world flew into flinders.

The stone dyke was not any longer between. Duncan Rowallan had overleaped it and stood by the side of Grace Hutchison.

* * * * *

The minister had come home to Howpaslet manse exceedingly elate. At last he had won the battle. The Kers had gone home gnashing their teeth. There was lament in the manse of the Calvins. After long endeavours he had got the farmer and the publican to vote for the dismissal of Duncan Rowallan. He smiled to himself as he came in. He was not a malicious man, but he could not bear being worsted in his own parish. His feeling against Duncan Rowallan was neither here nor there; but, indeed, the Kers were hard to bear.

His daughter met him with a grave face. The determined Hutchison blood ran still and sure in her veins.

"Father," she said, "what I am going to tell you will give you pain: I have promised to marry Duncan Rowallan."

The stern old minister swayed—doubting whether he had heard aright.

"Marry Duncan Rowallan, the dominie!" he said; "the lassie's gane gyte!
He's dismissed and a pauper!"

"No," she said; "on the contrary, he has got a mastership at the High
School. I have promised to marry him."

The old man said no word. He did not try to hector Grace, as he would have done any one outside the manse. Her household autocracy asserted itself even in that supreme moment. Besides, he knew that it would be so useless, for she was his own child. He put one hand up uncertainly and smoothed his brow vaguely, as though something hurt him and he did not understand.

He sat down in his great chair, and took up a little fire-screen that had stood many years by his chair. Grace had worked it as a sampler when as a little girl she went to the village school and had slept at night in his room in a little trundle-bed. He looked at it strangely.

"Grade," he said, "Gracie—my wee Gracie!"—and then he set the fire-screen down very gently. "I am an old man and full of years," he said. He looked worn and broken.

Grace went quickly and put her arms about his neck.

"No, no, father," she said; "you have only gained a son."

But the old man's passions could not turn so quickly, not having the pliancy of youth and love. He only shook his head sadly.

"Not so," he said; "I am left a lonely man—my house is left unto me desolate."

Yet, nevertheless, Grace was right. He stays with them for a month every Assembly time, and lectures them daily on the relations of Church and State.

II

A FINISHED YOUNG LADY

I

I cannot send thee gold
Nor silver for a show;
Nor are there jewels sold
One-half so dear as thou.

II

No daffodil doth blow
In this dull winter time,
Nor purple violet grow
In so unkind a clime.

III

To-day I have not got
One spray of meadow-sweet,
Nor blue forget-me-not
My posy to complete.

IV

Yet none of these can claim
So much goodwill as you;
Their lips put not to shame
Cowslip end Oxlip too.

V

But joy I'll take in this,
Pleasure more sweet than all,
If thou this book but kiss
As Love's memorial.

There were few bigger men in the West of Scotland than Fergus Teeman, the grocer in Port Ryan. He had come from Glasgow and set up in quite grand style, succeeding to the business of his uncle, John M'Connell, who had spent all his days selling treacle and snuff to the guidwives of the Port. When Fergus Teeman came from Glasgow, he found that he could not abide the small-paned, gloomy windows of the grocer's shop at the corner, so in a little while the whole shop became window and door, overfrowned by mere eyebrows of chocolate-coloured eaves.

He had a broad and gorgeous sign specially painted in place of the old "*John M'Connell, licensed to sell Tea, Coffee, and Tobacco,*" which had so long occupied its place. Then he dismounted the crossed pipes and the row of sweetie-bottles, and filled the great windows according to the latest canons of Glasgow retail provision-trade taste. The result was amazing, and for days there was the danger of a block before the windows. It was as good as a peep-show, and considerably cheaper. As many as four boys and a woman with a shawl over her head, had been counted on the pavement in front of the shop at once—a fact which the people in the next town refused to credit.

Fergus Teeman was a business man. He was "no gentleman going about with his hands in his pockets"—he said so himself. And so far he was right, for, let his hands be where they might, certainly he was no gentleman. But, for all that, he was a big man in Port Ryan, and it was a great day for the Kirk in the Vennel when Fergus Teeman led his family to worship within the precincts of that modest Zion. They made much of him there, and Fergus sunned himself in his pew in the pleasing warmth of his own greatness.

In the congregation from whence he had come he had not been accustomed to be so treated. He had held a seat far under the gallery; but in the Kirk in the Vennel he had the corner seat opposite to the manse pew. There Fergus installed his wife and family, and there last of all he shut himself in with a bang. He then looked pityingly around as his women-folk reverently bent a moment forward on the book-board. That was well enough for women, but a leading grocer could not so bemean himself.

In a few months Fergus started a van. This was a new thing about the Port. The van was for the purpose of conveying the goods and benefits of the Emporium to the remoter villages. The van was resplendent with paint and gilding. It was covered with advertisements of its contents executed in the highest style of art. The Kirk in the Vennel felt the reflected glory, and promptly elected him an elder. A man *must* be a good man to come so regularly to ordinances and own such a van. The wife of this magnificent member of society was, like the female of so many of the lower animals, of modest mien and a retiring plumage. She sat much in the back parlour; and even when she came out, she crept along in the shadow of the houses.

"Na," said Jess Kissock of the Bow Head, "it's no' a licht thing to be wife to sic a man"—which, indeed, it assuredly was not. Mrs. Fergus Teeman could have given some evidence on that subject, but she only hid her secrets under the shabby breast of her stuff gown.

There was said to be a daughter at a boarding-school employed in "finishing," whatever that might be. There were also various boys like steps in an uneven stair, models of all the virtues under their father's eye, and perfect demons on the street—that is, on the streets of Port Ryan which were not glared upon by the omniscient plate-glass of Teeman's Emporium.

There was no minister in the Kirk in the Vennel when Fergus Teeman came to Port Ryan. The last one had got another kirk after fifteen years' service, thirteen of which he had spent in fishing for just such a call as he got, being heartily tired of the miserable ways of his congregation. When he received the invitation, he waited a week before he thought it would be decent to say, that perhaps he might have seriously to consider whether this were not a direct leading of Providence. On the following Thursday he accepted. On the Monday he left Port Ryan for ever, directing his meagre properties to be sent after him. He shook his fist at the town as the train moved out.

So Fergus Teeman was just in time to come in for the new election, which seemed like a favouritism of Providence to a new man—for, of course, he was put on the committee which was to choose the candidates. Then there was a great preaching. All the candidates stopped with Mr. Teeman. This suited the Kirk in the Vennel, for it was a saving in expense. It also suited Fergus Teeman, for it allowed him to sound them on all the subjects which interested him. And, as he said, the expense was really a mere trifle, so long as one did not give them ham and eggs for their breakfast. It is not good to preach on ham and eggs. It spoils the voice. Fergus Teeman had a cutting out of the Glasgow *Weekly Flail*, an able paper which is the Saturday Bible of those parts. This extract said that Adelina Patti could not sing for five hours after ham and eggs. It is just the same with preaching. Fergus, therefore, read this to the candidates, and gave them for breakfast plain bread and butter (best Irish cooking, 6-1/2d. per pound).

Fergus was an orthodox man. His first question was, "How long are you out of the college?" His next, "Were you under Professor Robertson?" His third, "Do ye haud wi' hymn-singin', street-preachin', revival meetings, and novel-reading?"

From the answers to these questions Fergus Teeman formed his own short leet. It was a very short one. There was only the Rev. Farish Farintosh upon it. He took "cent.-per-cent." in the examination. Some of the others made a point or two in their host's estimation, but Farish Farintosh cleared the paper. He was just out of college that very month—which was true. (But he did not say that he had been detained a year or two, endeavouring to overcome the strange scruples of the Examination Board.) He had studied under Professor Robertson, and had frequently proved him wrong to his very face in the class, till the students could not keep from laughing (which, between ourselves, was a lie). He was no hypocrite, advanced critic, or teetotaler, and would scorn to say he was. (He smelled Fergus Teeman's breath. He had been a staunch teetotaler at another vacancy the Saturday before.) He would not open a hymn-book for thirty pounds. This was the very man for Fergus Teeman. So they made a night of it, and consumed five "rake" of hot water. Hot water is good for the preaching.

But, strange to say, when the day of the voting came, the congregation would by no means have the Reverend Farish Farintosh, though his claims were vehemently urged by the grocer in a speech, with strange blanks in the places where the strong words would have come on other occasions. They elected instead a mere nobody of a young beardless boy, who had been a year or two in a city mission, and whose only recommendation was that he had very successfully worked among the poor of his district.

Fergus Teeman stated his opinions of the new minister, across his counter, often and vehemently.

"The laddie kens nae mair nor a guano-bag. There's nocht in him but what the spoon pits intil him. He hasna the spunk o' a rabbit. I tell ye what, we need a man o' wecht in oor kirk. *Come up oot o' there, boy; ye're lickin' that sugar again*! Na, he'll ken wha he's preachin' till, when he stands up afore me. My e'e wull be on him nicht and day. *Hae ye no thae bags made yet? Gin they're no' dune in five meenits, I'll knock the heid aff ye*!"

The new minister came. He was placed with a great gathering of the clans. The Kirk in the Vennel was full to overflowing the night of his first sermon. Fergus Teeman 'was there with his notebook, and before the close of the service more than two pages were filled with the measure of the new minister's iniquity. Then, on the Tuesday after, young Duncan Stewart, seeking to know all his office-bearers, entered like the innocentest of flies the plate-glass-fronted shop where Fergus Teeman lay in wait. There and then, before half a score of interested customers, the elder gave the young minister "sic a through-pittin' as he never gat in his life afore." This was the elder's own story, but the popular opinion was clearly on the side of the minister. It had to be latent opinion, however, for the names of most of the congregation stood in the big books in Fergus Teeman's shop.

The minister commended himself to his Maker, and went about his own proper business. Every Sabbath, after the sermon, often also before the service, Fergus Teeman was on hand to say his word of reproof to the young minister, to interject the sneering word which, like the poison of asps, turned sweet to bitter. Had Duncan Stewart been older or wiser, he would have showed him to the door. Unfortunately he was just a simple, honest, well-meaning lad from college, trying to do his duty in the Kirk in the Vennel so far as he knew it.

There was an interval of some months before the minister could bring himself to visit again the shop and house of his critical elder. This time he thought that he would try the other door. As yet he had only paid his respects at a distance to Mrs. Teeman. It seemed as if they had avoided each other. He was shown into a room in which a canary was swinging in the window, and a copy of Handel's *Messiah* lay on the open piano. This was unlike the account he had heard of Mrs. Teeman. There was a merry voice on the stairs, which said clearly in girlish tones—

"Do go and make yourself decent, father; and then if you are good you may come in and see the minister!"

Duncan Stewart said to himself that something had happened. He was right, and something very important, too. May Teeman was "finished."

"And I hope you like me," she had said to her father when she came home. "Sit down, you disreputable old man, till I do your hair. You're not fit to be seen!"

And, though it would not be credited in the Port, it is a fact that Fergus Teeman sat down without a word. In a week her father was a new man. In a fortnight May kept the key of the cupboard where the square decanter was hidden.

A tall, slim girl with an eager face, and little wisps of fair hair curling about her head, came into the room and frankly held out her hand to the minister.

"You are Mr. Stewart. I am glad to see you."

Whereupon they fell a-talking, and in a twinkling were in the depths of a discussion upon poetry. Duncan Stewart was so intent on watching the swift changes of expression across the face of this girl, that he made several flying shots in giving his opinions of certain poems—for which he was utterly put to shame by May Teeman, who instantly fastened him to his random opinions and asked him to explain them.

To them entered another Fergus Teeman to the militant critic of the Sabbath morning whom Duncan knew too well.

"Sit down, father. Make yourself at home," said his daughter. "I am just going to play something." And so her father sat down not ill-pleased, and, according to her word, tried to make himself at home, till the hours slipped away, and Duncan Stewart was induced to stay for tea.

"He's mellowin' fine, like a good blend o' Glenlivet!" said the grocer next day, in his shop. (He did not speak nearly so loud as he used to do.) "He's comin' awa' brawly. I'll no' say but what I was owre sharp wi' the lad at first. He'll mak' a sound minister yet, gin he was a kennin' mair spunky. Hear till me, yon was a graun' sermon we got yesterday. It cowed a'! Man, Lochnaw, he touched ye up fine aboot pride and self-conceit!"

* * * * *

"What's at the bottom o' a' that, think ye, na?" asked Lochnaw that night as his wife and he dodged home at the rate of five miles an hour behind the grey old pony with the shaggy fetlocks.

"Ye cuif," said his wife; "that dochter o' his 'ill be gaun up to the manse. That boardin'-schule feenished her, an' she's feenished the minister!"

"Davert! what a woman ye are!" said Lochnaw, in great admiration.

III

THE LITTLE LAME ANGEL

In the field so wide and sunny
Where the summer clover is,
Where each year the mower searches
For the nests of wild-bee honey,
All along these silver birches
Stand up straight in shining row,
Dewdrops sparkling, shadows darkling,
In the early morning glow;
And in gleaming time they're gleaming
White, like angels when I'm dreaming.

*There among its handsome brothers
Was one little crooked tree,
Different from all the others,
Just as bent as bent could be.
  First it crawl'd along the heather
Till it turn'd up straight again,
Then it drew itself together
Like a tender thing in pain;
Scarce a single green leaf straggled
From its twigs so bare and draggled—
And it really looks ashamed
When I'm passing by that way,
Just as if it tried to say—
  "Please don't look at such a maim'd
Little Cripple-Dick as I;
Look at all the rest about,
Look at them and pass me by,
I'm so crooked, do not flout me,
  Kindly turn your head awry;
Of what use is my poor gnarl'd
Body in this lovely world?"*

Once I wrote[10] about two little, boys who played together all through the heats of the Dry Summer in a garden very beautiful and old. The tale told how it came to pass that one of the boys was lame, and also why they loved one another so greatly.

[Footnote 10: Jiminy and Jaikie (*The Stickit Minister*).]

Now, it happened that some loved what was told, and perhaps even more that which was not told, but only hinted. For that is the secret of being loved—not to tell all. At least, from over-seas there came letters one, two, and three, asking to be told what these two did in the beautiful garden of Long Ago, what they played at, where they went, and what the dry summer heats had to do with it all.

Perhaps it is a foolish thing to try to write down in words that which was at once so little and so dear. Yet, because I love the garden and the boys, I must, for my own pleasure, tell of them once again.

It was Jiminy's garden, or at least his father's, which is the same thing, or even better. For his father lived in a gloomy study with severe books, bound in divinity calf, all about him; and was no more conscious of the existence of the beautiful garden than if it had been the Desert of Sahara.

On the other hand, Jiminy never opened a book that summer except when he could not help it, which was once a day, when his father instructed him in the Latin verb.

The old garden was cut into squares by noble walks bordered by boxwood, high like a hedge. For it had once been the garden of a monastery, and the yews and the box were all that remained of what the good monks had spent so much skill and labour upon.

There was an orchard also, with old gnarled, green-mossed trees, that bore little fruit, but made a glory of shade in the dog-days. Up among the branches Jiminy made a platform, like those Jaikie read to him about in a book of Indian travel, where the hunters waited for tigers to come underneath them. Ever since Jaikie became lame he lived at the manse, and the minister let him read all sorts of queer books all day long, if so he wished. As for Jiminy, he had been brought up among books, and cared little about them; but Jaikie looked upon each one as a new gate of Paradise.

"You never can tell," said Jaikie to Jiminy; "backs are deceivin', likewise names. I've looked in ever so many books by the man that wrote *Robinson Crusoe*, and there's not an island in any of them."

"Books are all stuff," said Jiminy. "Let's play 'Tiger.'"

"Well," replied Jaikie, "any way, it was out of a book I got 'Tiger.'"

So Jaikie mounted on the platform, and they began to play 'Tiger.' This is how they played it. Jaikie had a bow and arrow, and he watched and waited silently up among the green leaves till Jiminy came, crawling as softly beneath as the tiger goes *pit-pat* in his own jungles. Then Jaikie drew the arrow to a head, and shot the tiger square on the back. With a mighty howl the beast sprang in the air, as though to reach Jaikie. But brave Jaikie only laughed, and in a moment the tiger fell on his back, pulled up its trouser-legs, and expired. For that is the way tigers always do. They cannot expire without pulling up their trouser-legs. If you do not believe me, ask the man at the Zoo.

Now, as the former story tells, it was Jaikie who used always to do what Jiminy bade him; but after Jaikie was hurt, helping Jiminy's father to keep his church and manse, it was quite different. Jiminy used to come to Jaikie and say, "What shall we do to-day?" And then he used to wheel his friend in a little carriage the village joiner made, and afterwards carry him among the orchard trees to the place he wanted to go.

"Jiminy," said Jaikie, "the flowers are bonnie in the plots, but they are a' prisoners. Let us make a place where they can grow as they like."

Perhaps he thought of himself laid weak and lonely, when the green world without was all a-growing and a-blowing.

"Bring some of the flowers up to this corner," said Jaikie, the lame boy. And it was not long till Jiminy brought them. The ground was baked and dry, however, and soon they would have withered, but that Jaikie issued his commands, and Jiminy ran for pails upon pails of water from the little burn where now the water had stopped flowing, and only slept black in the pools with a little green scum over them.

"I can't carry water all night like this," said Jiminy at last. "I suppose we must give up this wild garden here in the corner of the orchard."

"No," said Jaikie, rubbing his lame ankle where it always hurt, "we must not give it up, for it is our very own, and I shall think about it to-night between the clock-strikes."

For Jaikie used to lie awake and count the hours when the pain was at the worst. Jaikie now lived at the manse all the time (did I tell you that before?), for his father was dead.

So in the little room next to Jiminy's, Jaikie lay awake and hearkened to the gentle breathing of his friend. Jiminy always said when he went to bed, "I'll keep awake to-night sure, Jaikie, and talk to you."

And Jaikie only smiled a wan smile with a soul in it, for he knew that as soon as Jiminy's head touched the pillow he would be in the dim and beautiful country of Nod, leaving poor Jaikie to rub the leg in which the pains ran races up and down, and to listen and pray for the next striking of the clock.

As he lay, Jaikie thought of the flowers in the corner of the orchard thirsty and sick. It might be that they, like him, were sleepless and suffering. He remembered the rich clove carnations with their dower of a sweet savour, the dark indigo winking "blueys" or cornflowers, the spotted musk monkey-flowers, smelling like a village flower-show. They would all be drooping and sad. And it might be that the ferns would be dead—all but the hart's-tongue; which, though moisture-loving, can yet, like the athlete, train itself to endure and abide thirsty and unslaked. But the thought of their pain worked in Jaikie's heart.

"Maybe it will make me forget my foot if I can go and water them."

So he arose, crawling on his hands and knees down-stairs very softly, past where Jiminy tossed in his bed, and softer still past the minister's door. But there was no sound save the creak of the stair under him.

Jaikie crept to the water-pail, and got the large quart tankard that hung by the side of the wall.

It was a hard job for a little lad to get a heavy tin filled—a harder still to unlock the door and creep away across the square of gravel. "You have no idea" (so he said afterwards) "how badly gravel hurts your knees when they are bare."

Luckily it was a hot night, and not a breath of air was stirring, so the little white-clad figure moved slowly across the front of the house to the green gate of the garden. Jaikie could only reach out as far as his arms would go with the tin of water. Then painfully he pulled himself forward towards the tankard. But in spite of all he made headway, and soon he was creeping up the middle walk, past the great central sundial, which seemed high as a church-steeple above him. The ghostly moths fluttered about him, attracted by the waving white of his garments. In their corner he found the flowers, and, as he had thought, they were withered and drooping.

He lifted the water upon them with his palms, taking care that none dripped through, for it was very precious, and he seemed to have carried it many miles.

And as soon as they felt the water upon them the flowers paid him back in perfume. The musk lifted up its head, and mingled with the late velvety wallflower and frilled carnation in releasing a wonder of expressed sweetness upon the night air.

"I wish I had some for you, dear dimpled buttercups," said Jaikie to the golden chalices which grew in the hollows by the burnside, where in other years there was much moisture; "can you wait another day?"

"We have waited long," they seemed to reply; "we can surely wait another day."

Then the honeysuckle reached down a single tendril to touch Jaikie on the cheek.

"Some for me, please," it said; "there are so many of us at our house, and so little to get. Our roots are such a long way off, and the big fellows farther down get most of the juice before it comes our way. If you cannot water us all, you might pour a little on our heads." So Jaikie lifted up his tankard and poured the few drops that were in the bottom upon the nodding heads of the honeysuckle blooms.

"Bide a little while," said he, "and you shall have plenty for root and flower, for branch and vine-stem."

There were not many more loving little boys than Jaikie in all the world; and with all his work and his helping and talking, he had quite forgotten about the pain in his foot.

Now, if I were telling a story—making it up, that is—it is just the time for something to happen,—for a great trumpet to blow to tell the world what a brave fellow this friend of the flowers was; or at least for some great person, perhaps the minister himself, to come and find him there alone in the night. Then he might be carried home with great rejoicing.

But nothing of the kind happened. In fact, nothing happened at all. Jaikie began to creep back again in the quiet, colourless night; but before he had quite gone away the honeysuckle said—

"Remember to come back to-morrow and water us, and we will get ready such fine full cups of honey for you to suck."

And Jaikie promised. He shut the gate to keep out the hens. He crept across the pebbles, and they hurt more than ever. He hung up the tin dipper again on its peg, and climbed the stairs to his bedroom. Jiminy was breathing as quietly and equally as a lazy red-spotted trout in the shadow of the bank in the afternoon. Jaikie crept into his bed and fell asleep without a prayer or a thought.

He did not awake till quite late in the day, when Jiminy came to tell him that somebody had been watering the flowers in their Corner of Shadows during the night.

"*I* think it must have been the angels," said Jiminy, before Jaikie had time to tell him how it all happened. "My father he thinks so too."

The latter statement was, of course, wholly unauthorised.

Jaikie sat up and put his foot to the floor. All the pain had gone away out of it. He told Jiminy, who had an explanation for everything. *He* knew how the foot had got better and how the flowers were watered.

"'Course it must have been the angels, little baby angels that can't fly yet—only crawl. I did hear them scuffling about the floor last night."

And this, of course, explained everything.

BOOK FIFTH

TALES OF THE KIRK

I

THE MINISTER-EMERITUS

Ho, let the viol's pleasing swifter grow—
  Let Music's madness fascinate the will,
  And all Youth's pulses with the ardour thrill!
Hast thou, Old Time, e'er seen so brave a show?

Did not the dotard smile as he said "No"?
  Pshaw! hang the grey-beard—let him prate his fill;
  Men are but dolts who talk of Good and Ill.
These grapes of ours are wondrous sour, I trow!

They sneer because we live for other things,
  And think they know The Good. I tell the fools
We have the pleasure—We! Our master flings
  Full-measured bliss to all the folk he rules,

Nor asks he aught for quit-rent, fee, or tithe—
Ho, Bald-head, wherefore sharpenest thy scythe?

In the winter season the Clint of Drumore is the forlornest spot in God's universe—twelve miles from anywhere, the roads barred with snowdrift, the great stone dykes which climb the sides of apparently inaccessible mountains sleeked fore and aft with curving banks of white. In the howe of the hill, just where it bends away towards the valley of the Cree, stood a cottage buried up to its eyes in the snow. Originally a low thatch house, it had somewhat incongruously added on half a story, a couple of storm-windows, and a roof of purple Parton slates. There were one or two small office-houses about it devoted to a cow, a Galloway shelty, and a dozen hens. This snowy morning, from the door of the hen-house the lord of these dusky paramours occasionally jerked his head out, to see if anything hopeful had turned up. But mostly he sat forlornly enough, waiting with his comb drooping limply to one side and a foot drawn stiffly up under his feathers.

Within the cottage there was little more comfort. It consisted, as usual, of a "but" and a "ben," with a little room to the back, in which there were a bed, a chair, and a glass broken at the corner nailed to the wall. In this room a man was kneeling in front of the chair. He was clad in rusty black, with a great white handkerchief about his throat. He prayed long and voicelessly. At last he rose, and, standing stiffly erect, slipped a small yellow photograph which he had been holding in his hand into a worn leather case.

A man of once stalwart frame, now bowed and broken, he walked habitually with the knuckles of one hand in the small of his back, as if he feared that his frail framework might give way at that point; silvery hair straggling about his temples, faded blue eyes, kindly and clouded under white shocks of eyebrow—such was the Reverend Fergus Symington, now for some years minister-emeritus. Once he had been pastor of the little hill congregation of the Bridge of Cairn, where he had faithfully served a scanty flock for thirty years. When he resigned he knew that it was but little that his people could do for him. They were sorry to part with him, and willingly enough accepted the terms which the Presbytery pressed on them, in order to be at liberty to call the man of their choice, a young student from a neighbouring glen, whose powers of fluent speech were thought remarkable in that part of the country. So Mr. Symington left Bridge of Cairn passing rich on thirty pounds a year, and retired with his deaf old housekeeper to the Clints of Drumore. Yet forty years before, the Reverend Fergus Symington was counted the luckiest young minister in the Stewartry; and many were the jokes made in public-house parlours and in private houses about his mercenary motives. He had married money. He had been wedded with much rejoicing to the rich daughter of a Liverpool merchant, who had made a fortune not too tenderly in the West Indian trade. Sophia Sugg was ten years the senior of her husband, and her temper was uncertain, but Fergus Symington honestly loved her. She had a tender and a kindly hearty and he had met her in the houses of the poor near her father's shooting-lodge in circumstances which did her honour. So he loved her, and told her of it as simply as though she had been a penniless lass from one of the small farms that made up the staple of his congregation. They were married, and it is obvious what the countryside would say, specially as there were many eyes that had looked not scornfully at the handsome young minister.

"This, all this was in the golden time,
        Long ago."

The mistress of the little white manse on the Cairn Water lived not unhappily with her husband for four years, and was then laid with her own people in the monstrous new family vault where her father lay in state. She left two children behind her—a boy of two and an infant girl of a few weeks.

The children had a nurse, Meysie Dickson, a girl who was already a woman in staidness and steadfastness at fifteen. She had been in a kind of half-hearted way engaged to be married to Weelum Lammitter, the grieve at Newlands; but when the two bairns were left on her hand, she told Weelum that he had better take Kirst Laurie, which Weelum Lammitter promptly did. There was a furnished house attached to the grieveship, and he could not let it stand empty any longer. Still, he would have preferred Meysie, other things being equal. He even said so to Kirst Laurie, especially when he was taking his tea—for Kirst was no baker.

So for twenty years the household moved on its quiet, ordered way in the manse by the Water of Cairn. Then the boy, entering into the inheritance devised to him by his mother's marriage-settlement, took the portion of goods that pertained to him, and went his way into a far country, and did there according to the manner of his kind. Meysie had been to some extent to blame for this, as had also his father. The minister himself, absorbed in his books and in his sermons, had only given occasional notice to the eager, ill-balanced boy who was growing up in his home. He had given him, indeed, his due hours of teaching till he went away to school, but he had known nothing of his recreations and amusements. Meysie, who was by no means dumb though she was undoubtedly deaf, kept dinning in his ears that he must take his place with the highest in the land, by which she meant the young Laird of Cairnie and the Mitchels of Mitchelfleld. Some of these young fellows were exceedingly ready to show Clement Symington how to squander his ducats, and when he took the road to London he went away a pigeon ready for the plucking. The waters closed over his head, and so far as his father was concerned there was an end of him.

Elspeth Symington, the baby girl, turned out a child of another type. Strong, masculine, resolute, with some of the determination of the old slave-driving grandfather in her, she had from an early age been under the care of a sister of her mother's. And with her she had learned many things, chiefly that sad lesson—to despise her father. It had never struck Mr. Symington in the way of complaint that he had no art or part in his wife's fortune, so that he was not disappointed when he found himself stranded in the little cottage by the Clints of Drumore with thirty pounds a year. He was lonely, it was true, but his books stood between him and unhappiness. Also Meysie, deaf and cross, grumbled and crooned loyally about his doors.

This wintry morning there was no fire in the room which was called by the minister the "study"—but by Meysie, more exactly and descriptively, "ben the hoose." The minister had written on Meysie's slate the night before that, as the peats were running done and no one could say how long the storm might continue, no fire was to be put in the study the next day.

So after Mr. Symington had eaten his porridge, taking it with a little milk from their one cow—Meysie standing by the while to "see that he suppit them"—he made an incursion or two down the house to the "room" for some books that he needed. Then Meysie bustled about her work and cleaned up with prodigious birr and clatter, being utterly unable to hear the noise she made. The minister soon became absorbed in his book, and a light of contentment shone in his face. Occasionally his hand stole to his pocket. Meysie, whose eyes never wandered far from him, knew that he was feeling for the leather case in which he kept the photographs of his boy and girl. He liked to know that it was safe. Elspeth had recently sent him a new portrait of herself in evening dress, with diamonds in her hair. It came from London in a large envelope with the florid monogram of Lady Smythe, the widow of the ex-Lord Mayor, upon it. The minister considered it the last triumph of art, and often took it out of his pocket to look at when he thought Meysie was not looking. She always was, however. She had little else to do. Nevertheless, Meysie knew, for all that, the worn yellow "card" of the lost son who never wrote or sent him anything, to be the dearest to him.

While the minister sat pondering over his book, Meysie went to the back door, and stood there a moment vaguely gazing out on the snow. As she did so, a figure came slouching round the corner of the byre. Meysie quickly shut the door behind her, and turned the key. Any visitor was a strange surprise in winter at the Clints of Drumore. But this figure she knew at the first glance. It was the Prodigal Son come home—the boy whom she had reared from the time that she took his sister from his dying mother's arms. Some deadly fear constrained her to lock the door behind her. For the lad's looks were terribly altered. There was a sullen, callous dourness where bright self-will had once had its dwelling. His clothing had once been fashionable, but it was now torn at the buttonholes and frayed at the cuffs.

"Clement Symington, what brings ye to the Clints o' Drumore?" asked the old woman, going forward and taking hold of the skirts of his surtout, her face blanched like the blue shadows on the winter snow.

"Why, Mother Hubbard—" he broke out.

But Meysie stopped him, holding up her hand and pointing to her slate, which hung by a "tang" round her neck.

"Ha!" he murmured, "this is awkward—old woman gone deaf."

So he took the pencil and wrote—

"*Very hard up. Want some cash from the old man*," just as if he had been writing a telegram.

With her spectacles poised on the end of her nose, Meysie read the message. Her face took a hue greyer and duller than ever.

She looked at the lad she had once loved so well, and his shifty eye could not meet hers. He looked away over the moor, put his hands into his pockets, and whistled a music-hall catch, which sounded strangely in that white solitude.

"Weel do you ken that your faither has no sillar!" said Meysie. "You had a' the sillar, and what ye hae done with it only you an' your Maker ken. But ye shallna come into this hoose to annoy yer faither. Gang to the barn, and wait till I bring you what I can get."

The young man grumblingly assented, and within that chilly enclosure he stood swearing under his breath and kicking his heels.

"A pretty poor sort of prodigal's return this," he said, remembering the parable he used to learn to say to his father on Sunday afternoons; "not so much as a blessed fatted calf—only a half-starved cow and a deaf old woman. I wonder what she'll bring a fellow."

In a little while Meysie came cautiously out of the back door with a bowl of broth under her apron. The minister had not stirred, deep in his folio Owen. The young man ate the thick soup with a horn spoon from Meysie's pocket. Then he stood looking at her a moment before he took the dangling pencil again and wrote on the slate—

"*Soup's good, but it's money I must have!*"

Meysie bent her head towards him.

"Ye shallna gang in to break yer faither's heart, Clement; but I hae brocht ye a' I hae, gin ye'll promise to gang awa' where ye cam' frae. Your faither kens nocht aboot your last ploy, or that a son o' his has been in London gaol."

"And who told you?" broke in the youth furiously.

The old woman could not, of course, hear him, but she understood perfectly for all that.

"Your ain sister Elspeth telled me!" she answered.

"Curse her!" said the young man, succinctly and unfraternally. But he took the pencil and wrote —"*I promise to go away and not to disturb my father*."

Meysie took a lean green silk purse from her pocket and emptied out of it a five-pound note, three dirty one-pound notes, and seven silver shillings. Clement Symington took them and counted them over without a blush.

"You're none such a bad sort," he said.

"Now, mind your promise, Clement!" returned his old nurse.

He made his way at a dog's-trot down the half-snowed-up track that led towards the Ferry Town of the Cree; and though Meysie went to the stile of the orchard to watch, he ran out of sight without even turning his head. When the old woman went in, the minister was still deep in his book. He had never once looked up.

The short day faded into the long night. Icy gusts drove down from the heights of Craig Ronald, and the wind moaned mysteriously over the ridges which separated the valley of the Cree Water from the remote fastnesses of Loch Grannoch. The minister gathered his scanty family at the "buik," and his prayer was full of a fine reverence and feeling pity. He was pleading in the midst of a wilderness of silence, for the deaf woman heard not a word.

Yet it will do us no harm to hearken to the prayer of yearning and wrestling.

"O my God, who wast the God of my forefathers, keep Thou my two bairns. They are gone from under my roof, but they are under Thine. Through the storm and the darkness be Thou about them. Let Thy light be in their hearts. Though here we meet no more, may we meet an unbroken family around Thy heavenly hearth. And have mercy on us who here await Thy hand, on this good ministering woman, and on me, alas! Thine unworthy servant, for I am but a sinful man, O Lord!"

Then Meysie made down her box-bed in the kitchen, and the minister retired to his own little chamber. He took his leather case out of his breast-pocket, and clasped it in his hand as he began his own protracted private devotions. He knelt on a place where his knees had long since worn a hole in the waxcloth. So, kneeling on the bare stone, he prayed long, even till the candle flickered itself out, smelling rankly in the room.

At the deepest time of the night, while the snow winds were raging about the half-buried cot, the dark figure of a young man opened the never-locked door and stepped quickly into the small lobby in which the minister's hat and worn overcoat were hanging. He paused to listen before he came into the kitchen, but nothing was to be heard except the steady breathing of the deaf woman. He came in and stepped across the floor. The red glow from the peats on the hearth revealed the figure of Clement Symington. He shook the snow from his coat and blew on his fingers. Then he went to the door of his father's room and listened. Hearing no sound, he slowly opened it. His father had fallen asleep on his knees, with his forehead on his open Bible. The red glow of the dying peat-fire lighted the little room. "I wonder where he keeps his cash," he murmured to himself; "the sooner it's over the better." His eye caught something like a purse in his father's hand. As he took it, something broad and light fell out. He held it up to the moonbeam which came through the narrow upper panes. It was his own portrait taken in the suit which his father had bought him to go to college in. He had found the old man's wealth. A strangeness in his father's attitude caught his eye. With a sudden, quick return of boyish affection he laid his hand on the bowed shoulder, forgetting for the moment his evil purpose and all else. The attenuated figure swayed and would have fallen to the side, had Clement Symington not caught it and laid his father tenderly on the bed. Then he stood upright and cried aloud in agony with that most terrible of griefs—the repentance that comes too late. But none heard him. The deaf woman slept on. And the dead gave no answer, being also for ever deaf and dumb.

II

A MINISTER'S DAY

On either side the great and still ice sea
  Are compassing snow mountains near and far;
  While, dominant, Schreckhorn and Finsteraar
Hold their grim peaks aloft defiantly.

Blind with excess of light and glory, we,
  Above whose heads in hottest mid-day glare
  The Schreckhorn and his sons arise in air,
Sink in the weary snowfields to the knee;

Then, resting after peril pass'd in haste,
  We saw, from our rock-shelter'd vantage ledge,
  In the white fervent heat sole shadowy spot,

Familiar eyes that smiled amid the waste—
  Lo! in the sparsed snow at the glacier edge,
  The small blue flower they call Forget-me-not!

The sun was glinting slantwise over the undulating uplands to the east. Ben Gairn was blushing a rosy purple, purer and fainter than the flamboyant hues of sunset, when the Reverend Richard Cameron looked out of his bedroom window in the little whitewashed manse of Cairn Edward. His own favourite blackbird had awakened him, and he lay for a long while listening to its mellow fluting, till his conscience reproached him for lying so long a-bed on such a morning.

Richard Cameron was by nature an early riser, a gift to thank God for. Many a Sabbath morning he had seen the sun rise from the ivy-grown arbour in the secluded garden behind the old whitewashed kirk. It was his habit to rise early, and, with the notes of his sermon in hand, to memorise, or "mandate," them, as it was called. So that on Sabbath, when the hill-folk gathered calm and slow, there might be no hesitation, and he might be able to pray the Cameronian supplication, "And bring the truth premeditated to ready recollection"—a prayer which no mere "reader" of a discourse would ever dare to utter.

But this was not a morning for "mandating" with the minister. It was the day of his pastoral visitation, and it behoved one who had a congregation scattered over a radius of more than twenty miles to be up and doing. The minister went down into the little study to take his spare breakfast of porridge and milk. Then, having called his housekeeper in for prayers—which included, even to that sparse auditory, the exposition of the chapter read—he took his staff in hand, and, crossing the main street, took the road for the western hills, on which a considerable portion of his flock pastured.

As he went he whistled, whenever he found himself at a sufficient distance from the scattered houses which lined the roads. He was everywhere respectfully greeted, with an instinctive solemnity of a godly sort—a solemnity without fear. Men looked at him as he swung along, with right Scottish respect for his character and work. They knew him to be at once a man among men and a man of God.

The women stood and looked longer after him. There was nothing so striking to be seen in Galloway as that clear-cut, clean-shaven Greek face set on the square shoulders; for Galloway is a country of tall, stoop-shouldered men—a country also at that time of shaven upper lips and bristling beards, the most unpicturesque tonsure, barring the mutton-chop whisker, which has yet been discovered. The women, therefore, old and young, looked after him with a warmth about their hearts and a kindly moisture in their eyes. They felt that he was much too handsome to be going about unprotected.

Notwithstanding that the minister had a greeting in the bygoing for all, his limbs were of such excellent reach, and moved so fast over the ground, that his pace was rather over than under four miles an hour. Passing the thirteen chimneys of the "Lang Raw," he crossed Dee bridge and bent his way to the right along the wide spaces of the sluggish river. The old fortress of the Douglases, the castle of Thrieve, loomed up behind him through the wavering heat of the morning. Above him was the hill of Knockcannon, from which Mons Meg fired her fatal shots. The young minister stood looking back and revolving the strange changes of the past. He saw how the way of the humble was exalted, and the lofty brought down from their seats.

"Some put their trust in horses, and some in chariots," said the minister, "but we will trust in the Lord."

He spake half aloud.

"As ye war sayin', sir, we wull trust the Lord—Himsel' wull be oor strength and stay."

The minister turned. It was a middle-aged man who spoke—David M'Kie, the familiar good spirit of the village of Whunnyliggate, and indeed of the whole parish. Wherever sickness was, there David was to be found.

"I was thinking," said the minister sententiously, "that it is not the high and lofty ones who sit most securely on their seats. The Lord is on the side of the quiet folk who wait."

"Ay, minister," said David M'Kie tentatively.

It was worth while coming five miles out of a man's road to hear the minister's words. There was not a man who would have a word to say, except himself, in the smiddy of Whunnyliggate that night—not even the autocratic smith.

"Yes, David, it was grand, no doubt, to hear Clavers clattering down the Lawnmarket and turning the West Port like a whirlwind, with all his pennons fluttering; but it was the Westland Levies, with their pikes and their Bibles, that won the day at Dunkeld in the hinder-end. The king and his men were a bonnie sicht, with their lace collars and their floating love-locks; but the drab-coats beat him out of the field, because the Lord was on their side, at Naseby and Marston Moor."

The two men were now on the final rise of the hillside. The whole valley of the Dee lay beneath them, rich with trees and pasture-lands, waving crops and the mansions of the great. The minister shaded his eyes with his hand, and looked beneath the sun. He pointed with his finger to Thrieve, whose tall keep glimmered up from its island amid the mists of the river.

"There is the castle where the proud once dwelt and looked to dwell for ever, having no fear of God or man. The hanging-stone is there that never wanted its tassel, the courtyard where was the ready block, the dungeon for the captive, the banquet-hall and the earl's chamber. They are all there, yet only the owl and the bat dwell in them for ever."

"There is a boy that makes poetry aboot the like o' that," said David M'Kie, who loved to astonish the minister.

"And who, pray, is the boy who makes poetry? I would like to see him."

"'Deed, minister, gin ye're gaun up to Drumquhat the day, as I jalouse ye are, ye may see him. They ca' him Walter Carmichael. He's some sib to the mistress, I'm thinkin'."

"Yes, I have seen him in church, but I never had speech with the lad," said the minister.

"Na, I can weel believe that. The boy's no' partial-like to ministers—ye'll excuse me for sayin'—ever since he fell oot wi' the minister's loon, and staned him aff the Drumquhat grund. Saunders lickit him for that, an' so he tak's the road if ever a minister looks near. But gin ye come on him afore he can make the Hanging Shaw, ye may get speech o' him, and be the means o' doing him a heap o' guid."

At this point their ways parted. The minister held on up the valley of the Ken, curving over the moorland towards the farm of Drumquhat. He went more leisurely now that he had broken the back of his morning's walk. The larks sprang upward from his feet, and their songs were the expression of an innocent gladness like that which filled his own heart.

He climbed the high stone dykes as they came in his way, sometimes crossing his legs and sitting a while on the top with a sort of boyish freedom in his heart as though he too were off for a holiday —a feeling born in part of the breezy uplands and the wide spaces of the sky. On his right hand was the dark mass of the Hanging Shaw, where it began to feather down to the Black Water, which rushed along in the shadow to meet the broad and equable waters of the Ken.

As the minister came to one of these dykes, treading softly on a noiseless cushion of heather and moss, he put his foot on a projecting stone and vaulted over with one hand lightly laid on the top stone. He alighted with a sudden bound of the heart, for he had nearly leapt on the top of a boy, who lay prone on his face, deeply studying a book. The boy sprang up, startled by the minister's unexpected entrance into his wide world of air, empty of all but the muirfowls' cries.

For a few moments they remained staring at each other—tall, well-attired minister and rough-coated herdboy.

"You are diligent," at last said the minister, looking out of his dark eyes into the blue wondering orbs which met his so squarely and honestly. "What is that you are reading?"

"Shakespeare, sir," said the boy, not without some fear in telling the minister that he was reading the works of the man who was known among many of the Cameronians as "nocht but the greatest of the play-actors."

But the minister was placable and interested. He recognised the face as that of the boy who came to church on various occasions; but with whom he had found it so difficult to come to speech.

"How many plays of Shakespeare have you read?" queried the minister again.

"Them a'—mony a time," said the boy. The minister marvelled still more. "But ye'll no' tell my gran'mither?" said the boy beseechingly, putting the minister upon his honour.

Mr. Cameron hesitated for a moment, and then said—

"I will not tell your grandmother unless you are doing something worse than reading Shakespeare, my boy. You are from Drumquhat, I think," he continued. "What are you doing here?"

The boy blushed, and hung his head.

"Cutting thistles," he said.

The minister laughed and looked about. On one hand there was a mown swathe of thistles, on the other they still grew luxuriantly all down the slope to the burnside.

"I suppose you are cutting down the thistles in Shakespeare? There are a good many of them," he said; "but is that what your master keeps you for?"

The boy looked up quickly at this imputation on his honesty.

"I'm on piecework," he said, with a kind of defiance in his tone.

"On piecework?" asked the minister, perplexed; "how is that?"

"Weel, sir, it's this way, ye see. Gran'faither used to pay me a penny an hour for cuttin' the thistles. He did that till he said I was the slowest worker ever he had, an' that by the time that I was done wi' ae side o' the field, the ither was ready to begin owre again. I said that I was quite willin' to begin again, but he said that to sit doon wi' a book and cut as far roon' ye as the hook could reach, was no' the kind o' wark that he had been accustomed to on the farm o' Drumquhat. So he took me off working by time and put me on piecework. I dinna get as muckle siller, but I like it juist as weel. So I can work and read time aboot."

"But how do you know how the time goes?" asked the minister, for watches were not at that date to be found in the pockets of herdboys on the Galloway hills.

The boy pointed to a peeled willow-wand which was stuck in the ground, with a rough circle drawn round it.

"I made that sun-dial. Rab Affleck showed me," he said simply, without any of the pride of genius.

"And are ye sure that the working hour is always the same length as the reading time?" asked the minister.

Walter looked up with a bright twinkle in his eye.

"Whiles when I'm workin' at the thistles, she may get a bit kick forrit," he said.

The minister laughed a low, mellow laugh. Then he quoted a text, as was customary with him:

"'And Hezekiah said, It is a light thing for the shadow to go down ten degrees in the dial of Ahaz.'"

The minister and Walter sat for a long time in the heat of the noonday regarding one another with undisguised interest. They were in the midst of a plain of moorland, over which a haze of heat hung like a diaphanous veil. Over the edge there appeared, like a plain of blue mist, the strath, with the whitewashed farmhouses glimmering up like patches of snow on a March hillside. The minister came down from the dyke and sat beside the boy on the heather clumps.

"You are a herd, you tell me. Well, so am I—I am a shepherd of men, though unworthy of such a charge," he added.

Walter looked for further light.

"Did you ever hear," continued Mr. Cameron, looking away over the valley, "of One who went about, almost barefoot like you, over rocky roads and up and down hillsides?"

"Ye needna tell me—I ken His name," said Walter reverently.

"Well," continued the minister, "would you not like to be a herd like Him, and look after men and not sheep?"

"Sheep need to be lookit after as weel," said Walter.

"But sheep have no souls to be saved!" said Richard Cameron.

"Dowgs hae!" asserted Walter stoutly.

"What makes you say so?" said the minister indulgently. He was out for a holiday.

"Because, if my dowg Royal hasna a soul, there's a heap o' fowk gangs to the kirk withoot!"

"What does Royal do that makes you think that he has a soul?" asked the minister.

"Weel, for ae thing, he gangs to the kirk every Sabbath, and lies in the passage, an' he'll no as muckle as snack at a flee that lichts on his nose—a thing he's verra fond o' on a week day. An' if it's no' yersel' that's preachin', my gran'faither says that he'll rise an' gang oot till the sermon's by."

The minister felt keenly the implied compliment.

"And mair nor that, he disna haud wi' repeating tunes," said Walter, who, though a boy, knew the name of every tune in the psalmody—for that was one of the books which could with safety be looked at under the bookboard when the minister was laying down his "fifthly," and when some one had put leaden clogs on the hands of the little yellow-faced clock in the front of the gallery—a clock which in the pauses of the sermon could be heard ticking distinctly, with a staidness and devotion to the matter in hand which were quite Cameronian.

"Repeating tunes!" said the minister, with a certain painful recollection of a storm in his session on the Thursday after the precentor had set up "Artaxerxes" in front of him and sung it as a solo without a single member of the congregation daring to join.

"Ay," said Walter, "Royal disna hand wi' repeats. He yowls like fun. But 'Kilmarnock' and 'Martyrs' fit him fine. He thumps the passage boards wi' his tail near as loud's ye do the Bible yersel'. Mair than that, Royal gangs for the kye every nicht himsel'. A' that ye hae to say is juist 'Kye, Royal—gae fetch them!' an' he's aff like a shot."

"How does he open the gates?" queried the minister.

"He lifts the bars wi' his nose, but he canna sneck them ahint him when he comes back."

"And you think that he has a soul?" said the minister, to draw the boy out.

"What think ye yersel', sir?" said Walter, who at bottom was a true
Scot, and could always answer one question by asking another.

"Well," answered the minister, making a great concession, "the Bible tells us nothing of the future of the beasts that perish—"

"Who knoweth," said Walter, "the soul of the beast, whether it goeth upward or whether it goeth downward to the ground?"

The minister took his way over the moor, crossing the wide peat-hags and the deep trenches from which the neighbouring farmers of bygone generations had cut the peat for their winter fires. He went with a long swinging step very light and swift, springing from *tussock* to *tussock* of dried brown bent in the marshy places.

At the great barn-door he came upon Saunders M'Quhirr, master of the farm of Drumquhat, whose welcome to his minister it was worth coming a hundred miles to receive.

"Come awa', Maister Cameron, and the mistress will get you a drink o' milk, an' ye'll hae a bite o' denner wi' us gin ye can bide half an hour!"

The minister went in and surprised the goodwife in the midst of the clean and comely mysteries of the dairy. From her, likewise, he received the warmest of welcomes. The relation of minister and people in Galloway, specially among the poorer congregations who have to work hard to support their minister, is a very beautiful one. He is their superior in every respect, their oracle, their model, their favourite subject of conversation; yet also in a special measure he is their property. Saunders and Mary M'Quhirr would as soon have contradicted the Confession of Faith as questioned any opinion of the minister's when he spoke on his own subjects.

On rotation of crops, and specially on "nowt" beasts, his opinion was "no worth a preen." It would not have been becoming in him to have a good judgment on these secularities.

The family and dependants were all gathered together in the wide, cool kitchen of Drumquhat, for it was the time for the minister's catechising. Saunders sat with his wife beside him. The three sons—Alec, James, and Rob—sat on straight-backed chairs; Walter near by, his hand on his grandmother's lap.

Question and answer from the Shorter Catechism passed from lip to lip like a well-played game in which no one let the ball drop. It would have been thought as shameful if the minister had not acquitted himself at "speerin'" the questions deftly and instantaneously as for one of those who were answering to fail in their replies. When Rob momentarily mislaid the "Reasons Annexed" to the second commandment, and his very soul reeled in the sudden terror that they had gone from him for ever, his father looked at him as one who should say, "Woe is me that I have been the responsible means of bringing a fool into the world!" Even his mother looked at him wistfully, in a way that was like cold water running down his back, while Mr. Cameron said kindly, "Take your time, Robert!"

However, Rob recovered himself gallantly, and reeled off the Reasons Annexed with vigour. Then he promised, under his breath, a sound thrashing to his model brother, James, who, having known the Catechism perfectly from his youth up, had yet refused to give a leading hint to his brother in his extremity. Walter had his answers as ready as any of them.

Walter had, on one occasion, begun to attend a Sabbath school at the village, which was started by the enthusiastic assistant of the parish minister, whose church lay some miles over the moor. Walter had not asked any permission of his seniors at the farm, but wandered off by himself to be present at the strange ceremonies of the opening. There the Drumquhat training made him easily first of those who repeated psalms and said their Catechism. A distinguished career seemed to be opening out before him, but a sad event happened which abruptly closed the new-fangled Sunday school. The minister of the parish heard what his young "helper" had been doing over in Whunnyliggate, and he appeared in person on the following Sabbath when the exercises were in full swing. He opened the door, and stood silently regarding, the stick *dithering* in both hands with a kind of senile fury.

The "helper" came forward with a bashful confidence, expecting that he would receive commendation for his great diligence. But he was the most surprised "helper" in six counties when the minister struck at him suddenly with his stick, and abruptly ordered him out of the school and out of his employment.

"I did not bring ye frae Edinburgh to gang sneaking aboot my pairish sugarin' the bairns an' flairdyin' the auld wives. Get Oot o' my sicht, an' never let your shadow darken this pairish again, ye sneevlin' scoondrel!"

Then he turned the children out to the green, letting some of the laggards feel his stick as they passed. Thus was closed the first Sabbath-school that was ever held in the village of Whunnyliggate. The too-enthusiastic "helper" passed away like a dream, and the few folk who journeyed every Sabbath from Whunnyliggate to the parish kirk by the side of the Dee Water received the ordinances officially at noon each Lord's Day, by being exhorted to "begin the public worship of God in this parish" in the voice which a drill-sergeant uses when he exhorts an awkward squad. Walter did not bring this event before the authorities at Drumquhat. He knew that the blow of the minister's oaken staff was a judgment on him for having had anything to do with an Erastian Establishment.

After the catechising, the minister prayed. He prayed for the venerable heads of the household, that they might have wisdom and discretion. He prayed that in the younger members the fear of the Lord might overcome the lust of the eye and the pride of life—for the sojourners, that the God of journeying Israel might be a pillar of fire by night and of cloud by day before them, and that their pilgrimage way might be plain. He prayed for the young child, that he might be a Timothy in the Scriptures, a Samuel in obedience, and that in the future, if so it were the will of the Most High, he might be both witness and evangelist of the Gospel.

III

THE MINISTER'S LOON

Saw ye ae flour in a fair garden,
Where the lilac blossom blooms cheerily;
"Fairest and rarest ever was seen,"
Sing the merle and laverock merrily.

Watered o' dew i' the earliest morn,
Lilac blossom blooms cheerily;
Bield aboot wi' a sweet hawthorn,
Where the merle and lark sing merrily.

Wha shall pu' this flour o' the flours?
Lilac blossom blooms cheerily;
Wha hae for aye to grace their booers,
Where the merle and lark sing merrily?

This is the note that came for me this morning. It was the herd of Hanging Shaws that brought it. He had been down at the smiddy getting the horses shod; and Mr. Marchbanks, the minister, handed it to him himself as he was passing the manse on his way home. The herd said that it was "bound to be something pressing, or the minister wadna hae been so soon oot o' his bed." So he waited till I had opened it to hear what it was about, for the wife of Hanging Shaws would be sure to be asking. I read it to him, but he did not seem to be much the wiser. Here is the letter, written in an ill, crabbed hand-of-write, like all ministers' writings:—

"*Nether Dullarg.*

"DEAR MR. M'QUHIRR,—*I made strict inquiry subsequent to my return from your hospitable dwelling last evening regarding the slight accident which happened to my son, Archibald, whilst I was engaged in suitable converse with your like-minded partner. I am of opinion that there is no necessity for proceeding to extreme measures in the case of your son, Alexander—as in my first natural indignation, I urged somewhat strongly upon your good wife. It may not ultimately be for the worse, that the lads were allowed to settle their own differences without the intervention of their parents. I may say, in conclusion, that the application of a portion of uncooked beef to the protuberance has considerably reduced the swelling upon my son's nose during the night. I intend (D.V.) to resume the visitation of my congregation on Thursday next, unaccompanied either by my own son or yours.—Believe me, dear sir, to remain your most obedient servant,*

July 3rd.

"JOHN MARCHBANKS."

Now, Mr. Marchbanks is not my own minister, but there is not a better respected man in the countryside, nor one whom I would less allow any one belonging to me to make light of. So it behoved me to make inquiry. Of the letter itself I could make neither head nor tail; but two things were clear—that that loon of a boy, my son Alec, was in it, and also that his mother was "accessory after the fact," as the Kirkcudbright lawyers say. In the latter case it was necessary to act with circumspection. In the other case I should probably have acted instantly with a suitable hazel rod.

I went into the house. "Where's Alec?" I asked, maybe a kenning sharper than ordinary.

"What may ye be wantin' wi' Alec?" said my wife, with a sting in her accent which showed that she was deep in the ploy, whatever it had been. It now came to my mind that I had not seen Alec since the day before, when I sent him out to play with the minister's son, till Maister Marchbanks had peace to give us his crack before I went out to the hill sheep.

So I mentioned to Mrs. M'Quhirr that I had a letter from the minister about the boy. "Let us hear it," says she. So I read the letter word for word.

"What does he mean by a' that screed?" she asked. "It's like a bit o' a sermon."

Now, my wife takes the general good out of a sermon, but she does not always trouble to translate pulpit language into plain talk.

"He means that there's six o' yin an' half a dizzen o' the ither," I explained, to smooth her down.

"Na, they're no' that," said Mrs. M'Quhirr; "my laddie may be steerin', I'm no' denyin'; but he's no' to be named in the same day as that misleered hound, the minister's loon!"

It was evidently more than ever necessary to proceed with circumspection.

"At any rate, let us hear what the laddie has to say for himsel'. Where is he?" I said.

"He's in the barn," said his mother shortly.

To the barn I went. It is an old building with two doors, one very large, of which the upper half opens inwards; and the other gives a cheery look into the orchard when the sugar-plums are ripening. One end was empty, waiting for the harvest, now just changing into yellow, and the other had been filled with meadow hay only the week before.

"Alec!" I cried, as I came to the door.

There was an answer like the squeaking of a rat among the hay, and I thought, "Bless me, the boy's smothered!" But then again I minded that in his times of distress, after a fight or when he had been in some ploy for which he dared not face his father, Alec had made himself a cave among the hay or corn in the end of the barn. Like all Lowland barns, ours has got a row of three-cornered unglazed windows, called "wickets." Through one of these I have more than once seen Alec vanish when hard pressed by his mother, and have been amused even under the sober face of parental discipline. For, once through, no one could follow the boy. There was no one about the farm slender enough to scramble after. I had not the smallest doubt that the scapegrace was now lying snugly in his hole, impregnable behind the great hay-mow, provisioned with a few farls of cake from his mother, and with his well-beloved *Robinson Crusoe* for sole companion of the solitary hours.

I went round to the opening and peered in, but could see nothing.
"Alec," says I, "come oot this moment!"

"Nae lickin', then, faither?" says a voice out of the wicket.

"No, if ye come oot an' tell the truth like a man."

So I took him ben to the "room" to be more solemn-like, and bade him tell the whole story from the start. This he did fairly on the whole, I am bound to confess, with sundry questions and reminders here and there from his mother and me.

"Weel, mither, the way o' it was this. We had only a half-day yesterday at the schule," he began, "for the maister was gaun to a funeral; an' when I cam' oot at denner-time I saw Airchie Marchbanks, an' he said that his faither was gaun up the lochside veesitin', that he was gaun, too, an' if I likit I could hing on ahint. So I hid my buiks aneath a stane—"

"Ye destructionfu' vagabond, I'll get yer faither to gie ye a guid—"

"But, mither, it was a big braid stane. They're better there than cadgin' them hame an' maybe lossin' them. An' my faither promised that there was to be nae lickin' if I telt the truth."

"Weel, never mind the buiks," said I, for this had nothing to do with the minister's letter. "Gae on wi' your story."

"The minister startit aboot twa o'clock wi' the auld meer in the shafts, Airchie on the front seat aside his faither, an' me sittin' on the step ahint."

"Did the minister ken ye war there?" asked his mother.

"Nae fears!" said Alexander M'Quhirr the younger, unabashed. It is a constant wonder to his mother whom he takes after. But it is no great wonder to me. It had been indeed a greater wonderment to me that Alec should so readily promise to accompany the minister; for whenever either a policeman or a minister is seen within miles of Drumquhat, my lad takes the shortest cut for the fastnesses of Drumquhat Bank, there to lie like one of his hunted forebears of the persecution, till the clear buttons or the black coat have been carefully watched off the premises.

"The first place where the minister gaed," continued my son, "was the clauchan o' Milnthird. He was gaun to see Leezie Scott, her that has been ill sae lang. He gaed in there an' bade a gey while, wi' Airchie haudin' ae side o' the horse's heid an' me the ither—no' that auld Jess wad hae run away if ye had tied a kettle to her tail—"

"Be mair circumspect in yer talk," said his mother; "mind it's a minister's horse!"

"Weel, onyway, I could see through the wundy, an' the lassie was haudin' the minister's haun', an' him speakin' an' lookin' up at somebody that I didna see, but maybe the lassie did, for she lay back in her bed awfu' thankfu'-like. But her mither never thankit the minister ava', juist turned her back an' grat into her peenie. Mr. Marchbanks cam' oot; but I saw nae mair, for I had to turn an' rin, or he wad hae seen me, an' maybe askit me to hae a ride!"

"An' what for wad ye no' be prood to ride wi' the godly man?" asked my wife.

"He micht ask me my quaistions, an' though I've been lickit thirteen times for Effectual Callin', I canna get mair nor half through wi't. ['Yer faither's wi' ye there, laddie,' said I, under my breath.] Gin Mr. Marchbanks wad aye look like what he did when he cam oot o' Leezie Scott's, I wadna rin for the heather when he comes. Then he had a bit crack in twa-three o' the hooses wi' the auld wives that wasna at the wark, though he has nae mair members in the clauchan, them bein' a' Auld Kirkers. But Mr. Marchbanks didna mind that, but ca'ed on them a', an' pat up a prayer standin' wi' his staff in his hand and wi' his hair owre his shoother."

"Hoo div ye ken?" I asked, curious to know how the boy had sketched the minister so exactly.

"I juist keekit ben, for I likit to see't."

"The assurance o' the loon!" cried his mither, but not ill-pleased. (O these mothers!)

"Then we cam' to the auld mill, an' the minister gaed in to see blin' Maggie Affleck, an' when he cam' oot I'm sure as daith that he left something that jingled on the kitchen table. On the doorstep he says, wi' a bricht face on him, 'Marget, it's me that needs to thank you, for I get a lesson frae ye every time that I come here.' Though hoo blind Mag Affleck can learn a minister wi' lang white hair, is mair nor me or Airchie Marchbanks could mak' oot. Sae we gaed on, an' the minister gied every ragged bairn that was on the road that day a ride, till the auld machine was as thrang as it could stick, like a merry-go-roon' at the fair. Only, he made them a' get oot at the hills an' walk up, as he did himsel'. 'Deed, he walkit near a' the road, an' pu'ed the auld meer efter him insteed o' her drawin' him. 'I wish my faither wad lend me the whup!' Airchie said, an' he tried to thig it awa' frae his faither. But the minister was mair gleg than ye wad think, and Airchie got the whup, but it was roon the legs, an' it garred him loup and squeal!"

My wife nodded grim approval.

"When we got to Drumquhat," continued Alec, "it was gey far on in the efternune, an' the minister an' my mither lowsed the powny an' stabled it afore gaun ben. Then me an' Airchie were sent oot to play, as my mither kens. We got on fine a while, till Airchie broke my peerie an' pooched the string. Then he staned the cats that cam' rinnin' to beg for milk an' cheese—cats that never war clodded afore. He wadna be said 'no' to, though I threepit I wad tell his faither. Then at the hinner-en' he got into my big blue coach, and wadna get oot. I didna mind that muckle, for I hadna been in 't mysel' for six months. But he made faces at me through the hole in the back, an' that I couldna pit up wi'—nae boy could. For it was my ain coach, minister's son or no' minister's son. Weel, I had the cross-bow and arrow that Geordie Grier made me—the yin that shoots the lumps o' hard wud. So I let fire at Airchie, just when he was makin' an awfu' face, and the billet took him fair atween the een. Into the hoose he ran to his faither, *ba-haain'* wi' a' his micht; an' oot cam' the minister, as angry as ye like, wi' my mither ahint him like to greet."

"'Deed, I was that!" said Mrs. M'Quhirr.

"'What for did ye hit my son's nose wi' a billet of wood through the hole in your blue coach?' the minister asked me.

"'Because your son's nose was *at* the hole in my blue coach!' says I, as plain as if he hadna been a minister, I was that mad. For it was my coach, an' a bonny-like thing gin a boy couldna shoot at a hole in his ain blue coach! Noo, faither, mind there was to be nae lickin' gin I telt ye the truth!"

There was no licking—which, if you know my wife, you will find no difficulty in believing.

IV

THE BIOGRAPHY OF AN "INEFFICIENT"

White as early roses, girt by daffodillies,
  Gleam the feet of maidens moving rhythmically,
  Roses of the mountains, flowers of the valley,
Hill rose and plain rose and white vale lilies.

Dewy in the meadow lands, clover blossoms mellow
  Lift their heads of red and white to the bride's adorning;
  Sweetly in the sky-realms all the summer morning,
Joyeth the skylark and calleth his fellow.

In the well-known precincts, lo the wilding treasure
  Glows for marriage merriment in my sweetheart's gardens,
  Welcoming her joy-day, tenderest of wardens—
Heart's pride and love's life and all eyes' pleasure.

Bride among the bridesmaids, lily clad in whiteness,
  She cometh to the twining none may twain in sunder;
  While to marriage merriment wakes the organ's thunder,
And the Lord doth give us all His heavenly brightness.

Then like early roses, girt by daffodillies,
  Goes the troop of maidens, moving rhythmically,
  Roses of the mountains, flowers of the valley,
Hill rose and plain rose and white vale lilies.

PART I

There is no doubt that any committee on ministerial inefficiency would have made short work of the Reverend Ebenezer Skinner, minister of the Townend Kirk in Cairn Edward—that is, if it had been able to distinguish the work he did from the work that he got the credit for. Some people have the gift, fortunate or otherwise, of obtaining credit for the work of others, and transferring to the shoulders of their neighbours the responsibility of their blunders.

Yet, on the whole, the Townend minister had not been fairly dealt with, for, if ever man was the product of environment, that man was the minister of the "Laigh" or Townend Kirk. Now, Ebenezer Skinner was a model subject for a latter-day biography, for he was born of poor but honest parents, who resolved that their little Ebenezer should one day "wag his head in a pulpit," if it cost them all that they possessed.

The early days of the future minister were therefore passed in the acquisition of the Latin rudiments, a task which he performed to the satisfaction of the dominie who taught him. He became letter-perfect in repetition of all the rules, and pridefully glib in reeling off the examples given in the text. He was the joy of the memory-lesson hour, and the master's satisfaction was only damped when this prodigy of accurate knowledge applied himself to the transference of a few lines of English into a dead language. The result was not inspiring, but by perseverance Ebenezer came even to this task without the premonition of more egregious failure than was the custom among pupils of country schools in his day.

Ebenezer went up to Edinburgh one windy October morning, and for the first time in his life saw a university and a tramcar. The latter astonished him very much; but in the afternoon he showed four new comers the way to the secretary's office in the big cavern to the left of the entrance of the former, wide-throated like the portal of Hades.

He took a lodging in Simon Square, because some one told him that Carlyle had lodged there when he came up to college. Ebenezer was a lad of ambition. His first session was as bare of interest and soul as a barn without the roof. He alternated like a pendulum between Simon Square and the Greek and Latin class-rooms. He even took the noted Professor Lauchland seriously, whereupon the latter promptly made a Greek pun upon his name, by which he was called in the class whenever the students could remember it. There was great work done in that class-room—in the manufacture of paper darts. Ebenezer took no part in such frivolities, but laboured at the acquisition of such Greek as a future student of theology would most require. And he succeeded so well that, on leaving, the Professor complimented him in the following terms, which were thought at the time to be handsome: "Ye don't know much Greek, but ye know more than most of your kind—that is, ye can find a Greek word in the dictionary." It was evident from this that Ebenezer was a favourite pupil, but some said that it was because Lauchland was pleased with the pun he made on the name Skinner. There are always envious persons about to explain away success.

Socially, Ebenezer confined himself to the winding stairs of the University, and the bleak South-side streets and closes, through which blew wafts of perfume that were not of Arcady. Once he went out to supper, but suffered so much from being asked to carve a chicken that he resolved never to go again. He talked chiefly to the youth next to him on Bench Seventeen, who had come from another rural village, and who lived in a garret exactly like his own in Nicolson Square.

Sometimes the two of them walked through the streets to the General Post Office and back again on Saturday nights to post their letters home, and talked all the while of their landladies and of the number of marks each had got on Friday in the Latin version. Thus they improved their minds and received the benefits of a college education.

At the end of the session Ebenezer went back directly to his village on the very day the classes closed and he could get no more for his money; where, on the strength of a year at the college, he posed as the learned man of the neighbourhood. He did not study much at home but what he did was done with abundant pomp and circumstance. His mother used to take in awed visitors to the "room," cautioning them that they must not disturb any of Ebenezer's "Greek and Laitin" books, lest in this way the career of her darling might be instantly blighted. Privately she used to go in by herself and pore over the unknown wonders of Ebenezer's Greek prose versions, with an admiration which the class-assistant in Edinburgh had never been able to feel for them.

Such was the career of Ebenezer Skinner for four years. He oscillated between the dinginess and dulness of the capital as he knew it, and the well-accustomed rurality of his home. For him the historic associations of Edinburgh were as good as naught. He and Sandy Kerr (Bench Seventeen) heard the bugles blaring at ten o'clock from the Castle on windy Saturday nights, as they walked up the Bridges, and never stirred a pulse! They never went into Holyrood, because some one told Ebenezer that there was a shilling to pay. He did not know what a quiet place it was to walk and read in on wet Saturdays, when there is nothing whatever to pay. He read no books, confining himself to his class-books and the local paper, which his mother laboriously addressed and sent to him weekly. Occasionally he began to read a volume which one of his more literary companions had acquired on the recommendation of one of the professors, but he rarely got beyond the first twenty pages.

Yet there never was a more conscientious fellow than Ebenezer Skinner, Student in Divinity. He studied all that he was told to study. He read every book that by the regulations he was compelled to read. But he read nothing besides. He found that he could not hold his own in the give-and-take of his fellow-students' conversation. Therefore more and more he withdrew himself from them, crystallising into his narrow early conventions. His college learning acted like an unventilated mackintosh, keeping all the unwholesome, morbid personality within, and shutting out the free ozone and healthy buffeting of the outer world. Many college-bred men enter life with their minds carefully mackintoshed. Generally they go into the Church.

But he found his way through his course somehow. It was of him that Kelland, kindliest and most liberal of professors, said when the co-examiner hinted darkly of "spinning": "Poor fellow! We'll let him through. He's done his best." Then, after a pause, and in the most dulcet accents of a valetudinarian cherub, "It's true, his best is not very good!"

But Ebenezer escaped from the logic class-room as a roof escapes from a summer shower, and gladly found himself on the more proper soil of the philosophy of morals. Here he did indeed learn something, for the professor's system was exactly suited to such as he. In consequence, his notebooks were a marvel. But he did not shine so brightly in the oral examinations, for he feared, with reason, the laughter of his fellows. In English literature he took down all the dates. But he did not attend the class on Fridays for fear he should be asked to read, so he never heard Masson declaim,

"Ah, freedom is a noble thing!"

which some of his contemporaries consider the most valuable part of their university training.

After Ebenezer Skinner went to the Divinity Hall, he brought the same excellent qualities of perseverance to bear upon the work there. When the memorable census was taken of a certain exegetical class, requesting that each student should truthfully, and upon his solemn oath, make record of his occupation at the moment when the paper reached him, he alone, an academic Abdiel,

"Among the faithless, faithful only he,"

was able truthfully to report—*Name*, "Ebenezer Skinner"; *Occupation at this Moment*, "Trying to attend to the lecture." His wicked companions—who had returned themselves variously as "Reading the *Scotsman*," "Writing a love-letter," "Watching a fight between a spider and a bluebottle, spider weakening"—saw at once that the future of a man who did not know any better than to listen to a discourse on Hermeneutics was entirely hopeless. So henceforth they spoke of him openly and currently as "Poor Skinner!"

Yet when the long-looked-for end of the divinity course came, and the graduating class burst asunder, scattering seed over the land like an over-ripe carpel in the September sun, Ebenezer Skinner was one of the first to take root. He preached in a "vacancy" by chance, supplying for a man who had been taken suddenly ill. He read a discourse which he had written on the strictest academical lines for his college professor, and in the composition of which he had been considerably assisted by a volume of Mr. Spurgeon's sermons which he had brought home from Thin's wondrous shop on the Bridges, where many theological works await the crack of doom. The congregation to which he preached was in the stage of recoil from the roaring demagogy of a late minister, and all too promptly elected this modest young man.

But when the young man moved from Simon Square into the Townend manse, and began to preach twice a Sunday to the clear-headed business men and the sore-hearted women of many cares who filled the kirk, his ignorance of all but these theological books, as well as an innocence of the motives and difficulties of men and women (which would have been childlike had it not been childish), predoomed him to failure. His ignorance of modern literature was so appalling that the youngest member of his Bible-class smiled when he mentioned Tennyson. These and other qualities went far to make the Reverend Ebenezer Skinner the ministerial "inefficient" that he undoubtedly was.

But in time he became vaguely conscious that there was something wrong, yet for the life of him he could not think what it was. He knew that he had done every task that was ever set him. He had trodden faithfully the appointed path. He was not without some ability. And yet, though he did his best, he was sadly aware that he was not successful. Being a modest fellow, he hoped to improve, and went the right way about it. He knew that somehow it must be his own fault. He did not count himself a "Product," and he never blamed the Mill.

PART II

[Reported by Saunders M'Quhirr of Drumquhat.]

SKINNER—HALDANE.—On the 25th instant, at the Manse of Kirkmichael, by the Rev. Alexander Haldane, father of the bride, the Rev. Ebenezer Skinner, minister of Townend Church, Cairn Edward, to Elizabeth Catherine Haldane.—*Scotsman*, June 27th.

This was the beginning of it, as some foresaw that it would be. I cut it out of the *Scotsman* to keep, and my wife has pasted it at the top of my paper. But none of us knew it for certain, though there was Robbie Scott, John Scott's son, that is herd at the Drochills in the head-end of the parish of Kirkmichael—he wrote home to his father in a letter that I saw myself: "I hear you're to get our minister's dochter down by you; she may be trusted to keep you brisk about Cairn Edward."

But we thought that this was just the lad's nonsense, for he was aye at it. However, we had news of that before she had been a month in the place. Mr. Skinner used to preach on the Sabbaths leaning over the pulpit with his nose kittlin' the paper, and near the whole of the congregation watching the green leaves of the trees waving at the windows. But, certes, after he brought the mistress home he just preached once in that fashion. The very next Sabbath morning he stood straight up in the pulpit and pulled at his cuffs as if he was peeling for a "fecht"—and so he was. He spoke that day as he had never spoken since he came to the kirk. And all the while, as my wife said, "The mistress sat as quate as a wee broon moose in the minister's seat by the side wall. She never took her een aff him, an' ye never saw sic a change on ony man."

"She'll do!" said I to my wife as we came out. We were biding for a day or so with my cousin, that is the grocer in Cairn Edward, as I telled you once before. The Sabbath morning following there was no precentor in the desk, and the folk were all sitting wondering what was coming next, for everybody kenned that "Cracky" Carlisle, the post, had given up his precentorship because the list of tunes had come down from the manse to him on the Wednesday, instead of his being allowed to choose what he liked out of the dozen or so that he could sing. "Cracky" Carlisle got his name by upholding the theory that a crack in the high notes sets off a voice wonderfully. He had a fine one himself.

"I'll no' sing what ony woman bids me," said the post, putting the saddle on the right horse at once.

"But hoo do ye ken it was her?" he was asked that night in Dally's smiddy, when the Laigh End folk gathered in to have their crack.

"Ken?" said Cracky; "brawly do I ken that he wad never hae had the presumption himsel'. Na, he kenned better!"

"It was a verra speerited thing to do, at ony rate, to gie up your precentorship," said Fergusson, whose wife kept the wash-house on the Isle, and who lived on his wife's makings.

"Verra," said the post drily, "seein' that I haena a wife to keep me!"

There was a vacancy on the seat next the door, which the shoemaker filled. But, with all this talk, there was a considerable expectation that the minister would go himself to Cracky at the last moment and beseech him to sing for them. The minister, however, did not arrive, and so Cracky did not go to church at all that day.

Within the Laigh Kirk there was a silence as the Reverend Ebenezer Skinner, without a tremor in his voice, gave out that they would sing to the praise of God the second Paraphrase to the tune "St. Paul's." The congregation stood up—a new invention of the last minister's, over which also Cracky had nearly resigned, because it took away from his dignity as precentor and having therefore the sole right to stand during the service of song. The desk was still empty. The minister gave one quick look to the manse seat, and there arose from the dusky corner by the wall such a volume of sweet and solemn sound that the first two lines were sung out before a soul had thought of joining. But as the voice from the manse seat took a new start into the mighty swing of "St. Paul's," one by one the voices which had been singing that best-loved of Scottish tunes at home in "taking the Buik," joined in, till by the end of the verse the very walls were tingling with the joyful noise. There was something ran through the Laigh Kirk that day to which it had long been strange. "It's the gate o' heeven," said old Peter Thomson, the millwright, who had voted for Ebenezer Skinner for minister, and had regretted it ever since. He was glad of his vote now that the minister had got married.

Then followed the prayer, which seemed new also; and Ebenezer Skinner's prayers had for some time been well known to the congregation of the Laigh Kirk. The worst of all prayer-mills is the threadbare liturgy which a lazy or an unspiritual man cobbles up for himself. But there seemed a new spirit in Ebenezer's utterances, and there was a thankful feeling in the kirk of the Townend that day. As they "skailed," some of the young folk went as far as to say that they hoped that desk would never be filled. But this expression of opinion was discouraged, for it was felt to border on irreverence.

Cracky Carlisle was accidentally at his door when Gib Dally passed on his way home. Cracky had an unspoken question in his eye; but Gib did not respond, for the singing had drawn a kind of spell over him too. So Cracky had to speak plain out before Gib would answer.

"Wha sang the day?" he asked anxiously, hoping that there had been some sore mishap, and that the minister, or even Mrs. Skinner herself, might come humbly chapping at his door to fleech with him to return. And he hardened himself even in the moment of imagination.

"We a' sang," said Gib cruelly.

"But wha led?" said the ex-precentor.

"Oh, we had no great miss of you, Cracky," said Gib, who remembered the airs that the post had many a time given himself, and did not incline to let him off easily in the day of his humiliation. "It was the minister's wife that led."

The post lifted his hands, palm outwards, with a gesture of despair.

"Ay, I was jalousing it wad be her," said he sadly, as he turned into his house. He felt that his occupation and craft were gone, and first and last that the new mistress of the manse was the rock on which he had split.

Mrs. Ebenezer Skinner soon made the acquaintance of the Cairn Edward folk. She was a quick and dainty little person.

"Man, Gib, but she's a feat bit craitur!" said the shoemaker, watching her with satisfaction from the smiddy door, and rubbing his grimy hands on his apron as if he had been suddenly called upon to shake hands with her.

"Your son was nane so far wrang," he said to John Scott, the herd, who came in at that moment with a coulter to sharpen.

"Na," said John; "oor Rob's heid is screwed the richt way on his shoothers!"

Now, in her rambles the minister's wife met one and another of the young folk of the congregation, and she invited them in half-dozens at a time to come up to the manse for a cup of tea. Then there was singing in the evening, till by some unkenned wile on her part fifteen or sixteen of the better singers got into the habit of dropping in at the manse two nights a week for purposes unknown.

At last, on a day that is yet remembered in the Laigh Kirk, the congregation arrived to find that the manse seat and the two before it had been raised six inches, and that they were filled with sedate-looking young people who had so well kept the secret that not even their parents knew what was coming. But at the first hymn the reason was very obvious. The singing was grand.

"It'll be what they call a 'koyer,' nae doot!" said the shoemaker, who tolerated it solely because he admired the minister's wife and she had shaken hands with him when he was in his working things.

Cracky Carlisle went in to look at the new platform pulpit, and it is said that he wept when he saw that the old precentor's desk had departed and all the glory of it. But nobody knows for certain, for the minister's wife met him just as he was going out of the door, and she had a long talk with him. At first Cracky said that he must go home, for he had to be at his work. But, being a minister's daughter, Mrs. Skinner saw by his "blacks" that he was taking a day off for a funeral, and promptly marched him to the manse to tea. Cracky gives out the books in the choir now, and sings bass, again well pleased with himself. The Reverend Ebenezer Skinner is an active and successful minister, and was recently presented with a gown and bands, and his wife with a silver tea-set by the congregation. He has just been elected Clerk of Presbytery, for it was thought that his wife would keep the Records as she used to do in the Presbytery of Kirkmichael, of which her father was Clerk, to the great advantage of the Kirk of Scotland in these parts.

[My wife, Mary M'Quhirr, wishes me to add to all whom it may concern,
"Go thou and do likewise."]

V

JOHN

Shall we, then, make our harvest of the sea
 And garner memories, which we surely deem
  May light these hearts of ours on darksome days,
When loneliness hath power, and no kind beam
 Lightens about our feet the perilous ways?
   For of Eternity
This present hour is all we call our own,
 And Memory's edge is dull'd, even as it brings
 The sunny swathes of unforgotten springs,
And sweeps them to our feet like grass long mown.

Fergus Morrison was in his old town for a few days. He was staying with the aunt who had brought him up, schooled him, marshalled him to the Burgher Kirk like a decent Renfrewshire callant, and finally had sent him off to Glasgow to get colleged. Colleged he was in due course, and had long been placed in an influential church in the city. On the afternoon of the Saturday he was dreamily soliloquising after the plain midday meal to which his aunt adhered.

Old things had been passing before him during these last days, and the coming of the smart church-officer for the psalms and hymns for the morrow awoke in the Reverend Fergus Morrison a desire to know about "John," the wonderful beadle of old times, to whose enlarged duties his late spruce visitor had succeeded. He smiled fitfully as he brooded over old things and old times; and when his aunt came in from washing up the dinner dishes, he asked concerning "John." He was surprised to find that, though frail, bent double with rheumatism, and nearly blind, he was still alive; and living, too, as of yore, in the same old cottage with its gable-end to the street. The Glasgow minister took his staff and went out to visit him. As he passed down the street he noted every change with a start, marvelling chiefly at the lowness of the houses and the shrunken dimensions of the Town Hall, once to him the noblest building on earth.

When he got to John's cottage the bairns were playing at ball against the end of it, just as they had done thirty years ago. One little urchin was making a squeaking noise with a wet finger on the window-pane, inside which were displayed a few crossed pipes and fly-blown sweatmeats. As the city minister stood looking about him, a bent yet awe-inspiring form came hirpling to the door, leaning heavily on a staff. Making out by the noise the whereabouts of the small boy, the old man turned suddenly to him with a great roar like a bull, before the blast of which the boy disappeared, blown away as chaff is blown before the tempest. The minister's first impulse was likewise to turn and flee. Thirty added years had not changed the old instinct, for when John roared at any of the town boys, conscious innocence did not keep any of them still. They ran first, and inquired from a distance whom he was after. For John's justice was not evenhanded. His voice was ever for open war, and everything that wore tattered trousers and a bonnet was his natural enemy.

So the minister nearly turned and ran, as many a time he had done in the years that were past. However, instead he went indoors with the old man, and, having recalled himself to John's clear ecclesiastical memory, the interview proceeded somewhat as follows, the calm flow of the minister's accustomed speech gradually kindling as he went, into the rush of the old Doric of his boyhood.

"Ay, John, I'm glad you remember me; but I have better cause to remember you, for you once nearly knocked out my brains with a rake when I was crawling through the manse beech-hedge to get at the minister's rasps. Oh, yes, you did, John! You hated small boys, you know. And specially, John, you hated me. Nor can I help thinking that, after all, taking a conjunct and dispassionate view of your circumstances, as we say in the Presbytery, your warmth of feeling was entirely unwarranted. 'Thae loons—they're the plague o' my life!' you were wont to remark, after you had vainly engaged in the pleasure of the chase, having surprised us in some specially outrageous ploy.

"Once only, John, did you bring your stout ash 'rung' into close proximity to the squirming body that now sits by your fireside. You have forgotten it, I doubt not, John, among the hosts of other similar applications. But the circumstance dwells longer in the mind of your junior, by reason of the fact that for many days he took an interest in the place where he sat down. He even thought of writing to the parochial authorities to ask why they did not cushion the benches of the parish school.

"You have no manner of doot, you say, John, that I was richly deserving of it? There you are right, and in the expression I trace some of the old John who used to keep us so strictly in our places. You're still in the old house, I rejoice to see, John, and you are likely to be. What! the laird has given it to you for your life, and ten pound a year? And the minister gives you free firing, and with the bit you've laid by you'll juik the puirhoose yet? Why, man, that's good hearing! You are a rich man in these bad times! Na, na, John, us Halmyre lads wad never see you gang there, had your 'rung' been twice as heavy.

"Do ye mind o' that day ye telled the maister on us? There was Joe Craig, that was lost somewhere in the China seas; Sandy Young, that's something in Glasgow; Tam Simpson, that died in the horrors o' drink; and me—and ye got us a' a big licking. It was a frosty morning, and ye waylaid the maister on his way to the school, and the tawse were nippier than ordinar' that mornin'. No, John, it wasna me that was the ringleader. It was Joe Craig, for ye had clooted his lugs the night before for knockin' on your window wi' a pane o' glass, and then letting it jingle in a thousand pieces on the causeway. Ye chased him doon the street and through the lang vennel, and got him in Payne's field. Ye brocht him back by the cuff o' the neck, an' got a polisman to come to see the damage. An' when ye got to the window there wasna a hole in't, nor a bit o' gless to be seen, for Sandy Young had sooped it a' up when ye were awa' after Joe Craig.

"Then the polisman said, 'If I war you, John, I wadna gang sae muckle to the Cross Keys—yer heid's no as strong as it was, an' the minister's sure to hear o't!' This was mair than mortal could stan', so ye telled the polisman yer opinion o' him and his forebears, and attended to Joe Craig's lugs, baith at the same time.

"Ye dinna mind, do ye, John, what we did that nicht? No? Weel, then, we fetched ye the water that ye were aye compleenin' that ye had naebody to carry for ye. Twa cans fu' we carried—an' we proppit them baith against your door wi' a bit brick ahint them. Ay, just that very door there. Then we gied a great 'rammer' on the panels, an' ye cam' geyan fast to catch us. But as ye opened the door, baith the cans fell into the hoose, an' ye could hae catched bairdies an' young puddocks on the hearthstane. Weel, ye got me in the coachbuilder's entry, an' I've no' forgotten the bit circumstance, gin ye have.

"Ill-wull? Na, John, the verra best of guid-wull, for ye made better boys o' us for the verra fear o' yer stick. As ye say, the ministers are no' what they used to be when you and me were sae pack. A minister was a graun' man then, wi' a presence, an' a necktie that took a guid half-yard o' seeventeen-hunner linen. I'm a minister mysel', ye ken, John, but I'm weel aware I'm an unco declension. Ye wad like to hear me preach? Noo, that's rale kind o' ye, John. But ye'll be snuggest at your ain fireside, an' I'll come in, an' we'll e'en hae a draw o' the pipe atween sermons. Na, I dinna wunner that ye canna thole to think on the new kirk-officer, mairchin' in afore the minister, an 's gouns an' a' sic capers. They wadna hae gotten you to do the like.

"Ye mind, John, hoo ye heartened me up when I was feared to speak for the first time in the auld pulpit? 'Keep yer heid up,' ye said, 'an' speak to the gallery. Never heed the folk on the floor. Dinna be feared; in a time or twa ye'll be nae mair nervish than mysel'. Weel do I mind when I first took up the buiks, I could hardly open the door for shakin', but noo I'm naewise discomposed wi' the hale service.'

"Ay, it is queer to come back to the auld place efter sae mony year in Glesca. You've never been in Glesca, John? No; I'll uphaud that there's no' yer match amang a' the beadles o' that toun—no' in yer best days, when ye handed up yer snuff-box to Maister M'Sneesh o' Balmawhapple in the collectin' ladle, when ye saw that he was sore pitten til't for a snuff. Or when ye said to Jamieson o' Penpoint, wee crowl o' a body—

"'I hae pitten in the fitstool an' drappit the bookboard, to gie ye every advantage. So see an' mak' the best o't.'

"Ay, John, ye war a man! Ye never said that last, ye say, John? They lee'd on ye, did they? Weel, I dootna that there was mony a thing pitten doon to ye that was behadden to the makkar. But they never could mak' ye onything but oor ain kindly, thrawn, obstinate auld John, wi' a hand like a bacon ham and a heart like a bairn's. Guid-day to ye, John. There's something on the mantelpiece to pit in the tea-caddy. I'll look in the morn, an' we'll hae oor smoke."

VI

EUROCLYDON OF THE RED HEAD

There's a leaf in the book of the damask rose
 That glows with a tender red;
From the bud, through the bloom, to the dust it goes,
 Into rose dust fragrant and dead.

And this word is inscribed on the petals fine
 Of that velvety purple page—
"Be true to thy youth while yet it is thine
 Ere it sink in the mist of age,

 "Ere the bursting bud be grown
 To a rose nigh overblown,
 And the wind of the autumn eves
 Comes blowing and scattering all
 The damask drift of the dead rose leaves
 Under the orchard wall.

"Like late-blown roses the joy-days flit,
 And soon will the east winds blow;
So the love years now must be lived and writ
 In red on a page of snow.

"And here the rune of the rose I rede,
 'Tis the heart of the rose and me—
O youth, O maid, in your hour of need,
 Be true to the sacred three—
Be true to the love that is love indeed,
 To thyself, and thy God, these three!

 "Ere the bursting bud is grown
 To a rose nigh overblown,
 And the wind of the autumn eves
 Comes blowing and scattering all
 The damask drift of the dead rose leaves
 Under the orchard wall."

Euroclydon of the Red Head was the other name of the Reverend Sylvanus Septimus Cobb during his student days—nothing more piratical than that. Sylvanus obtained the most valuable part of his training in the Canadian backwoods. During his student days he combined the theory of theology with the practice of "logging," in proportions which were mutually beneficial, and which greatly aided his success as a minister on his return to the old country. Sylvanus Cobb studied in Edinburgh, lodging with his brother in the story next the sky at the corner of Simon Square, supported by red herrings, oatmeal, and the reminiscence that Carlyle had done the same within eyeshot of his front window fifty years before.

"And look at him now!" said Sylvanus Cobb pertinently.

Sylvanus had attained the cognomen of Euroclydon of the Red Head in that breezy collegiate republic whose only order is the Prussian "For Merit." He was always in a hurry, and his red head, with its fiery, untamed shock of bristle, usually shot into the class-room a yard or so before his broad shoulders. At least, this was the general impression produced. Also, he always brought with him a draught of caller air, like one coming into a close and fire-warmed room out of the still and frost-bound night.

But Edinburgh, its bare "lands" and barren class-rooms, in time waxed wearisome to Sylvanus. He grew to loathe the drone of the classes, the snuffy prelections of professors long settled on the lees of their intellects, who still moused about among the dusty speculations which had done duty for thought when their lectures were new, thirty years ago. "A West Indian nigger," said Sylvanus quaintly, "ain't in it with a genuine lazy Scotch professor. Wish I had him out to lumber with me on the Ottawa! He'd have to hump himself or git! I'd learn him to keep hag-hagging at trees that had been dead stumps for half a century!"

At this time of life we generally spent a part of each evening in going round to inform our next neighbours that we had just discovered the solution of the problem of the universe. True, we had been round at the same friend's the week before with two equally infallible discoveries. Most unfortunately, however, on Sunday we had gone to hear the Great Grim Man of St. Christopher's preach in his own church, and he had pitilessly knocked the bottom out of both of these. Sometimes our friends called with their own latest solutions; and then there was such a pother of discussion, and so great a noise, that the old lady beneath foolishly knocked up a telephonic message to stop—foolishly, for that was business much more in our line than in hers. With one mind we thundered back a responsive request to that respectable householder to go to Jericho for her health, an it liked her. Our landlady, being long-suffering and humorously appreciative of the follies of academic youth (O rare paragon of landladies!), wondered meekly why she was sent to Coventry by every one of her neighbours on the stair during the winter months; and why during the summer they asked her to tea and inquired with unaffected interest if she was quite sure that that part of the town agreed with her health, and if she thought of stopping over this Whitsunday term.

When Sylvanus Cobb came up our stairs it was as though a bag of coals on the back of an intoxicated carter had tumbled against our door.

"That's yon red-headed lunatic, I'll be bound; open the door to him yersel'!" cried the landlady, remembering one occasion when Euroclydon had entered with such fervour as almost to pancake her bodily between wall and door.

Sylvanus came in as usual with a militant rush, which caused us to lift the kitchen poker so as to be ready to poke the fire or for any other emergency.

"I'll stop no more in this hole!" shouted Euroclydon of the Red Head, "smothered with easter haar on the streets and auld wife's blethers inby. I'm off to Canada to drive the axe on the banks of the Ottawa. And ye can bide here till your brains turn to mud—and they'll not have far to turn either!"

"Go home to your bed, Euroclydon—you'll feel better in the morning!" we advised with a calmness born of having been through this experience as many as ten times before. But, as it chanced, Sylvanus was in earnest this time, and we heard of him next in Canada, logging during the week and preaching on Sundays, both with equal acceptance.

One night Sylvanus had a "tough" in his audience—an ill-bred ruffian who scoffed when he gave out his text, called "Three cheers for Ingersoll!" when he was half through with his discourse, and interjected imitations of the fife and big drum at the end of each paragraph. It may be said on his behalf that he had just come to camp, had never seen Sylvanus bring down a six-foot pine, and knew not that he was named Euroclydon—or why.

The ruddy crest of the speaker gradually bristled till it stood on end like the comb of Chanticleer. He paused and looked loweringly at the interrupter under his shaggy brows, pulling his under lip into his mouth in a moment of grim resolve.

"I'll attend to you at the close of this divine service!" said Euroclydon.

And he did, while his latest convert held his coat.

"An almighty convincing exhorter!" said Abram Sugg from Maine, when Sylvanus had put the Ingersollian to bed in his own bunk, and was feeding him on potted turkey.

On the hillsides, with their roots deep in the crevices of the rocks, grew the pines. One by one they fell all through that winter. The strokes of the men's axes rang clear in the frosty air as chisel rings on steel. Whenever Sylvanus Cobb came out of the door of the warm log-hut where the men slept, the cold air met him like a wall. He walked light-headed in the moistureless chill of the rare sub-Arctic air. He heard the thunder of the logs down the *chute*. The crash of a falling giant far away made him turn his head. It was a life to lead, and he rubbed his hands as he thought of Edinburgh class-rooms.

Soon he became boss of the gang, and could contract for men of his own. There was larger life in the land of resin and pine-logs. No tune in all broad Scotland was so merry as the whirr of the sawmill, when the little flashing ribbon of light runs before the swift-cutting edge of the saw. It made Sylvanus remember the pale sunshine his feet used to make on the tan-coloured sands of North Berwick, when he walked two summers before with May Chisholm, when it was low-water at the spring-tides. But most of all he loved the mills, where he saw huge logs lifted out of the water, slid along the runners, and made to fall apart in clean-cut fragrant planks in a few seconds of time.

"That tree took some hundreds of years to grow, but the buzz-saw turns her into plain deal-boards before you can wink. All flesh is grass," soliloquised the logger preacher.

A winter in a lumber camp is a time when a man can put in loads of
thinking. Dried fish and boiled tea do not atrophy a man's brain.
Loggers do not say much except on Sundays, when they wash their shirts.
Even then it was Sylvanus who did most of the talking.

Sometimes during the week a comrade would trudge alongside of him as he went out in the uncomfortable morning.

"That was the frozen truth you gave us on Sunday, I guess!" said one who answered placably to the name of Bob Ridley—or, indeed, to any other name if he thought it was meant for him. "I've swore off, parson, and I wrote that afternoon to my old mother."

Such were the preacher's triumphs.

Thus Sylvanus Cobb learned his lesson in the College of the Silences, to the accompaniment of the hard clang of the logs roaring down the mountain-side, or the sweeter and more continuous ring of his men's axes. At night he walked about a long time, silent under the thick-spangled roofing of stars. For in that land the black midnight sky is not thin-sprinkled with glistening pointlets as at home, but wears a very cloth of gold. The frost shrewdly nipped his ears, and he heard the musical sound of the water running somewhere under the ice. A poor hare ran to his feet, pursued by a fox which drew off at sight of him, showing an ugly flash of white teeth.

But all the while, among his quietness of thought, and even in the hours when he went indoors to read to the men as they sat on their rugs with their feet to the fire, he thought oftenest of the walks on the North Berwick sands, and of the important fact that May Chisholm had to stop three times to push a rebellious wisp of ringlets under her hat-brim. Strange are the workings of the heart of a man, and there is generally a woman somewhere who pulls the strings.

Euroclydon laid his axe-handle on the leaves of his Hebrew Bible to keep them from turning in the brisk airs which the late Canadian spring brought into the long log-hut, loosening the moss in its crevices. The scent of seaweed on a far-away beach came to him, and a longing to go back possessed him. He queried within himself if it were possible that he could ever settle down to the common quiet of a Scottish parish, and decided that, under certain conditions, the quiet might be far from commonplace. So he threw his bundle over his shoulder, when the camp broke up in the beginning of May, and took the first steamer home.

His first visit was to North Berwick, and there on the sands between the East Terrace and the island promontory which looks towards the Bass, where the salt water lies in the pools and the sea-pinks grow between them, he found May Chisholm walking with a young man. Sylvanus Cobb looked the young man over. He had a pretty moustache but a weak mouth.

"I can best that fellow, if I have a red head!" said Sylvanus, with some of the old Euroclydon fervour.

And he did. Whether it was the red head, of which each individual hair stood up automatically, the clear blue eyes, which were the first thing and sometimes the only thing that most women saw in his face, or the shoulders squared with the axe, that did it, May Chisholm only knows. You can ask her, if you like. But most likely it was his plain, determined way of asking for what he wanted—an excellent thing with women. But, any way, it is a fact that, before eighteen months had gone by, Sylvanus Cobb was settled in the western midlands of Scotland, with the wife whose tangles of hair were only a trifle less distracting than they used to be between the East Cliff and Tantallon. And this is a true tale.

VII

THE CAIRN EDWARD KIRK MILITANT

Out of the clinging valley mists I stray
  Into the summer midnight clear and still,
And which the brighter is no man may say—
  Whether the gold beyond the western hill

Where late the sun went down, or the faint tinge
  Of lucent green, like sea wave's inner curve
Just ere it breaks, that gleams behind the fringe
  Of eastern coast. So which doth most preserve

My wistful soul in hope and steadfastness
  I know not—all that golden-memoried past
  So sudden wonderful, when new life ran

First in my veins; or that clear hope, no less
  Orient within me, for whose sake I cast
    All meaner ends into these ground mists wan.

"We've gotten a new kind o' minister the noo at Cairn Edward," said my cousin, Andrew M'Quhirr, to me last Monday. I was down at the Mart, and had done some little business on the Hill. My cousin is a draper in the High Street. He could be a draper nowhere else in Cairn Edward, indeed; for nobody buys anything but in the High Street.

"Look, Saunders, there he is, gaun up the far side o' the causeway."

I looked out and saw a long-legged man in grey clothes going very fast, but no minister. I said to my cousin that the minister had surely gone into the "Blue Bell," which was not well becoming in a minister.

"Man, Saunders, where's yer een?—you that pretends to read Tammas Carlyle. D' ye think that the black coat mak's a minister? I micht hae a minister in the window gin it did!" said he, glancing at the disjaskit-looking wood figure he had bought at a sale of bankrupt stock in Glasgow, with "THIS STYLE OF SUIT, £2, 10s." printed on the breast of it. The lay figure was a new thing in Cairn Edward, and hardly counted to be in keeping with the respect for the second commandment which a deacon in the Kirk of the Martyrs ought to cultivate. The laddies used to send greenhorns into the shop for a "penny peep o' Deacon M'Quhirr's idol!" But I always maintained that, whatever command the image might break, it certainly did not break the second; for it was like nothing in the heavens above nor in the earth beneath, nor (so far as I kenned) in the waters under the earth. But my cousin said—

"Maybes no'; but it cost me three pound, and in my shop it'll stand till it has payed itsel'!" Which gives it a long lifetime in the little shop-window in the High Street.

This was my first sight of Angus Stark, the new minister of Martyrs' Kirk in Cairn Edward.

"He carries things wi' a high hand," said Andrew M'Quhirr, my cousin.

"That's the man ye need at the Martyrs' Kirk," said I; "ye've been spoiled owre lang wi' unstable Reubens that could in nowise excel."

"Weel, we're fixed noo, rarely. I may say that I mentioned his wearin' knickerbockers to him when he first cam', thinkin' that as a young man he micht no' ken the prejudices o' the pairish."

"And what said he, Andrew?" I asked. "Was he pitten aboot?"

"Wha? Him! Na, no' a hair. He juist said, in his heartsome, joky way, 'I'm no' in the habit o' consulting my congregation how I shall dress myself; but if you, Mr. M'Quhirr, will supply me with a black broadcloth suit free of charge, I'll see aboot wearin' it!' says he. So I said nae mair.

"But did you hear what Jess Loan, the scaffie's wife, said to him when he gaed in to bapteeze her bairn when he wasna in his blacks? She hummered a while, an' then she says, 'Maister Stark, I ken ye're an ordeened man, for I was there whan a' the ministers pat their han's on yer heid, an' you hunkerin' on the cushion—but I hae my feelin's!"

"'Your feelings, Mrs. Loan?' says the minister, thinking it was some interestin' case o' personal experience he was to hear.

"'Ay,' says Jess; 'if it was only as muckle as a white tie I wadna mind, but even a scaffie's wean wad be the better o' that muckle!'

"So Maister Stark said never a word, but he gaed his ways hame, pat on his blacks, brocht his goun an' bands aneath his airm, and there never was sic a christenin' in Cairn Edward as Jess Loan's bairn gat!"

"How does he draw wi' his fowk, Andra?" I asked, for the "Martyrs" were far from being used to work of this kind.

"Oh, verra weel," said the draper; "but he stoppit Tammas Affleck and John Peartree frae prayin' twenty meenits a-piece at the prayer-meetin'. 'The publican's prayer didna last twa ticks o' the clock, an' you're not likely to better that even in twenty meenits!' says he. It was thocht that they wad leave, but weel do they ken that nae ither kirk wad elect them elders, an' they're baith fell fond o' airin' their waistcoats at the plate.

"Some o' them was sore against him ridin' on a bicycle, till John Peartree's grandson coupit oot o' the cart on the day o' the Sabbath-schule trip, an' the minister had the doctor up in seventeen minutes by the clock. There was a great cry in the pairish because he rade doon on 't to assist Maister Forbes at the Pits wi' his communion ae Sabbath nicht. But, says the minister, when some o' the Session took it on them to tairge him for it, 'Gin I had driven, eyther man or beast wad hae lost their Sabbath rest. I tired nocht but my own legs,' says he. 'It helps me to get to the hoose of God, just like your Sunday boots. Come barefit to the kirk, and I'll consider the maitter again.'"

"That minister preaches the feck o' his best sermons *oot* o' the pulpit," said I, as I bade Andrew good-day and went back into the High Street, from which the folk were beginning to scatter. The farmers were yoking their gigs and mounting into them in varying degrees and angles of sobriety. So I took my way to the King's Arms, and got my beast into the shafts. Half a mile up the Dullarg road, who should I fall in with but "Drucken" Bourtree, the quarryman. He was walking as steady as the Cairn Edward policeman when the inspector is in the town. I took him up.

"Bourtree," says I, "I am prood to see ye."

"'Deed, Drumquhat, an' I'm prood to see mysel'. For thirty year I was drunk every Monday nicht, and that often atweenwhiles that it fair bate me to tell when ae spree feenished and the next began! But it's three month since I've seen the thick end o' a tumbler. It's fac' as death!"

"And what began a' this, Bourtree?" said I.

"Juist a fecht wi' M'Kelvie, the sweep, that ca's himsel' a *pugilist*!"

"A fecht made ye a sober man, Bourtree!—hoo in the creation was that?"

"It was this way, Drumquhat. M'Kelvie, a rank Tipperairy Micky, wi' a nose on him like a danger-signal"—here Bourtree glanced down at his own, which had hardly yet had time to bleach—"me an' M'Kelvie had been drinkin' verra britherly in the Blue Bell till M'Kelvie got fechtin' drunk, an' misca'ed me for a hungry Gallowa' Scot, an' nae doot I gaed into the particulars o' his ain birth an' yeddication. In twa or three minutes we had oor coats aff and were fechtin' wi' the bluid rinnin' on to the verra street.

"The fowk made a ring, but nane dared bid us to stop. Some cried, 'Fetch the polis!' But little we cared for that, for we kenned brawly that the polisman had gane awa' to Whunnyliggate to summon auld John Grey for pasturing his coo on the roadside, as soon as ever he heard that M'Kelvie an' me war drinkin' in the toon. Oh, he's a fine polisman! He's aye great for peace. Weel, I was thinkin' that the next time I got in my left, it wad settle M'Kelvie. An' what M'Kelvie was thinkin' I do not ken, for M'Kelvie is nocht but an Irishman. But oot o' the grund there raise a great muckle man in grey claes, and took fechtin' M'Kelvie an' me by the cuff o' the neck, and dauded oor heids thegither till we saw a guano-bagfu' o' stars.

"'Noo, wull ye shake hands or come to the lock-up?' says he.

"We thocht he maun be the chief o' a' the chief constables, an' we didna want to gang to nae lock-ups, so we just shook haun's freendly-like. Then he sent a' them that was lookin' on awa' wi' a flee in their lugs.

"'Forty men,' says he, 'an' feared to stop twa men fechtin'—cowards or brutes, eyther o' the twa!' says he.

"There was a bailie amang them he spoke to, so we thocht he was bound to be a prince o' the bluid, at the least. This is what I thocht, but I canna tell what M'Kelvie thocht, for he was but an Irishman. So it does not matter what M'Kelvie thocht.

"But the big man in grey says, 'Noo, lads, I've done ye a good turn. You come and hear me preach the morn in the kirk at the fit o' the hill.' 'A minister!' cried M'Kelvie an' me. A wastril whalp could hae dung us owre with its tail. We war that surprised like."

So that is the way "Drucken" Bourtree became a God-fearing quarryman. And as for M'Kelvie, he got three months for assaulting and battering the policeman that very night; but then, M'Kelvie was only an Irishman!

EPILOGUE

IN PRAISE OF GALLOWAY

New lands, strange faces, all the summer days
  My weary feet have trod, mine eyes have seen;
  Among the snows all winter have I been,
Rare Alpine air, and white untrodden ways.

From the great Valais mountain peaks my gaze
  Hath seen the cross on Monte Viso plain,
  Seen blue Maggiore grey with driving rain,
And white cathedral spires like flames of praise.

Yet now the spring is here, who doth not sigh
  For showery morns, and grey skies sudden bright,
  And a dear land a-dream with shifting light!
Or in what clear-skied realm doth ever lie,

Such glory as of gorse on Scottish braes,
  Or the white hawthorn of these English Mays?

Night in the Galloway Woods.

Through the darkness comes the melancholy hoot of the barn owl, while nearer some bird is singing very softly—either a blackcap or a sedge-warbler. The curlew is saying good-night to the lapwing on the hill. By the edge of the growing corn is heard, iterative and wearisome, the "crake," "crake" of the corn-crake.

We wait a little in the shade of the wood, but there are no other sounds or sights to speak to us till we hear the clang of some migratory wild birds going down to the marshes by Loch Moan. Many birds have a night cry quite distinct from their day note. The wood-pigeon has a peculiarly contented chuckle upon his branch, as though he were saying, "This here is jolly comfortable! This just suits *me*!" For the wood-pigeon is a vulgar and slangy bird, and therefore no true Scot, for all that the poets have said about him. He is however a great fighter, exceedingly pugnacious with his kind. Listen and you will hear even at night

"The moan of doves in immemorial elms,"

or rather among the firs, for above all trees the wood-pigeon loves the spruce. But you will find out, if you go nearer, that much of the mystic moaning which sounds so poetic at a distance, consists of squabblings and disputings about vested rights.

"You're shoving me!" says one angry pigeon.

"That is a lie. This is my branch at any rate, and you've no business here. Get off!" replies his neighbour, as quarrelsome to the full as he.

Birds at Night.

A dozen or two of starlings sit on the roof of an out-house—now an unconsidered and uninteresting bird to many, yet fifty years ago Sir Walter Scott rode twenty miles to see a nest of them. They are pretty bird enough in the daytime, but they are more interesting at night. Now they have their dress coats off and their buttons loosened. They sit and gossip among each other like a clique of jolly students. And if one gets a little sleepy and nods, the others will joggle him off the branch, and then twitter with congratulatory laughter at his tumble. Let us get beneath them quietly. We can see them now, black against the brightening eastern sky. See that fellow give his neighbour a push with his beak, and hear the assaulted one scream out just like Mr. Thomas Sawyer in Sunday-school, whose special chum stuck a pin into him for the pleasure of hearing him say "Ouch!"

As the twilight brightens the scuffling will increase, until before the sun rises there will be a battle-royal, and then the combatants will set to preening their ruffled feathers, disordered by the tumults and alarms of the wakeful night.

The bats begin to seek their holes and corners about an hour before the dawn, if the night has been clear and favourable. The moths are gone home even before this, so that there is little chance of seeing by daylight the wonderfully beautiful undervests of peacock blue and straw colour which they wear beneath their plain hodden-grey overcoats.

The Coming of the Dawn.

It is now close on the dawning, and the cocks have been saying so from many farm-houses for half an hour—tiny, fairy cock-crows, clear and shrill from far away, like pixies blowing their horns of departure, "All aboard for Elfland!" lest the hateful revealing sun should light upon their revels. Nearer, hoarse and raucous Chanticleer (of Shanghai evidently, from the chronic cold which sends his voice deep down into his spurs)—thunders an earth-shaking bass. 'Tis time for night hawks to be in bed, for the keepers will be astir in a little, and it looks suspicious to be seen leaving the pheasant coverts at four in the morning. The hands of the watch point to the hour, and as though waiting for the word, the whole rookery rises in a black mass and drifts westward across the tree-tops.

Flood Tide of Night.

In these long midsummer nights the twilight lingers till within an hour or two of dawn. When the green cool abyss of fathomless sky melts into pale slate-grey in the west, and the high tide of darkness pauses before it begins to ebb, then is the watershed of day and night. The real noon of night is quite an hour and a half after the witching hour, just as the depth of winter is really a month after the shortest day. Indeed, at this time of the year, it is much too bright at twelve for even so sleepy a place as a churchyard to yawn. And if any ghost peeped out, 'twould only be to duck under again, all a-tremble lest, the underground horologes being out of gear, a poor shade had somehow overslept cockcrow and missed his accustomed airing.

Way for the Sun.

By two o'clock, however, there is a distinct brightening in the east, and pale, streaky cirrus cloudlets gather to bar the sun's way. Broad, equal-blowing airs begin to draw to and fro through the woods. There is an earthy scent of wet leaves, sharpened with an unmistakable aromatic whiff of garlic, which has been trodden upon and rises to reproach us for our carelessness. Listen! Let us stand beneath this low-branched elder.

"We cannot see what flowers are at our feet,"

but that there is violet in abundance we have the testimony of a sense which the darkness does not affect, the same which informed us of the presence of the garlic. Over the hedge the sheep are cropping the clover with short, sharp bites—one, two, three, four, five bites—then three or four shiftings of the short black legs, and again "crop, crop." So the woolly backs are bent all the night, the soft ears not erected as by day, but laid back against the shoulders. Sheep sleep little. They lie down suddenly, as though they were settled for the night; but in a little there is an unsteady pitch fore and aft, and the animal is again at the work of munching, steadily and apparently mechanically. I have often half believed that sheep can eat and walk and sleep all at the same time. A bivouac of sheep without lambs in the summer is very like an Arab encampment, and calls up nights in the desert, when, at whatever hour the traveller might look abroad, there were always some of the Arabs awake, stirring the embers of the camp fire, smoking, story-telling, or simply moving restlessly about among the animals. As we stand under the elder-bushes we can look down among the sheep, for they have not the wild animal's sense of smell, or else the presence of man disturbs them not. One of the flock gives an almost human cough, as if protesting against the dampness of the night.

The Early Bird.

Swish! Something soft, silent, and white comes across the hedge almost in our eyes, and settles in that oak without a sound. It is a barn-owl. After him a wood-pigeon, the whistling swoop of whose wings you can hear half a mile. The owl is just going to bed. The pigeon is only just astir. He is going to have the first turn at Farmer Macmillan's green corn, which is now getting nicely sweet and milky. The owl has still an open-mouthed family in the cleft of the oak, and it is only by a strict attention to business that he can support his offspring. He has been carrying field mice and dor-beetles to them all night; and he has just paused for a moment to take a snack for himself, the first he has had since the gloaming.

But the dawn is coming now very swiftly. The first blackbird is pulling at the early worm on the green slope of the woodside, for all the world like a sailor at a rope. The early worm wishes he had never been advised to rise so soon in order to get the dew on the grass. He resolves that if any reasonable proportion of him gets off this time, he will speak his mind to the patriarch of his tribe who is always so full of advice how to get "healthy, wealthy, and wise." 'Tis a good tug-of-war. The worm has his tail tangled up with the centre of the earth. The blackbird has not a very good hold. He slackens a moment to get a better, but it is too late. He ought to have made the best of what purchase he had. Like a coiled spring returning to its set, the worm, released, vanishes into its hole; and the yellow bill flies up into the branches of a thorn with an angry chuckle, which says as plainly as a boy who has chased an enemy to the fortress of home, "Wait till I catch you out again!"

Nature is freshest with the dew of her beauty-sleep upon her. The copses are astir, and the rooks on the tops of the tall trees have begun the work of the day. They rise to a great height, and drift with the light wind towards their feeding-grounds by the river. Over the hedge flashes a snipe, rising like a brown bomb-shell from between our feet, and sending the heart into the mouth. The heron, which we have seen far off, standing in the shallows, apparently meditating on the vanity of earthly affairs, slowly and laboriously takes to flight. He cannot rise for the matter of a stone's-throw, and the heavy flaps of his labouring wings resound in the still morning. There is no warier bird than the heron when he gets a fair field. Sometimes it is possible to come upon him by chance, and then his terror and instant affright cause him to lose his head, and he blunders helplessly hither and thither, as often into the jaws of danger as out of it.

Did you see that flash of blue? It was the patch of blue sky on a jay's wing. They call it a "jay piet" hereabouts. But the keepers kill off every one for the sake of a pheasant's egg or two. An old and experienced gamekeeper is the worst of hanging judges. To be tried by him is to be condemned. As Mr. Lockwood Kipling says: "He looks at nature along the barrel of a gun Which is false perspective."

Full Chorus.

In the opener glades of the woods the wild hyacinths lie in the hollows, in wreaths and festoons of smoke as blue as peat-reek. As we walk through them the dew in their bells swishes pleasantly about our ankles, and even those we have trodden upon rise up after we have passed, so thick do they grow and so full are they of the strength of the morning. Now it is full chorus. Every instrument of the bird orchestra is taking its part. The flute of the blackbird is mellow with much pecking of winter-ripened apples. He winds his song artlessly along, like a *prima donna* singing to amuse herself when no one is by. Suddenly a rival with shining black coat and noble orange bill appears, and starts an opposition song on the top of the next larch. Instantly the easy nonchalance of song is overpowered in the torrent of iterated melody. The throats are strained to the uttermost, and the singers throw their whole souls into the music. A thrush turns up to see what is the matter, and, after a little pause for a scornful consideration of the folly of the black coats, he cleaves the modulated harmony of their emulation with the silver trumpet of his song. The ringing notes rise triumphant, a clarion among the flutes.

The Butcher's Boy of the Woods.

The concert continues, and waxes more and more frenzied. Sudden as a bolt from heaven a wild duck and his mate crash past through the leaves, like quick rifle shots cutting through brushwood. They end their sharp, breathless rush in the water of the river pool with a loud "Splash! splash!" Before the songsters have time to resume their interrupted rivalry a missel thrush, the strident whistling butcher's boy of the wood, appears round the corner, and, just like that blue-aproned youth, he proceeds to cuff and abuse all the smaller fry, saying, "Yah! get along! Who's your hatter? Does your mother know you're out?" and other expressions of the rude, bullying youth of the streets. The missel thrush is a born bully. It is not for nothing that he is called the Storm Cock. It is more than suspected that he sucks eggs, and even murder in the first degree—ornithologic infanticide—has been laid to his charge. The smaller birds, at least, do not think him clear of this latter count, for he has not appeared many minutes before he is beset by a clamorous train of irate blue-tits, who go into an azure fume of minute rage; sparrows also chase him, as vulgarly insolent as himself, and robin redbreasts, persistent and perkily pertinacious, like spoiled children allowed to wear their Sunday clothes on week-days.

The Dust of Battle.

So great is the dust of battle that it attracts a pair of hen harriers, the pride of the instructed laird, and the special hatred of his head keeper. Saunders Tod would shoot them if he thought that the laird would not find out, and come down on him for doing it. He hates the "Blue Gled" with a deep and enduring hatred, and also the brown female, which he calls the "Ringtail." The Blue and the Brown, so unlike each other that no ordinary person would take them for relatives, come sailing swiftly with barely an undulation among the musical congregation. The blackbird, wariest of birds —he on the top of the larch—has hardly time to dart into the dark coverts of the underbrush, and the remainder of the crew to disperse, before the Blue and the Brown sail among them like Moorish pirates out from Salee. A sparrow is caught, but in Galloway, at least, 'tis apparently little matter though a sparrow fall. The harriers would have more victims but for the quick, warning cry of the male bird, who catches sight of us standing behind the shining grey trunk of the beech. The rovers instantly vanish, apparently gliding down a sunbeam into the rising morning mist which begins to fill the valley.

Comes the Day.

Now we may turn our way homeward, for we shall see nothing further worth our waiting for this morning. Every bird is now on the alert. It is a remarkable fact that though the pleasure-cries of birds, their sweethearting and mating calls, seem only to be intelligible to birds of the same race, yet each bird takes warning with equal quickness from the danger-cry of every other. Here is, at least, an avian "Volapuk," a universal language understood by the freemasonry of mutual self-preservation.

While we stood quiet behind the beech, or beneath the elder, nature spoke with a thousand voices. But now when we tramp homewards with policeman resonance there is hardly a bird except the street-boy sparrow to be seen. The blackbird has gone on ahead and made it his business, with sharp "Keck! keck!" to alarm every bird in the woods. We shall see no more this morning.

Listen, though, before we go. Between six and seven in the morning the corn-crake actually interrupts the ceaseless iteration of his "Crake! crake!" to partake of a little light refreshment. He does not now say "Crake! crake!" as he has been doing all the night—indeed, for the last three months—but instead he says for about half an hour "Crake!" then pauses while you might count a score, and again remarks "Crake!" In the interval between the first "Crake!" and the second a snail has left this cold earth for another and a warmer place.

Now at last there is a silence after the morning burst of melody. The blackcap has fallen silent among the reeds. The dew is rising from the grass in a general dispersed gossamer haze of mist. It is no longer morning; it is day.

BALLAD OF MINE OWN COUNTRY[11]

[Footnote 11: *Rhymes à la Mode* (Kegan Paul, Trench & Co.)]

Let them boast of Arabia, oppressed
  By the odour of myrrh on the breeze;
In the isles of the East and the West
  That are sweet with the cinnamon trees:
Let the sandal-wood perfume the seas,
  Give the roses to Rhodes and to Crete,
We are more than content, if you please,
  With the smell of bog-myrtle and peat!

Though Dan Virgil enjoyed himself best
  With the scent of the limes, when the bees
Hummed low round the doves in their nest,
  While the vintagers lay at their ease;
Had he sung in our Northern degrees,
  He'd have sought a securer retreat,
He'd have dwelt, where the heart of us flees,
  With the smell of bog-myrtle and peat!

O the broom has a chivalrous crest,
  And the daffodil's fair on the leas,
And the soul of the Southron might rest,
  And be perfectly happy with these;
But we that were nursed on the knees
  Of the hills of the North, we would fleet
Where our hearts might their longing appease
  With the smell of bog-myrtle and peat!

ENVOY.

Ah! Constance, the land of our quest,
  It is far from the sounds of the street,
Where the Kingdom of Galloway's blest
  With the smell of bog-myrtle and peat!

ANDREW LANG.

Printed in Great Britain
by Amazon